SUNSETS & OTHER DANGEROUS THINGS

DANI FRANK

To Grandma,

~~*who wouldn't approve of a book with two girls kissing, but would be so proud I wrote a book.*~~

~~*the first to warn me of blasphemous books...after I'd already read them.*~~

for being the best thing about Catholicism. Miss you.

AUTHOR NOTE

I wrote this book many moons ago with the intention of writing something purely indulgent. This is my ode to young, high school Dani who read this book called *Twilight* and thought something really dramatic and emo like "What if I could love forever?"

This book was written by someone who grew up on the campy *Buffy* and blue-tinted joy of the *Twilight* saga, but I feel like I need to warn people about this book before diving in. Heads up for mild spoilers in the following paragraph.

While this story was written as a fun, rompy ode to romance and all the silly vampire tropes, it still has vampires in it. This book contains alcohol consumption, internalized and addressed biphobia, mentions of blood, cursing, abandonment by a romantic partner (in the past), fight scenes with and without weapons, off page death of two named characters (NOT one of the two main characters), death of a grandparent (in the past), occasionally negative views on vampires, Catholicism, Twilight jokes, open door and consensual sex scenes.

Take care of yourself, merry reader.

1

———

Ashley was on the cusp of getting everything she ever wanted. This year was about getting her life back for the first time...well, for the first time since she died.

She turned to the vanity she'd rescued during post-graduation moveout season nine years ago and pointed at a five-by-seven of her senior portrait taped to the center of the mirror. One from the series in her cheer uniform.

"You are a twenty-year-old girl—I mean, woman." Crap, she'd forgotten she'd changed that part of her mantra. She shook out her hands, bouncing back and forth on the balls of her feet, her socks sinking into the white faux-fur rug, and then returned her attention to the mirror. "You are a twenty-year-old woman. Always have been. Always will be." She struck a superhero pose, channeling confidence from her core to the soles of her feet. "You've got this."

The photo was two years younger than she was meant to

be and taken in a cornfield just outside her hometown but worked better than a mirror reflecting an empty room back at her. The point was no one would know her age if she... well, acted her age, and she'd gotten pretty good at acting twenty over the past decade. It helped that, aside from one big, vampire-shaped difference, not much had changed. She was still going to school, didn't own any property, had no real career aspects, lived in a home full of roommates, and was rich in student loans.

And being late for class again was not going to help.

Ashley peered through her curtain's sliver-sized opening.

Another beautiful, sunny day in upstate New York shone back at her—she was definitely going to be late for class. She tucked the blackout curtain into place with a sigh. She would do unspeakable things for a cloudy day. Well, nothing too awful. But she would do several softly whispered things if the sun would hide for the next ten minutes.

But being late might mean she got to sit next to a certain unspeakable someone. Ashley's mind wandered to crimson lips and slender fingers caressing her throat before waking from the daydream.

These were not safe thoughts to have before class.

A knock at her door pulled her focus.

"Shouldn't you be in class already?" Cynthia—her mentor, not babysitter—leaned against the doorjamb, impressively pulling off a denim jumper with flared pants in the twenty-first century.

Crap. How long had she been daydreaming? Maybe she should have offered just one unspeakable thing to the universe.

"Right. Of course. I was just heading out." Ashley pulled

out her sunny day gear—gloves, Ray-Ban category 4 high altitude sunglasses, lightweight shawl, and a wide-brimmed fedora.

Cynthia didn't look impressed by her hustle. "I mean, it's not my business, but maybe try taking your future seriously."

Ashley nodded as she pulled on her gloves, keeping her protective smile in place and ignoring the tightness in her chest whenever she was reminded how important this year was. She'd heard the speech a million times, and it never got easier.

"This isn't one of your sappy movies," Cynthia said. "The Family isn't known for giving second chances, let alone third."

"I know." Her words came out tighter than she intended as she slipped her arms into her J. Crew trench coat, cinched it, and eased past Cynthia and downstairs, desperate to escape the foreboding message hidden in her mentor's nagging.

Cynthia stuck to the shadows as Ashley slipped on her boots and opened the front door. "Maybe this year, try not obsessing over a pretty face."

Her cackle followed Ashley out the door.

The last rays of daylight coasted the treetops as Ashley stepped out on the creaking porch, breathing deeply and feeling her shoulders relax. Her smile weighed heavier every day as the only people who knew the real her saw her as a burden at best and a liability at worst.

Twelve years of this crap. She was the last twenty-year-old millennial in existence and trying to finish this same school year over and over again without incident was growing old. But if all went as planned, this was her last year. This was her last chance to join the Family and gain the sense of security she'd hunted for the past decade. She just needed to keep her head down and finish one school year without letting her impulsive tendencies grab the wheel and careen off the road to happiness.

She needed this year to be perfect.

Ashley pulled up her collar and slunk into the shadows along the hedge. This year, she'd be a normal college student in a normal college town where the only supernatural characters were actors on TV. She just had to play a twenty-year-old. Not the impulsive romantic she had actually been at twenty. She followed streets canopied in old oaks and crept along the southern edge of the library until sprinting the final stretch across the quad.

At her lecture hall, she slid into the first available seat while her professor's back was turned, dropping her Platt U tote by her feet and ignoring any feelings she might have about the chair's proximity to a certain classmate. She dug in her bag, fishing for a gel pen. She removed the sparkly pen's cap and set to work coloring in the bubbled title of her list.

Ashley's Rules for Succeeding in Undergrad

- Rule 1: Do NOT discuss your roommates
- Rule 2: Do NOT do weird stuff where others can see you
- Rule 3: Do NOT make friends ~~or obsess over you-know-who~~

Cynthia's warning floated back to her. But if she were obsessing, she would write about it in a notebook. And see? She'd crossed it out, and therefore, she was not obsessing.

"Would anyone care to summarize the reading from last week?" Professor Jenkins stalked the small lecture hall of Anthropology 101, hunting for prey. The wooden floors creaked beneath her kitten heels, growing louder as she approached Ashley's desk.

Ashley kept her gaze firmly on her list, avoiding eye contact. Maybe she could disguise the crossed-out bit with flowers like she never wrote it. She uncapped another pen.

It wasn't that she hadn't done the reading. She'd glanced at it—something to do with cultural relativism? But there was this party with Cynthia last night, and Ashley had lost track of time.

The floor in front of Ashley creaked, followed by a long-suffering sigh from Professor Jenkins. Ashley tensed, letting her curtain of blond hair shield her while she curated a list of buzzwords from the two pages she did read.

"Esther," called Professor Jenkins. An endorphin rush like nailing a perfect back handspring shot down Ashley's spine. "I know this isn't your job, but would you share your thoughts on today's reading? Just to get us started."

Don't look. Don't look. Don't look. Ashley's betraying eyes tracked to the seat at the opposite corner. The seat where Professor Jenkins's hot graduate assistant always sat. Not that Ashley kept track of where Esther Green sat. That was something someone obsessive would write about in a notebook somewhere, and Ashley wrote nothing of the sort.

She couldn't see Esther from this angle, another pitfall of the front row. Not that Ashley knew which seat had the best view of Esther—two seats back and three over.

"I guess a part that stood out to me was the discussion on cannibalistic practices and the different approaches to it." Something about Esther's matter-of-fact tone had Ashley envisioning Esther behind a library desk pressing spectacles up her nose while giving Ashley a stern look, maybe biting the end of a pen. "You have the spiritual with Christian communion in holy human sacrifice versus the militaristic eat-your-enemies-and-reduce-them-to-waste approach. But I liked the description of cannibalism as a communal funerary practice. I suppose this is a bit of a personal take and probably borders on moral relativism, but the idea of your ashes being put in a stew and consumed by your closest friends and family so you are literally carried with them, even in death, sounds... poetically beautiful."

A shiver ran down Ashley's spine. If Esther was into being eaten, Ashley wouldn't push her out of bed. Hypothetically of course. She'd never spoken to Esther. Never so much as made eye contact with her from Ashley's usual place in the back of the class.

Ashley leaned forward. However, with Fadl reclining and Taylor leaning over their notes, her view was blocked.

Forming friendships was off-limits, but Ashley took pride in her ability to remember names. Plattsburgh was a small enough college town that she'd run into at least half the class on weekends.

"Thank you, Esther. And that segues into our discussion on what Franz Boas meant when he used the term *cultural relativism* and how it differs from *moral relativism*. Would anyone else care to give us a quick definition?"

When Fadl leaned over his notes, Ashley performed a backward-stretch-and-lean to catch a sight of the woman on the other side of the room. The woman she was absolutely not obsessing over. Esther's face was blocked as she twirled a lazy finger around a lock of brown hair that had escaped from her messy bun—the motion mesmerizing in its slow and steady rhythm.

"Ashley."

Ashley dropped her arms and whipped her head back to where Professor Jenkins waited. What was the question again? "Cultural relativism...is culture...relative to...other cultures?"

"Their own culture. Relative to their own culture, Ashley." Professor Jenkins continued up the center aisle. "Would anyone else like to continue the definition?"

Ashley snatched up her pencil to pantomime taking notes. Despite her better judgment, she glanced to the far side of the room. If she slouched back just right... Esther's slender fingers returned to her notes, revealing a touch of pale, sharp cheekbones and blood red lips. If this were a romance, Esther and Ashley would be enemies. She pictured Esther in a forest green tunic and impractically tight leather leggings, holding a knife to Ashley's throat. Ashley sighed dreamily.

And then something happened that never happened two rows back and three seats over—Esther and her deep-set eyes glanced back at Ashley.

She had the aura of Winona Ryder from the early nineties.

Ashley shifted in her chair, unable to blink. *Jesus, I'm in trouble.*

Fadl chose that moment to lean back again, blocking her view. The snap of Ashley's pencil splintering in her fist startled her back to reality. Someone in the back of the class eloquently discussed Franz Boas's work in the growing field of anthropology, how racist views of the time shaped and emphasized the novelty of his research on Inuit culture. Ashley took this monologue in like the cold shower she needed.

She most definitely did not need distractions like pools of deep, brown eyes and talk of the romantic elements of cannibalism calling her long history of falling too fast and too hard. Ashley's crushes led to obsession, which led to oversharing, which led to discovery, failure, banishment, and starting over again in a room full of her previous classmates who had magically forgotten her name.

"Thank you, Charlotte. That was quite thorough." Professor Jenkins's smile looked genuine for the first time. She returned to the SMART board, clicking to the next slide. "Now, your assignment for next week. We're doing ethnographies focusing on everyday rituals. Preparing dinner, putting on makeup, making the bed. Big or small, as long as you can fit it within the—"

The high-pitched scatting of "The HampsterDance Song" filled the classroom, echoing off the ancient wooden floors and matching wood-paneled walls, traveling up the vaulted ceiling and sharply contrasting with the neo-Gothic look of Plattsburgh University. The floor groaned as desks shifted to face the corner of the room, where the sound emanated from the tote by Ashley's desk. Ashley couldn't recall ever wishing to be smitten from the earth more.

"Ashley, could you please silence your phone?"

She dove for her bag as her phone encouraged everyone to stomp their feet and clap their hands. Everything inside fell to the floor—loose gel pens, her favorite Lisa Frank notepad, a flyer for a party this weekend. Finally, she grasped the hard rectangle and flipped it to silent. She flopped into her seat and dropped her phone onto her desk, mortified. What were the chances Esther heard that?

"As I was saying," Professor Jenkins continued, "the assignment will be—"

Ashley's desk vibrated under her fingers, her phone dancing across the surface as if to mock any hope of ever having a positive standing in this class.

"Ashley," Professor Jenkins hissed. "Please take that outside."

Ashley grabbed her phone and scampered from the classroom, leaving a whispered "sorry" as she passed her professor.

She followed the corridor to the common area where the last dregs of daylight lit the stained glass and coated the room in a deep orange. Less than shocked to see her mother in the missed calls, Ashley took a calming breath and sat on a hard, wooden pew to return the call.

"Hi, Mom. Did you need something?" She glanced at the wall clock, doing quick mental math. "It's the middle of the night."

"Hey, sweetie. It's Mom."

Ashley held the phone away from her face so it wouldn't pick up her sigh.

"Sorry to wake you. I won't keep you. I just wanted to know your Christmas plans." Her mom said this like it was a quick check-in and not the start of a multi-day negotiation process. And the thing about her mom was, despite treating her like a child, she knew Ashley's real age. Her mom continued to fill the silence while Ashley grasped for something to say. "It's just we haven't seen you in so long." Pans clanged and Schatzi yipped in the background. "Your father and I talked about it and decided to buy your plane ticket home from Romania. Think of it as an early Christmas present."

Ashley felt a stomach cramp and the start of a headache. They must have saved for months to afford this, and Ashley wasn't even in Romania. A few years ago, she'd spent exactly three seconds looking at a map while her mom asked when she was coming home for Christmas. So, Ashley did the logical thing and picked a random country as far from Iowa as she dared, declaring she was transferring there for her bachelors. And then a couple years for her masters. And now a lengthy Ph.D. She cringed, realizing the excuse may be running thin, but limited funds as a student made her story about being unable to return each holiday nearly plausible—and put off having to tell them she was never coming back.

"It's not that I don't want to come home for Christmas." Ashley's class ticked by. She should get back to hear about the next assignment.

"Ashybear, it's been years. I won't take no for an answer."

But she needed her mom to take no for an answer. Just a little longer before she had to say goodbye for good. A classmate came down the hall, followed by a second. Her professor was going to be pissed.

"I'll see what I can do. Gotta go. Love you, bye." Ashley hung up before her mom could respond.

She wove through the exiting tide of students. The room was empty save for one person crouched by Ashley's desk, gathering gel pens off the floor. Her stomach clenched.

Esther.

Ashley squashed her excitement as soon as she recognized it.

"Oh my god, you don't have to do that." The creaky floor drowned out her words as she scurried to help Esther. "Thanks for watching my stuff though."

"Sure, I guess." Esther snatched the last rogue pen from under the desk just as Ashley reached for it. A faint perfume lingered behind the motion. The earthy vanilla of old books. This was officially the closest she had ever been to Esther. She should write this down somewhere.

Every day, Esther left another tempting crumb, be it a casual comment on cannibalism or the way she smiled like it was a secret. The way she wore these tiny rings but never on her ring fingers or her daily insistence on sporting the loudest black boots, even back when the nights were still hot before the leaf tips colored and a cool breeze stirred over Lake Champlain.

Ashley stood, dusting off her skinny jeans, reeling her libido in, and offering Esther a hand. In that small contact, she registered her Midwest manners betraying her in the worst way.

Everything changed to slow motion.

Esther's gaze flicked up, sparkling in the overhead lights. Her hand slid into Ashley's, smooth as silk. Music from the movie *Troy* played in Ashley's head as Esther rose. The one with a single woman singing mournful vowels accompanied by a booming and unsteady drum, emphasizing the tragic yet epic significance of this moment.

Esther, for her part, seemed not to notice the life-changing contact, her boots stomping as she adjusted her stance and freed her hand from Ashley's.

"I was waiting for you, actually," Esther said.

Ashley bit her lip to keep from groaning aloud. *There was some dialogue she'd rewind later.* She was her own worst enemy. Maybe they weren't enemies to lovers at all. They could be long-lost childhood friends.

"You don't happen to be from Iowa, do you?" *Be cool, Ashley.* She planted her hip on a nearby desk.

Esther blinked at her. "Florida."

"Oh." Well, there went that option.

"Anyway." There—a slight tug at the corner of Esther's mouth as she turned her face away, her secret smile. "Professor Jenkins paired up the class to do the ethnographies while you were gone. We're uneven, so I offered to work with the odd student." She shrugged before shoving a fistful of pens at Ashley. "Hey, odd student, I guess you're stuck with me."

Sweet baby Jesus, Ashley didn't know whether to thank her mom or curse her for putting her in the path of this marvelous temptation. Her fingers brushed Esther's as she fumbled with the pens. She wanted to live in this awkward moment with Esther for a century at least. This was definitely a bad idea.

The back of her throat tingled, and she coughed it away. "Cool."

"Right." Esther nodded, as though that settled things. "We should exchange numbers to plan when to meet."

When to meet. As in, with another student, outside of class, on purpose. Did this break rule three? It was for class after all. Sure, she'd failed her list twice already, but she'd grown. She was totally in control and ready for a one-on-one with a person she was not obsessing over.

The tingling in her throat increased, and she coughed again, trying to clear out the agitation. "Cool."

She would need a better vocabulary the next time they met.

Again, Esther shoved something into Ashley's unprepared hands. Her phone this time.

"Just put it in, and I'll text you so you have my number." Esther shifted her weight to one side, tapping the toe of her loud boot in a hurried beat while Ashley weighed the pros and cons.

There was a light knock on the door.

"Hey, Esther." A bushy-browed, long-haired behemoth filled the doorway. "I was hoping to catch you. Oh. Still busy?" He spotted Ashley and stilled, blocking the exit.

Ashley's throat now tingled like she'd swallowed an entire bag of Pop Rocks.

That's when she remembered what that tingling meant.

Ashley plugged in her number and returned the phone without considering any further Family-related complications. But she kept focus on the man in the doorway. He'd just made her life exponentially more difficult.

Esther fumbled the phone Ashley shoved at her. "I'm just wrapping up with class stuff. What did you need?"

"Just checking if you're coming over tomorrow." His eyes continued to flick back to Ashley. "There's something I wanted to talk about."

"Of course." Esther waved away his concern, rings flashing in the overhead light, and adjusted the strap of her cross bag. "I'll see you then, August."

Ashley's shoulders stiffened. The name was ringing some sort of bell but that didn't matter right now because Esther knew him. And not in a casual "hi, fellow classmate" way but an "of course I'll be at the place where you live and we regularly meet" way. Just another reason Ashley should be avoiding Esther. Maybe they were destined to be enemies to lovers after all.

"Ashley," Esther said.

Ashley pasted on her everything-is-fine smile before tearing her eyes away from the man and turning to Esther.

"I'll text you," Esther said, "and we can coordinate a time to meet up. Maybe this weekend?"

"Sure. Sounds great." *Please leave.* She didn't need the stranger in the doorway saying anything suspicious in front of Esther.

Esther nodded and strolled to the door. "You leaving too, August?"

"I just have to check a thing." He threw a thumb over his shoulder indicating farther into the building before giving Ashley another side-eye. "You go on ahead."

Esther shrugged and clomped down the corridor, disappearing from view.

Ashley returned her full attention to the man dripping with the tingling spark of magic before dropping her fangs. "What are you doing here, witch?"

2

Ashley

The witch had the audacity to raise a brow at her. Like finding a witch in vampire territory was perfectly normal and perhaps it was *her* reacting incorrectly.

"Yeah, I had a feeling you'd make a scene." He leaned out the door, checking if Esther had exited before turning back to Ashley. "Listen, how about you leave her alone and we'll forget we saw each other?"

He backed slowly out the door and turned in the opposite direction of Esther's exit.

Ashley knew she should pretend this hadn't happened and continue on her way as though someone with the ability to ruin her life—someone who instinctively knew what she was, and was apparently close with her newest project partner—wasn't out there bending the rules.

She stood in the classroom doorway listening to the shush of the main entrance closing behind Esther and their romantic comedy in one direction and the brisk step of retreating witch feet in the other.

Go home and pretend this didn't happen—or make *sure* nothing happened.

This year—the year she'd finally succeed and join the Family—was meant to be more Dawson's Creek and less Buffy. She couldn't just go around as the heroic blond destroying paranormal bad guys. That should have been rule number one, now that she thought about it—no destroying. She'd add it later. But this witch didn't have to know that. She could run in, huffing and puffing, and scare him off.

After all, she was a vampire.

Scary was their thing. Being scary and sexy. Or so sexy it's scary. She smirked before remembering she was in the middle of something important. Right.

Ashley took off, following the hall deeper into the building. The lingering trail of his magic bubbled in her throat as she passed rows of empty classrooms, listening. Her ankle boots clipped against the tiled hallway. A bat squeaked and fluttered around the insect-laden streetlight by the western entrance, and...a lone heart beat in a lab to the right. She took the corner, following the *thud thud* to the second door. Her hand stilled over the doorknob.

This had better be her year.

She turned the knob and flashed inside. Her face smacked into something cold and slimy and stinking of formaldehyde.

It dropped to the floor in front of her with a wet smack.

"I had a feeling you wouldn't take the *let's part ways amiably* plan," he said, "so if you'll give me a second to explain."

Ashley bent in half and dry heaved over the crumpled

carcass on the floor. A dead frog. The damn witch had levitated a dead frog knowing she would run into it. Oh god, she still felt it on her face. Was her mouth open? She tasted its salty chemical-soaked skin on her tongue. She needed a hot shower and toothbrush, stat.

The witch stood by the far window silhouetted by a streetlamp. "Long story short, she's my aunt, so there's this sort of general agreement."

"The frog?" Ashley looked down at the sad, disgusting creature. Witches were gross. It made sense they were related to frogs.

"Not the frog." The witch scoffed. "Were you even listening to me?"

She checked her top, making sure frog goo hadn't ruined it as well. There, at the right shoulder, was a pea-sized wet spot that would forever stink of dead frog and embalming fluids. "This was one of my favorite tops!"

Screw Dawson's Creek.

Buffy was back on the table.

Two rows of sturdy and sterilized lab desks separated them. Not enough to stop her. Her fangs dropped from her gumline as she stepped toward him.

He muttered something, and a sick sucking sound drew her attention to the side.

The frog squelched, limb by limb, off the floor and back into the air.

"You wouldn't dare," she growled. "I can have you in the lake with the rest of the frogs before you take your next breath."

She took another step.

"Hannah!" The witch's hands shot out in front of him like he was calming a wild animal but dropped the frog back to the floor. "Hannah Comstock."

That stopped her. "How do you know Hannah?"

"Like I was saying, she's my aunt."

Ashley burst out laughing, gripping her side and forgetting about the frog on the floor as she nearly fell over with this ridiculous claim. The laugh surprised her almost as much as the witch's comment. The witch thought Hannah, head of the Plattsburgh vampire Family, was his aunt.

"Hey," his tone came out grumbly. "I'm not lying. She's just a very great aunt. I've lost count of the number of greats. What is she now, two hundred?"

Ashley wiped tears from her eyes. "Are you serious? She's over two-fifty." She looked him up and down. "She never mentioned any living relatives. And certainly not any..."

"Of course she wouldn't mention me." He laughed without humor. "My dad married a witch and made another one. Why would she share that kind of information?"

Ashley squinted at him, trying to see anything to connect him to Hannah, but nothing obvious stood out aside from them both being white. The hair was all wrong, he was much too tall and bulky, and she couldn't recall what color eyes Hannah had so there was no way of knowing if his hazel eyes matched Hannah's until Ashley saw her next. She wouldn't let a chance run-in with, and subsequent disposal of, a secret nephew ruin her chances of joining the Family—even if he was a witch.

She took a step toward the door. "If you're lying, I'll be back."

"Tell Hannah August said hi. She'll hate to hear from me."

August. Of course. She hadn't fit it together until now. He was August *Platt*, as in Plattsburgh Platts, town legacy.

And apparently nephew of one of the oldest vampires in Plattsburgh.

⌣ ⌣ ⌣

Ashley

The Family lived in the old part of town in a gothic Victorian straight out of a slasher film. When she first came to Plattsburgh ten years ago, Ashley was convinced this was a mistake. The house was obviously full of vampires, and everyone must know it. But she quickly learned post-transformation—humans were very good at rationalizing away the odd or unexplainable. The old house also blended in among other paint-chipped Victorians, so it wasn't entirely out of the ordinary.

Forgoing the peeling railing, she hopped up the steps and paused with her hand at the doorbell and took a deep breath in the twilight. Ashley had lived here for years before her banishment and been back for two months. She pulled her hand back from the bell. Yes, today she'd enter unannounced.

The door swung open before she could properly grab the handle.

"Ash, darling. I thought I heard you lurking. Come in, come in." Claribel materialized from the shadows in a full, black-velvet-and-taffeta contraption from a seamstress she'd found on Etsy. She had a hard time with the idea of a girl named Ashley but loved the idea of ashes—hence the nickname.

Ashley let it pass. She needed to fit in, and it wasn't a big deal.

A pure Victorian, lover of poetry, and wild story-teller, it was hard to tell if anything Claribel said was true. Supposedly, as a child, she took a nap under an ancient cemetery oak and inspired Lord Alfred Tennyson to write a poem about her. Later, as a new vampire, she sought to extract the essence of Edgar Allan Poe and instead ended up draining him in a gutter.

"University was well, I hope," Claribel said.

"It was fine. Is Hannah still in?" Ashley's skin felt tighter the longer she didn't notify Hannah of a rogue witch gallivanting through town.

"She should still be in her chambers." She passed Claribel and entered the foyer, its vaulted ceiling painted midnight blue and spangled in gold stars. Carved oak arches traced from the center of the vault down to the four corners, finishing in spiraled columns. From the center of the vault hung a curling, iron chandelier decked with five globes, their warm glow enough to make the gilded stars pop but not near enough to drown the shadows lurking in the corners.

Claribel took up her post on the settee, an open mystery novel in hand. Her black gown and updo blended with the rich damask walls and heavy wood accents of the house giving her face an extra ghost-like pallor.

Through the columned entryway into the front sitting room, Gus hung from the ceiling, his small, furry body nestled among the blood-toned velvet curtains. He preferred his bat form to human, so all she knew of him was his name and that he preferred the southeast corner of the front sitting room.

Ashley ran to the curved, double stairs at the back of the foyer, taking the steep steps two at a time.

"We don't need another girl," a male voice said on the other side of the door to Hannah's room.

Ashley stopped, her fist poised to knock. Her chest squeezed as she recognized the voice as John's and the complaint to be her greatest fear.

"Where is she going to go?" Hannah's voice was short and clipped. She had a brisk, no-nonsense way about her that carried into her speech. "We have the room, and she's done her time."

"Five years is hardly any time."

They were definitely talking about Ashley. This was her third attempt to pass the trial to officially join the Family. After her last slip-up, she was sent from the house for five years while they cleaned up her mess, erasing the memory of her from everyone she'd ever come in contact with. It was the longest five years of her life.

"We don't need to be taking in charity cases," John said. "I can—"

"You can leave her be." Hannah enunciated each word.

"Woman, I am the man of this household and over a hundred years your senior."

"Old man, this is my house, and you may leave if it no longer suits you."

John huffed. "You regency women and your liberal views. In my day, a woman knew her place."

"Your day is long past, John Proof-of-Christ's-Everlasting-Love Peters."

Hannah and John's on-again, off-again vibe—which currently sounded off again—was Ashley's favorite form of entertainment at the house. This was basically *Dark Shadows*. She would watch the box set with her mom after dinner when her dad worked night shifts. Her mom would love to hear about the Family. Not that she could tell her anything. She did her best to ignore the tightening in her chest.

"Hey there, chickadee," a voice whispered, inches from Ashley's ear.

Ashley nearly jumped out of her skin.

Cynthia, the fifth and last of the core vampire Family, stood so close she nearly smacked Ashley in the face with the gold hoop earrings cutting through her straight, blond hair. She let out a cackle at Ashley's flinch.

"Shh," Ashley hissed.

Changed sometime in the 1970s at twenty-three, Cynthia was the closest in both apparent age and actual age to Ashley.

Ashley turned back to the door, answering in a hushed voice. "I'm waiting for them to finish."

"Oh, sure. No worries," Cynthia said. "We still on for this weekend?"

She couldn't hear Hannah and John anymore, which meant they'd probably heard her and Cynthia out in the hall. She tried pulling Cynthia away from the door, anything to look less suspicious.

"Yes. I got the flyer you left." Ashley wasn't sure what else to add to make Cynthia get the hint and leave. "Looks good."

"Cool beans." Cynthia shot her a finger gun, jumped onto the stair banister, and shot out of sight as Hannah's door squeaked open behind Ashley.

She took a moment to contemplate that, if they'd accepted the lawless Cynthia into the Family, surely Ashley could make it in too, before turning to find John glowering down at her.

"H-hi, John."

He was in his usual costume—starched white button-down and black slacks purchased presumably a half-century ago and meticulously maintained for longevity. During a speech about the "frivolity of modern dress," she learned that he possessed an excessive six sets of this outfit and a "finer" one reserved for Sundays and important guests. Not that they ever had guests.

"Are you in need of assistance?" he drawled.

Ashley was not short, but John and his lean frame towered over her. Weren't people short back in the 1600s? John must have come from the same stock as Lincoln.

"I was just looking for—" Ashley started.

"Is that the new child?" Hannah said from behind John.

Ashley cringed at the label but schooled her expression when Hannah pushed her way past him. It was impressive how much space such a small person could take up. Hannah came to Ashley's shoulder and John's chest. Her yellow hair was parted in the middle and fastened into a low bun in the back. What she lacked in height and adventurous hair, she made up for in loud, floral prints. Today was a high-waisted, cobalt maxi dress with a matching blue blazer covered in bold red poppies.

"I need to speak with you." Ashley sneaked a glance at John. "In private."

Hannah squinted at her. Maybe she didn't think Ashley's comment was worth the effort of privacy, but she turned to John and nodded him away before gesturing for Ashley to follow her into her room and closing the door behind them.

The original dark oak accents and walls of the master bedroom had been painted a pale, pea-soup green. Their steps faded in the truly horrendous hunter green-and-gold floral carpet. The four-poster bed, which dominated half the space, sported another pattern and a slightly different shade of green, and Ashley again marveled at how Hannah could be so fastidious and so gaudy at the same time. Was there some spark she couldn't see that drew Hannah to the stiff and colorless John, or was it just a lack of better options? What did that do to their sex life?

Nope. Not going there. Ashley shook the thought out of her head and turned back to Hannah. Best to get this over with.

"I met someone claiming to be your nephew," Ashley said.

Hannah didn't answer but gave a small huff of disapproval or acknowledgment that Ashley had spoken. After five years apart, she'd lost her ability to read people in this house. She wasn't even sure Hannah and John were still doing the will-they, won't-they thing.

So, Ashley kept talking. "And I know what he is. I told him his kind wasn't allowed in vampire territory, but he seemed to know this and felt exempt." It wasn't a question, but her sentence curled up at the end.

"He is an exception." Hannah's response started slowly then picked up to her usual clip as her thought finalized. "And we do not talk about him."

That was an answer. Not a satisfying one, but at least she was getting somewhere.

"I guess that's all I really had to say." Ashley regretted bringing up the topic. She'd just jeopardized her precarious position over a witch. "Just wanted to make sure everything was cool and all. I'll just..."

She backed slowly toward the door.

"Wait."

Crap. There went her third and final chance. And she was so sure she'd done the right thing this time. What happened when she ran out of second chances? Would they kick her out of the house? Leave her to find her own source of blood, figure out ever-changing and more necessary government documents, and evade vampire-hunting witches by herself? Or would it be something more permanent? What were the chances they let a lone and clueless vampire out into the world with the chance of exposing their existence to the humans? They might as well hand her over to the witches.

"He's attending the university?" Hannah picked at invisible lint on her sleeve.

"I think so. He was on campus."

Hannah nodded slowly, her gaze distant, and Ashley assumed her fate was at the end of whatever mental gymnastics were going on in Hannah's head. This could be very good news or very bad, and she honestly didn't know what either option would look like.

"I'd like for you to check on him," Hannah said at length.

Ashley blinked. Okay. She wasn't getting kicked out, but Hannah knew her nephew was a witch. This felt like a trap.

"Now?" Ashley asked. "He seemed fine when I left him." She didn't mention her previous threat to drown him.

"I'll give you his address." Hannah went to her secretary and pulled out a sheet of paper and quill. These old vampires and their reluctance with new technology.

The only reason Ashley had found them was that Cynthia was fascinated by "the World Wide Web" and had made a site only accessible through hearsay channels and links. Ashley had lucked out and found a business card with the address when she was most desperate. She'd hitchhiked halfway across the country to show up on their door with nothing but the clothes on her back and a slight hunch they could help her.

Hannah scratched out a few lines on the page, her calligraphy perfect, and gently shook the paper a few times to dry the ink before handing it to Ashley.

Ashley had so many questions but was too relieved that she wasn't being flung from the house or worse, so she kept them to herself. She noted the address before folding the page and cramming it in her back pocket.

"I expect regular updates—nightly if you can," Hannah said. "Just that he is well and how he's spending his time. He'll know you're there on my behalf, but...don't be explicit."

Again, Ashley wanted to ask why. He was a witch and a liability. Was this a test? Hannah must have heard the witch was up to something. Ashley would be sure to figure out what it was.

"All right." Ashley nodded and left the room. One more thing to add to her list of Things to Not Screw Up. Now she was babysitting the world's most annoying witch and trying to uncover his secret plot. This was going to be a long year.

3

───────

Esther

Esther's phone rang. Checking the ID, she answered the video call and threw it on her bed while she finished packing for work.

"Ah, yes," came the tinny voice on the phone. "The tapestry-like face of my oldest and dearest friend. How are you today, Esther, my love? Would you call yourself a ceiling or an under-roof?"

Esther shoved her laptop into her bag. "Is that your way of calling me old, Uther, my oldest and most faithful comrade?"

"I would never. But if I did, words could never part us. We are the peas of a single pod. The Gimli and the Legolas. The Geralt and the Jaskier..."

"The annoyer and the annoyed?" She blew at a lock of hair tickling her nose.

"Esther. Come, let me see your face so I may properly profess my love for you."

"Is that really necessary?"

"It very much is, yes. Thank you in advance."

Esther dropped her bag and plopped onto her bed with a huff. He wanted something. Which was fair. When she'd left her tranquil solitude—nearly one year ago to this day—to attend an open game night at the local board game café, she'd wanted something too. What she'd wanted was a casual acquaintance—an accountability partner, if you will—to check in and make sure they were both completing their homework and to alert the local authorities if she ever went missing.

What she'd ended up with was her fellow wallflower, Uther.

"What do you want, Uther?" she asked.

"Please, let me come to work with you. I'll behave. You'll barely notice me. I can help you, even. I love books or papers or whatever crap you're working with."

Esther stood, taking her phone with her. There wasn't any great way to make a serious face while lounging tummy-first on her bed, and he needed to know she would not be manipulated by his puppy eyes this time. "Uther, you are not coming with me. This is my job, and I can't just bring people with me willy-nilly."

"One, I can't believe you just willy-nilly-ed at me, and two, you visit me at work all the time."

"You work at a restaurant. It's a public place. I work in a private residence."

"Bitch, you just want him for yourself."

"Hey!" She shot a warning finger at the screen. "You know how I feel about using that word."

Uther sighed dreamily, ignoring Esther's comment. "He's like a young, queer Aragorn, which is literally my dream man."

She couldn't argue that point. It was probably August's

long hair. Or his brow ridge. God, that man could rock a strong brow ridge. But— "I'm more of a team Legolas, personally."

Although, that wasn't quite right either. If she was honest with herself, she was drawn to boldness with a hint of danger. But the closest comparison was when Eowyn ripped off her helmet, long blond hair flying in the wind, proclaiming, "I am no man," before stabbing the Nazgul. There wasn't a male example quite as sexy.

"You and your pretty guys. Just date a girl already." Uther and the camera spun so she was looking down on him as his hair fanned out in a golden halo. "What I wouldn't do for a hot, chauvinistic pig like *New Hope* Han."

She ignored his joke about dating women. "We've been over this. You are a treasure and deserve to be treated like one."

He flipped over again, forcing her to look away to avoid motion sickness. "You know I like them alpha. This is kink shaming, and I will not stand for it."

The corner of her mouth twitched, despite her best efforts to remain serious. She'd had her doubts when first befriending an undergrad, but god, she was so lucky to have found Uther. He was just as quiet around new people as she was, but once he got going, there was no shutting him up. She wasn't born with one of those personalities that opened up to people. Or even gave off an approachable vibe.

She thought of the blond girl at the front of her anthro class, Ashley. Always with the brightest smile and this vibe like she knew everyone, even when she was meeting them for the first time. It was unfair. There was something enticing about her. Like she had a glow you wanted to be around. Speaking of Ashley, Esther needed to text her to set up a time to meet for that assignment. She didn't want to be the reason Ashley did poorly in class.

"Hey." Uther snapped in front of the camera, drawing her attention back to the screen. "Stop daydreaming about men with long, blond hair and remember that I am your bestest friend and in need of this gesture of love from you. I can't actually talk to him, so I need any opportunity for face time outside of class that I can get. Pleeeeeeease."

He put on his puppy face, and Esther rolled her eyes. She knew this was coming, and yet some annoying muscle in her chest contracted as his bright, blue eyes doubled in size. "Okay—"

"Yay!" The camera shook as Uther leaped from the bed and ran around his room.

"Uther, sit down and look in my eyes."

He plopped belly-down onto his bed, his legs kicking behind his head, and bit his lip to hide his smile. It was the best she would get.

"Because you're my friend," she said, "I will *not* let you come to work with me and embarrass both of us."

"Esther! I thought you loved me I'm going to cry how dare you say that to my face." His entire run-on sentence was a single breath.

She winced at his use of the L-word. He was using it more and more lately, and maybe she needed to talk to him about that. But not right now. "But because you are my friend, and I need a ride, you can pick me up from work. And if you happen to come a few minutes early, you can hang out for a bit and wait."

Uther was back up and dancing around his room. She did her best to look serious and not laugh with him.

"Do not abuse this," she yelled as he continued to dance. "I need this job to graduate."

"You are the love of my life. I would never let you down. I will name our first child in your honor. Not your name because, um, Esther? Blah. But I will think of your beautiful face while naming Baby Han."

"Didn't you just say you thought Han was hot? This feels like a conflict of interest."

"Legolas then. Again, in your honor."

Esther grabbed her bag, bid Uther adieu, and set off for the historic Platt house. She didn't need a ride. Plattsburgh was such a small town. It was barely half a mile to the place. But it would be dark by the time she clocked out, and she felt better getting a ride. And Uther would never let her be if she didn't give him something.

She pulled out her phone while she walked and stared at the blank text addressed to Ashley. *Don't overthink it.* This was a school assignment, not some chance to form a closer relationship with another human being.

ESTHER

Hey Ashley, it's Esther.

Did she really use proper punctuation in a text? It looked like a letter. She deleted the message and tried again.

ESTHER

Hi.

Wow, that was a creepy one. Delete.

ESTHER

This is Esther.

Too direct. Was she a robot?

Time to consider this text objectively. What was her goal?

Ashley must think she forgot and that Esther was sabotaging her assignment. But every time she pulled out her phone, nothing came out right. She'd think of Ashley's giant blue eyes and golden mane and that smile she had that was almost a laugh and—

Esther stumbled on a sidewalk crack and lost her grip. Her phone bounced back and forth against her hands before landing with a wet thud in a puddle. *Serves me right.* She pulled the contraption out by a corner and dried it on her shirt. It sported a new crack bisecting one corner of the screen. *Great.*

At least it was working. Her phone pinged.

ASHLEY

Hey girl! When do you want to meet up? I'm free Friday after 6.

Oh, sweet Jesus, it sent the last message. Now she was a robot. She put her phone, The Betrayer, back into her pocket and walked the last block to the Platt house in ashamed silence. She'd text Ashley after work when she cooled down and had something brilliant to say.

Esther hopped up the steps to the two-story, redbrick house and rang the doorbell, one of those fun, manual twist ones that trilled through the house. It was the oldest private residence in town, built in the Neoclassical style.

August answered the door. "Hey, Esther. Come on in."

She entered the foyer and slipped off her shoes, placing them in their usual spot under the half-moon console by the door, and followed August from the muted seafoam and beige of the foyer into the gilded white of the sitting room.

Two days a week, every week, since the start of school a month ago, this was Esther's routine. Plattsburgh University required a practicum for the master's degree in library and information science, and she had happened upon a posting looking for an archivist to catalog the Platt family's historic records—soon to be donated to the local historical society.

"Do you have a minute?" August's words stopped her progress to the stairs.

Her neck strained to find him—still standing in the living room—while the rest of her body remained frozen, facing the steps in its determined retreat to the upper floors.

"Yes?" She honestly wasn't sure. This was not part of the routine, and routines were what kept her out of harm's way.

"Good." He gestured to the couch and sat cross-legged on the white-and-gilt chaise lounge across from it.

She approached the couch, giving him a once-over for anything else out of the ordinary. His long hair was pulled half back, as usual, and he was wearing a black tunic over black distressed jeans, making him stand out boldly from the white and gold and sunlight.

"Right." He nodded as she settled into the couch, took a deep breath, and suddenly, he was normal August, chin up, shoulders broad. He transformed his perch on the chaise into a king holding court. "We're looking for a book."

"We?" She shifted uncomfortably on the couch's old springs.

"I need you to find a book for me." He waved generally at the ceiling. "While you're going through the collection anyway."

"Any particular book in mind? I've found several. There was a fascinating journal by Zephaniah Platt on the creation of the town charter."

August made a face. "Not that. This is more of... Well, it's older, for one. Kind of like a weird cookbook maybe."

Now it was Esther's turn to make a face. She warred between frustration that he wouldn't just say what he wanted and annoyance that she wasn't upstairs already doing her work. "I think there was a collection of family recipes by Zephaniah's daughter, Hannah Comstock."

"Definitely not that. Just, if you see anything...weird, let me know, okay?"

"Besides this conversation?" Esther hadn't meant to say that out loud, but she was terrible at filtering her thoughts before speaking.

He rolled his eyes. "Just help me out, Esther."

"Fine." She stood and adjusted her bag. "I will look for a weird, old cookbook. Anything else?"

He sat a moment longer, a finger tapping at his knee like he was debating adding something more. But he shook his head, so she went upstairs to the collection—as usual.

4

Esther pressed the spring-tensed button at the top of the stairs, illuminating the space in a stale yellow.

The third floor had held the Platt family's staff quarters back in the house's heyday then was leased out as rooms when the house could no longer support staff, and finally—after gathering the requisite layer of dust—the inner walls were torn away one by one for the sake of storage. Now, overflowing shelves of earthy browns and fading jewel-toned manuscripts lined the sloping walls, while boxes of loose-leaf piled into a maze across the worn floorboards. An old, wooden desk was crammed under the window at one end, nearly hidden under the stacks of acid-free tissue, Mylar sleeves, and piles of moldy paper Esther still needed to dry wash before labeling, recording, and fitting safely in their sleeves.

She tossed her bag by the desk and dropped into the old wooden chair. The chair listed backward, wooden wheels finding the undetectable tilt to the floorboards, and forcing Esther to grab the desk before it carried her across the room.

"Not today, Trouble."

Its rusty springs groaned a reply as she pulled back into place. She couldn't be sure if the sound was reluctant acquiescence or a threat of future mischief. Probably both. But Esther couldn't complain. This was her ideal environment— quiet solitude and the control over her work that came with no one watching.

She'd underestimated the level of conservation this project needed, and part of her worried she wouldn't finish by the time her nine months were up. She still hoped to digitize the bound books for her final report.

When she'd first moved to Plattsburgh for her LIS degree, the fight for internships was competitive and some people were doubling up to pad their resumes. Through luck or timing or both, Esther had stumbled on one of the few paid openings in town through a fellowship program with the Plattsburgh Historical Society. When her year was up, they would box up the documents and continue whatever conservation and cataloging she hadn't finished. That plus the free housing she snagged in her uncle's spare bedroom and the GA position with Professor Jenkins meant she was able to cover the cost of food and even pay upfront some of the tuition her scholarship didn't cover.

She placed her hand fondly on the stack of yellowed paper awaiting her attention. Loose pages should be addressed first and save the easier, bound books for last. But with August's request to find this missing book, her plans had to change. She scooped up the papers from the desk, placed them lovingly into an acid-free box in the corner, and covered them in fresh silica gel packets, assuring them she would return soon.

Most of the sorting was done. Bound books in one spot, journals in another. Loose-leaf had its own space and odds and ends like photographs, portraits, and maps in another. There were labels and rules and procedures, simple steps so whoever took up this project next could continue with ease. Rules cut back on recommendations. If she messed up, it was because she missed a step or a rule was faulty. Not because her recommendation was a bad one. Not because her suggestion had impacted someone's life.

She pulled out her laptop and fired up the catalog system, letting that load while she grabbed a small stack of books from the shelf. Here in this attic, she lost herself in the easy movement of checking off lists and following the natural and well-researched order of archival work.

First up, and probably all she'd have time for today, was a small, handwritten journal. The leather cover remained soft but cracked near the spine, its edges hardened from the touch of decades of curious fingertips. She slid on her cotton gloves, cradling it in her palm as she turned the tissue-thin pages, yellowed with age and filled with tight but neat cursive. There was only a couple dozen pages. If she was diligent, she could finish transcribing by the end of the week.

Her transcription slowed as the journal drew her into a manifesto. Or maybe the making of a gothic romance. The nameless author spoke of duty handed down for generations, a secret society with the task of "containing the contagion of the night." With another flip of a flimsy page, she reached the end, only to realize she'd read the whole thing and only transcribed the first page. She checked again for an author but found no clue. Maybe August knew more, or she could ask a family member familiar with the collection. She would love to interview an elder Platt on some of the obscure things she'd found, but that wasn't part of her internship. She shouldn't be stepping outside the tasks outlined to her.

The clock downstairs chimed, breaking her focus. That couldn't be right. Six already? Esther pulled out her phone and confirmed the number of chimes matched what the modern world was touting as the current hour. She finished transcribing the sentence she was on, left enough notes in her notebook to remember where she'd left off, and packed up her bag to leave. Chair with a capital Trouble took its final opportunity for mayhem and shot out the second she stood, leaving Esther to chase it across the room and back into place.

"And stay there!" she commanded, stuffing a fistful of acid-free tissue under one of its wheels, pinning it under the desk where it belonged. It was a waste of resources but worth it if that damn chair would behave. "I'll see you next week."

"Well, that's no bigger than a womp rat," came Uther's voice.

Oh, Uther. Midway down the stairs, she cringed in the secondhand embarrassment wafting up from the floor below. She'd completely forgotten her promise to him until now. And that wasn't even a sexy movie quote.

She raced down the last flight, the creaking wood covering any further conversation until she joined them. "All right, I'm ready to go."

Uther turned to her, his face somehow conveying both relief and disappointment.

"No luck today," she said to August, "but I'll continue on

the books next week. Do you know if it's a bound book or more of a journal?"

"No worries," August said. "You'll know it when you see it."

Not helpful, but the one joy of hourly minimum wage was dropping everything at the end of the day and not thinking about it again until clocking back in.

Esther adjusted the strap on her bag and headed for the door when Uther coughed pointedly. She spun to see what she'd forgotten. Uther's eyes widened in a silent plea as he nodded toward August.

Right. She was supposed to be a supportive friend and get her bestie laid. Or at least a coffee date. Though she wasn't sure how salvageable that prospect was at this point.

She scrunched half her mouth and tilted her head, silently asking Uther if he was sure because they could bail now and save face.

He narrowed his eyes and shook his head just enough for her to see.

Well, if he insisted.

"Hey, August," she said.

August turned back from his retreat to the other room, and she had to hurry to come up with something—anything—to say that might keep him there.

"I hope it's okay," she said. "I asked Uther if he would give me a ride home. Now that it's getting dark earlier."

"Oh, that's no problem." He turned to Uther. "You're in my photojournalism class, right? With Dr. Welch?"

"Yes."

Esther waited for Uther to say more, but he seemed to have short-circuited.

Telepathically, she fed him the start of conversations: Was August also majoring in journalism? What were his thoughts on the teacher? The freaking weather, for goodness's sake. Anything.

But he just stood there like a statue until the tension was too much for Esther to stand and her thoughts shifted from conversation starters to ways to get out of there. Maybe she could start a small fire.

"Well, I suppose I'll see you at class." August released them from this purgatory, patting Uther's arm as he did so.

Esther knew she'd be helping him analyze this interaction the entire car ride home.

"Sure," Uther responded, his body finally reanimating. "It was good catching up."

They left the house, Esther first, Uther lagging as August closed the door for them with a smile. Maybe Uther still had a chance.

"You were kind of floundering a little there, friend," Esther said. They walked down the porch steps to the curb where Uther had parked.

"Not all who wander are lost," Uther replied with the smallest smile. "Did you see when he touched my arm?"

She nodded along, hiding her smile. "I did. It's getting pretty serious."

A breeze smelling of the chilled earth of fall pulled at her hair and stirred the leaves. She paused in the patch of grass between the sidewalk and curb and closed her eyes, letting the moment wash over her.

"Esther?" The newcomer's voice, bright and sweet as a peach, surprised Esther. She thought she'd imagined it, some piece of magic blown in with the wind. "How funny running into you here."

A cool hand touched Esther's arm, and she opened her eyes to look up into the face of Ashley—there on this sidewalk, of all sidewalks, in all the world.

Was Ashley always so tall? She was like an Amazon. That time after class, she must have been leaning against a desk because now she was like a tree towering over her. A curvy tree with impressive arms. How did she find the time to work out?

Ashley was still touching Esther's arm, a fact Esther noticed but did not point out. There was something nice about her touch. Calming in a way, like a cool breeze on a hot day. The red sky framed her long, blond hair and ocean eyes. For a moment, the rest of the world faded away, and they were the only two people on this street, in this galaxy.

"You didn't answer my text," Ashley said.

"Right." Esther backed away a step, returning from her journey through the stars.

Ashley's hand slid from her arm, and she remembered she was supposed to set up a date—or not a date—but a meeting of some sort. A get-together? Appointment? The name didn't matter. She was digressing.

"Yes. Sorry. I was..." She gestured vaguely at the Platt house, as though that was a real answer.

"Oh, right." Ashley glanced at the house, her face temporarily obscured, before turning with her usual smile. "You were seeing your guy."

"Excuse me?" Uther chose this moment to hop into the conversation. Because of course he did. "Are you talking about August? August is not *her guy*. He's not your guy, right? Esther, answer me!"

She rolled her eyes. "He's not my guy. Calm down, Uther."

His gaze ping-ponged between her and Ashley, brows furrowed before lifting to his hairline and nodding. She had no idea what he was nodding about, but whatever it was, she didn't like it.

"Hi, I'm Uther, Esther's best friend in the entire world." He offered his hand, and Ashley took it.

A vision flashed before Esther's eyes. The two of them, Ashley and Uther, going to brunch and laughing together, sitting on the little stools at the window table of that café downtown because the hostess knew to put the happiest-looking people on display. They were free marketing. *Come eat brunch here and you can be as happy as these two.* Ashley would claim him as her friend to whoever asked with no restraint, and Uther would return every text she sent him with the utmost punctuality.

"Nice to meet you. I'm Ashley." Ashley shifted a lock of hair behind her ear, nails the soft pink of clouds passing in and out of sight. "I'm in Esther's Anthro 101 class."

"Oh, the one where she's GA?" Uther tucked a fist under his chin as though this was the most fascinating conversation.

Esther could let this happen. They would make the perfect best friend pair. Ashley was fun and outgoing, and Uther, while shy in a crowd, made an excellent confidant. She could fade into the background and let nature take its course. He was supposed to be temporary, a phase to get her through school. Maybe it was for the best to let him go now. But picturing that future carved a hollow tunnel in her chest and a feral part of her extended its claws.

"Yes," Esther said. "They're partnering up to do an ethnography in her class, and I agreed to pair up with Ashley."

"You did, did you?" Uther said the words slowly and with a meaning Esther couldn't quite follow. She was still reeling from the unmoored feeling of losing Uther.

Ashley jumped in. "And it was so nice of you to offer to help like that. I had a family emergency when everyone was pairing up. Anyway, we still need to set up a date, or umm, a time to meet up and, you know, study each other?"

"Oh, studying each other." Uther turned to Esther, still using that weird, slow voice and nodding like some knowing idiot. Behind a hand, he mouthed the name Legolas before nodding to Ashley, and Esther glared at him. Maybe losing her best friend wouldn't be a bad thing.

"She means for the ethnography," Esther said. "Obviously."

"Obviously. Well." Uther clapped his hands and rubbed them together, backing up toward his car. "I don't want to keep you two from planning your not-date to study each other."

"Uther," Esther hissed, but he continued to open the door and get inside without her. "You are my ride home."

"It's not that far," he said. "Ashley can walk you. Give you time for that planning."

Esther was going to murder Uther. This was not the plan.

"I'll see you for brunch this weekend." He put on his sunglasses, despite the sun being long gone, and took off.

"Oh god, I miss brunch." Ashley sighed, her eyes soft and her gaze distant.

Right. Now she was here. Alone. With Ashley.

Deep breath.

"Warm butter melting over a fluffy pancake." Ashley's gaze was a mile away. "And when you heat up the syrup just right so it drizzles over the side and you have to soak it up with each cakey bite."

Esther's mind followed Ashley's, slicing into the pancake with the side of her fork, lapping up syrup until the piece was dripping, then for some reason, reaching across the table and offering the bite to Ashley, who waited, her lips soft and expectant, her gaze hungry.

Esther's stomach rumbled, breaking the silence. She needed a glass of water. For some reason, all the moisture had left her mouth.

"Sorry." Ashley clapped once, breaking them from the daydream and turned to Esther with a smile. This did nothing to settle Esther's nerves. "Which way are we walking?"

Thank goodness, a question she could answer. Or at least something to break her silence. "You don't have to walk me. You're obviously here for something else. I can walk myself."

"Oh." Ashley's smile wobbled and seemed like she might lose it, but she got it back in line. "It's no trouble, really. Plus, buddy system and all."

Fine. Esther turned and began down the path, a merry tap of heels behind her the only clue that Ashley was following.

"So. how does this ethnography thing work?" Ashley's shoulder brushed hers, and Esther course corrected to make space for her. The contact tangled their orbits. No matter how closely Esther hugged the edge of the sidewalk, she remained aware of the exact distance between her shoulder and Ashley's. "You just watch people and...write down what they do? Sounds a little creepy."

Esther shrugged. "That happens. The point is to try to keep as much of your personal bias out of your summary. For example, I could see someone wandering the sidewalks at night in ankle boots and assume she has no sense of preservation for her ankles, but maybe she just came from an event that required formal footwear."

"Or maybe," Ashley flipped a lock of gold over her shoulder, "the extra inches make her feel powerful, like every step she takes is at a starter block. So, she wears heels constantly, but ankle boots are the best for wandering sidewalks at night."

Esther's cheek tugged into a smile. She let a lock of hair block it from sight. "You realize you're already a giant, don't you?"

"Jealous much?" Ashley propped the back of her hand under her chin like it was a pedestal and laughed at her own antics. "What else?"

"What do you mean, what else?"

"This ethnography thing is fun. What else do you see?"

What else did she know about Ashley? Not much really. Esther always sat at the front of the class, so the only time she saw Ashley was when she walked into class, her hair long and shiny like some anime character, heels as previously described. She wore that trench coat every day, rain or shine, but some days, it was thrown artfully over her shoulder as she sauntered into the classroom, shouting a greeting at the first person she saw and three others before taking a seat. It was always a production. What did they do that weekend? How was that project they were working on?

"You care about people," Esther said. "Which works because you're an extrovert that thrives under being perceived."

"What?" Ashley's laugh stuttered. "You got all that from my choice in footwear?"

But there was something more. All that energy projected outward, a grand and last-minute entrance that always centered the conversation around others. Was she hiding something? Or maybe she was just a private person. Esther understood and appreciated privacy, though boisterous conversation wasn't an approach she'd ever considered.

"It's just the way you carry yourself," Esther said.

"Like a tall badass, right?" Ashley bumped Esther's shoulder and gave her a wink, crashing into her orbit again. "I'm going to have to watch you. Looks like there's more I could learn."

Esther's gut clenched. Despite that being exactly the point of their shared assignment, being noticed was not high on Esther's list of fun.

"So, what were you doing at the Platt house?" Ashley asked. "If you're not..."

In the unfinished sentence, Esther remembered Ashley assumed Esther was with August. "My internship," Esther explained. "I'm cataloging their records, the Platt family's. It's going to be donated to the historical society. So, I'm there two days a week going through papers."

"And you're a GA the other two weekdays? Plus classes. Sounds like a busy schedule."

"That's how grad school works." Esther shrugged. She knew when she signed on it would cost her two years of her life on top of tuition. "I have classmates with two internships and two student work jobs. Everyone feels the need to work harder, but there will always be someone doing more or better."

"How does anthropology fit in?"

The memory filled the space behind Esther's sternum with a warm fuzzy feeling. "It was my undergraduate degree. I loved anthropology. Every class was more story-telling than lecture. Humans are fascinating."

"Ha, you don't say. But you didn't stay in it?"

"You're good at these ethnographies already." She

needed to sidestep, to delay Ashley's probing questions. Their quickfire was sending her arm hairs to standing attention and making her long for a dark cave to hide in. Luckily, they rounded a corner and came in sight of her uncle's house. "I wanted...I guess I wanted something more behind the scenes. Something stable."

Ashley nodded earnestly. "Stability. I get that."

The front porch light flickered on behind Ashley's head. Her uncle's signal that she was in sight and expected. He would be setting out dinner soon.

"Friday works, by the way," Esther said. "Did you want to come by for dinner? I think the assignment was to watch an everyday ritual, so dinner should fit."

"Sure, I could come by for dinner." Ashley's smile grew at the invitation, the brightness drawing Esther's eyes like a tractor beam.

She cut her gaze to over Ashley's shoulder, trying to avoid the funny feeling she got when she met Ashley's eye. "Before you agree, I should mention," Esther said. "I'm staying with my uncle and cousin. They can be a lot, and I know family wasn't part of the deal for this assignment. We could do another time if that doesn't work."

"Oh, that's not a problem. I love meeting family."

"Great," said Esther, surprised at how cool Ashley was by the situation. But she could be just being polite. Who loved meeting family? "Well, I should get to dinner. Can you be by at six?"

"I can," Ashley cheered.

Esther chuckled at the enthusiasm. It was refreshing. Maybe she could take a leaf from Ashley's book.

"All right then."

There was a pause like Esther was supposed to say

something more but didn't know what. Of course, she had to make this awkward. Maybe Ashley's bubbly and friendly personality would rub off on her. In the meantime, she made a gesture she hoped looked like a wave and jogged back to the house.

5

Ashley could die of embarrassment. She loved family? Was she a creep trying to hit on other people's innocent relatives? Who said things like that? And Esther took her babbling like a champ.

Of course, all the embarrassing things she said came back to her as she mounted the steps to Esther's house that Friday, promptly at six. And empty-handed. She was claiming to be good with family and yet not even flowers or a bottle of wine. Except that the vampires reset all her government IDs to twenty when she came back, so no wine purchasing for her. She suspected this was part of her punishment, though no one outright told her.

So much for being the smart and put-together human she was trying to embody. Esther's family was stuck with an empty-handed fool of a vampire for dinner.

She sighed as she knocked on the door.

The door opened a crack, and a small boy somewhere between the age of five and ten—based on her limited knowledge of children—with dark, floppy brown hair wearing a T-shirt with what looked like a hyper-pixelated pie poked out his head.

"You're not allowed in here," he said.

Did she have the right house?

"Hi, I'm Ashley." She hadn't interacted with kids in literal decades, but surely, they responded similarly to adults or semi-adults—wherever she fell on the spectrum— with a direct approach. "Does Esther live here?"

"Stranger danger," he yelled at her and hissed.

Esther's voice called from farther inside. "Leave her alone, Jason. Don't listen to him, Ashley. He's just joking."

The boy scowled before running away, leaving the door swinging on its hinge. This was awkward. She'd never been in a situation like this before. Curious, she reached through the open doorway. As she suspected, her hand met an invisible wall. This was the dumbest piece of nonsensical lore and served no purpose whatsoever. Yet here it was, ruining her life. She tried feeling along the opening for—for what? A weak spot where a vampire needing permission to enter a human's house didn't count? It was smooth like glass, but when she tried knocking, the magical force field wouldn't make a sound.

Interesting. If only she could write her ethnography on the struggles of being a new vampire in the twenty-first century. But then she *really* wouldn't get into the Family. As much as Hannah and Claribel supported Ashley's education, none of them would be keen on the idea of her revealing the existence of vampires to Professor Jenkins. Not that her professor would believe it anyway.

But back to the problem at hand.

"Hey, Esther," she called, hoping Esther was still within hearing distance. "Is it okay if I come in?"

"Yes, yes. I'm just finishing up with the side. Make yourself comfortable."

Ashley reached out again, and this time, her hand felt no resistance. What a ridiculous curse. Was there any vampire lore more outdated than not being able to walk through a freaking door when she wanted to?

She stepped into the entryway, and a wave of energy blew over her, heat lapping at her skin like someone had left a giant oven open. She hissed, covering her face with her arms to try to block whatever was attacking her. She pressed against the opposite wall.

Through her fingers, she made eye contact with an extremely mopey-looking Jesus, nailed to a cross. Dammit, there had to be a crucifix right there at the entryway?

Esther came around the corner then. "Is something wrong?"

Ashley dropped her arms from her face. "No, I just, umm... I bumped my elbow on the door is all. Funny bone."

She rubbed her elbow for show and tried putting on the most authentic-looking smile she could, despite burning alive standing there.

They needed to move. Now. Before her face turned red and started sizzling.

"Is there somewhere I can leave my coat?" She ducked past Esther into what looked like the living room.

More flames came at her from all directions.

Figurines and shadow boxes and ornate crosses covered the walls and tables of the living room.

"That's a lot of Jesus." Ashley tried her best to sound casual. "And some Marys as well. Is your uncle Catholic?"

"Oh." Esther's voice softened, and she toyed with a piece of her hair, looking around the room.

Ashley internally kicked herself. If she wasn't so

distracted by the pain of each object burning into her skin, she would have remembered religion was a taboo topic for first-time visitors.

"Yes," Esther said. "This whole side of my family is very religious."

"Well, they're charming." Ashley gestured at a nearby Mary trying to burn her hand to a nub. If she kept her distance, she could hopefully make it through this evening without looking like a boiled lobster. "Sometimes it's nice to have a community with a common pursuit. Makes us feel less alone in the world."

Esther looked around as though just noticing how many religious objects surrounded them. Her cheeks pinkened appetizingly. If Ashley were able to function at full capacity instead of ignoring angry effigies radiating invisible fire at her, she would take this moment to curve the conversation into something light and easy. The weather, classwork, hobbies. She'd used these go-to conversations so often that even now they came to her in this fiery hell, but only as buzzwords.

Short of shouting, "Weather!" at Esther, she wasn't sure how to fix this.

"I have a complicated relationship with Catholicism, to be honest." Esther brushed her hair behind one ear and tapped her socked toe on the hardwood floor behind her. "It has its faults, but there's also what you said, the community aspect. It's my childhood. I've identified with it so long that to deny it would feel like denying I was born." She chuckled lightly, and Ashley begged her silently to continue. "It has its merits. I like that it leaves room for the gray parts of us."

"The gray parts?" Ashley had grown up in a casually Methodist household, so her knowledge of Catholicism was slim. She knew generally about the idea of saints and Mary being a big deal but had hoped there was enough of a cross-over that she could still keep up with the conversation.

"The idea that an imperfect person can still go to heaven. Purgatory specifically. Heaven and hell are so all-or-nothing. Purgatory leaves the door open so you don't end up condemning anyone. I like the idea that a whole religion left room for the gray."

"Oh my god, you're a marshmallow."

"I'm a what?" Esther's brows furrowed, and her nose scrunched in an adorably put-off way.

Ashley was being unfiltered again. She blamed Jesus. "No, wait. If there's a redemption arc available for everyone, would anyone go to hell?"

"If it were my cosmology..." Esther blushed and looked off somewhere over Ashley's shoulder. "I guess everyone would get a chance at a redemption arc, as you put it."

Ashley laughed with delight at the new depths she'd discovered. "Yes, you're a marshmallow. You give off this hot, badass, goth chick vibe, but in your heart of hearts, you're an optimist who believes, even in death, everyone deserves a second chance. You're a hard shell with a soft, gooey center."

Esther's foot tapped faster, and her face got so red Ashley wondered if the heat from the relics was getting to her as well.

Despite how much physical pain she was in, Ashley loved this. When was the last time she had a conversation with someone that meant something? Even before her transformation, she had a reputation to keep up. You didn't become cheer captain and class president by discussing politics, life goals, and people's thoughts on the universe. You won by knowing everyone's name, one fun fact about them, and constantly providing an aura of happiness through easy, mindless conversation.

Well, screw the weather, what were Esther's thoughts on reincarnation?

Hurried stomping echoed from the other room before the boy from earlier burst in, grabbing the door frame as he ran so that only the top half of him swung in to look at them.

"Dinner's ready," he screeched before running back to wherever he came from.

"I guess that's our cue," said Esther.

"Please, let's pick this up again later. I am fascinated." Ashley wanted nothing more than to hear Esther describe her views on right and wrong, good and evil, and the ideal cosmology of Esther. She touched Esther's arm lightly, giving a gentle caress with her thumb, and heard Esther's heart rate increase. That was a fun trick. She let Esther lead her through the door the small boy had scampered through.

"Did you bring your notebook? I wasn't sure if I should tell them about the project or not. On the one hand, it's ethical to let people know they're part of a project, but on the other hand, they will be weirder than normal in an attempt to not be weird, which will inevitably ruin your study."

Ashley smiled. "Let's tell them. I like weird."

6

Esther

Esther prayed to all that was holy and listening Uncle Pete and Jason behaved themselves for one evening.

"Soup's up," called Uncle Pete from the kitchen. He wore his usual ratty T-shirt, vintage only because he'd kept it for so long, and his "comfy jeans." She knew he owned nicer clothes. He just didn't like to wear them unless they were going out. And she never would have asked that of him. She didn't ask things of family—her whole housing situation had been negotiated through her mom's insistence. But this was Ashley's first time in Esther's personal life, and a jittery energy in her leg wouldn't rest until everything was perfect.

He carried the soup to the table, a reindeer oven mitt on each hand as he lugged the heavy pot by the handles. Jason scampered behind him with a set of crocheted hot pads for the table.

"Can I help with anything?" Ashley dove into the action, adjusting the hot pads Jason threw onto the table and following Uncle Pete into the kitchen for the bowls and utensils.

"Ashley, you're a guest." Esther followed them, partially to retrieve her side salad but mostly to monitor the situation.

"I don't believe we've been properly introduced. I'm Ashley." Ashley was shaking hands with Uncle Pete by the time Esther caught up.

"Well, it's nice to meet you, Ashley. Call me Pete. Uncle Pete if you're feeling feisty. And that's Jason running around somewhere. So, you're Esther's friend." It wasn't a question, more an accusation. As though Ashley was the first human Esther had brought to the house.

"I like to think so. Esther's helping me out with my anthropology project. I'm here to see how dinner ticks. Any chance you'd be willing to walk me through it?"

"This your first time eating dinner?" He laughed at his own joke.

Without missing a beat, Ashley countered, "It's my first time eating *your* dinner, Uncle Pete."

She threw in some finger guns, and Uncle Pete laughed even more.

"Well, welcome aboard, Ashley." He handed her some bowls, and she saluted sharply before turning back to the table.

She gave Esther a quick wink while passing her in the doorway, as though they were both in on some joke, though Esther wasn't sure what the joke was. A spark zapped down her sternum, a part of her excited to be in on the secret and nearly distracting her from the mortification of Ashley being forced to set her own place at the table.

"Jason," Uncle Pete called. "You're in charge of spoons. Esther, come help me with drinks and toppings."

She dropped the salad off on the table and ran back for cups before Ashley could be enlisted for another round.

In no time, the table was set, grace was said, bowls were filled with Uncle Pete's Famous Taco Soup, and dinner was on.

"Hey, Jason, pass the sour cream. Ashley, you have to try a dollop of this. It's what makes the soup." Uncle Pete handed the tub back to Jason, who made a face and pushed it away.

"Yuck."

Esther rolled her eyes. They went through this every time he made Taco Soup.

"Yuck?" Ashley squinted dramatically. "Are you trying to trick me, Uncle Pete?"

"Me?" Uncle Pete placed a hand on his chest, hamming up the moment. "I would never."

This was the most animated they'd been together for a meal in a while. Esther marveled at Ashley's ability to seamlessly ingrain herself in their routine and even bring out her uncle's playful side. Why had she worried about her family when Ashley was here to smooth it all over?

"Esther," Ashley said.

Esther jumped, forgetting she was at the table and not watching a dinner documentary.

Ashley was looking at her. "What do you say? Sour cream or no sour cream?"

Sour cream or no sour cream? Well, there were many factors to consider. Had the sour cream unknowingly expired? Can Ashley handle dairy? What were her taste preferences? So many variables with answers she didn't have access to. On the one hand, it was her uncle's recipe, and he preferred sour cream on his soup, which made sour cream truer to the experience. But on the other hand, there were many dietary risks of consuming sour cream. Should she risk putting Ashley's stomach in danger of digestive issues or suggest she skip what was considered the true experience?

Her hands started to sweat, and she wondered how long she'd remained silent considering both options and their endless variables. A part of her knew this was the lowest of stakes. What was the worst that could happen if she gave the wrong answer? Her mind helpfully filled in the blank with an allergic reaction and calling 9-1-1, Ashley being so offended by the flavor she'd choke and die, and Ashley never speaking to her again after learning Esther had kept her from a full experience.

Her spiral into panic was interrupted by Jason's laughter.

"Don't ask Esther," he said. "She gives bad advice."

Ashley chuckled but stopped when no one joined her. "You're serious?"

"She does have a bit of a reputation." Uncle Pete took another spoonful of soup with a perfectly proportioned dollop of sour cream. "I mean, there was Aunt Clare's hair." He laughed to himself now. "You don't recommend bangs a week before your wedding."

"Oh, oh!" Jason bounced in his seat, eager to add to Esther's humiliation. "What about that road trip where everyone threw up?"

"The family reunion!" Uncle Pete was roaring with laughter now. "I forgot Esther was the one to pick the restaurant. We all got food poisoning. Took out a whole public bathroom by the end of the night."

Esther sank into her seat, her face heated. They weren't wrong, but did they have to relive this now? In front of Ashley, the perfect person who could do no wrong. It only drew their differences into sharper relief. There was something wrong with Esther. Something that made her always choose the wrong option and only reiterated her need to avoid making decisions and to avoid people altogether. Uncle Pete and Jason hadn't even brought up Esther's worst suggestion on record. She needed to end this conversation before it got any worse.

"Well, that just sounds like a bunch of coincidences. I'd still like to hear Esther's opinion on the sour cream." Ashley smiled at Esther, her teeth bright, her head slightly tilted in the most encouraging way. As though saying, *Go ahead, Esther. Prove your family wrong. Break the cycle.*

But that wasn't how this worked. It didn't matter what answer Esther gave—it would be the wrong one, and she'd be to blame for whatever negative outcome. It could be small. It could even be nothing this time. But it could be something, and it could be life-changing. And she wasn't ready to shoulder something like that. Not again.

"I don't give advice," Esther said.

"Esther, I—" Ashley started.

"Just leave it alone, okay," she snapped. "Eat the soup however you want to eat it and leave me out of it."

Esther continued eating her soup without the sour cream, and dinner was blissfully silent, aside from spoons scraping bowls. Ashley typed out a few notes on her phone but didn't ask any more questions. Which was perfectly fine with Esther. This dinner was a reminder that people made her life difficult, and the sooner it was over, the sooner she could return to her peaceful solitude.

When Esther had scraped the last bit from her bowl, she stood, her chair screeching against the wood floor. "I'm finished. Can I take anyone else's bowl?"

Jason passed her his, and she hurried off to the kitchen. She turned the sink to scalding and let the heat and menial task of rinsing dishes wash away the stress of the moment and the memory of her embarrassing outburst. The truth was Esther didn't give bad advice—it was just that when she was presented with two options, a voice in her head rooted for the one that made the most waves. But she'd learned her lesson over and over again. The problem with picking the more exciting option was that it rarely worked out the way she might hope and people got hurt in the process. People she cared about. And they wouldn't let her forget.

As she lowered the bowl to put it in the dishwasher, it was scooped up, and another dirty bowl was placed in her hand. Ashley had joined her, wordlessly loading the dishwasher while Esther rinsed the dishes.

"Hey," Uncle Pete said.

Esther turned to find her uncle hanging in the doorway of the kitchen.

"Let me and Jason finish that up. You girls head upstairs and work on that project."

"Are you sure, Uncle Pete?" Ashley was faster to answer, placing the last bowl in the dishwasher as Uncle Pete carried in the pot with the last of the soup. "It's no trouble."

"We are highly capable men, who happen to know our way around a kitchen. Isn't that right, Jason?"

Leftover containers clattered to the floor as Jason climbed through the Tupperware cupboard.

"Well, holler if you need backup." Ashley toweled off her hands and waited expectantly by the door.

A second passed before Esther registered it was her Ashley was waiting for. She toweled off and followed Ashley out of the kitchen. Esther wasn't sure where they were going or if Ashley was leaving. Surely, she would say something. But Ashley continued putting one determined step in front of the other as she passed the front entryway and returned to the living room on the far end of the house. When she reached the exact center of the room, she turned on her heel to face Esther and placed her hands on her hips. The whole move was snappy and neat like she'd performed it hundreds of times. Her golden hair flew like a flag as it flipped over her shoulder and landed in the most delicate and perfect position, half of it trailing over the opposite shoulder and an artful tendril shadowing one eye.

"I don't want to impose on you or anything," Ashley said, "but if you wanted to show me around or just hang out, I don't have anywhere to be."

Something about that tendril of hair was distracting and making Esther's thoughts go all fuzzy. Was it the nearness to Ashley's eye? It was dangerous and precarious, and she wanted to brush it away to somewhere safer.

Esther's fingers twitched at her side. She couldn't touch her classmate's hair. What if she accidentally swiped a finger across Ashley's face, her cheek that rounded when she smiled. She wondered how soft it would be, how warm. She stepped forward, her feet betraying the warning signal going off in her mind, bringing her closer and closer like a moth to a flame until they were only an arm's length apart.

Ashley's smile dimmed as Esther drew nearer, her breaths growing slower and shallower, and as the smile faded, a spark in her eye grew brighter. A sea of fathomless sapphire, depths Esther could only imagine opened, as though her smile was nothing but a shield and, without it, a deeper and darker Ashley shone forth.

Esther craved this Ashley, the open and real one. But how to make her stay? Ashley's lips parted, and Esther stared, transfixed, waiting for whatever would come out of them.

A pot clanged from the kitchen, followed by the long

chiming of church bells. Right. Uncle Pete had put on his favorite AC/DC album.

"Did you want to go upstairs?" Esther asked as electric guitar accompanied the chiming of *Hells Bells*.

"Yes," Ashley whispered then coughed and shook her head. "Yeah, sure. That sounds great." Her smile was back in place.

7

—————

Ashley

Esther had looked at her mouth. That was a classic romance move. It'd been a few years, but Ashley read romance. She knew that was a move. And now they were walking up the stairs—where bedrooms were kept—Esther's cute ass right there in front of her, rocking those black jeans, and Ashley had to wonder, was this night shifting into date territory? Sure, Uncle Pete was down there mucking up the atmosphere but also pushing them upstairs to some privacy.

No, she was getting carried away by the moment. What would twenty-year-old Ashley do? Ashley spun around, pointing like a compass at the three doors at the top of the stairs. "Which one is yours?"

"Oh, these are Uncle Pete, Jason, and the bathroom." Esther pointed at each door, eliminating them one by one.

Ashley stopped her spinning. Did Esther not have a room? She knew Esther didn't live here permanently, but she assumed they were headed to Esther's room. Ashley's pondering was interrupted by the squeaking of old springs. Esther had pulled a cord from the ceiling, opening a hatch and unfolding a ladder staircase.

"I'm up here." Esther climbed the steps, disappearing into the empty, black rectangle.

Ashley grabbed the ladder, waiting until a yellow glow illuminated the hatch before starting up. A waft of cool, stale air and dust molecules flowed down to her as she climbed. As though the space hadn't been properly aired out in a while.

"Sorry, it's a bit of a mess. It's technically only half-finished. But rent is free, and it's close to campus, so I can't complain."

Ashley reached the top, her hand resting on the rough plywood floor as she pulled herself up the rest of the way. The space in front of her was a mess. On top of the bare plywood was a tightly packed maze of boxes and stuffed trash bags. In the far corner was a fully assembled Christmas tree. And over all of it, the sloping ceiling showed bare beams filled with puffy insulation, trimmed professionally in brown paper as though waiting to be properly covered in drywall and made into a real room if only someone had the time. Ashley scanned the boxes of old toys and out-of-season clothing, wondering where Esther could possibly fit.

When she turned, it was like she was in a different world.

A thick layer of blue and red vintage rugs hid the rough floors. The brown paper ceiling was disguised beneath mandala tapestries tacked in place. And the bare wood beams running horizontally between the arches of the ceiling were looped with strings of lights, giving the space a warm, yellow glow. A plain mattress, propped on recycled pallets and covered with a slightly mussed, white linen duvet, dominated the center of the space, and in the far corner under the round window rested a vintage tufted armchair next to a small, overflowing bookshelf.

As though entering a holy place, Ashley stepped cautiously, reverently into Esther's room.

"It's beautiful."

Esther stood in a corner by the chimney separating the two halves of the attic, her attention on Ashley, as though waiting and judging Ashley's reaction. There was something disarming about the way Esther watched the world. Like she saw through the face Ashley presented, the smiles and the cheerful words, to whatever she was in the dark.

They certainly couldn't have that, so Ashley pasted on an especially bright smile and moved to the far side of the room, plopping into the armchair. It wasn't until she was seated on the worn cushion that she noticed the record player on the floor and the crate nearby with a handful of vinyl. She combed through them like the nosy busybody she was. It was a small collection of about ten. All vintage and mostly classical music, though there was Barbra Streisand's album, *Wet*. She plucked it up and held it so Esther could see, only raising a brow in question. Esther walked closer. A blush traveled up her neck and colored her cheeks. Delicious.

"It's my mom's." Her answer was almost apologetic.

"Barbra's a classic," Ashley said, tucking the album back with a shrug. "What do you have in the player? Please tell me it's Debussy."

"Are you a fan of Debussy?"

The quick way Esther asked had Ashley regretting making the reference. Here she was, trying and failing to make *Twilight* references when Esther actually cared about Ashley's musical taste.

"He has some good ones." *Probably*. But Ashley only knew the one.

A glance at the bookshelf proved *Twilight* was nowhere to be found. Bram Stoker's *Dracula* was there though, which also made sense. Esther seemed like the type to enjoy the darker classics. She'd probably love talking to Claribel about the authors Claribel had met and eaten over the years.

On second thought, she should probably keep Esther away from Claribel.

Ashley picked up the book resting on top of the shelf, half-heartedly flipping through the pages. "I used to love to read, but..." She broke off, years of solitude flashing before her eyes. She pulled them back into the box in the back of her mind where she kept them. "I haven't had a chance in a while."

"You could borrow one," Esther offered. "If you'd like."

If she'd like? Sharing books was a sacred thing. "Are you sure?"

"Of course." Esther shifted from her spot by the bed and knelt in front of the shelf. "I couldn't fit my whole collection. Some of these I'm borrowing from Uncle Pete." Her fingers combed through the spines.

Ashley slid off the chair to join Esther on the floor. The space was small, and she sat close enough that only a whisper of space separated her knee from Esther's.

"Which one would you suggest?" Ashley asked.

Esther's smile faded, and her shoulders pulled up. Her hand fiddled with her ear, hidden within her curls, as her gaze—darting across the shelves—turned more frantic than loving, and Ashley realized her mistake. Esther didn't give advice.

"I mean, which is your favorite?" Ashley asked quickly.

The tension in Esther's shoulders loosened at the change in wording. Ashley resisted the urge to rub Esther's back like she was soothing a scared animal.

"They're mostly old reads," Esther said, "so I don't know how many you've read already. I've always loved Poe."

Maybe she would hate Claribel.

"What's your favorite of his?" Ashley's legs were losing feeling from kneeling for so long, so she shifted off her legs, her knees pointing to Esther. In a burst of confidence, or maybe recklessness, she placed her hand on Esther's ankle in that small stretch between jean and sock, her thumb resting lightly on the knob at her joint. Esther didn't move or say anything, but Ashley heard her heart rate pick up.

A chuckle that was only a quiet puff of air escaped Esther, and she turned her attention from the books to Ashley. "You want me to pick a favorite? Impossible. And where would I begin? Favorite short story? Favorite poem? Something scary, romantic, a mystery?"

Esther shifted to her side too, and Ashley's hand was brushed away in the motion, but their socked feet ended up touching. This felt more intimate.

"Start where you want," said Ashley. "I want to hear everything."

"I probably sound like a creep, but when it comes to short stories, I love his dark stuff. 'The Pit and the Pendulum,' 'Masque of the Red Death,' 'The Cask of Amontillado.' More revenge and torture than mystery. But with his poetry, I'm all about the tragic love like 'The Raven' and 'Annabel Lee.' Though there's something to the hopeless fortitude of 'Eldorado.'"

"I think I read 'The Raven' in school." Ashley laughed. She was way out of her element but wanted to keep Esther talking.

"Here." Esther pulled a large black book from the shelf without even looking for it and shoved it into Ashley's lap with a thump. *The Complete Tales and Poems of Edgar Allan Poe.*

"Esther, this is your copy." She didn't know how to express what this meant to her. "He's your favorite."

"Please, I have half of them memorized." She shifted closer, and her next words were confident. "Besides, you'll bring it back to me."

Ashley was still unsure. Taking this book was a commitment, a promise that this one-time not-date would happen again, but she hugged the book to her all the same. "Why don't you give advice, Esther? I know it's not because of silly things like recommending a bad haircut or a restaurant where everyone got food poisoning. Everyone does that from time to time."

Esther's mouth opened and closed like she might say something and changed her mind. Ashley stared, riveted, until Esther settled with, "Read a few of the stories. You don't have to read them all, but tell me which one you liked, or hated, and when you bring it back, I'll tell you."

A lock of hair fell in front of Esther's face, taunting Ashley. It was cliché. Super cliché. But her hand moved anyway as she shifted forward and brushed the piece of hair back behind Esther's ear. Ashley still wasn't even sure if this was a date or friends or just two classmates hanging out. Was Esther leaning forward?

Ashley leaned in too, ever so slowly. She heard Esther's heart beating fast as they inched closer. She counted the pale freckles speckling Esther's nose. Felt her warm breath ghosting Ashley's cheek. It was important Esther made the final move.

Something behind Esther's ear stung Ashley's finger, and she yelped and jumped back. The sting turned into a burn that sank into her skin as she tried to keep back tears and hold in her fangs from their instinctual fight-or-flight reflex. They extended anyway, and she had to pout slightly and turn her head to hide the canines poking out between her lips. With a shuddering breath, she pulled them in and turned back, studying Esther's face to see if she noticed.

"Are you all right? What happened?" Esther reached for her hand, and Ashley reluctantly released her fist so they could both look.

At the end of her ring finger was a perfectly burned cross, still steaming from the contact. Ashley pulled her hand back and looked at Esther's ear. As she suspected, a small cross dangled from the end.

This was a mistake.

She shouldn't be up here in this private space, sharing books and pushing back hair.

She was a vampire. Even if she didn't have the Family telling her to keep apart from the humans, there was so much baggage that came with being with her—with being with a vampire—and she couldn't put that on someone.

"I should go." Ashley stood, practically jumping over Esther in her haste to get out of this close romantic setting. She stubbed a toe on Esther's platform bed but ignored the shooting pain. It took the last of her control to keep a human speed while descending the steps.

"Ashley, wait."

But she couldn't wait. Maybe Esther hadn't seen her teeth, but she'd seen the burn. It wasn't subtle. Anyone that knew the lore knew what that meant. Esther had *Dracula* on her freaking shelf.

"Tell your uncle I said thank you for the dinner," she called over the creaking of Esther running down the stairs. She slipped on her shoes, praising the speed of ankle boots, and ran out the door without looking back.

Outside, Ashley didn't bother with human speed. She needed to get out of there. She couldn't see Esther ever again. Maybe she could drop the class. Would this night compromise her entire mission?

It wasn't until she was back at the Family's house and in her room that she realized she still had *The Complete Tales and Poems of Edgar Allan Poe* tucked safely under her arm.

8

———

Ashley

Ashley used both hands to turn the knob of the doorbell, maintaining a steady stream of ringing. It only took three minutes of persistence before the door wrenched open.

August, with his tingling cloud of magic, stuck out his head. "Hey, that's an antique!" He spotted Ashley, and his frown deepened. "Dammit, it's you."

"Let me in, witch."

"Pass." He slammed the ancient door in her face.

She went back to ringing. Five minutes passed before the door flung open again.

"What do you want?" August asked.

"Invite me in."

"Not going to happen."

"I'll bring your aunt here next time."

His eyes narrowed. "That's a bluff. She hasn't been here in years."

"Years mean nothing to her. Besides, it's no fun hassling

you from the windows." She put on her best pleading face, as though she hadn't threatened his life only a week ago.

A week of following the witch to and from his one evening class then staring through the window like some sad puppy looking for a home while he twiddled endlessly at his computer. It was the most boring week of her life, and she was now convinced that Hannah was just being paranoid when she'd assigned Ashley to keep an eye on him. The witch did nothing with his life. Even when she yelled through the window, demanding he be more exciting, the most she could get out of him was a glower and an extra burst of his annoying magic for her troubles. She'd entertained herself by singing show tunes and tapping on his windows until he growled and sulked upstairs where she couldn't follow him. Hannah's request to be subtle no longer seemed important when she was so bored.

"Are you kidding me?" There was that higher register in his voice that was her daily goal to reach. She didn't even bother hiding her smile. "Are you planning on trying to kill me?"

"I wouldn't try. I would *do*. Do or do not, and all that jazz." She added jazz hands to emphasize her point.

"As Yoda sagely proclaimed." He opened the door farther and turned back inside. "Fine, you can come in, but take off your shoes and don't touch anything."

"Yay," she trilled, following after him and kicking her shoes at the corner just to watch him cringe as they smacked the ugly blue wallpaper. She hadn't expected demanding entry to work. Maybe all that singing had finally worn him down.

"I regret this already." He sighed, snapping his fingers to turn on the lights in the next room.

"The light switch was literally right next to you." She pushed the off button, demonstrating her point.

"Hey!" He snapped the light back on again. "What did I say about touching things? That's an antique."

"They're all antiques." She flailed her arms, indicating the room at large. "You literally live in an antique."

"That's why you can't touch any of it. Do you want me to rescind your invitation? It'll be entertaining to see you magically flung from here."

"Is that a thing?" Ashley paused mid-tapping a portrait of a tightly buttoned woman with a cat on her lap to lay slightly askew. She checked his expression for sincerity.

"Care to find out?"

She thought about it. Being magically flung sounded pretty cool, but something told her he wouldn't try it. Whatever changed his mind about letting her in wasn't going to change in the first five minutes. To be nice, she played along, opening her eyes wide and blinking playfully, the picture of innocence. He scoffed and took a seat in his gaudy sitting room.

"So why do you live in an antique anyway?" Her fingers trailed along a console, leaving a line in the thin layer of dust.

"Easy. My parents retired to Florida and left me the house since I'm the only Platt left in town." He shifted Cat Lady back into a mostly straight alignment.

Ashley moved on to a bowl of glass fruit, picking up and inspecting each one individually. "Yeah, but you could move. Sell this place and get your own wherever you want, with light switches and doorbells from this century."

He looked at her like she'd suggested dancing naked in the street. "This is a bicentennial house. A historical landmark."

"I didn't suggest murder." She realized she was shaking a banana at him and put it back.

"Hey, August," called a voice from upstairs. "I think I found your weird cookbook."

The stairs creaked with the familiar sound of someone descending, and a tingling sensation like magic coursed down Ashley's spine and through her fingertips in anticipation. She knew today was Esther's work day, but in the past, she always stayed in the attic. Should Ashley leave and avoid her? She glanced to August and a look of panic crossed his face. Something was afoot. Well, she had to stay to find out what that was about. Was Hannah actually right about him?

They both called up the stairs, yelling over each other.

"What cookbook?"

"Wait there. I'll be up in a sec."

Ashley met August's gaze for a split second before darting for the steps. Vampire speed and the fact she was standing gave her the obvious advantage. But she only made it to the bottom step before her ankle snapped out of place, and she tumbled to all fours. The damn witch had dislocated her ankle. August tried to climb past her, but she grabbed his leg and pulled him down. He wasn't getting by that easily.

"Dammit, witch," she said. "What are you hiding?"

"Let me go!"

"Are you two okay?" Esther stood on the landing, a large leatherbound book tucked under her arm, staring down at them like they'd both lost their marbles. Her gaze snagged a second longer on Ashley, sprawled across the stairs.

Ashley pulled August's body in front of her while she snapped her ankle back in place with a pop. "Perfectly fine." Speaking over the sound of her ankle snapping into its socket, she ground her teeth into a smile to hide the pain. "What have you got there?"

August interrupted Esther's response. "Platt business. Nothing for you to bother with."

Ashley scowled at him and caught Esther with a similar expression.

Esther held up the book, and August's shoulders slumped. It was bound in dark leather, almost black, with silver decals on the corners and a matching lock fastening it shut. Embossed on the cover were the phases of the moon aligned in a circle.

"If I had to guess," Esther said as she flipped the book to inspect the back, "I'd say this isn't exactly a cookbook in the traditional sense."

"A grimoire, huh?" Ashley stood, dusting herself off. "What would the Platt family be doing with a grimoire? In New York of all states?"

"I don't know what being in New York has to do with it, but it's fascinating. Based on this binding, it's quite possibly the oldest piece in the collection." Esther continued to look over the spine while descending the stairs. "Do you know if your family had a history of collecting objects from the occult?"

"You could say that." August stood as well and gestured for Esther to pass him the book.

"Let me see it." Ashley grabbed the book from August's outstretched hand, ignoring the stupid smirk on his face. She fiddled with the latch.

A red heat nipped at her fingertip.

"Ouch!" She dropped it like a hot potato.

"Ashley," scolded Esther. "It's fragile.

"Dammit, August!" Ashley said.

But he was too busy laughing to pay attention to her

scolding. Ashley popped her finger in her mouth and glared at him.

"Here, let me see it." Esther gestured for Ashley's hand, but Ashley shifted out of her grasp and away from Esther's gaze that always noticed a pattern. "Do you have a metal allergy? This is the second time you've reacted like this."

Too late.

Ashley hadn't dropped Anthropology 101 like she'd promised herself. There just wasn't another class at such a convenient time. And until now, Esther hadn't said anything about her rushing off into the night like a weirdo. She'd successfully cut back her Esther-watching from longing gazes to an occasional casual look. Okay, maybe it was more like stolen glances, but a girl couldn't help herself. When she fixated, she Fixated.

"Sure." August huffed a laugh. "A *metal allergy*." He used air quotes around 'metal allergy.'

Ashley raised a choice finger at him. "Shut up, August."

Esther snatched Ashley's hand while she had it raised and gently pried open her fist. Inside, they found a perfect cross christening her pointer finger.

"Well, at least your other rash is gone." Esther gently trailed her fingertips down the length of Ashley's palm. Her expression remained absent, as though she didn't even notice the effect she had.

Ashley wanted Esther's hand to continue its gentle stroll everywhere on her. And strangely, she wanted to know what holding Esther's hand was like as well.

"Probably for the best." Ashley pulled her hand back, attempting to laugh off her overactive feelings. "My hand was looking like a cathedral."

Right then, obnoxious hamsters started singing.

Because, of course, now was the right time for a phone call, and of course, her phone had fallen out of her pocket when she and August had their mad dash for the stairs. August got to it first.

"It's your mom," he called, lifting the phone so she could see.

Of course it was her mom. "Tell her I'll call her back."

She realized her mistake two seconds too late.

"Hello, Ms. Ashley's mom." August reclined onto his chaise lounge. "This is August speaking."

Total panic followed, and Ashley flashed to his side. "Give me the phone."

"Her boyfriend?" August rolled off the chaise and out of Ashley's grasp. "No, nothing as official as that."

Ashley hissed through her teeth, barely remembering to keep in her fangs. "August, I will end you."

The front door closed, and everyone turned to Uther in the foyer. "I tried knocking because I don't know how that doorbell works. I guess no one heard me. What do you mean boyfriend?"

"I'm going to have to let you go, Ms. Ashley's mom. Here's Ashley." He shoved the phone into her hand and walked to the front door while Ashley scrambled to not drop her mom.

"Hi, Mom?" How much damage had August done? Her mom knew she was gay. Why was she asking about a boyfriend?

"Ashley? Who was that friend of yours? He sounds handsome."

So much damage.

"People don't sound handsome, Mom. That's not a thing." She kept her voice low, but one look at August's smug face, and she knew he'd heard. "Actually, he has a very unfortunate face. I'm really only around him out of obligation."

"Is he an intern at the lab?"

Okay, she couldn't talk about fake Romania in front of everyone. Time to change the subject. She put extra cheer in her voice so her mom wouldn't infer correctly that she wanted her off the phone. "Was there something you wanted, Mom?"

"Just calling to gab. I was talking to your father about Thanksgiving plans. Apparently, your aunt called dibs on hosting. After what happened last year, you'd think she knows it's too much for her to handle. So now I'm offering to help with food prep, and we'll have to be quicker on the draw for next year. Maybe I'll say something at dinner."

"Yeah, that's great, Mom. Listen, now isn't a great time for me to talk."

"Oh, I won't keep you long. I know you have a busy schedule. What was your research on again?"

"A certain mushroom. I'm kind of in the middle of something, so I'll have to let you go."

"Sure thing, honey. Did you think any more about Christmas? I know it's still early, but your father and I are hosting. You know, since your aunt got Thanksgiving. We can keep it low-key since you're coming in from so far off. Just the aunts and uncles and cousins."

"So, the usual crowd?"

"Well, our neighbor Colleen was talking about a get-together for the neighborhood, but I think we're going to do that earlier. You know, before people leave to go be with their families."

How was she still on the phone? Hadn't she tried to hang up five minutes ago?

"Okay, cool, well I'll see you then, Mom."

"So, you're coming? Dale!" By the sound of it, her mom had moved the phone the smallest fraction from her face before bellowing across the house.

Ashley moved the phone away from her ringing ear. What had she done?

"Ashley says she's coming for Christmas! Dale! Did you hear me?" Quiet mumbling, presumably from her dad, followed, then her mom was talking again. "He's thrilled honey. We both are. Just let me know how much plane tickets are, and I'll send you some money through that online website you were talking about. PayPal? Was that the one you liked? I'll find the email where you explain it. I know I saved it somewhere."

"It's not a— You know what, yeah, look up the email. But also, you don't have to pay for my ticket. I'll be fine."

"Bring that boyfriend of yours too, honey."

"I don't have a boyfriend, Mom. Remember?"

"Sure, sure, honey. Listen, I'm going to go call everyone and let them know we're on board for Christmas. You can bring your *special someone*, but I'll leave that up to you. I'll talk to you later, dear. Love you, bye."

The phone clicked before Ashley had a chance to process what had happened. Had she just agreed to Christmas with her entire family? How would she possibly pull that off? She should call her back and shut this down. Her mom didn't know she was a vampire for the same reason Ashley still hadn't faked her death and cut ties with her parents. She didn't want them to worry. It wasn't rational, but neither was her mother-daughter relationship.

But this was her year—the year she passed the Family's test and they finally accepted her as an official member. It also meant this was her last year to cut ties with her parents. Her last Christmas.

"Well, I'm done for the day. You ready to go, Uther?" Esther's words brought Ashley out of her panic spiral.

"I can walk you home, Esther." Ashley needed something to take her mind off of this Christmas debacle.

"Oooh!" the boys said in singsong from the foyer.

Ashley glared at them.

"Oh." Esther adjusted the strap of her shoulder bag, looking between Ashley and Uther. "I mean, Uther came all this way. I don't want to put him out."

Right. In her need for distraction, she'd completely forgotten she was supposed to give Esther space.

Uther waved Esther over. "Can I talk to you for a second?"

He opened the front door, and they both walked out to the porch, leaving Ashley and August alone in the house.

"That was weird, right?" Ashley turned to August for confirmation.

"So, you and Esther, huh?" His gaze was on his nails, but his tone said they weren't the focus of his attention.

Ashley narrowed her eyes. "I don't know what you mean."

She wasn't sure why she was talking to the witch. She went back to leaning against the wall and waiting for Esther.

"She's cute. I get it." He'd stopped playing with his nails, done pretending to be uninterested in the conversation he'd started. "The brooding goth girl. Plus, she's a hottie. Who isn't into that type?"

"Watch yourself, witch."

August held up his hands. "Hey, hey, no worries. I've made my peace with that. Set my sights elsewhere, if you will."

Ashley huffed. She would not.

"I was just going to say...I don't know. Are you sure?"

She pushed from the wall. "I have no idea what you're talking about. And if I did, it would be none of your business."

He ignored her statement. "It's just, you know. You're you, and she's...well. Her."

"I know I'm a vampire. I'm not an idiot."

"Not that." He laughed and plopped down on that damn chaise. "I mean you, with your"—he waved his hand at her in a fluttery manner—"sparkly, talk-to-everyone-and-sings-show-tunes-outside-my-window vibe. And she's Esther, lives and works in an attic and would rather not talk to anyone ever please and thank you. I guess I just don't see it."

His shrug was the final straw on Ashley's self-control. Her fangs came out, and she was mid-hiss when the door opened. Quick as she could, she retracted her fangs and resumed her post against the wall as Esther and Uther stepped inside.

"You may walk with Esther," declared Uther with a hand flourish. "I have further to discuss with August."

"Smooth." Ashley walked to the door, ready to leave everything August had said behind. "That sounded really natural and not at all rehearsed." She touched Esther's arm, mostly to hear her heart pick up. "Ready to go?"

"I... Let me grab my bag." She raced up the stairs.

Ashley had to wait for the creaking to stop before she could be heard. She leaned against the doorway, studying her own nails now. "So, what are you and Uther up to these days?"

"Nosy, much?" August snapped.

Bingo. Two could play at this game of poking into other people's personal lives.

"August was telling me about this gardening club in Vermont," offered Uther, ever the excited one. If Ashley didn't have to focus on vampire stuff, she'd have befriended him weeks ago. She'd seen him once or twice at some of the smaller weekend parties. He gave off strong supportive friend vibes.

The noisy stairs interrupted any attempt to continue the conversation, and then Esther was there. "Ready."

Ashley gave August a parting glare before following Esther out the door and down the steps to the narrow side-walk. The sun had long set, the stars shone overhead, and Ashley returned to imagining what it would feel like to hold Esther's hand.

"So," said Esther. "You're kind of different, aren't you?"

"I like to think I'm exceptional." Ashley flicked her hair over her shoulder. Was this when Esther noticed her? Dating was a bad idea. But she was feeling a little reckless this evening. Maybe something casual could be okay. She didn't have to tell Esther anything—

"No, I mean... Well, the super speed thing."

Ashley stopped walking. Record scratch. *What? Shit-shit-shit.*

"What do you mean?" Maybe Ashley wasn't understanding her correctly. No one noticed her little slips.

"I thought I'd just imagined it after dinner the other night." Esther looked everywhere except at Ashley. "You were gone so fast. But today when August had your phone, you were on one side of the room and then suddenly the other." She locked eyes with Ashley. "I know what I saw."

Crap. This was bad. This was very, very bad. Esther and her beautiful brown eyes missed nothing.

"It's... I used to do track. That's all." Ashley forced a

laugh, looking around to make sure none of the vampires were within listening distance. "You must have had a longer blink than you thought." If anyone heard what Esther was saying, it would be sayonara to Ashley's chances of joining the Family. And who knew what they would do to Esther. Ashley still wasn't sure what happened to the last people that found out about her.

She took Esther's arm and steered them in the other direction. All those times she'd heard Esther's heart race—was Esther was afraid of her? Maybe she was a monster, and Esther had figured it out.

"No one's that fast," Esther said. "I know what I saw. Where are we going?"

"Okay, look." Ashley stopped at an intersection, waiting for the light to change. "I can't have this conversation here, okay? So, you have two options." This was such a bad idea. But things were already bad. She needed to handle the situation. "I can walk you home, and we'll never talk about this again. I promise. I'll leave you alone. I can transfer classes or take them online. Whatever. Or..."

Tornado sirens were going off in Ashley's head. *Take cover. Get out of danger.*

But like any true and terrible Midwesterner, she studied Esther's face for any hint at what was going on in her head, her curiosity keeping her on the porch, flirting with danger instead of seeking cover.

"Or I can take you somewhere private," Ashley said, "and we can keep talking."

Esther's attention snapped back to her. "So, my choices are going home and we continue life as though nothing is different, or I come with you and ...you reveal some myste-rious secret that's potentially life-changing?"

That about summed it up. She knew Esther didn't like choices, but there wasn't a way around it. Ashley didn't have the fortitude to answer, so she just nodded.

Reflected in Esther's eyes, Ashley watched the walk sign change from red to white.

"I want to keep talking."

9

____

Ashley

Lake Champlain was quiet at this time of night, too late for the usual crowd to venture off the walking path to the shoreline. The full moon carved a jagged path across the water, stirred by the gentle fall breeze. Ashley pulled her jacket tight out of habit. She didn't need it anymore. It was all an act now. Pretending to be human. Walking along the pebbled shore with Esther like this was just any other conversation they were about to have.

They were silent as they walked, listening to the push and tug of water slipping between time-smoothed rocks and the breeze rustling fall leaves until they came to a log just out of reach of the light from the nearby pier. Ashley took a seat, making sure to leave room for Esther.

Ashley waited until she couldn't take the silence any longer. Until the chirp of crickets and the lapping water were deafening. "All right, then. What do you know?"

Esther pulled at a loose string on her hoodie's sleeve.

"I've been trying to think of some way to explain you since that time at my uncle's."

Ashley nodded encouragingly. This was it. Esther could say it, and it would be out there. Esther and her observant gaze, seeing through all the shields Ashley put up. She could be one person Ashley didn't have to hide from. But she was also terrified of Esther's reaction when—no, *if*—she confirmed her suspicion. She dug her nails into the log to keep her hands from shaking, hoping Esther didn't notice this detail as well.

"And do you have any guesses?"

"One." Esther lifted a shoulder, letting her hair shield part of her face. "But it's ridiculous, and you'd probably laugh."

Something about this moment felt déjà vu. The lake, the trees, the conversation. When it clicked, and the quiet piano from the movie came to mind, Ashley had to use all her weak willpower to keep from laughing. Should she say the line? No, it was too cheesy. But this might be the only chance anyone in the history of time had to use the quote properly.

"Say it," Ashley said, trying her best to keep a serious face. "Out loud." She covered her mouth to hide her snickering.

Esther looked away, clearly embarrassed by what she was going to say and missing Ashley's hidden laughter. "A genetically modified human from a government experiment."

"What?" Ashley jumped from the log, shaking it enough that Esther had to hold on while Ashley stared down at her. "You think I'm Spider-Man?"

"I think Captain America is a more accurate comparison." Esther looked past her to the lake, but pink crept across Esther's cheeks. "But I haven't crossed out injection of radioactive venom yet either."

"Wow, you're messing up the movie reference so much right now."

"What movie?" Esther looked up at her. "I haven't watched all of the Avengers franchise. There's so many of them. It's hard to keep up."

"Not Avengers, *Twilight*."

Crap. She hadn't meant to just blurt it out.

"*Twilight*? I remember that being a big deal, but never actually saw it." She raised a curious brow and looked Ashley up and down. "It was a little before our time, don't you think? I mean, I guess some...okay, maybe a lot of my classmates were reading it, but what are you? Nineteen? You're a lot younger still."

"I'm twenty, sort of, but I also read *Twilight* when it first came out and saw the movie."

"When it came out? That book was early two thousands. You would have been like four."

"Okay. I really need you to figure out what I am already." This conversation was more frustrating than sexy. Why were they out here? Esther didn't know what she was, and she wasn't going to guess it. Ashley had all but told her the answer, and she was still none the wiser. "Are you out of guesses?"

"That was vampires and werewolves fighting over a girl, right? So, like, gang stuff?" Esther shrugged. "I don't really understand how a gang would make you run that fast. Is it a drug?"

All right. Maybe it was time to call it a night. Esther knew something, but she didn't know the specifics, and as far as Ashley was concerned, that meant they were still in the clear. No one knew her secret. Well, no one except the witch, but he didn't count. Oh god. The only mortal who knew her secret was a witch.

"You're looking too sci-fi when you need to go paranormal." *Shut up, Ashley.*

"Paranormal?" Esther's head tilted skeptically. "Like ghosts? Are you a ghost?" She took Ashley's hand, and damn it, Ashley was so excited until she realized Esther was checking Ashley's solidity. She held it anyway, letting the warmth of Esther's hand seep into her own.

Don't say it. Don't say it. Don't say it. "Have you considered vampire?"

"Like you're anemic? Or wait…" Esther flipped over Ashley's hand, touching her fingertips, but the cross-shaped burn from earlier had healed. She snatched Ashley's other hand and checked it as well. "Well, the speed and the healing and…and the crosses, okay." A slight tremble made its way from Esther's hand to Ashley's. "But the teeth? Yes! The teeth. You smile all the time. It's a lovely smile and not very umm… teethy."

"Thanks." Ashley flashed her signature grin, and for half a reckless second, let her fangs slip as well.

"What the fuck?" Esther tumbled over the log, tossing Ashley's hand in her haste to get away.

"No, no, Esther, I'm so sorry. I didn't mean…" This might have been the greediest thing Ashley had ever done.

Esther crawled across the ground to the woods, and it was all Ashley's fault.

It was just that, for one selfish second, Ashley thought maybe she could have it all.

Esther opened her mouth to scream, and Ashley snapped back into action, covering her mouth and setting her back on the log before she made a sound.

"Look, Esther. I realize I could have eased you into this a

little better, probably. On the one hand, you told me you wanted this conversation, but on the other hand, it has become very clear you had no idea where this conversation was going. So, I want to apologize now for how...jarring this was."

She waited with her hand still over Esther's mouth, but Esther remained frozen in place.

"Can I take my hand away," Ashley said, "and you won't scream, and we can have a normal conversation like two normal people?"

Esther remained frozen.

Ashley tentatively moved her hand away from Esther's face.

Two beats passed.

Esther screamed, and Ashley covered her mouth again.

Ashley was the worst no-longer-human on the planet. She needed to fix this. "Esther, I'm so sorry. Telling you was really selfish of me. Just because you think cannibalism is sexy doesn't mean—"

Esther mumbled something from under Ashley's hand that didn't sound like screaming. Tentatively, Ashley moved her hand away again.

"Never in my life have I ever said cannibalism is *sexy*." Esther was yelling. She looked pissed even. But she wasn't screaming or running for her life.

Ashley took this as an improvement. "I mean, it was a couple of weeks ago. But that one lecture on cultural relativism? You said you thought eating a loved one was romantic or something."

"And you took that as me wanting to be eaten?"

"No, of course not." Ashley almost took her hand to assure her before thinking better of touching her right now. "I'm not going to—I would never! I just...I mean, I guess I hoped maybe you'd understand that I'm...me. And I wanted one person that knew that. That's it."

Esther's eyes were wide, her brows near the middle of her forehead. She huffed out a breath and turned to the lake. So, Ashley followed suite, giving Esther time to process everything.

It was a beautiful night. The moon nearly full. For a moment, Ashley pretended it was the sun and Esther wasn't angry-scared about Ashley's undead status and instead they sat on the beach together, sunning. They could walk along the bike path and listen to the water and people out on their boats and cars passing. On the weekend, they would go to brunch, but she'd have to call in a reservation because the trendy, new place she wanted to try was so busy on Saturday mornings. They could go to the museum or a card shop or the yarn store with the cute seasonal displays in its window that always closed promptly at five. She'd entered a world of sunsets and dark, empty streets. A few more decades and even sunsets would be too bright as her vampire skin grew more sensitive with age.

The wind blew Esther's hair, drawing Ashley's attention back to the moment and the girl sitting next to her staring out into the lake like she had a world of thoughts going through her head as well.

It wasn't right of Ashley to take her into the darkness with her. Not when she couldn't promise any sort of future.

The truth was, Ashley changed into a vampire because she read about a love that would last forever and she wanted that. Now might not be the right time to start a new relationship, not when her connection to the Family was still on shaky ground, but she'd already sacrificed her human life for love. What was poor timing when she had all the time in the world?

She shifted closer so the tips of their fingers touched.

When Esther didn't move away, Ashley decided it was all right to talk again. "I read some of your book. It was really messed up. Just when I thought you were a marshmallow, you give me a book full of psychotic and bloody stories."

Esther's gaze stayed out on the lake, but the corner of her mouth ticked up. "Which one did you read?"

Good, she was talking again.

"'The Black Cat.' I thought, surely, a story about a cat can't get too dark. I was wrong. And it wasn't even the cat's fault. It was that dick owner of his."

Esther chuckled and Ashley cheered internally. Maybe this night was salvageable.

"I tried some poems too," Ashley went on. "There was this one where half the words were 'bell,' and I don't know if it had any point, and like three about dreams being inside each other that probably had some meaning I missed. I'm not sure I'm into his poetry. Maybe he just can't top 'The Raven.'"

"No, you missed it." Esther turned to Ashley, a spark from the moon catching in her eye. "'The Bells' is an evolution of the different uses of bells in our everyday lives paralleled to show the passing of time from birth to death. And 'A Dream Within a Dream.' That's also about time and how intangible and fleeting it is. Trying to hold on to life is like holding on to a dream. 'Is all that we see or seem but a dream within a dream?'"

Ashley had missed those themes, but if Esther wanted to explain her favorite poems to her, she'd sit by this lake and listen until the sun came up. She'd never seen Esther this fired up. Hungry for more, Ashley moved her hand closer, draping her fingers across Esther's resting hand.

"I thought you promised me some fated love poems."

Ashley's thumb glided across the ridges of Esther's knuckles, exploring her hills and valleys—down and back once, twice.

Esther turned her hand, gripping Ashley's fingers. For a moment, the world flashed white, and on it, Ashley filled it like text from a typewriter with reasons why this was happening, all while keeping absolutely still so as not to draw attention to it.

"You were supposed to read 'Annabel Lee,'" Esther said. "I thought you'd like that one. It's tragic but beautiful."

"And tragic beauty reminds you of me?" Ashley loved how that sounded.

"Yes." Esther's voice was soft but certain.

"Do you know any of it?" Ashley didn't have the patience to wait until she got home to read the poem that reminded Esther of her. She shifted closer, testing the limits Esther allowed until their knees pressed together.

"It was many and many a year ago, in a kingdom by the sea." Esther smiled, her gaze on the lake. "That a maiden there lived whom you may know, by the name of Annabel Lee. And this maiden she lived with no other thought than to love and be loved by me."

The words were familiar. Ashley couldn't place why she knew them, but she continued where Esther had left off. "I was a child and she was a child, in this kingdom by the sea."

Esther turned to Ashley, her look mirroring Ashley's surprise. Tendrils of her long, dark hair floated around her in the light breeze, and Ashley caught a lock with her free hand and tucked it behind Esther's ear, this time watching for the dangling cross. Instead of dropping her hand back to her side as she should, Ashley let her fingertips follow along Esther's jawline, tilting her face to meet Ashley's.

"But we loved with a love, that was more than love. I and my Annabel Lee."

In one slow and steady motion, and without thinking much further on the idea, Ashley leaned in. No cross, no nosy friends, no AC/DC playing from the other room. Their lips met in a sweet embrace. Gentle, but with a satisfying and full pressure behind it. Esther's lips were just as soft as Ashley imagined. She caressed Esther's cheekbone with her thumb as she pulled away.

Esther remained frozen, her eyes still closed, her body leaning slightly forward before she opened her eyes. The brown of them shone like liquid in the moonlight then grew wider in shock.

"Wait," said Esther. "Wait wait."

Ashley was doing nothing but waiting, but she attempted to wait more.

"But I'm straight."

Okay. For some reason, that wasn't what she'd expected. Ashley had decided Esther was queer on some scale of the spectrum. She might not be interested in Ashley, especially considering the whole vampire thing, but she hadn't expected her to claim to be straight.

"Like, all the way?" Ashley said.

Esther's eyes shifted back and forth, solving an equation only she saw. "I-I thought so. I guess I never really thought about it before?"

"Okay. Cool cool cool." Ashley retreated, moving her hands back into her personal space. This was a lot. Maybe it was time for her to leave.

10

———————

Esther

Esther's thoughts pulled in a million directions. When she'd agreed to this "life-changing secret," she hadn't prepared herself for it to include a short-circuiting kiss. Ashley being a vampire—a vampire!—was more on-brand with what she saw coming. Definitely lived up to the hype, so bravo to Ashley on that front. But she hadn't expected any life-altering reveals about *herself*.

"You really never thought about it before? How old are you?" Ashley's question broke through the hurricane of thoughts flying through Esther's mind.

"How old am I? I'm twenty-five. And you're twenty, so really this is highly inappropriate."

"That's what you're going with? My *age* is throwing you off? Because I'll have you know that by romance standards our age gap is not even remarkable enough to warrant a trope tag." Ashley looked skeptical, which was a reasonable reaction because Esther was not being reasonable. It wasn't

Ashley's age that was a problem, though she had no idea what she meant by "a trope tag."

The vampire reveal followed by that kiss had broken something loose in her head and she was still reeling trying to get her thoughts back on track.

Ashley had kissed her. She kissed Ashley.

The girl from class who was practically perfect in every way. With the cheerful smile and the strong arms. Who knew everyone's name and everyone wanted to be around, and she had kissed Esther—of all the forgettable people in the world.

And also, Ashley was a vampire. How did that fit in with what she was feeling?

Ashley stood. "I'm pretty sure I know what the issue is here, and it's not my age—which is not inappropriate by the way."

"How old are you? Like really?"

Apparently, her mind was stuck on the age thing. It was the least of her problems, but that was what made the topic so appealing. It was safe. Talking kept Ashley here, and what she wanted most was for Ashley to stay where she was, framed by the lake, the moon making her blond hair glow. She was beautiful and powerful, and she'd kissed her.

But also, Esther knew nothing about her. "How long have you been twenty?"

Ashley scowled. "You can't win me over with *Twilight* references."

Esther made a note to watch this movie the second she got home. She scooted on the log and patted the spot next to her—hopeful. Ashley was making her hopeful. For what, Esther had no idea, but something in her said if Ashley just sat, they could talk this through and the world would stop spinning so fast. Ashley looked to the distant dock, as though debating leaving her here, but she sat down.

"So." Esther took a second to collect her thoughts, snagging the first one she could put to words. "Vampires are old, right? The moon landing, Civil Rights Movement, the Civil War and the Revolutionary. Did you cross over from Europe, or were you born here?"

As she listed events, the anthropologist inside her took out a notebook and pen. A firsthand account of the big moments in history that were fading from living memory. This was the opportunity of a lifetime.

Ashley chuckled. "A 'where are you *really* from' question. As blond as I am, I haven't experienced one of those before. Well, I was born in Iowa and grew up in the time when our solar system had nine planets and 150 Pokémon."

"Pluto?" Esther did the math in her head, but Ashley cut her off.'

"I'm a nineties child. Born in '88 and changed 2008."

"So, wait." Esther computed again. Her list of historic questions shrinking exponentially. "You're thirty?"

"Okay, 32, and I don't think I like the tone you just took."

"You're only seven years older than me."

Ashley shrugged. "I could tell you where I was during 9/11."

She wasn't ancient at all. Vampires were still made in the twenty-first century? Strange this was her first thought when she'd only just discovered vampires were real. As though Esther had thought herself an expert in vampire lore, and Ashley was crumbling all her assumptions.

"And you thought I was too young for you." Ashley smirked. "Like I said, if this was a romance novel, we wouldn't even qualify as an age gap."

"So that's how *Twilight* and Pluto and..." Esther's words faded as she fit the pieces together.

"*Holes!*" Esther jumped at Ashley's outburst. "They quote that poem in the movie. With Shia LaBeouf. Did you ever watch that one? I *loved* the book and the movie. I basically had it memorized."

Esther shook her head, barely listening. This was a lot. All of it. Vampires were real.

And also, Ashley had kissed her, and...maybe Esther liked it?

Did that make her a lesbian? She pulled up childhood celebrity crushes. Legolas, Rick O'Connell, Ryan Gosling, several interchangeable abs from the Avengers franchise probably named Chris. Yup, those still did it for her. Maybe she needed to call Uther and talk this through. But that thought scared her too. Since when had her casual study buddy and check-in-to-make-sure-she-wasn't-murdered friend become the first person she wanted to talk to when an identity crisis popped up?

"Hey."

Ashley placed a hand on Esther's shoulder, and Esther's attention snapped back to her. Phantom sparks traveled down her jaw where Ashley had touched her. Would she kiss her again? Esther's heart beat at her chest, and her entire being channeled a forward motion. She was the sea and Ashley the moon.

"I'm sorry about how forward I was just now. I guess I was reading into something that wasn't there. But don't worry." She hopped up from the log, jostling Esther from her trance. "I promise not to do that again." She reached a hand down to Esther. "In fact, I was hoping we could start over. I'd like to be friends. Unless you're uncomfortable, in which case it's totally cool. I can back off. I just find you fascinating, and I think we could be good together. Even in a strictly platonic sense."

Esther took her hand without thinking. But Ashley just pulled her up and let go, an impenetrable wall of a smile on her face.

"Okay. Friends." Friends. Esther could be friends.

They started toward Esther's house—the streets empty at this time of night—and the whole time, a gnawing feeling in the pit of Esther's stomach told her she'd missed an opportunity she'd soon regret.

11

Ashley

Ashley adjusted her hair bow and took another picture to make sure it was centered. The silver in her vanity mirror might not show her reflection, but at least her smartphone camera was silver free. Her phone buzzed, and a notification dropped down, covering her bow.

ESTHER

> Wasn't there a Friends episode about the nonexistence of a selfless gift? I think they had a point. Change my mind.

All thoughts of accessories vanished, and a quick dopamine rush sent warm tingles up and down Ashley's arms. She took a beat to remind herself they were just friends before replying. This week's lecture had been on gift giving. They were just two classmates discussing a lecture. Nothing sexy whatsoever.

ASHLEY

what happened to you being a forever optimist?

ESTHER

Not condemning anyone to hell is different from not believing in the existence of a selfless gift.

ASHLEY

ok. counterpoint. free suckers at the bank. BAM!

ESTHER

Corporate America's attempt to commoditize the human desire for community through trivial acts of goodwill.

ASHLEY

WOOOOOOOOOOOOOOOOOOW

I'm not giving up but I'm going to need a min after that

Ashley's door opened, taking her focus from her game with Esther and her constant debate on whether Esther was flirting or not.

"Ready to go?" Cynthia's blond hair feathered away from her face in deep, dramatic curls. She wore a baggy, red zip-up, belled denim jeans, and white Nikes.

"Cynthia, this is a Halloween party. You're supposed to dress up."

"I am dressed up." Cynthia spread her arms wide and spun for Ashley to take it all in.

Ashley sighed. "How are you dressed up?"

"I'm Farrah Fawcett in Charlie's Angels." She jumped into a crouch, spreading her arms wide like she was surfing.

"I don't know what you're talking about."

"Maybe it would make more sense with a skateboard, but I'm not carrying that around."

"Whatever." Ashley waved her comment away. She was ready to go party. "How do I look?" She did a quick about-face and lifted a pom-pom to sell it.

"Isn't cheerleader a bit obvious?"

"Isn't seventies' icon a bit obvious?" she retorted. "Besides, it still fits." She twirled, showing off the flare in her shirt. She hadn't worn this outfit in over a decade. She wasn't sure why she'd grabbed it from her parents' house all those years ago except she was her most confident in this outfit, and at the time, she could really use some of that. Now wouldn't hurt either, come to think of it.

"What are you going to do with the pom-poms?" Cynthia crossed her arms, tapping a finger against her biceps as she inspected Ashley's outfit. "Carry them the whole night?"

"Good point. Hate that plan. We pregaming first?"

Cynthia tossed a bag of blood at her from somewhere unknown, and Ashley dropped her pom-poms to catch it.

"Drink up," Cynthia said. "You have to finish that before we go out. No slip-ups. Remember?"

"This isn't exactly the pregaming I had in mind," Ashley grumbled, as she popped open the straw. "Ack! It's cold."

"Hurry up. I brought a vodka chaser." She pulled an entire bottle of Smirnoff out of her jacket, unscrewed the lid, and took a pull.

Ashley wasn't much of a vodka drinker, but the existence of a chaser was enough motivation for her to drain the bag. "Done. Gimme."

They passed the bottle, then another. They needed to leave before John noticed they were going out again and queued up another lecture. Hannah and Claribel didn't care either way. Don't draw attention and don't form human attachments. Aside from those two rules, they hardly cared. Which was why Ashley hadn't invited Esther out with her. At best, if they were caught, she could expect a lengthy sermon from John on the long-term repercussions and complications of associating with something as fleeting as humans. At worst...well, she wouldn't risk that.

After that night at the lake, she'd kept up a semi-regular stream of texts with Esther. Usually light and school-related, nothing suspicious. After blowing through the whole "don't tell people about vampires" rule, she was determined to be fastidious about the others. But she couldn't help if their texting bordered on flirty.

Esther is straight. You are just friends. Don't make this complicated. But being friends was complicated. And now, she was addicted to the adrenaline rush she got each time her phone buzzed and Esther's name popped up on the screen.

Ashley finished the bottle and made a face as Cynthia took a swig from a third bottle before tucking it back in her jacket. Where were these all coming from? Her jacket couldn't possibly have that much space in it. Ashley hoped they had rum at the party. Alcohol took longer to hit since her change. And she was still kind of figuring out her tolerance level, but they'd finished over half of the third bottle when they booked it out of the house.

With the help of vampire speed, they were there in two Mississippis. The house was one of a string of McMansions along the lake shore—clearly a parents-out-of-town situation. She followed the music around to the backyard, Cynthia trailing along, where a majority of the party coalesced around a fabricated sound system and in-ground swimming pool. Being October in New York, no one was in the pool, but the blue light from it reflected off people's faces, adding to the Halloween atmosphere.

"All right, well, I think I'm going to take off." Cynthia hitched a thumb over her shoulder.

"What?" Ashley whirled on her. They had *just* gotten there. They hadn't even spoken to anyone yet.

"Hannah wanted me to watch out for you, but you've got this under control." She grasped Ashley's shoulders and spoke like a coach to her star player before a game. "We've been doing this for weeks, and I kind of have my own life."

"I thought you liked going out?" Ashley pushed Cynthia's hands away. She'd thought Cynthia was maybe her friend. That maybe Cynthia went to these things with her because she enjoyed it. Ashley wasn't looking for a babysitter.

"Yeah yeah, you're totally fun, babe. But I've hit this scene, and I got a tweet from this band I'm following. They're doing a pop-up show in Montreal like now-ish, so I'm going to go hit that up."

"But Montreal is over an hour from here, and you don't even have a car." And she could have invited Ashley to this other thing if she didn't want to go to the party. Ashley was flexible. She would have understood. Maybe she'd like the band, and they could bond over their similar taste in music. It wasn't too late. Maybe she could still tag along.

"Hey, no worries. You got this." Cynthia winked and gave Ashley a peace sign as she backed into a shadowed corner behind some shrubs. "Catch you on the flip side."

"Wait. Cynthia." Ashley realized what Cynthia was planning, but it was too late to stop her.

She tossed Ashley the half-empty vodka bottle before

slipping out of sight behind a shrub. A second later, a bat fluttered out of the branches and off into the night.

Ashley's shoulders slumped. Of course Cynthia was going bat to travel. It was easier than learning how to drive a car. Easier for Cynthia at least. Ashley still hadn't managed anything useful in the transformation department, and Cynthia knew this. Ashley was just a burden slowing her down.

All right, Ashley was on her own tonight. Again. Not a problem. She could handle herself. Plus, she could probably name everyone here. For example, there was Fadl from her anthro class wearing a Big Lebowski cardigan and standing with a group of his friends. Time to put on a smile and make the best of the night. She took a fortifying swig from the bottle that was getting much lighter than she expected and set her shoulders.

"Fadl! Saleh! Taylor!" Ashley called.

"Heyyyy!" They all cheered, lifting their hands above their heads in greeting.

She wasn't sure if any of them remembered her name, but they were always a welcoming crowd. She returned the dramatic hey and jogged over.

"Who's jumping in?" She nodded to the pool where they congregated. It was best to take control of the conversation early. If there was a lull, people started in on the small talk which inevitably led to the dreaded, *What's your major?* And she really didn't want the concerned, *Oh you're undecided?* Or worse still, the falsely supportive, *Wow, how brave* and, *You have plenty of time to make a decision.*

"Taylor can go first." Saleh, always the jokester, had on something that looked like a khaki fisherman's vest and had shaved his stubble into a goatee.

"Hey, man!" Taylor in a Pikachu onesie stepped back

from the pool, raising their palms in the universal *I'm out* gesture. "I'm not going in. It's cold in there. She can go ahead."

Inspired, Ashley took a long swig of her vodka—yuck, she needed to check out that drink table—placed the near-empty bottle on the ground, and lifted both arms over her head.

"I said brrr," *stomp, clap, clap*, "it's cold in here," *stomp clap*. "There must be some Clovers in the atmosphere."

"Oh. My. God." Taylor was smiling hard. "You know that cheer? My aunt and I spent a whole summer trying to learn it."

"I have no idea what you people are talking about." Fadl looked between her and Taylor, brow raised like he was unsure if he should laugh or change the subject.

"It's from this old cheerleading movie from like 2000," Taylor said. "*Bring it On.*"

Thanks, Taylor. Now Ashley felt old.

"Can you show me how to do it?" Taylor asked.

"Yes." Pepped back up, Ashley slowed down the move, and soon others were joining in. Someone pulled up the song on their phone, and in a matter of minutes, she had a handful of people performing a passable routine. This devolved into Ashley performing different jumps for people. The third time she landed a front handstand, she wobbled, rising to her final pose. Was she getting tired, or was the alcohol starting to get to her? Maybe she should move away from the pool. She cleaned out the last of her vodka while scanning the crowds for an excuse to move on when she spotted a flash of familiar blond hair.

"Uther!" she called and waved, excited to recognize another person.

And that wave was the final straw on her balance. She

pitched backward, her foot catching on a stone tile, and arms twirling, crashed into the pool behind her.

Cool water enveloped her, blocking out the noise of the party and shocking her senses. Maybe the alcohol was getting to her after all. As a vampire, she couldn't die of hypothermia or drowning, but it didn't feel good. She kicked off the bottom and broke through the surface, lifting her arms in victory and showing she was okay.

Everyone cheered. Then a song she didn't recognize started, and everyone cheered again, her tumble forgotten.

She leaned back and floated on the surface of the water, letting it muffle the sounds of the party like she was in another space, another room—apart. That was the goal, right? *Good job, Ashley. You're living the vampire dream.* The pool must have been heated or still carrying some heat from the day because a shallow fog lingered on the surface. She let it play between her fingers, not caring if she looked like an idiot, because she wasn't here with anyone, so there wasn't anyone to care.

Eventually, she got tired of feeling sorry for herself. This was a party. She didn't need to feel sad if she didn't want to. Because that was definitely how happiness worked. Of course, this rule only applied to her. She sighed and pulled herself out of the Pool of Introspection before she cried in the middle of a party and ruined it for everyone. Water streamed from her clothes and hair, sloshing onto the tile that had tripped her. She looked back. Her bow remained floating in the pool. It was time for that drink table.

She wove her way toward the house—the ground gently swaying beneath her feet and people jumping out of her way to avoid getting wet—and finally found the table set up on the back patio. Legions of liquor bottles surrounded the punch bowl, a mysterious red concoction with a semi-melted, frozen hand floating on its surface. When at a Halloween party, she thought and filled a red cup. She took a sip. There was that rum she was looking for. And a lot of other things, but her vodka was gone and this was dangerously good.

A short brunette dressed as Wonder Woman appeared at her side. "Hey! Don't we have anthro together?"

Ashley gave the girl another once-over. She did look familiar now that she mentioned it. "Charrrrrlotte?" Names were coming a little slower. What was in this drink?

"Char, actually. Well, I go by Charlotte in class, so that makes sense you would remember that. But most people just call me Char."

"Cool cool coolio." She performed some obnoxious version of finger guns, and Char giggled. Ashley still had it.

"Are you okay?" Char reached like she might pat Ashley's arm before changing her mind. "You're kind of wet."

"You're kind of wet." *Oh wow.* Ashley needed to slow down with this drink. Char laughed it off though. What a good person.

"Do you want a change of clothes?" She looked Ashley over, and Ashley did a twirl for her, earning another squeak of laughter as water flew from her skirt. "You're a bit taller than me, but I have an extra pair of pajamas inside."

"Cool cool." She wasn't sure if that was the right answer. *Decisions are hard.*

"Let's go in." Char guided her through a fancy white-and-chrome kitchen, over some empty beer boxes, and into the nearest available bathroom. "Here."

Ashley wasn't sure when, or if, Char had left. Maybe she fell asleep. But it felt like time had passed because now she was sitting on a closed toilet seat as Char pulled a matching set of fluffy kitty-and-rainbow pajamas out of a duffel bag. A wave of love for all of womankind washed over her, and her eyes watered. Char barely knew her, and these pajamas were super cute.

"You can keep them." Char said. "They're getting a little short for me. Do you have someone I can call to come get you?"

Oh god. She felt an actual tear sliding down her cheek now. She pressed the pajamas to her face to hide it before answering. Or she would have answered if there was anyone she *could* call. Instead, she was left pinching her eyes shut to focus as she ran through an embarrassingly short list of names followed by why she very much couldn't call them.

Hannah or John, obviously not.

Cynthia was out of the country by now and hardly answered her phone anyway.

Claribel didn't even have a phone—apparently, Dr. Bell said something at a dinner party once, for which she still hadn't forgiven him.

"I'm fine," Ashley said with a smile. She just needed a minute to sober up. Then she could walk home on her own. The house was only a mile from here.

She peeled off her spankies and slipped a foot into the kitty pajama pants. Char jumped up and passed her a towel before backing out of the bathroom, apologizing and insisting she would give her some privacy. Ashley shrugged and peeled off her top while Char closed the door. There were no words for the feeling of being soft and fluffy after being cold and wet. She did a little shimmy before deciding this bathroom was too small and wrestled the door open.

The living room was huge. Open floor plan and two floors high at least. She made a popping sound with her mouth to check for an echo, but the music from outside was too loud to tell. Her super hearing was crap when there were too many sounds. She did catch an indecipherable grumble from the pile of blankets on a nearby couch.

"Can I get you a drink?" A guy in a ripped and dirty shirt with the word Brian written in sharpie across it appeared out of thin air. Well, probably not actually out of thin air, but Ashley was fairly confident he hadn't been there five blinks ago. Or seven. Who counts blinks? What was she doing again?

"Oh. No, I got this." Ashley lifted her much lighter red cup, which was still miraculously in her hand. How had she put on these pajamas? They were so fuzzy. Maybe she could turn the bottoms into capris and keep them forever. Would her body always be the same size? Did this mean she never had to buy new clothes again because they would always fit her? Being a vampire was sweet.

Brian lifted a bottle of rum that also appeared out of nowhere. "I'll just top you off then."

He filled her cup back up to the top.

"Wow, that's a lot," said Ashley, watching him pour into her cup like it was someone else's. How irresponsible of them to have that much. Who knew what it was mixed with? She sniffed it curiously, and her eyes watered. That was strong all right.

"You're a lot." He put his free hand on her waist, and his thumb tucked into the hem of her pajama bottoms.

"Wow." She backed up to move out of his reach. "That's not okay."

But he stepped forward with her.

Okay then, Brian. This was where the night was going.

An idea slowly formed. She sipped her drink, contemplating, before coughing because she forgot it was mostly pure rum now. That settled it. She needed to practice drinking without draining—and she didn't mean rum. She was forming a brilliant plan with no flaws whatsoever. She could even practice memorizing! Mesmerizing? Glamouring? Hypnosis. What was that vampire trick called again? Didn't matter. She was confident tonight was the night she could accomplish both, and then Hannah and the rest of the vampires would be so proud of her and welcome her into their home with open arms.

"All right, Brian." She poked his chest and swayed a little.

"It's Jeff, actually."

"Jeff?" She stepped back and looked at his shirt again. "But your shirt says Brian."

"My shirt says Brains." He pulled down the hem to straighten out the wrinkles. "I'm a zombie. Obviously."

"Okay, cool." She set down her drink on a nearby surface —her mother's voice asked about coasters, but she ignored it—and grasped Not-Brian's face with both hands so she could focus on his eyes. Focusing her mesmerizing muscles that she was sure existed, she intoned, "You want to go somewhere private with me."

"Heck yeah, I do."

Hmm. It was unclear if that had worked or not. She decided to say yes it did, and now they were walking down the hall to find an open bedroom, or that was what he was hoping for at least. But it turned out there weren't any bedrooms on the first floor, and she didn't want to go upstairs because that was more of a commitment to the house than she wanted, and she liked that it was easier to exit on the first floor. So, they settled on an office-looking room instead.

The window at the back overlooked the lake and the party still going on outside. Not-Brian pulled half the curtain closed to provide some privacy like the gentleman he was then sat at the desk and slapped his legs in a universal "sit here" gesture. Wow. What a winner. He even turned his hat backward so the bill wouldn't hit her face.

Be still her beat-less heart.

All right, it was going to be gross and embarrassing, and this guy was kind of the worst. She wasn't even into men on a good day. He probably tasted horrible. But she would just have a sip. Enough to say she did it. She'd had a whole bag of blood before leaving, so it wasn't like she was even hungry. Did blood work to absorb alcohol?

Focus, Ashley.

First step, sit on his lap. She perched herself as close to his knees as possible. No need for any more surprises from him.

And that was it. No stalling. Just get it over with. She extended her teeth, and his head pulled back from her in surprise. "Whoa. Wicked body mods. Are you supposed to be Caroline? I loved *Vampire Diaries*."

She had no idea what he was talking about, and she frankly didn't care. She looked deeply into his eyes. "Don't freak out."

Ashley wrenched his head to the side.

Before she could bite down, he leaped from the chair, knocking her to the floor. "Whoa, man. I'm not into that kind of stuff. Just because I'm supposed to be a zombie doesn't mean I'm into the whole biting thing. You're like hot and whatever, but umm yeah, I'm out."

He left the room, and Ashley was disappointed to conclude that perhaps she hadn't figured out the whole glamouring thing after all. What a waste of an evening. Maybe it was time to go home. With the help of the nearby desk, it took her two—no, three—tries to stand back up again, but she did it. Because she was a champion. She wobbled and leaned against the window, letting the cool glass press against the back of her head. That felt nice.

"Has anyone seen Ashley?" a voice called through the pane. "I'm trying to find Ashley. She's tall and blond and dressed like a cheerleader. Is she still here?"

She was Ashley and also tall and blond and dressed like a cheerleader. She looked down and was shocked to find her uniform was gone. Who put her in these pajamas? They were cute. She turned her head, smooshing her cheek against the glass to look out the window. The party was clearing out. Only a handful of people lingered around the pool. Flitting among them was someone that looked like Esther.

Esther was so cool. She wished Esther was here. She tapped lightly at the glass, but maybe it was loudly, because the girl turned, and it *was* Esther.

They made eye contact before Ashley sank to the floor. A few minutes later, Esther was in the same room as her.

"Hey, Ashley. I heard you were about ready to go home. I'm here to give you a ride."

"My hero," Ashley proclaimed, lifting her arms. Stuck that landing.

Esther's car was full of cutesy bobbleheads and fast-food wrappers. Also, Esther didn't have a car. "Esther, you don't have a car."

"That's right." Esther continued to buckle herself in and adjust the mirrors. "Uther lent me his car."

"I hate it." Ashley pulled at her seat belt, but it kept snapping back against her neck. Why did Uther have seat belts that were trying to strangle her? "It's only like a mile from here. We can walk. I wanna walk."

"It was enough work to get you from the house to the

car." Esther put the car in drive. Not even a debate from her! "I'm not carrying you a mile home as well."

"Uther's seatbelt hates me." She tugged on her shoulder strap. "It's trying to kill me."

"Stop tugging on it," said Esther, keeping her eyes on the road. "You're going to—"

"Esther!"

The car stopped, and the momentum flung Ashley forward. She was stopped by the crappy seat belt and Esther's hand in the center of her ribcage.

"Did you just mom block me?" Ashley asked, her eyes tearing up from a sudden outburst of emotion.

"Are you okay?" Esther looked her over. "Why did you yell? Did you see something?"

"What?"

"You yelled my name. I thought you saw someone crossing the road or something."

"Oh, that. My seat belt locked." She fiddled with the latch, trying to get it to release.

Two hands appeared on each of Ashley's cheeks, and she looked up into Esther's serious eyes.

"Stop fiddling with your seat belt," Esther said.

Sweet baby Jesus, she was gorgeous.

Esther unbuckled and buckled her so the strap wasn't stuck then leaned over Ashley to adjust some contraption by her head. Ashley didn't know or care what she was doing. She was close enough that Ashley felt heat radiating off Esther's body. If she breathed in deeply, maybe their boobs would touch. Could she handle that sensation, or would her mind self-destruct from sensory overload? She was starting to inhale when Esther finished her work and sat back in her seat. Ashley's seat belt rested comfortably across her shoulder instead of her neck, and she hated it.

"You're like a super mom." Ashley felt the need to inform her. "Not that I'm projecting kids onto you if that's not something you're into. You would also be amazing at herding the drunk. Not that I'm drunk. Just a little tipsy. Good practice for when you get a real-life drunk person to herd."

"Can't wait for that day." Esther rolled her eyes and put the car back into motion.

"Esther," Ashley said. "My mom forgot I'm gay. My own mother! Who made me. From her womb. How gay is that? And yet she forgets?"

"I'm pretty sure some not-so-gay things happened that led up to you being born, but sure. I don't know your mom."

"And now I have to go home, and they don't know I'm all vampire-like." She lifted her hands into claws so Esther got what she meant. "And she forgot I'm gay. I mean, I guess it's been a while since I've been home, but what did she think happened in the meantime? I was just out trolloping with the peniae, penises, dickory? Not that penises are a bad thing. I mean, you're into the peen, right?"

"I have imbibed in a penis or two. That is true. Not that we're conflating genitalia with gender, correct?"

"Touché." It sucked that Esther wasn't gay, but it was still so nice that she was here to give Ashley a ride. "You're so nice, Esther. You should come home for Christmas with me."

Shocking as it might have sounded, Ashley hadn't thought this idea through before saying it aloud, but now she was obsessed with it. Her and Esther holding hands on the couch under the light of a Christmas tree, sipping hot chocolate while her mom played her favorite Christmas music and her dad told stories from his early firefighting days.

"I mean, my parents are out of the country." Esther's

words drew Ashley's attention back. "So, my uncle invited me to join Jason and his annual Disney trip, which kind of sounds like the worst. But I don't want to impose on your family."

"Oh my gosh, Esther!"

The car halted, and again, Ashley was flung forward and caught by Esther and the seat belt.

"Stop doing that!" Esther scolded. "You keep startling me."

"No, but Esther. Esther!"

Esther silently fixed Ashley's seatbelt.

"This would be perfect. You could be my girlfriend."

Esther froze with her hand on the release, and Ashley realized her mistake. Esther didn't like her that way.

"No, no!" she corrected. "Not a real girlfriend. You would be like my pretend girlfriend. So my mom knows I'm still gay. But also! Also, you can help me with the whole vampire thing. Because they don't know about that, and I kind of want to keep it that way."

Esther was driving again, and Ashley waited for an answer. And waited. Maybe Esther hadn't understood her. Did she say the idea out loud, or was she talking in her head again? Sometimes she did that when she was drinking. But Ashley was basically sober now, and this was the best idea she had ever had since that time she thought about drinking from Not-Brian in the middle of a Halloween party.

Esther pulled to the side of the road and turned off the car. "How serious are you right now?"

"So serious. Super serious." How could she emphasize this properly? The only thing she wanted for Christmas was for Esther to come home with her.

"I'm pretty sure you're going to forget this conversation

in the morning, so I don't want to commit to anything you'll regret the next day."

"Oh, wow. That sounds like not a no." Ashley bounced excitedly in her seat. Esther unbuckled her, which only made her more excited.

"Well, we're here. Text me in the morning if you remember this conversation, okay?"

"Yessss." That was definitely a yes. No doubt about it. "An unmemory never elephants," she proclaimed and leaped from the car before Esther could change her mind. Her shoe caught on the curb, and she face-planted into the grass. Damn curb, making her look like a drunken fool when she was clearly sober. A car door slammed, and then Esther was there in front of her looking beautiful and concerned.

"Are you okay?" Esther asked. "I'll walk you to the door."

She helped Ashley up, and nearly on her own, Ashley walked up the porch steps and opened the front door.

"Are you going to be okay?" Esther's brows were puckering most adorably. Ashley wanted to kiss that spot. So, she did, leaving behind a pink lip print in the middle of Esther's forehead like a flag on the moon.

"You are the best fake girlfriend who ever fake girlfriended."

And then Ashley sprinted to the bathroom and threw up.

12

____

Esther

Esther tapped the toe of her boot against the gravel parking lot of the marina and debated leaving for the thousandth time. After staying up late last night only to be woken for eight a.m. Mass by Uncle Pete—you can't skip on All Saints' Day—she wanted nothing more than to crawl back into bed, pull the covers over her head, and forget the world. She checked her phone again. Maybe Uther forgot. She'd canceled brunch with him every week for a month. She wouldn't blame him if he'd fallen out of the habit and forgotten her.

She hadn't told him about the whole Ashley-is-a-vampire thing, and her sense of keeping Ashley's confidence warred with her loyalty to her friend. And what made her think he would believe her to begin with? Uther had stuck with her for over a year, despite her recent flakiness. She'd only known Ashley for a couple of months, and they were what? Classmates? Acquaintances?

Her mind flashed to a night by a lake almost a month

ago now, the water lapping at the shore as Ashley's lips coaxed softly against Esther's. She regretted having to wash the lipstick off her forehead this morning. It felt like rubbing off the ashes from Ash Wednesday before school so your classmates wouldn't ask about the smudge on your face, even though the point was to leave it on. But it was scary to broadcast something that intimate to the world.

"Esther, I'm here!" Uther trudged up the path, pulling up the collar of his coat and pushing sunglasses tighter against his face.

"Hiding from the law?" she asked.

"Not so loud." He cringed and massaged his temple. "Who knew board game club was that into Halloween?"

"Hey, about last night—"

Uther held up his palm. "Please, can we get a seat and some coffee first? I am not a full human being at the moment. It's much too early for brunch."

"It's eleven. I don't think this place even serves breakfast. Why are we here?" The waterfront bar and grill was just opening for the day as they pushed through the door. There were more nets among the myriad of random fishing supplies crowding the ceiling and walls than there were customers.

"My parents took me here a few times as a kid, and I need greasy food right now. Lay off."

"Wait, you grew up here?"

"Esther," he grumbled, pulling the collar of his coat so it covered his face. "Of all days for you to be interested in talking about personal stuff. My parents are history teachers in Burlington."

"Burlington?" She stopped and looked him over. "Vermont? You grew up across the lake this whole time, and I never knew?"

In lieu of a response, Uther grumbled indecipherably as he stomped over to the bar. "So much coffee please."

He snagged two menus and took a seat at the back near a window overlooking the lake.

Esther followed, carefully pulling out her chair and flipping through the novel of a menu in silence until someone plopped two steaming cups of coffee in front of them with a dish of sugar packets and another of creamer cups.

Uther took a long drag from his mug and sighed, slumping back into his chair. "All right, I'm ready. Go ahead."

Esther paused while reaching for the creamer. "Sorry, what were we talking about again?"

"Fish and chips," Uther called across the room to the waiter headed their way then pointed to Esther. "And a quesadilla with the sour cream on the side."

"What makes you think you know what I want?"

Uther tilted his head. "I pay attention. Besides, I was planning on splitting with you—hence the sour cream on the side because I know you don't like it." He tapped the side of his nose, as though this was a witty yet obvious observation. "Don't worry. The quesadilla is amazing. And by amazing, I mean cheesy, which is just what I need."

He knew she didn't like sour cream, and she didn't even know where he was from. Over a year of claiming to be his friend and Esther hadn't even cared to ask the most basic questions. But if she had, she'd have had to answer the same questions in return. That was how conversations and friendships worked. A give and take, tit for tat.

"Well, don't leave me in suspense," he said. The coffee must have kicked in. He even removed his sunglasses. "What happened last night? I passed out on the couch after calling you. Like, Char had to help me inside. Did you find the keys all right?"

"Right, sorry." Esther fished in her pocket and dropped the keys on the table. "Thanks again for letting me borrow your car." Her mind wandered to that ride with Ashley. To feeling the softness, the weight of her, as she helped Ashley up the steps to her house. She was inhuman and yet so real.

"You're welcome." Uther pulled the keys back and stuffed them in his pocket. "And I mean that for more than just the ride." He gave her a wink and a quick finger gun.

"What's that?" She gestured to all of him. "What are you doing? What's going on?"

"For being your wingman, obviously." He lifted his coffee to his lips and gave her a saucy look, doing something funny with his eyebrows. She wasn't sure she liked it.

"Wingman?" She hadn't meant to shout the word. The couple at the table in the other corner looked over at them. Esther ducked her head to the level of her coffee, as though a lower elevation would save her from observation. "What do you mean wingman?" she hissed.

Uther opened his mouth to answer.

"That's fish and chips for you." A poorly timed server dropped a basket of fried things in front of Uther, whose eyes grew wide and shiny. Esther shot back up in her seat. "And quesadilla for the lady. Anything else I can get you?"

"No," she snapped.

"I think we're good for now." Uther gave a charming smile, and the server left.

When she was sure he was out of earshot, Esther started again. "What do you mean wingman?"

"I mean, okay, so I was a little drunk at the time...." He paused, looked at the items on the ceiling, then crammed a steaming chunk of battered and fried fish in his mouth, pointing to his face and shaking his head.

Esther glared at him. "You can't chew forever."

He did his best.

She started in on a slice of her quesadilla while waiting, and unfortunately it was quite cheesy and delicious, and she couldn't hate Uther for ordering something she actually liked.

Finally, he swallowed and reached for another bite of fish.

"Uther, I'm warning you"—she shot a finger at his face—"if you take one more bite, I will make sure you regret it."

He gulped, but his hand dropped from the basket. "Okay, so don't hate me."

"That's not an encouraging way to start a story."

"Yeah, well, that wasn't a promise to not hate me." He took her plate and divided their food, shoving a generous pile of fries onto hers. "So, you know how we're both amazing people, but we're also kind of wallflowers?"

"Just get to the point."

Uther pushed her plate, now piled with food, back to her side of the table. "You don't talk about personal stuff, Esther. And that's totally fine. You don't owe anyone your backstory." He paused to eat a fry. "It's just that we've been friends for a year and you haven't opened up about anything. So, I figured it was me and maybe if you had a more outgoing friend, you would feel comfortable talking to them. And you and Ashley, I thought I saw something there. Some natural chemistry."

"That's not—" But she didn't know how to finish that thought. She didn't open up because she didn't open up. No one was interested, and she shouldn't be imposing more on people's lives. If she shared personal anecdotes, the next thing you knew, she'd be giving advice and someone could get hurt. She could ruin lives, and she couldn't be responsible for that again.

He waved off her half-comment. "I was drunk and not thinking straight. I saw Ashley being so comfortable in a crowd and everyone engaging with her and thought, hey, why not hook Esther up with a better friend? So, when she fell in the pool, it seemed like the perfect chance..."

"Uther." She took his hand. The warmth of it startled her. Had they ever done this before? They weren't hand-holding friends. She took her hand back again. Touching was too much. "You're already a better friend."

But that wasn't enough. Uther was right. She was holding back, and maybe it was fine to trust him with her secrets. She was struck with the sudden realization she could lose him—his friendship—and she didn't want that.

"Sorry, I wasn't trying to fish for compliments, but thanks all the same." He plucked a fry from the pile. "So how was the ride? You got her number, right?"

"She kissed me."

Uther coughed on his bite of fry. "She did what? Do I need to have a word with her? I mean, she was drunk, but that's no excuse to get handsy without consent."

"No, not last night." She wasn't sure what made her mention the kiss. Clearly, the whole agreeing-to-be-Ashley's-pretend-girlfriend was a more pressing matter. Or maybe the whole vampire thing. Maybe all of it was a pressing matter and she should start from the beginning. "She kissed me about a month ago. While we were both sober. I've had her number for over a month now."

"Oh. Oh!" His gaze flickered across her face, assessing. "Esther, I'm so sorry. I didn't know you were avoiding her. I never would have... I would have called someone else to get her. I swear. I just thought...”

“No, no! I wasn’t avoiding her.” She bit her lip. How to explain that Uther’s call to get Ashley, to be in a vehicle with Ashley like they were people that rode in vehicles together, had shot through Esther’s system faster than coffee ever had?

Uther nodded and ate some more of his fish, giving her time before asking, “Did you want to talk about it?”

She nibbled at a fry. “What do you mean?”

He was sipping his coffee and looked out the window, as though this wasn’t the most terrifying conversation Esther had been a part of in recent memory. “What happened after she kissed you?”

“Well, then I told her I was straight.” Maybe it was nice he wasn’t looking at her. She couldn’t make eye contact with anyone right now.

There was a pause as he took another sip of coffee. “Why’d you tell her that?”

“Well, because...because I thought it was true?”

He nodded and went back to eating. And for a while, that was where they left it. No pressure to say more. She could change the subject if she wanted. The pause was long enough that it wouldn’t seem odd. And it was Uther. He wouldn’t judge her if she didn’t say anything. But he wouldn’t judge her if she did either. They finished their food in silence, Esther both unsure how to continue and also not ready to change the subject. So, she left it floating there until she was eating her last bite of quesadilla and the check materialized.

“Toss a coin to your server,” sang Uther, while pulling out his wallet. “Oh, valley of plenty.”

Finances settled, they stood to leave.

"Uther?"

"Hmm?"

"How did you know? I mean, I guess you always knew. And if at some point you didn't...know. Or something different. I don't think I'm saying this right."

"I'm going to be honest," He held the door for her. "I'm not sure what you just said, but I have a good idea where this conversation is headed." He nodded toward the lake. "Did you want to take a walk?"

Esther turned to the lake and took one fortifying inhale through the nose and out through the mouth then nodded. "All right."

The gravel crunched beneath their feet as they walked to the shoreline. The summer season was long past, and most of the boats were dry-docked for winter, the piers along with them. They took the path through a miniature forest of boats and masts, following the gravel jetty out into the lake.

"So, you like Ashley, huh?" Uther kicked at a rock, sending it skidding to the edge of the water.

"Okay, so..." Esther grabbed the rock and hurled it as far into the water as she could. It made a satisfying plunk and inspired her to look for more rocks. "I never considered dating a woman before, or...I guess I was only considering men? I was interested in them so—you know, the men, I mean. It's easy to just not think any harder about it." She found another rock and threw it. This one sounded more like a pink than a plunk. "There were probably signs. Occasionally, I'd think 'that girl is hot. I'd like to be her friend,' and then be flattered when the friendship got territorial. I can't be friends with that other person because I'm already friends with her. You know, girl stuff." She threw a stick this time, and it made an unsatisfying splash and floated to the surface. She watched it bob for a while. "And even if it wasn't just girls being girls, that's a handful of cases to a life-time of Orlando Bloom posters and Sadie Hawkins dances. I mean even if I am..."

Gay. The word echoed in her head, pushing to come out, but if she said it out loud and to another human, it would be real. Recorded in history for all time. In her head, it was a rough draft. Something bold to consider, but maybe too hastily written for the final draft.

"How much is enough to count?" She braved looking up and found Uther seated on a discarded, plastic chair under one of the two trees, one leg resting across the other.

"Okay." He steepled his hands, squinting at something invisible in front of him like he was using his mind to unravel the tangles of Esther's life. "I think the best analogy I've heard for this discussion is the purple metaphor."

"Okay." Esther nodded like this was the most normal conversation in the world. Uther was her gay Jesus speaking in parables, ready to present her with all the answers.

"So purple is thought of as blue and red, right? But the proportions aren't set in stone. Like fifty percent blue and fifty percent red is called purple, but so is twenty percent blue and eighty percent red. Lavender, plum, fuchsia, electric purple. They're wildly different, but if we were told to pick a Roy G. Biv category, we'd stick them all into purple. Right?"

"Yeah, that sounds right." Esther was pacing along the shore, nodding like a bobblehead ready for him to wrap this up with something all-knowing and personal to her life. She waited. And waited. "Is that it?"

"Oh. Did I need to spell it out for you?"

"Damn it, Uther. You just gave me an art lesson on the color purple. I learned this in grade school."

"It's called bi, Esther. Or pan or queer or whatever label

you're comfortable with. You can like men eighty percent of the time and women or any other gender the other twenty percent, and it's still enough to count. There isn't a cut-off on how gay you need to be to fit. Labels are inherently a social construct made to both help us understand and categorize ourselves and also to needlessly stress us the fuck out."

"Oh."

"The label doesn't matter, Esther. So stop stressing over it. Just be you and know, whatever that looks like, it's all right."

"Okay." She was back to nodding and pacing. Taking in everything he'd said.

She knew gender and sexuality were on a spectrum and also the labels used for them were all social constructs. Anthropologists, sociologists, and plenty of others had written on this concept for decades. But hearing it out loud, that labels don't matter? She felt like a balloon freed from its tether. Both exhilarated and terrified.

"Okay, thanks" she said. "I can live with that."

"You feeling good?" He scrutinized her. "Did you need to talk about it some more?"

"No." Esther shook her head. "No, this is plenty to process already. Let's move on."

"Great." He jumped up from the chair and skipped over to her. "Friend level, upgraded. Now, on that note, can we talk about my problems?"

"Oh. Sure, what's happening?" She dusted off her hands, retuning to the sharp change in focus.

"I have man problems. Did you think this conversation was going to pass the Bechdel test?"

"I, umm...no?"

"Are you free this afternoon?"

This felt like a trap. But he'd just talked her through her fumbling identity crisis.

"I was going to work on my final project some," she said. "Why?"

"August is being suspicious. He's invited me to this 'gardening club'" —Uther used finger quotes— "but he was all cagey and nondescript about it. Something is afoot."

"Oh." Esther shrugged. "Maybe it's a date."

"To a gardening club?" Uther raised a skeptical brow.

"I don't kn—"

"In November?"

"Okay, well, it does sound a little weird."

Uther snatched her hand. "Can you come with me?"

"What?" Esther pulled her hand back. "Uther, I'm not going on a probable date with you and August."

"But, Esther." He propped his hands under his chin to emphasize how large and puppy-like his eyes were growing.

She glared and pointed at his face. "Stop it."

"Esther, my one true friend and the apple of my eye, come to this thing with me that's probably not a date for moral support."

She huffed, resting her fists on her hips. "And if it turns out to be a date?"

Uther scoffed, waving away her concerns. "It's not a date. You just said. Who takes someone to a gardening club as a date?"

"*I* didn't say it wasn't a date! *You* said that."

"Esther." He took her hand and dropped to one knee.

Her eyebrows shot up to her hairline. "Uther," she hissed, looking around to see if anyone was watching. "People are going to think you're proposing."

"I *am* proposing." Uther pressed one hand solemnly to

his heart. His other remained a vice on hers. "I'm proposing we spend the afternoon together at this gardening club."

"Stop it. All right, fine. Get up, and I'll go with you, okay?"

"Yay!" He leaped to his feet and wrapped his arms around her, spinning her so fast her legs lifted from the ground. "She said yes!" he shouted to the two people smoking by the backdoor of the restaurant.

They cheered their support and Esther's face heated.

She would not smile and encourage his antics. "This better not be a date."

13

Esther

Esther looked at her phone again. Twelve hours since Ashley's drunken proposal and she still hadn't texted to confirm she remembered their exchange.

She rolled down the car window and watched the ever-approaching shoreline of Grand Isle, Vermont, the large island in the middle of Lake Champlain.

It was chilly that afternoon, and Esther had never taken the ferry before. August got some sort of special discount for being a descendant of a founder—or the guy in the booth recognized him—because he just waved their car on by. The sun glistened off the wakes from the boat, the sound of its engine fought with the churning of the water, and the chatter of other mingling passengers filled the day like white noise.

"Hey, roll that up," Uther called back to her. "I'm freezing up here."

Esther rolled her eyes but complied. "Tell me again why a Vermont gardening club is meeting in November."

"It's a social club as well as gardening," snapped August. He was tapping his finger on the steering wheel again.

August hadn't seemed excited to see her when they arrived, but Uther had called shotgun, and the two of them had carried on a steady stream of playful conversation the entire ride, leaving Esther forgotten in the backseat.

Not a date, my ass. Which left Esther's mind wandering to things outside this car.

Like how Ashley still hadn't texted her.

Ashley was a mess yesterday and Esther...well, Esther was kind of into it. Ashley was kicking down a door Esther didn't know she'd locked. Maybe it was the whole vampire thing. She was into this new dark and edgy side to Ashley. But it was also Ashley being open and funny and brave. And god, she was hot as hell. Even in those ridiculous pajamas that were way too short for her and her makeup all a mess like she'd been tossed in the lake.

Over a month had passed since Ashley had kissed her by this very lake, and it was still all Esther could think about. Not even the coming out as a vampire part distracted her—which, to be fair, was an important part. Ashley had kissed her and Esther had liked it, and maybe Esther wanted to do it again.

And what did that mean? She'd dated men in the past. Did her sheltered upbringing imprint such a strong heteronormative view into her psyche, she hadn't even conceived of the idea that two women could be interested in each other without falling into the narrow view she was familiar with that, if you weren't straight, you were a lesbian? Or it was a phase, something you were trying. Or it was just performative for the male gaze.

That was a lot to take in. Esther hadn't lied that night. Until that moment, she really had thought she was straight. But now a million memories ran through her mind, making her question this claim. The time in middle school when she told a group of girls she found it easier to tell if a girl was attractive than a guy and was met with silence instead of agreement. That time in high school when a boyfriend requested she not date a girl after him because his last girlfriend had come out as a lesbian and he was worried about getting a reputation. And her problematic thought, that she needed to date an in-between guy quickly in case a cute girl asked her out.

Still straight though.

She was like one of those women in fairy tales that was asleep their whole life, then one kiss and bam! They're checking their phone every minute in the hopes that that cute girl would just freaking text her back already.

Seriously, if fake dating meant she could kiss Ashley again, she would say yes in a heartbeat. It had taken everything in her not to agree right there on the spot. But she knew Ashley was wasted, and she couldn't take advantage of her like that. If Ashley wanted to date her—even if it was pretend—she needed to ask her sober. Esther looked at her phone for the hundredth time since waking up that morning to a screen with no new notifications.

"She's probably still sleeping." Uther gave her a knowing look.

"Who?" Esther shoved her phone back in her pocket before meeting his gaze.

"She had a lot to drink at that party. I think she cleaned out a whole bottle of vodka by herself. I wouldn't be up for a few hours still if I'd kept up with her."

Esther looked out the window again. She didn't need

Uther digging into her romantic life while in the middle of flirting his way into one of his own. She still wasn't sure why she was the third wheel to this supposed not-date. Uther had insisted he needed her, but she was sure he would have been fine. August even laughed at Uther's last Star Wars joke.

The ferry docked, and they waited their turn as the line of cars started their engines and crawled one by one to solid ground. They followed the two-lane highway past pale yellow bungalows and red brick farmhouses broken up with cow pastures, empty cornfields, and small towns with their two-pump gas stations and white-steepled churches. After ten minutes of driving, August turned off onto a small gravel road. At the end sat a white, two-story house facing the bay, mainland Vermont providing a shoreline of scattered stick-looking trees just beyond the water.

"Why's the window slanted like that?" Esther pointed up at the house where an addition sported a window set on a diagonal like someone had taken an old farm window and fit it as best they could into the new crevice the addition made to the front of the house.

August crouched over the steering wheel to see where she pointed. "Oh that's... It's nothing. They put in an addition, and that's just how they fit the window. It happens all over the place around here. It's a quirky Vermont thing."

"We call them witch windows," Uther added, clearly proud to be the resident Vermonter for this conversation.

"Right." August's knuckles went white as he gripped the steering wheel. "Listen, this trip isn't exactly going how I'd planned. If you want to go back..."

Esther flicked Uther's ear and he scowled back at her. *Not a date, my ass.*

The front door to the house opened, and a brown blur

whizzed for the car. Barking followed, and Uther locked the doors as a dog assaulted his window.

"Greg." A woman with a severe braid and a large Carhartt jacket stepped out on the porch. "Come."

The dog whizzed back to her side and stood, a single paw raised and eyes trained on the newcomers.

"Great." August sighed. "They know we're here."

With a fortifying breath, he unbuckled and opened his car door.

"Hey, Meg," he called. The door slammed shut, and the rest of his greeting was muffled.

Esther looked at Uther.

"After you." They both spoke in unison. "Jinx. Stop it."

She glared at him. This was his idea. He should be the one to lead the way into the strange house in the middle of nowhere with an intense-looking dog. Seriously, that dog still hadn't moved. He just stood there, staring at them.

Another woman came out of the house, this one much shorter, and beelined it for August with a squeal and upraised arms. She jumped, and he caught her, lifting her in a full twirl before setting her down. Uther was watching now.

"Did he just kiss her?" He threw off his seat belt and was fighting with the door lock.

At least that got him moving.

"It was on the—" The door slammed shut behind him before she finished with "cheek." She rolled her eyes and got out of the car. Uther was getting so territorial lately. He and August needed to define that relationship before Uther fretted himself into the grave. She should have a talk with him about giving people their space.

The second woman let go of August and turned to

Esther and Uther as they cautiously approached, Esther keeping her distance from the dog.

"Hi, I'm Gwen. Is it okay if I hug you?" She had green corduroy overalls and a pink cardigan that popped against her earthy brown skin. Her black curls were pulled back into two fluffy buns.

"Sure," said Esther. She wasn't much of a hugger, but she didn't mind them, and she liked that Gwen had asked permission first, like she cared about Esther's comfort.

Gwen swooped in, and it was worth it. She gave good hugs.

"Did you bring the book?" The woman with the dog—Meg—asked August.

"It's in the car," he replied. "I'll grab it."

"You found it?" Gwen chased after him, her run more of a frolic than anything else.

Gwen wore cute vintage lace-ups. Esther looked at her own scuffed, black boots wondering if she needed to get something new yet. And that was when she noticed the grass around her feet. A November frost had sapped the color from them, but a circle of dewy emerald radiated out from her grungy boots. Smaller patches trailed off from the larger like someone had dropped the green from a bucket but spilled along the way. She followed the trail with her eyes to the car. Did she have something on her shoes that was reacting to the grass? Balancing on one foot, she pulled her other up to check the bottom of her boots. Nothing there that she could tell.

"It's the book!" called Gwen. She jumped up and down, and...

Flowers sprouted from the ground around her. Esther tumbled out of the patch of green and away from the car and growing flowers. What the hell was going on?

"August?" Esther tried to sound calm while continuing to back away from the encroaching green but heard the waver in her voice.

"What's wrong?" His brows furrowed into his classic grumpy stance as his gaze shifted from her to the growing patch of flowers.

"Damn it, Gwen. I haven't told them yet." He sighed.

"Oh my god, what are these flowers?" said Uther, jumping over patches to join Esther.

August opened his mouth to answer, but no words came out.

"Oops." Gwen twirled, looking at all the winter greenery she'd awakened. "Did I do that again?"

"Let's do this inside," said Meg. She whistled, and the dog reanimated and ran back into the house, Meg following behind. Gwen frolicked after her, small twists of flowers and vines sprouting in her wake.

Esther turned to Uther and nodded to the house. He could go first.

Uther's eyes widened and he shook his head.

She replied with her sternest look, and he countered with a mocking stern look and tilted his head to her. She squeezed her eyes, focusing lasers on him, and he matched her look with a glare of his own.

Esther was about to up the debate to a foot stomp when a hand grabbed her at the elbow. August dragged both of them up the porch steps and into the house.

"Hey, hey! No need to manhandle us." Esther pulled her arm free once they were in the doorway.

Inside reminded her of her grandparent's house if her grandparents lived in a cottage. A green gingham couch was accompanied by two faded red armchairs, each topped with a doily and centered around a braided circle rug. The wood-paneled walls were decorated with shelves of knickknacks and macramé wall hangings. She followed August through a doorway and into the cramped kitchen dinette at the back of the house. A lace-curtained window by the oval table showcased the lake just outside.

Meg grabbed the book from August and plopped it on the table, rifling through the pages like she had a certain one in mind.

Gwen fumbled around in the kitchen, opening cupboards and starting a kettle of water.

"Is anyone interested in tea?" she said in singsong. No one responded, but she pulled out a handful of mismatched teacups all the same.

"Is someone going to explain what's going on?" Esther looked at August, judging him to be the easiest to bully into talking.

The dog whined at the back door.

August ran his hand through his hair. "I'm not sure where to begin. How much do you know?"

"How about you just assume we know nothing," said Uther, apparently also put out by all that was happening.

The dog whined again, and without looking up from the book, Meg snapped her fingers. The back door opened on its own, slamming shut behind the dog.

"Like that!" Uther pointed at the door. "What was that?"

"We're witches. Obviously." Meg flipped another page. "Start there, August."

"Damn it, Meg," said August. "These are my friends, and I was kind of hoping they wouldn't run away screaming by the end of this."

"No one's screaming, love," called Gwen, combing through bundles of dried plants hanging from the kitchen ceiling. The tea kettle whistled, and she hurried to lift it from the heat.

"So, you're witches." Uther looked pointedly at August. "All of you?"

A pause before August nodded. "I meant to ease you into the idea on the ride over, but I wasn't expecting... Well, I thought it would just be you."

Esther glared at Uther. "I told you it was a date." She slumped in her chair, taking in all this new information. "I'd just gotten used to the idea of vampires. What's next? Were-wolves? Ghosts?"

"Hold up. Vampires?" Uther turned to Esther, but luckily Gwen showed up with the tea.

"Officially, there isn't witch territory or vampire territory." Gwen placed a delicate flowered teacup in front of Uther and a matching sugar dish in the middle of the table. "But unofficially, New England is witch territory, with little pockets elsewhere across the country. So, of course, that Family of vampires decided to camp out in New York, right across the border from us, a couple of years ago."

"By a couple of years, you mean over two hundred." August sounded insulted. "My family set up that town and lived in the same house for over two hundred years."

"Well, it wasn't Zephaniah that caused the problem, now, was it?" Gwen placed two more steaming cups on the table in front of Esther and August, her voice remaining as gentle as the teacups. "It was his daughter, Hannah. She's the one that started that house and brought them all to the area."

"Who's Hannah?" asked Esther.

"She's my aunt." August was messing with the small gold hoop in his ear. "A distant aunt."

"Are you a vampire?" whispered Uther.

"No, I'm not a vampire." August sounded tired. "That's not how vampires work. You're made a vampire, not born one."

"Just checking," Uther said.

"But you're a witch?" asked Esther.

August nodded, still keeping an eye on Uther like he might run screaming from the house. Uther remained quiet, his attention zoning out like someone trying to escape an overstimulating situation.

"It's not here." Meg slammed the book shut, making everyone jump. "There's a page torn out. You're going to have to ask your aunt for it."

"Is your aunt a witch too?" asked Uther.

August was massaging his temples. "Are you sure it's not in there?"

Meg snapped, sending the book careening at him. August caught it just before it could smash into his nose.

"Check for yourself. It's gone and we need it. Talk to your aunt or get someone to do it for you. I don't care. But we need that spell, and she's the only one that had access to it."

Esther was still piecing everything together. "If you have weird unofficial territory disputes with the vampires, why is Ashley over at your place all the time?"

Everyone turned to August.

"Esther." He hissed her name like this conversation might still be a secret. "Could we please talk about this later?"

"You let a vampire in your house?" Meg had the same laser-focused expression her dog was wearing earlier. "You invited her in?"

"August." Gwen's voice was gentle and motherly, despite her appearing to be around the same age as them. "You know that's not a safe thing to do."

"It's fine!" August snapped. "She's not going to do anything while living under Hannah's roof. I can take care of myself."

"Wait. *Ashley*?" Uther turned to Esther, his voice soft and vulnerable. "And you knew? This whole time?"

"I…" Esther couldn't do this. She thought she could do a deep and meaningful friendship, but she was already failing. Instead of answering his question, she turned to Meg and changed the subject. "Why do you need the missing page?"

The three witches exchanged looks, none of them willing to speak, and that was what finally broke her patience.

"I have homework to do!" Esther got up from the table, mid-speech, like her studies were calling to her this very moment. "I was perfectly happy not knowing any of this. I could be home, being productive with my own things, and not here, getting sucked into whatever paranormal drama is starting. And you decide now—*now*—is the time to be cryptic? Keep your witchy secrets. I'm done here."

Esther wished she had her bag or something to dramatically gather to emphasize how much she was leaving, but she hadn't even taken off her coat. She hesitated, doing her best to school her expression, but while the conclusion of her speech meant she was leaving, she hadn't driven herself here and, therefore, had no ride.

Gwen broke the silence first. "Would you like a tour? Meg, dear. You could show them the garden."

Esther did not want a tour. She wanted answers.

But actually, no. Her wants were all flipped around. She didn't want answers. She wanted to go home and mind her own business. Not following her supposed friend on his date with a bunch of witches while they hunted some spell in an old book she'd found for them. She was already more involved than she'd intended. She'd let her inclination to observe situations get away from her.

"Fine." Meg shoved her chair from the table and walked to the back door, not waiting for anyone's answer.

"Are we meant to follow her?" Uther sounded just as unsure as Esther felt.

Gwen approached Esther, placing a warm hand at her elbow. "Some of this is easier to show than explain. I'm sorry that it's a lot, but...well, it's a lot."

"All right." Uther stood and walked to the door. "I came here to see a garden, and a garden I shall see."

The door closed behind Uther, Gwen following behind him, and the conversation was over. Her big speech about leaving was ignored. Esther was a joke.

"Esther." August bit his lip and tugged at the ring in his ear. "You should know. It's not...Whatever they show you, I know Ashley is off-limits, okay? So, don't freak out or anything. I mean, she's in Hannah's Family for starters, so she's off-limits anyway. But I know... Well, I get she means something to you, so I thought I'd let you know."

Off-limits from what? Did Uther say something to him?

"What are you talking about?" Esther asked.

There was a thwack from outside and an alarmed squeak from Uther.

August's gaze cut to the door and back at her. "Esther—"

But Esther was not interested in whatever vague thing August was talking about. She wrenched open the door everyone else had gone through. Her first thought was there was no garden out here.

Her next was *That's a crossbow Meg's shouldering.*

"You ready to give it a go?" Meg handed the contraption to a very reluctant Uther and faced him toward a scarecrow near the lake shore with a cloth head and stitched-on face, featuring two pointed canines—a dart protruding from its chest.

The door squeaked open behind her.

"You're vampire hunters," Esther said.

"That's a simplistic way of putting it." August joined her at the railing overlooking the scene below. "We consider it population control."

"Population control." What a simple yet nefarious phrase. A word pulled out by hunters every deer season. Or *conservationists* when dealing with an invasive species. A word used by one group to justify the death of another. For the sake of balance.

"There are rules," he said.

But Esther barely heard him over the rushing static in her head.

"No one wants to start a war," August continued. "Vampires in a Family are safe from hunters. We only go after the young and unaffiliated. Those without anyone to keep them in line."

That "we" echoed in her head. August had hunted vampires. Vampires like Ashley, who was a real person and not a deer.

"Uther."

Uther loosed the dart as Esther called to him, and the shot sailed past the target and into the lake.

"Watch it," Meg scolded him. "Greg. Fetch."

The dog shot out from under the porch and performed a perfect dive into the lake, beelining for the missing dart.

"I'm ready to go back now." Esther didn't wait for August's answer or even for Uther to catch up to her. She went back through the kitchen door and out the other side to the car. It was time to call it a day.

This time, Esther was happy to be the forgotten third wheel in the backseat—the ferry chugging along beneath them back to Plattsburgh. August was a member of a coven of vampire-hunting witches. And Esther was checking her phone to see if the hot vampire from class had texted yet. No, she had not. This was a problem.

"All right, here's the plan," said August.

Esther hated this plan already.

"I'm dropping Uther off on our way into town."

Uther raised his hand as though summoning a teacher. "Umm. Actually, I don't like this plan."

At least she wasn't the only one not on board.

"I'm dropping you off on our way into town," August continued, "and Esther, I'm taking you to the vampire house to get the missing page."

Esther and Uther had strong words on this idea, and both shared them—loudly, one over the other.

"You can't just dump me at home like this."

"Why do I have to go? You go."

"Just because I'm not some magical creature doesn't mean I'm not helpful."

"I just wanted to work on my paper in peace."

"Stop it!" August yelled, but they continued to argue their points, Esther fueling her anger from Uther's.

August finally resorted to holding down the horn until they both quieted, and everyone on the ferry glared daggers at their car.

"Here's the plan," August said. "I am going to take Esther to interview my aunt about Platt family history as part of her internship. You can actually benefit from this. Uther, you don't need to be there, so I'm taking you home, where you won't be in any danger. Ideally."

They sat in silence, both Uther and Esther fuming for

being treated like children. If August thought he was going to have two cooperative volunteers, he had another think coming. In the silence, Esther's mind went to the small journal she'd found days ago in the Platt collection talking of night contagions and a secret society. She had a feeling she'd just met a branch of that secret society. August's aunt was the perfect person to ask about that piece and the history of the collection in general.

Not that she'd admit that to August.

The ferry slid into the dock and other passengers started their engines. "Fine." August sighed. "What can I do to convince you two to help me?"

Esther was ready for this. "What's on the missing page? Why do they want it so much?"

"I don't know—a spell of some sort. I don't even know how they heard about it." He took a steadying breath. "Honestly, it sounds like some pet project of Meg's. But I really need to be the one that helps them get it. You heard them back there. How they feel about my family. I'm a witch with a vampire for an aunt. I need them to see me as an asset if I want to fit in. And I'd really like to fit in somewhere."

"Ah, yes." Esther rolled her eyes. "Because August *Platt*, on our way back to *Platt*sburgh, doesn't fit in anywhere." She looked to Uther to back her up, but Uther was looking at August like he was a lost kitten. Instead of acknowledging Esther's comment, he placed his hand on August's.

"We'll help you. Right, Esther?" Now Uther turned to her.

She glared back. "Fine. Whatever. I do this one thing and then I'm out. And I better get a good interview out of this."

14

Ashley stared at her phone's blank text screen, Esther's name glaring at her from the top, unsure how to proceed. That was why she'd trekked down to the front sitting room to ask advice from the absolute worst person yet the only one available.

"Did I ever tell you about my pendant?" Claribel lifted a silver chain from around her neck, revealing a spherical bauble at the end.

"No, I don't think you have." Ashley was pretty sure this had nothing to do with whether she should text Esther or not, but she'd humor Claribel. The longer Ashley delayed, the longer she didn't have to come up with a response to her dumb plan of inviting Esther home to her human family for Christmas. What had she been thinking? She obviously hadn't been. She'd spouted out the first thought that came to her, and Esther had been too polite to outright say no while Ashley was in her unmanageable drunken state. She needed to text Esther, but the question was—did she laugh it off like this whole plan was just her drunken babbling, or did she go with it and see if Esther had a real response?

Esther had told Ashley to text her. It wasn't a no.

"It's actually a vial," Claribel said. "I keep the blood of a past lover in it. Washington Irving. Have you heard of him? He had such a beautiful way with words."

Ashley was only half listening. Her mind composing and deleting messages to Esther. Maybe she needed a good pros and cons list. Her musing was interrupted when someone knocked on the door—in the middle of the day.

Claribel hissed in annoyance. "Be a dear and get that, Ash. You're the only one with a strong enough complexion at this hour."

It was a blessedly cloudy day, but strong complexion or not, Ashley still had to cover up. Who knocked in the middle of the day on a Sunday? She donned her cardigan, gloves, and hat, making sure her hair covered as much of her neck as possible. The porch blocked any direct sunlight, but she wouldn't be able to stand out there for long. She cracked the door and promptly closed it again.

"Who was it, dear?" called Claribel from the safe darkness of the front sitting room.

The knocker repeated, and Ashley looked down at the phone in her hand then back at the door. Shaking her head, she opened it.

"Esther," she breathed. That was too breathy. She should try again. "I mean, Esther. Hi."

She looked good. Tight black jeans and a black sweater with a white embroidered Peter Pan collar. Her hair hung in loose curls over her shoulders, and her lips were painted the sort of deep orange that had Ashley thinking of sunsets and other dangerous things. Esther's heart was beating fast, which was an intriguing touch.

Another figure stepped from behind Esther. "Are you going to let us in?"

Ashley's fangs dropped instinctively and she barely held back a hiss. August was such a mood wrecker.

She narrowed her eyes at him. "What are you doing here, witch?"

"Doesn't matter." He walked past Esther and pushed his way into the house. "Some of us don't have to ask for permission."

"That's called trespassing." Ashley scowled as he stepped onto the sitting room rug with his shoes still on.

"You knew?" Esther, still waiting to be let in.

Ashley was so fired up from August that she'd forgotten to hide that she knew what August was.

"Esther, I—" Ashley's response was cut off by a hiss from inside.

Abandoning her post at the door, Ashley rushed back to the sitting room to find August plopped on the settee facing Claribel with his dirty boots up on the coffee table.

"Ash!" Claribel cried from her chair. "You let a witch into the house? His magic is clawing." She massaged her neck and glared at August. Ashley also felt the now familiar fizzy tingling in her throat of August's magic. Like someone had told a joke just as she took a swig of pop and now the carbonation was trapped in her sinuses.

"Feet off the table, witch," Ashley demanded. "And tone down that wretched magic, or I'll burn your antique house to the ground."

He huffed but took his feet off the table, and the tingling went from mildly painful to a slight annoyance.

"We're here to see Aunt Hannah. Is she up?"

"*Aunt* Hannah?" Claribel pulled her cross-stitch from

between the couch cushions and began stitching excitedly. She was such a gossip.

"I'm guessing she doesn't talk about me." August shrugged.

Claribel huffed. "That would be a good guess."

"Well, I brought Esther to interview her for her practicum. She's archiving the Platt family records, and who better to talk to than a Platt intimately familiar with the collection."

"You did what?" Ashley grabbed August by the collar. "Whatever game you're playing, witch, you leave Esther out of it."

Gus squeaked from the commotion and rustled his way farther into the curtains.

"Interesting." The soft shush of thread pulling through cloth indicated Claribel was getting quite some cross-stitching in. "Who is this Esther?"

"That would be me." Without her loud boots on—because Esther was polite enough to take off her shoes—and in all the commotion, Ashley had lost track of her. Esther reached out her hand to Claribel. "It's good to meet you."

Ashley dropped August's collar and bolted between them before Esther took a step closer, blocking Esther from Claribel's view. "She's a classmate. That's it."

Slowly, Claribel lowered her stitching to her lap. "And she knows…"

Ashley glanced over at August, still fixing his collar over on the couch. "About witches. Yes. But that wasn't my doing."

"Hmm." Claribel moved her project to the cushion next to her and stood. "I see."

"No, it's fine." Ashley took another step back, pulling Esther farther behind her. "If the witches want to go around broadcasting who they are, that's their problem." She waved her hand like she was swatting away a fly. "You don't need to..."

Claribel waited. "I don't need to...what?"

"Ashley."

Ashley jumped as Hannah descended the ancient stairs without making a sound.

"What is he doing here?" Hannah asked.

"Nice to see you too, Aunt Hannah." August brushed imaginary dust off his shoulders and straightened his shirt as he stood.

She was a foot shorter than August, at least, but still managed to look down her prim nose at him. "What is it you're looking for, August?"

He took his time, returning her glower with one of his own. Ashley thought he might not answer until he finally gestured to Esther. "I've brought someone to interview you. This is Esther Green."

Esther broke free of Ashley's grasp and stepped out from behind her but didn't offer a hand this time.

"A graduate student at the college," August continued. "She's archiving the family records and has some questions about a particular piece that I thought you could help her with."

Hannah looked Esther up and down then nodded to the study. "This way, if you please."

Ashley tried to catch Esther's eye, but Esther followed Hannah without a second glance.

"Watch him," Hannah instructed, nodding to August before closing the door behind them.

The conniving witch definitely had some ulterior motive, and Hannah's recommendation to watch him was well warranted. But Esther was in a room alone with a powerful vampire who may or may not have heard that Esther was privy to too much information. So, Ashley went back to where Claribel sat and crouched near a floor vent she knew connected to the study.

"Aren't you watching me?" If she didn't know better, she'd think he sounded disappointed in her lack of interest.

"Shut up. I'm trying to listen." She waved aimlessly in his direction. "Go on with whatever nonsense you have planned and leave me alone."

There was a small pause before his boots clomped out of the room, and Ashley was able to listen in peace. Esther had come prepared with some journal. A few long pauses concerned Ashley, but then Esther asked a new question and Hannah would start again. When Esther asked about a night contagion, Ashley debated running in there and dragging Esther out.

"Someone has a little infatuation, it seems." Claribel picked up her cross-stitch again. She'd never finish if she only worked on it while gossiping. Although, she was getting a lot done today.

"You can have the witch," Ashley offered chivalrously.

"Ha! No, thank you." Claribel turned to the foyer where August had disappeared and muttered to herself, "Although, he does look tasty."

She stitched in silence while Ashley listened for any sign of distress in Esther's voice. How quickly could she get there if Esther cried out? Hannah could mesmerize her into silence and then make her forget so Ashley never knew. She should go in there now and stop whatever was happening. Esther had enough answers for her project.

"You're playing a dangerous game, my dear," Claribel said.

"Dangerous?" She hoped Claribel didn't keep this conversation up for long. Ashley needed to pay attention. Esther's life could be on the line.

"Humans are destined to die." While this was not a groundbreaking statement, it was enough to catch Ashley's attention. "Worse still, they know it."

"We all know it." Ashley went back to smooshing her face to the vent so Claribel would get the hint and stop talking to her.

"Yes, well. When you know you are a creature that dies, you want to spend the life you have with another creature that dies. Humans hold this sentimental value around growing old together. Nonsense, exacerbated by the greeting card industry, I'm sure, but real nonetheless."

"It's nothing," said Ashley. "I'm not looking for some happily ever after with any human you might be alluding to. I'm fine."

Claribel raised a brow, as though doubting that hovering over a floor vent to listen in on a secret conversation was the regular actions of someone who was "fine."

"Anyway," Claribel continued. "I was *fine* once too, living in the city before moving upstate to join the Family." She pulled out the vial Ashley was sure did not have Essence of Irving in it. Claribel didn't know Ashley checked the ages of all her supposed suitors, and they never quite matched up. She wasn't sure if Claribel lied on purpose or if after a couple of centuries, lies blurred into truth. She didn't doubt that *someone's* blood was in that vial. "It's an old story and not the sort that would make it on any greeting card. He gave me this token to remember him by."

The door to the study opened, and Ashley leaped to her feet and ran to the door, glad to get away from Claribel.

"Esther." Ashley caught her by the bicep, looking her up

and down to make sure she was okay. There was no way to know for sure that her memories were intact without asking her something specific. "Before you go, I was wondering..."

She wasn't sure what to ask.

"Did you remember something you wanted to ask me?" Esther asked.

Remember. Ashley's phone sat heavy in her pocket with an open text still waiting to send. This was her chance to ask Esther about Christmas. She was standing right there. But pretend it was a joke or ask for real?

Hannah walked out of the study.

Right. Ashley couldn't invite Esther to Christmas in front of this crowd. And there was a chance Esther didn't even want her to ask. She should think of another question to check Esther's memory.

"Something about an elephant never forgetting. Or unmemory-ing?" Esther's lashes lowered, and the corner of her mouth hitched playfully. "It was a little unclear what you were trying to say."

Sweet Jesus, Esther was *trying* to get Ashley to remember. Like Ashley could somehow forget. Okay, sure she was drunk at the time, but last night had haunted her all day. Also, was Esther flirting?

No, she's straight. Pay attention, Ashley. Her memories were still intact, but they could *not* do this here. She grabbed Esther's hand.

"Yes, school question. Don't mind us," she announced to the rest of the room, none of whom looked up as she pulled Esther up the stairs. "We'll just be studying, in my room. About school and such."

Ashley practically carried Esther up the stairs in her haste to get her alone. Down the hall and to the left. She didn't even bother closing the door.

Esther leaned in the open doorway, her eyes transfixed. Ashley waited. Maybe this was a terrible idea. Even now, she was watching the rise and fall of Esther's chest as she got her breath back, her long and graceful neck and that smooth expanse of skin. Ashley heard blood churning through Esther's veins, not slowing now that they stopped running but keeping their excited pace. So many temptations combined into one person. How could Ashley possibly expect to survive a whole week at her parents' house with her?

"Ask me." Esther breathed the command.

And then there was Esther. Quiet and fierce. Prickly with a mushy center that made Ashley want to dig for it every time. She was a kitten with claws. The scratches were worth a snuggle.

"Come home with me for Christmas."

"All right." Esther's smile was slow and heartbreaking. No wonder she hid them. It was a punch to Ashley's chest.

Ashley fisted her hand resting on the wall next to Esther's head, using every ounce of willpower in her body to not pull Esther into her arms and kiss her senseless.

"This is a terrible plan," said Ashley. Her cheeks were tired from smiling so much, but she couldn't help herself.

"Quite terrible." Esther laughed. A short, sweet puff of a laugh that felt like a treasure. "Don't wait so long to text me next time."

"I wouldn't dream of it." Testing her boundaries, Ashley ran a light finger down Esther's shoulder and along her arm, watching as Esther shivered in response. Their gaze met, and there was another question in Esther's eyes. Some want that Ashley hadn't yet addressed.

A light cough nearby had them jumping apart, Ashley with a hiss.

"Well, what do we have here?" August stood in Hannah's bedroom doorway across the hall, tucking a sheet of paper into the inside pocket of his coat before closing the door behind him.

"What have you got there, witch?"

"I'm sure you know. You were watching me the whole time, after all." He folded his arms in front of him and leaned against the doorway with a smile like some flirty school gossip. "What are you two up to?"

Ashley glared at him. "I will end you, witch."

She knew she should be more concerned about whatever he took, but she was still riding this high called Esther and couldn't manage to care too terribly much about some annoying witch. What was the worst that could happen from a single piece of paper?

"Not today, at least." He grabbed Esther by the arm and guided her down the stairs and out the front door, Ashley following behind.

Ashley stood in the doorway and watched helplessly as Esther strode down the porch steps and into the sunshine.

Esther turned back and mouthed, *Text me*, before getting in the car and driving away. It wasn't until they turned out of sight that Ashley noticed the red welts on her gloveless hand and stepped back inside.

"Ash." Claribel stood in the shadow of the column to the front sitting room. She tossed something small to her, and Ashley caught it. "I thought you could use your own. To remember her by."

A silver vial.

15

———

Ashley

Ashley strutted through August's back door like she did every evening. Ah, the luxury of walking through a door without first asking permission. Was there any simpler joy?

"Honey, I'm home," she sang while stepping, unimpeded, across the threshold.

"I'm going to take back your permission if you keep barging in like this," August called from the other room. "What if I didn't have pants on?"

"Why are you walking around without pants on?"

"Because this is my damn house, and I don't have to wear pants if I don't want to."

Ashley stopped at the kitchen door. "Are you wearing pants?"

There was a moment of silence and shuffling. "I am now. Hope you're happy."

"I am." She skipped into the other room, but he wasn't there. He wasn't anywhere on the first floor. She'd never been upstairs before. What a perfect excuse. She shot up the steps, looking in every door and ignoring the one he was in to finish snooping.

Satisfied, she returned to where August was sitting at a desk in rumpled pajama pants and a gray tee, his hair a mess. The room was an office. Or maybe a study. Was that what people with old houses called their room lined with bookshelves and a desk so immovable it must have grown there a century or two ago? Maybe it was called a library. The house was snobby enough to pull it off.

A book cart of textbooks lined up against the side of the desk, their subjects all over the place—interior design, philosophy, graphic design.

She peered over his shoulder at what appeared to be something for a world history class. "Is your major undecided too?"

"Nosy, much?" He shifted his computer away from her like she was going to cheat off some quiz. "I happen to have decided on history."

Ashley picked up the philosophy textbook. "Did you take your time deciding on that?"

He snatched the book back. "There might have been a few majors before landing on history. I'll just have a couple of minors to go with my degree. No biggie."

"A few minors? That must take forever to finish."

"If you don't mind, I'd rather not discuss my school schedule with you."

"Sure, whatever." She lifted her hands placatingly, and he went back to reading his screen. "Why do you have so many bedrooms?"

August sighed and closed the laptop. "There used to be more people that lived here than just me."

She felt it then. The quiet stillness of the house. It gave

her an itchy feeling like she needed to turn on some music to keep the vacuuming silence at bay. "Where's Uther?"

"Family dinner with his parents."

"You didn't get an invite?"

"Why would I?" He muttered something under his breath, and the philosophy textbook slid back onto the cart. "He knows what I am now."

Ashley stiffened and shifted away from him. She'd almost forgotten. Her regular evenings here had desensitized her to the electricity in her throat at his proximity. Her check-in was done. She could report back to Hannah that her nephew remained incredibly boring. But something about this moment felt distressingly familiar. She just couldn't quite put her finger on it. "You know you could always—"

"Don't say it." He lifted a hand, his palm a wall between them. "I know what you're going to say, and I'm not going to—"

"Move already, damn it!"

They both looked up at the ceiling where the third voice had come from.

"Well, I didn't say it." She shrugged and skipped to the door.

"Yeah, yeah." He opened the laptop, positioning it like a wall between them. "Go on and see what she's up to. I know you're not here for me."

Ashley deliberated at the doorway. Lonely. That was the familiar feeling.

August muttered something and a drawer slid open.

The static in her throat grew to an unbearable frequency, as though he knew she was still there watching him.

Right. They weren't friends, and they weren't going to be.

She left the room and headed to the set of stairs at the back of the hall.

⌣ ⌣ ⌣

Esther

Today, the chair decided not to move.

Esther ground her molars at the sound of wheels scraping against old wood as she wormed her way free, tumbling to the cold, hard floor. Another bound book cataloged, a few dozen more to go.

"Trouble?" Ashley leaned in the doorway with one of her perfect smiles pasted in place.

"Oh, so you know its name." Esther gestured at the heavy chair planted merrily and firmly by the desk before getting up and dusting off her knees.

Ashley had never been up here before. If Esther kept moving, she wouldn't have to think about how small the space was with Ashley in the doorway. Or how they hadn't been in the same room since All Saints' Day, over a week ago when Esther had basically begged Ashley to take her home. But Esther was a mature adult who was not thinking of the way Ashley had looked at Esther like she was a snack. Or the realization that if Ashley didn't bite her, Esther would bite Ashley herself. That was new—and complicated.

Grabbing the old stool in one hand and the finished book in her other, Esther hastened past the doorway to the bound books' shelf, eager to hide whatever expression was on her face. The stool groaned and shifted under her. They needed a new one, but she always forgot the moment she was downstairs. She'd be sure to bring it up with August on her way out today. The stool tilted again, and she latched onto the top shelf to keep her balance.

"Did you need help with that?" Ashley's heels tapped closer, but Esther was determined to do this herself.

"I'm fine." Esther tucked the book into place. "I've been shelving books for months now."

"Well, I brought back another one."

Esther glanced over her shoulder as Ashley held up a large, black book. This turn was the stool's final hurrah. With a crunch, a leg gave out, and Esther toppled backward, careening into the abyss. And then she was in Ashley's arms, cradled like Ashley would walk her over a threshold. Esther didn't even realize there was time to catch her in this position. But of course there was. Ashley was fast.

And cold. Not how an ice cube was cold. She wasn't emitting a chill. More like a rock. Like if Esther kept her hand resting here on Ashley's chest, Esther might sink beneath her skin and warm her all the way to the inside. Esther's thumb moved experimentally back and forth along the smooth curve of Ashley's collarbone. The rise and fall of Ashley's chest shuddered, and Esther moved her attention from her hand to Ashley's face.

Ashley's smile was gone, and she was looking at Esther... and Esther wasn't sure what this look meant, but it was dark and called to a deeper part of Esther.

Ashley blinked. "Sorry, sorry." Ashley set her down faster than Esther enjoyed but still safely so it wasn't like she could complain. "I brought you your book."

There was a swish of air, and what felt like a brick dropped into Esther's hands, nearly toppling her with the sudden weight. Poe was back.

"So, about Christmas." Ashley paced the room, her eyes everywhere but on Esther.

Oh no, Esther thought. Ashley probably realized how ridiculous this plan was. A fake girlfriend? And Esther at that. She had to have noticed how awkward Esther was and decided to nicely take back her request.

"I was thinking a scarf for Dad and a candle for Mom. I can just say it's from both of us. Do you mind being the type of girlfriend that does couple's gifts?"

A couple's gift, right.

"Sure. That's fine." This was all fine. Except now her mind raced from relief she wasn't being fake dumped to calculating the pressure of meeting the parents for the first time. What should she wear? *Was* a couple's gift a proper first impression?

"All right, perfect." Ashley grabbed the back of Trouble and swiveled it around. The chair complied with zero resistance, and Esther glared at it. Ashley pulled a notepad and pencil from her pocket and crossed something out. "Next item on the list: getting out of a large family gathering. I propose we milk Romania for all its worth."

"I...do not know what you're talking about. Is your family from Romania?"

"No." Ashley set down the notepad and crossed her legs.

She wore impossibly tight skinny jeans highlighting the curve of her hip and the athletic flex to her calves when she tipped her foot just right. Esther pulled her gaze back to Ashley's face.

"Studying abroad in Romania is the cover story I've been using for my extended absence," Ashley said. "I'll have to fake my death at some point, but I haven't quite worked up to it yet. And I'm not sure how to pull that off. Faking your death is surprisingly difficult. Even when you're technically dead already."

Esther nodded as though all of this made sense. It didn't,

but she was sure she could follow along. "Isn't Romania a little on the nose for a vampire cover story?"

Ashley stopped tapping her pen and looked at her. "What do you mean? Is Romania, like, a big fan of vampires or something?" She gave a timid chuckle. "It's not like I said Transylvania. That would have been..." Her words tapered off as she took in whatever face Esther was making. "No. I mean, I'm not great with maps, but there's no way—Transylvania is its own country, right?"

Esther cringed. "It's more like a region. In Romania."

"Dammit." Ashley turned to the ceiling and groaned, the vibrations of which sent goosebumps racing up Esther's forearms. "It's fine. We're fine." Ashley took a deep breath and shook out her hands. "If they haven't noticed in the decade I've been using this excuse, then they won't notice now. Let's just skip to the list." She picked up her notebook. "First up, large family gathering. I propose we tell them we're exhausted from travel and jet-lagged. We couldn't possibly function at a large gathering under such conditions."

"That could also be an excuse for why you're not going out during the daytime."

"What do you mean?"

"Well, jet lag. Maybe you have an important meeting when you get back and a week isn't enough time to switch your sleep schedule twice. So, we have to make the nights work instead. You did say they don't know you're a vampire, right?"

"Right."

"You'll probably want to do a better job of hiding that too."

"I do a perfectly adequate job of hiding my vampireness, thank you very much." Ashley flicked a lock of golden hair over her shoulder and tipped her chin up. Esther did her best not to be charmed by the dramatics.

There wasn't enough room on the desk to sit so Esther leaned instead. "I mean, I noticed something was up after spending time with you *once*. And I haven't known you your whole life."

"Well, that's just because you are very astute."

Esther gave her a skeptical look.

"Fine, what am I messing up on?"

"Well, the speed was the easiest giveaway. There's also the issue of body temperature, not aging, and presumably the whole blood thing. That's a real part of the equation, correct? I'm not making this up?"

"Are you asking if I drink blood? Yeah, that's still a vampire thing."

Esther clenched her thighs together. Now was not the time to analyze this new kink she was developing. "Well, that makes a whole other list of potential problems."

Ashley waved her comment away. "Don't worry about that list. I have it under control. One of the benefits of a vampire Family is they'll take care of getting you blood where and when you need it."

"And the other vampires are cool with you leaving town for a week? I thought you said you were supposed to be cutting ties with your family. How does this fit?"

Ashley pulled out her list again and began writing, but it looked more like doodling flowers and stars on the borders. "It's a farewell trip. I promised to fake my death at the end of the school year." She looked up and pointed her pencil at Esther. "And, no, I don't have a plan for that yet, but the vampires don't need to know that."

"Well, I'm certainly not planning on saying anything."

Ashley nodded and went back to doodling.

"That just leaves monitoring your speed, hiding your age, and making sure you aren't suspiciously cold all the time."

"Oh, is that it?" Ashley's tone was sarcastic, but she'd switched to taking actual notes. "Did you have any suggestions? I'll take anything you have to offer."

Esther froze. This wasn't a big deal. Except it was a very big deal.

Sour cream or no sour cream was the smallest of concerns compared to how Ashley should disguise her people-eating tendencies from the two people who knew her best in the world. The number of ways this could go wrong was staggering. Actual lives lay in the balance. She shouldn't be doing this. Going to Ashley's parents, pretending to be her girlfriend. This was a terrible idea. She was flirting with disaster.

"I can't," Esther said. "We shouldn't—"

"Actually..." Ashley closed her notepad and set it on the desk, her gaze fixed on Esther. "We should take a break from this discussion. Christmas break is over a month away, and we've laid some solid ground here. What if we switch the subject to something a little less anxiety-inducing?" She shifted Esther's computer so she could see the screen. "What are you working on?"

"Box and whisker plots." Esther snatched the computer and began typing notes.

Ashley pulled her hands back like Esther might bite them off, which was fair. Esther needed to write this idea down before she forgot it.

"I have no idea what that means," Ashley said. "Is it a cat thing?"

"It's a kind of graph," Esther answered over her typing. "I'm trying to format Professor Jenkins's data collection from last semester and organize it into easily digestible graphs and a box and whisker plot would be perfect for comparing the span of averages between groups. I don't know why I didn't think of this sooner."

"Did you want me to leave? I can let you work on this since it sounds like you just had a breakthrough."

"No, don't go." Esther grabbed Ashley's wrist as she shifted in the chair. "Sorry." She let Ashley's arm go. "It's just —I should let this idea simmer before investing more time and effort into it. I just wanted to get these basic notes down. There. Now, what were we talking about before?"

"Suggestions on how to make me seem less vampiric."

"Oh. Right." Esther regretted reviving this conversation. Her insides shrank as her heart raced.

"You know you're not responsible for everyone's actions, right?" Ashley said. "Whether you suggest it or not, whatever comes out of it is not on you."

A quick huff escaped Esther's lips, somewhere between a laugh and a scoff. "Well, either I give consistently bad advice, or I'm cursed to always give the advice that leads to the worst possible outcome."

"Okay. This is fascinating, and being cursed is something I can relate to." Ashley propped her elbow on the desk and rested her chin on her fist like she was a Gene Wilder meme. "Were you always cursed, or was there a moment when you first noticed it manifesting?"

Esther turned away to the bookshelves. "You think I'm being ridiculous."

Cool fingers enveloped Esther's hand, drawing her attention back to Ashley.

"I'm honestly fascinated by you, Esther Green." Ashley's face was so earnest.

"Oh." Esther's heart beat faster at the revelation. She was

fascinating? But Ashley was the one with the big personality and the gorgeous eyes. Ashley was a vampire, for crying out loud. And she was going around calling Esther Green, of the small voice and quiet demeanor fascinating. Esther needed to sit down. She slid down the desk, losing Ashley's hand in the process, and landing with a plop on the floor. "You really want to know?"

"I most definitely do."

Esther knew when the whole thing started. Or the first incident she noticed at least. There could have been smaller, unmemorable moments before then, but the big one— "It was my parents' divorce."

"Oh." Ashley slid down to the floor next to her, leaving Trouble to drift off to the middle of the room untethered. "That does sound like a big one. When was that?"

"Thirteen years ago now?" She tried waving it away like it was no big deal. "I was probably a couple of years older than Jason."

"Do you want to talk about it? I'm told I'm an excellent listener."

"I thought I was helping. They were so busy all the time and hardly talking. I just wanted them to be happy again. I heard about this radio giveaway for a free week-long cruise for two, all expenses paid. It felt like a sign, so I called the station, and I did it. I won. I gave my parents the tickets." Esther braced her forearm across her chest, holding herself in place, while she fiddled with the cross at her ear. "By the time they got back, Mom had taken a job as the cruise line's sous-chef and Dad had met Marjorie and their divorce was officially being filed. I'd failed at keeping them together."

"Are they happy now?"

"I think so."

"Then that's what really matters. You didn't wreck anyone's life."

"But that doesn't negate that my good intentions end up with negative results. You heard what Uncle Pete and Jason were saying. That was just the tip of the iceberg. I can't recommend the smallest thing without the worst possible outcome happening."

Ashley nodded along. "That's fair, but I still think you're taking on too much of the responsibility for other people's decisions."

Esther eyed her sideways, not trusting her words. What she hadn't told Ashley was that a part of her just wanted something new, something exciting, and sometimes she projected that desire onto others when giving suggestions. When she picked the restaurant for the family reunion, the final choices were either the new place or a couple of chains they'd been to a million times. When her aunt asked Esther for her thoughts on a new hairstyle, Esther had already overheard her aunt bemoaning the lack of control she had over her wedding and how she wanted something for herself. When her parents fought, her mom lamented never going anywhere new anymore and her dad would fire back that he needed more quality time. In the moment, her suggestions always sounded like the right ones.

"All right." Ashley's cool hand on her knee brought her back from her memories. "How about you continue to tell me your thoughts and suggestions. I'm immortal after all. You can't kill me, Esther."

"You say that now," she mumbled.

"I'm ready for whatever you throw at me. Trust me. It'll be fine." Ashley smiled, and it took some of the chill out of the room.

"All right," Esther said. "I'll try."

16

Ashley

The nice thing about taking anthropology was they didn't do a final exam. The awful thing about taking anthropology was the final project was a twenty-page report on a subject Ashley had lost interest in fifteen pages ago. She picked up her phone.

ASHLEY

Remind me again why I'm taking anthropology?

Esther replied in a matter of seconds.

ESTHER

Besides the fact that it's a fascinating subject and everyone should take at least one class? Probably because you of all people need to remember how to be human.

Ashley scoffed at her screen. She was plenty human. She took another sip of her Bloody Mary—with actual blood.

Well, it wasn't like she could stop drinking blood. That was just part of the package.

ESTHER

You're not doing anything tonight right?

ASHLEY

Wow. Presumptive.

ESTHER

I'm on my way over to pick you up.

ASHLEY

wait wut?

Ashley waited, but no response came. Not even the flashing thought bubble she hated so much. Esther was really on her way over, and Ashley was in her pajamas with her hair in a messy bun and a half-finished Bloody Bloody Mary. She was not ready to see Esther in the five minutes it took her to walk here.

Thank goodness for vampire speed.

In two minutes, she'd tried on and discarded two-thirds of her closet before finding something acceptable. Another two minutes for hair and makeup. With the last minute, she chugged her Bloody Mary and chomped the celery stir stick to dilute the sudden intake of vodka. Who drank vodka alone on a Thursday night while doing homework? She didn't even like vodka. But freaking Cynthia was her alcohol hookup, and beggars couldn't be choosers.

Ashley straightened her sweater, flipped off the heated blanket and therapy light, and took a quick selfie to check her makeup. When she heard steps on the sidewalk, she ran downstairs to meet Esther outside. Claribel might have noticed something was up, but Ashley needed to keep

Hannah in the dark about social visits. It was Hannah's house after all.

Ashley opened the door to find Esther walking up the porch, looking dark and sexy in a black overall skirt dress over a white turtleneck sweater, her lips a rich burgundy. She looked delicious, and Ashley had to bite her lip to stop from making any rash suggestions. Maybe she should've been drinking more blood and less vodka.

"Ready?" Esther had a tote bag on each arm and a pan in her hands.

"Can I carry something?" Ashley closed the door, anxious to move them away from the house.

Esther passed her the two tote bags, giving a happy sigh as the weight lifted off her arms. "Thanks. Those were getting heavy."

"Where are we going anyway?" She peeked in the bag to find a handful of Tupperware containers. It smelled like a feast inside. "Not that I'm complaining."

"Have you heard of Friendsgiving?" They started down the sidewalk together.

"Like friends having a Thanksgiving?"

"Exactly that. I wasn't sure if the phrase was around before you were... Well, I guess I don't know much about how or when you changed."

Ashley wasn't sure how to respond. She hadn't explained the story of her change because she didn't think about it. It was in the past, not relevant to her present. "Wait. What day is today?"

Esther laughed. "It's Thursday and Thanksgiving. Why'd you think class was canceled?"

"But you have family in town."

"Uncle Pete and Jason go back to Florida for the holidays."

"Without you?"

Esther stayed quiet for another block, and Ashley scolded herself for being too forward. Again. If she wasn't careful, Esther would realize Ashley and her complicated life and intrusive comments weren't worth this much effort. She should remember to be nice, smile more.

"I'm sorry. That was—" Ashley started.

"No, you're right. I could go with them. It's just...I tell myself it's because of the cost. I need to save up to pay back this student loan, but I kind of just use that as an excuse. It's my mom's family, and she's not even going to be there, so like, why bother, I guess? I don't see them often enough to be close, so I end up feeling like the odd one out."

"Where's your mom?"

"I think she said Naples today. But it's hard to remember, and with the time difference, I usually get it wrong. She calls when she can, and we catch up. She sounds happy, so that's good."

"Is it?" Ashley hadn't meant to ask, but Esther sounded so glum. And she couldn't fight her desire to dig deeper.

"Yeah. No, I'm happy she's happy. Sometimes I miss her, but...well, sometimes it's better to be on your own. I'm a threat to fewer people this way." She chuckled, but Ashley didn't join in.

"Hey." Ashley touched Esther's arm. "You're really cool to be around, and there are plenty of people that want to be around you on a holiday."

Esther blushed but didn't respond.

"So, where are we going?" Ashley hadn't paid attention to their progress, focusing on Esther's words and letting her take the lead.

They slowed in front of a familiar old house.

"No." Ashley stopped, cementing her feet firmly on the sidewalk. "I'm not going in there."

Esther stopped as well, balancing the dish on her hip. "Ashley, you're there basically every day already."

"And it's literally a chore, so thank you, but pass." Ashley folded her arms across her chest. She couldn't believe she was debating voluntarily *not* spending time with Esther. But at what cost?

"Why are you here all the time if you hate him so much?"

Well, this was a pickle. Did she tell Esther she was a glorified spy working for August's aunt or confess that she looked forward to her nightly visits as a chance to see Esther? She knew too much already.

Ashley settled on the truth only softer. "Hannah, his aunt. She asked me to check in on him. Like maybe she cares or something?"

"Oh. I guess that's almost sweet, maybe. In a totally inappropriate way. Couldn't she just do that herself?"

"I guess she has more of a reputation to uphold." Ashley kept her answers simple. As much as she wanted to vent everything, she needed to keep Esther safe from vampire business.

"Well, I know you two don't get along, and it was unfair of me to spring this on you." The toe of Esther's boot tapped at the sidewalk. "If you really want to go home, I won't hold it against you. I just wanted to be with people I care about."

Ashley narrowed her eyes. "This is manipulation at its finest."

"I'm Catholic." Esther shrugged. "Guilt is basically a love language."

She huffed once, walked around Esther, and stomped up

the steps. "I will not be held responsible if I have to kill him before the night is over."

"Your restraint is appreciated," Esther called back.

Ashley opened the door, not bothering with the doorbell. "All right, witch, I'm here."

"Could you not be?" August called from somewhere out of sight.

Uther's head popped up over the back of the couch, his hair disheveled. "Oh, you're early."

"Uther, you hussy!" Esther joined Ashley in the doorway. "We're supposed to be having Friendsgiving."

August's head popped up next to Uther's. "He was being quite friendly, in my opinion."

Ashley turned back to Esther, amusement sparkling in her eye. "How exactly does Friendsgiving work again?"

"All right," Esther announced to the room. "Ashley, you come with me to the kitchen to get this food started. Uther and August, you have three minutes to prepare yourselves accordingly and join us."

"Want to see what I can do in three minutes?" whispered Uther.

"Uther!" scolded Esther.

Ashley

Ashley set the stuffing on the table, turning the pan just right so the kitschy orange-and brown flower design faced out. Perfect. With the matching dishes the witch had scrounged up and the single sunflower someone had plopped in an empty cup in the middle of the table, it was almost worthy of a visit from Martha Stewart herself. Or at least someone's parents.

"Should we all go around and say what we're thankful for or something?" Uther sat primly in his seat, hands folded in front of him. Ashley took her seat next to him, purposefully away from a certain undesirable at the table.

"Can Ashley even eat this?" August asked.

Unfortunately, sitting as far away from the witch meant sitting directly across the table, and now she had to look at his ugly face all of dinner.

August made eye contact but continued to speak to the table at large. "I thought she was on a liquid diet these days."

"Commenting on someone's diet is tacky, you oaf." Ashley took a deep breath, trying to calm herself. Esther wanted her on her best behavior. "And I can eat all the food I want to. I just don't need it." To be petty, she grabbed one of the rolls he'd been eyeing all of set up and took a generous bite—to prove her point, of course.

"Esther," August growled, clutching his fork in a fist. "She knows the rolls are my favorite."

"I'm not your parent. Deal with it yourself." Esther scooped green bean casserole onto her plate and passed the dish to August. "Pretend you're mature adults for one night."

"She doesn't even need it." Under his breath so no one but Ashley heard, he muttered, "Probably suck us all dry if Esther wasn't here."

"You know what." Ashley was done with his childish behavior. "Take your damn roll." She picked up the one with a single bite missing and lobbed it at his stupid face, bonking him on the nose. His shocked expression made her stifle a giggle.

"Are you kidding me?" He scooped a hearty helping of

the green bean casserole, but instead of dropping it on his plate, he lifted the spoon and flung the serving across the table.

She gasped, leaping to avoid the projectile beans, but only dodged half the serving. "You ass, this is cashmere!"

Her fangs came out with a hiss.

"You want a fight?" August stood from his chair, letting it crash to the floor behind him. "Let's go."

Ashley threw her chair to the side, ignoring a resounding crash, as August muttered incantations under his breath. Uther's hand slapped over August's mouth.

"Stop it!" Esther slammed her hands on the table, making everyone jump. "I made that green bean casserole." She pointed at the mess splattered across the table. "Okay, I just dumped some stuff in a dish and stuck it in the oven, but I don't cook so this is a big deal. And Uther heated those bakery-fresh rolls in the oven by himself. There is more than enough food for everyone, so stop being asses and eat your food, or so help me, I will cut someone."

"She has a knife," Uther chimed in. "She'll do it."

Under Esther's glare, they righted their chairs and returned to their seats.

Esther sighed and dropped her chin. "What will it take for the two of you to stop being so scared of each other?"

The question must have been rhetorical. Instead of letting them answer, she picked up the platter with the canned cranberry sauce and resumed the passing and serving process.

A weight settled in Ashley's stomach that had nothing to do with the dinner roll, but she wasn't quite sure how to fix it. "Sorry about throwing your roll, Uther. I hope I didn't ruin your Thanksgiving."

"Are you kidding?" Uther reached for a second helping

of mashed potatoes. "I'd take this any day over a meal with my conservative uncle and his thinly veiled homophobia."

Esther accepted the tray from him. "How'd you get out of Thanksgiving with the family when they live so close?"

"I didn't." Uther looked down at his plate, mashing the already mashed potatoes with his fork. "We do family Thanksgiving the Saturday after so we can share Black Friday shopping stories and eat discount turkey. My family is clever like that. What does your family do, Ashley?"

"Oh, mine?" Ashley took another bite of turkey before answering. "I haven't been home in years, but they were pretty traditional around the holidays. Aunts, uncles, cousins. We'd all cram into the house of whoever called it first that year. Before that, Oma hosted each holiday."

Uther nodded along, like Ashley's story was a familiar tune, and that small gesture warmed a place deep in her chest.

"Do the vampires do anything to celebrate?" he asked.

Right. Ashley had been swept away in her own story. She wasn't human anymore. "Hannah and John are older than the holiday and generally don't see what the fuss is about. Claribel and Cynthia will sometimes agree to a meal, but when you don't need to eat anymore, a holiday around food doesn't make much sense." A return to a community was one of the main draws of joining the Family. She couldn't say she wasn't disappointed to learn of all the holidays they'd already outgrown. "When I officially join the Family, I plan on hosting some creative holiday parties where food is optional. But I don't want to rock the boat until then."

"When you join?" It was the first time August had spoken since their fight. She'd nearly tuned out his existence. "What do you mean 'when'?"

"Well, I haven't officially been accepted, so to speak."

She concentrated on shaping her potatoes into a unicorn, glad for once she was no longer able to blush. "They don't let just anyone into a Family. You have to prove you won't draw attention from the humans first." She looked up again, feeling more confident. "But this is my year. I can feel it. Third time's the—"

"*Third?*" August's voice raised a level, but Ashley didn't find it as entertaining this time. "What happens if you mess up again?"

Ashley fisted her fork, holding on to her patience and that positive energy. "I *won't* mess up again."

"Ashley, this is serious. The witches..." August trailed off. She wasn't sure he'd addressed her by her name before. His throat worked like he was trying to swallow his words. "If you aren't part of a vampire Family, you're their prime target. You need to get in."

"I know that," she snapped. "You think I'm not painfully aware of the stakes? Why do you even care?"

"I—I don't." He sat up straighter and resumed picking at his plate. "Just making conversation."

Ashley eyed him, unconvinced. They resumed eating to the tune of silverware scraping plates.

"Damn." Uther tapped at his phone. "My phone died. Does anyone have a charger?"

"Again?" August's brows pinched together. "Is it your battery?"

"No, I lost my charger." Uther gave him his trademark pouty face, fishing for sympathy.

"Again?" August rolled his eyes.

"I'd appreciate more sympathy and less victim-blaming, thank you."

"You're the victim of your own...never mind. I have one upstairs."

August rose, but Esther cut him off, jumping up and grabbing Uther's arm.

"We'll get it." She pulled Uther toward the stairs. "Uther and I cooked. You two can clean."

Ashley was left in the kitchen with the last person she wanted to be alone with, washing dishes. "Can't you just snap your fingers and finish this?"

"Shocking as it may sound, washing dishes is not as easy as snapping your fingers. It's less mental energy to just do it by hand."

"You're one of those people that never had a dishwasher growing up, so when you finally move into a place that has one, you use it as a large drying rack while you continue to hand wash dishes, aren't you?"

August didn't answer, which only confirmed her theory and annoyed her more.

"But if you snap your fingers, *I* won't have to do the dishes."

He gestured a soapy hand at the empty kitchen, losing a dollop of bubbles to the kitchen floor in the process. "No one's making you do the dishes,"

Sure, Esther wasn't here to make her do the dishes, but after Esther and Uther disappeared upstairs, August started clearing the table. Ashley hadn't even considered the idea of letting the host do the dishes on his own. She just wasn't raised that way.

"What do you think is taking them so long?" She snatched the plate he held out to her and started drying. They were almost done with the stack, and Esther and Uther were still missing.

"They're obviously talking about us."

"What?" The plate slipped back into the sink, splashing both of them.

"Watch it," August growled.

"You watch it," she snapped back. "What do you mean, they're talking about us?"

"Well, there are two obvious options." He rinsed the plate and handed it back to her. "The first is that they're talking about us as potential love interests. The pros and cons, if you will."

"Oh god." Ashley looked at the stairs and wondered if there was a way to stop them but couldn't think of an option that also turned back time. "Wait. Both of us? As in *I'm* a love interest?" Did August not know Esther wasn't interested in dating women?

August rolled his eyes and didn't answer, and Ashley continued to hate him.

"Well, what's the other option?" she asked.

"The other option is much worse."

"Worse than them discussing what's wrong with us?" Ashley squeaked.

He glanced at her through the hair that had escaped his hair tie. "The other option is that they want us to get along."

She waited a few seconds to see if he had more to add before she burst out laughing. "Could you imagine?" She grasped her side and wheezed in stuttered breaths. "You're the worst."

Her laughter was interrupted by a burst of water from the handheld nozzle. "Right back at you, bloodsucker."

Water dripped from the sleeve of her sweater. "Witch, I will end you!"

"You can't." He drained the sink, before turning to face her.

"You want to bet?" Ashley dropped her fangs. "We can be in the lake in ten seconds."

"Esther wants us to get along."

Dammit. She continued to glower at him but relaxed her fangs back into her gum line. Her mind whirled, but no answer came that would result in both destroying August and Esther not being upset with her. She huffed, unwilling to verbally acquiesce.

"Look," he continued. "I know you're leaving with her in a few weeks for the middle of nowhere Midwest to meet your family."

"And?" She didn't think she could handle a scolding from the witch. She still had the vial from Claribel in her pocket, reminding her how fleeting her non-relationship was. She was risking everything, letting herself be vulnerable, over something with an expiration.

August plucked her phone from the nearby counter and began typing. Stunned by his blatant disregard for private property, she watched in horror.

"The holidays can be tough, and new relationships are hard." He handed it back to her. "So, if you need someone to call or text, you have my number. Also, you should put a password on your phone."

Ashley's hand shook. She snatched her phone back before he noticed. There were a handful of numbers in her contacts, and the only one regularly used was Esther's. Ashley wasn't sure what to do with something this serious. He couldn't possibly know how alone she was in the world. Should she *not* threaten his life anymore?

"Are we friends now, witch?" she asked.

The corner of his mouth hitched. "Something like that, I guess."

17

———

Esther

Esther woke to a rumbling under her cheek and a kink in her neck. She sat up with a squeaky whine as she stretched. Her hand hit the overhead call button, and a small wind tunnel attacked her face. She slapped buttons furiously until it was back in line.

Right. They were on a plane headed to Ashley's parents in Iowa.

Neither of them could have predicted what a headache holiday flying would be. After traffic to the airport, followed by another hour through security, their plane was delayed because of bad weather—frost, if she remembered correctly. Two hours behind schedule, and she was really regretting forgetting to pack her water bottle. She swiped the top of her mouth with her tongue, trying to ease the dryness.

According to her phone, they were over halfway through their flight. Surely, the drink cart should be by soon. Esther craned her neck to check the back of the plane. A flight attendant offered a cup to the passenger two seats up the aisle.

She'd missed her chance. Her shoulders slumped. Maybe she could get up and ask for a cup of water. She turned to Ashley to see if she wanted anything as well and froze.

Ashley sat hunched in her window seat, a sheet of her long hair covering her face, but Esther saw the rough way she was breathing. Short jagged breaths like it pained her to take in air. "Ashley?"

A rumbling deep in Ashley's core was her only response.

Cautiously, Esther reached out and shifted Ashley's hair. "Are you all right?"

They had the row to themselves, which offered a bit of privacy. Esther wasn't sure what she would find behind that golden curtain, but she wasn't prepared for this. The golden smiling girl from class was gone, and in her place was a vampire in all sense of the word. Her cheeks hollowed, her jaw flexed with tension and her nostrils flaring.

Ashley gazed fixedly at the upright tray in front of her. "Are we close?"

The flight wasn't supposed to take this long. Neither of them had planned for the hours' delayed access to blood, and Esther cursed their naivety that everything would work out the way it should. She pulled out her phone with a shaking hand.

"We should be landing in about an hour." She did her best to keep her voice calm, but the way Ashley pinched her eyes shut told her that wouldn't be soon enough.

Ashley's gaze snapped to the front of the plane, following a man as he entered the small restroom.

"I have to pee." She fumbled with her buckle.

"Wait—" Esther placed a hand over Ashley's.

Her fangs came out with a snarl, fixing Esther with red-rimmed eyes, the skin around them pulled tight. Esther's heartbeat ratcheted up ten notches, and she pulled her hands back to safety.

Ashley retreated into herself, hands covering her mouth, shoulders hiked to her ears.

"Esther, I'm so sorry. I would never..." Her words mumbled through her hands, and her head shook as though rejecting her own actions.

She was scared.

This brave, confident, starburst of a woman was scared by the needs of her own body.

"Hey, listen." Esther didn't try touching her again but unbuckled her own seat. "I have a plan, okay? I need you to trust me."

Ashley's frantic gaze darted around at the other passengers as Esther stood.

"Ashley."

Ashley's gaze snapped back to her.

"Keep your eyes on me. You are going to be fine." She kept her words slow and measured. "I have a plan. Two minutes and you will feel better."

Ashley pulled tight, her movements more nervous cat in a new space than human. She slunk from her seat, following Esther. Maybe Esther hadn't thought this idea all the way through, but locking herself in a bathroom with Ashley seemed like a better plan than hoping Ashley didn't lose whatever control she had left and rampage across the plane. It was a choice that involved other lives, but this was clearly the best option available.

They made it to the stall just as the man slid the bathroom door open to leave. Ashley stared as he passed, and Esther had to pull her from her trance and into the bathroom with her. There was barely room for the two of them.

Esther straddled the small toilet while Ashley got the last two square feet in front of the door.

"All right." Esther took off her black cardigan and placed it on the closed toilet seat beneath her. "The arm is the easiest spot to hide."

She kept her tone methodical and confident, talking over the heavy beating of her heart. The last time she'd made a big decision involving Ashley, it had resulted in her kissing a vampire and led to this moment with her pretending to be her girlfriend. Try as she might to frame that as a bad thing, she had to work to keep the corner of her mouth from tugging up at the memory. She could offer a little bit of blood to get them through the flight.

Ashley's brows furrowed. "I don't know what you're talking about."

Away from the crowds of people, she almost looked better, her body more relaxed. Or maybe she just trusted Esther, which activated a fluttery feeling in the pit of Esther's stomach that could be flattery or nerves, depending on how she looked at it.

"Try to keep it near the elbow so my sleeve will cover it." She held up her arm so Ashley had a better angle.

"No!" Ashley shoved her, sending her tumbling onto the toilet seat as Ashley suctioned her body to the door.

Well, that could have gone better.

"We both know you're hungry." Esther tried to stay kind but needed to be firm here. "I don't mind."

"I can't... I've never—" Tears pooled and fell down Ashley's cheeks as she tried to look anywhere but at Esther.

"Hey." Pushing off the seat, Esther regained her footing and took Ashley's hand. "What's wrong?"

Ashley swallowed, her gaze fixed on the sink. Her words came out in barely a whisper. "I can't stop."

She sniffed and wiped her face with her sleeve.

"Okay." Esther nodded confidently, but that complicated things. Of course, even a choice she made for herself had to have consequences. But they were in this now. She didn't have an alternate option. "Okay, we'll make this work."

Distance. They just needed distance. And a lot of luck. She studied Ashley's shrunken posture one more time and knew what she had to do. She propped her boot on the toilet lid and pulled out her emergency switchblade.

Ashley jumped as she flipped it open. "How do you have that on a plane?"

"Never mind that." It was time to take action. Sucking in a fortifying breath, she cut down her arm. Nothing too deep, just an inch or so. Enough that red bubbled to the surface, spilling over the cut and dripping to her elbow.

A soft hiss came from Ashley as Esther tucked her blade away.

Confidence felt important at this moment. "Get on your knees and open your mouth."

Ashley's irises dilated to full black. She dropped to her knees at Esther's feet. It was a little exhilarating. Being dominant wasn't a usual kink for her, but the power of having someone like Ashley—a powerful, confident, sunflower of a vampire—obeying her was a heady cocktail in and of itself.

"You are not going to touch me, okay?" Esther said.

Ashley nodded. Esther braced one foot on the toilet seat and her healthy arm against the frame of the door so she hovered over Ashley.

At first, everything went as it should. Esther clenched her fist, and a drop of blood rolled down her elbow, landing on Ashley's eager tongue. The second hit her bottom lip before Ashley licked it away, and Esther imagined that tongue on her body. Those lips pressed to her skin. Another drop fell, and Esther cursed the space between them. The flow was too slow, and she felt Ashley growing just as impatient.

Her arm grew heavy. That was what Esther told herself as slowly, it lowered closer and closer to Ashley's lips until Ashley's cool fingers curled like lover's claws around her bicep and another around her wrist. She gasped at the feel of Ashley's lips on her inner elbow and sank into the moment.

No consequences, no danger. Just Ashley's skin on her own, Ashley's tongue running down that sensitive joint, Ashley's teeth scraping, testing the limit of her skin.

It wasn't until a gentle tug from Ashley nearly knocked Esther over that she realized how dizzy she was.

"Ashley." Her voice was barely a whisper.

Ashley didn't respond, and at first, Esther thought maybe she hadn't heard her. This was fine. What a way to go, really. All pleasure and no pain.

But Esther remembered she wasn't done living. She touched Ashley's cheek. "Babe, you're done."

The hand around Esther's bicep tightened. Ashley took a shuddering breath as she pulled away.

"Esther." Something in Esther's face must have been upsetting because Ashley's eyes watered and her arm wrapped around Esther's waist, helping her sit. "I'm so sorry. I didn't mean to go so long."

"It's all right." Esther touched Ashley's cheek, marveling at the slight flush to it. "Let's go back to our seats."

18

Ashley

Everything was exactly as Ashley remembered and also fit like a sweater that shrank two sizes in the wash. The black, empty cornfields passed by the window of the rental car as she drove, navigating by muscle memory. If someone had asked her how to get from the airport to her parents' house, she would have had no way of telling them. Twelve years had flown by, but the second she got into the car and Esther buckled in next to her, she pulled out of the parking lot, turned a confident left, and kept driving.

They drove in silence, Esther keeping to herself and Ashley fiddling with the radio, which never kept a station out on the country roads. It hadn't snowed yet, or at least not enough to stick, so driving wasn't difficult. The dark and barren fields kept bringing her back to her first few years post-transformation when she was all on her own and scared of her own shadow. She couldn't help hitting the accelerator to hurry their trip along.

"Did you want a break?" Esther asked after an hour of driving. "I could take a turn."

"No, we're almost there." Ashley kept her eyes glued to the road, the headlights giving her tunnel vision.

"Ashley." Esther's voice was cautious, as though she sensed something was wrong.

But nothing was wrong. She was just driving. They would be there any minute. Just a few more miles to go.

"Ashley, can you pull over?"

"No." The last thing Ashley wanted to do was stop out here in the middle of nowhere.

"Ashl—"

"I said no!" she yelled and cringed at how her voice took up the whole car.

She was fine. She was fine. *She was fine.*

"What's wrong?"

"Nothing is wrong!" Ashley didn't know how to stop yelling.

"Sorry, that was the wrong question." Esther kept her voice low.

The road blurred in front of her as her eyes watered. She was being managed. Esther thought she was out of control. And maybe she was, but she couldn't stop the car. Not here. Not in this infinite black.

"What I meant was, what are you thinking about?"

Ashley wiped her eyes on her sleeve, clearing her vision again. "I'm thinking I'm a terrible travel companion."

"Hush."

Ashley snuck glances at her but kept her eyes mostly to the road.

"Going home is hard," Esther continued, "and most people aren't vampires on top of it."

"It's not going home," said Ashley. "Well, it is going home. But right now, it's the nothing on the way there."

"The nothing?"

As counterintuitive as it seemed, discussing her lonely years took away the sting of seeing the darkness creep up around her, so she kept going. "When I changed, I wasn't exactly alone. Not at first at least."

She paused, not sure how much of this story to tell. But Esther wasn't her girlfriend. Not for real. She wasn't even gay. There was no reason to try to impress her or keep parts hidden.

"In the beginning, there was Konstantine." Ashley blushed, hearing the reverent way she still said her name. "She was my first crush in high school. Not that anything ever happened. I wasn't out then. It was the early 2000s in rural Iowa. No one was out." She was rambling and glanced at Esther to see if she was still listening. "Anyway, I went to college after high school, like the good middle-class daughter I was. But while I was gone, my Oma died, and she was kind of an important person."

But she couldn't go through all of that now. How her Oma was the one she made cookies with after school and taught her to curse in German when she was angry so she wouldn't upset her teacher. She showed Ashley how to cross-stitch and to speak louder, and going home would never be the same without her there.

"I came home for the funeral and wasn't all right. And it's a small town so, of course, Konstantine was there. We got to talking, and one thing led to another. In one weekend, I lost a grandma and gained a girlfriend and also agreed to become a vampire. Turns out Konstantine changed sometime during college out east." She paused to take a breath, stealing a glance at Esther to see she was still listening.

"Oma had this thing she would say, *Einmal ist keinmal*. Once is nothing. And I just thought, if I only have one life, I'll make the most of it. I'm probably butchering the German. I never did learn much more than cursing."

"So, did you live with her after that?"

"Yeah, I lived with Konstantine. Dropped out of school and started training to be a functional vampire. The first few days are the hardest, so it was nice to have someone to walk me through the process. Some things at least. I still have trouble stopping, once I start drinking."

"Where is she now?" Esther with the hard questions.

Ashley gripped the steering wheel until her knuckles turned white. "She's dead."

"Wait, I thought vampires couldn't die. Don't you live forever?"

"Well, there are some pretty classic ways to kill a vampire, but strangely enough, it wasn't burning or a stake to the heart. It was witches." Ashley took a deep breath and tried to focus on the road as that day came tumbling back to her. How she had come home from the farmer's market, so proud to have been in a crowd, and bore the fresh produce to prove her success. But the house was empty except for a clawing, fizzing sensation in her throat she would later recognize as residual magic.

"Witches?"

"I waited a couple of weeks before realizing she wasn't coming back, but her absence activated my anxiety, and I relapsed. I couldn't control the bloodlust like I had before. I decided to take myself away from temptation." The town lights grew on the horizon, and Ashley felt both relief to get out of the endless darkness and anxiety at the idea of being around people that knew her again. "I ran away, wandering cornfields for a time as I made my way over to western Nebraska to get away from the crowds."

"You walked to Nebraska?"

"Some. I hitchhiked a lot of it. It wasn't the safest option, so I tried not to do it often." Ashley didn't mention that it wasn't safe for the person giving her the ride, not herself.

That was her vigilante phase. She tried to live on deer blood, but if she got an especially handsy driver, she'd dispense of him as a service to humanity. It never settled quite right though, no matter how terrible the driver.

Esther was the first human she drank straight from in years.

The road curved through town and out again, and Esther left her in silent reflection for the rest of the drive. Her parents still lived in their country home just on the other side of town. She recognized the colorful lights over the porch and on the large pine in the front yard.

They pulled into the gravel drive, and Ashley turned off the engine. "We're here."

19

———

Esther

Esther pulled her bag from the car, still processing everything Ashley had shared on the ride over. She pressed a hand to her inner elbow, feeling a small sting, but the cut had mostly healed already. Which couldn't be natural, but neither was the situation she was in.

She had a lot to process in general, and they hadn't even set foot inside.

"Do you want to be Romanian or another foreign Ph.D. candidate in microbiology like myself?" Ashley paused next to her open car door. "Or was it environmental science? Crap, I forgot what my Ph.D. program was."

"What? Why would I be Romanian?" Standing in front of Ashley's parents' house with a suitcase ready to pretend to be their daughter's girlfriend was already a huge ask on Esther's acting skills. She'd never dated a woman before and certainly didn't go home to visit the parents.

"Well, I've been in Romania this whole time—as you remember—so that's where I would have met you. Long-distance seems too difficult." Ashley laughed. "It's just occurring to me now. We spent so much time working on making sure I looked human, we forgot to figure out our backstory."

Esther froze, her hand on the door to the car. They didn't have a backstory. How could they have missed something so obvious?

A door opened, and a slab of light cut across the front yard. "Ashybear, is that you? Come inside, I made hot toddies."

Ashley pointed up as though she had an idea. "There's my invitation into the house."

Momentarily distracted from panicking over a Ph.D. program she knew nothing about, Esther looked up. "Wait, is that a real vampire thing? I thought August was just being a dick when he said something about needing permission to enter a house."

Ashley gave her a wink before tugging her suitcase from the car. It thudded to the driveway. "All right, darling. Let's do this."

She grabbed Esther's hand with her free one. Esther snatched her bag and let Ashley lead her up the porch.

"Also, my mom will tell you that you don't have to eat all the food she offers. This is a lie. I'll try to give you an out when I can, but she will take it personally if you don't take her food."

Before Esther could respond, there was insistent barking on the other side of the red, wreath-decked door. A few seconds later, it opened, and a woman in a pullover and jeans appeared in the doorway. Her hair, blond with streaks of white, was up in a bun and laugh lines framed her eyes. It was like catching a glimpse of future Ashley. Or what could have been future Ashley.

"Ashybear!" She grabbed Ashley in a hug, nearly lifting her from the ground. "Come inside. Come inside. I saved you some strudel from the Christkindlmarkt. Don't let Schatzi out. We'll never find him at this time of night."

"Did someone say strudel?" called a male voice from farther in the house.

The woman rolled her eyes. "Your father finished off the Apfelstrudel, but I managed to hide the strawberry cheese-cake one for you."

Ashley pushed her way in the door. Esther followed close behind, using her suitcase as a barricade to block the small dachshund trying to wiggle his way past them and out into the night. The spacious living room was plushily carpeted in off-white. A brown leather sectional filled the room, with a colorful crocheted blanket thrown over the back. A man reclined at one end under a purple-and-gold quilt checkered with football helmets. His attention never strayed from the TV, but he lifted a hand in a distracted wave.

"And who is this?" Ashley's mom spotted Esther. "I thought you were seeing that nice boy."

"Mom." Ashley put an arm around Esther's shoulder. Esther noted Ashley's cringe at the nice boy comment. "This is Esther. My girlfriend. Who I have been dating for...a while now."

They needed a backstory fast.

"It's lovely to meet you, Mrs. Schafer." Esther offered her hand.

"So good to meet you, Esther. Call me Suzie." Mrs. Schafer ignored Esther's hand, diving in for a firm hug instead.

"Mom, where are we staying? I want to ditch our bags."

"In your room, obviously, dear." Mrs. Schafer—Suzie—

gave Esther a wink, and it was so much like Ashley, Esther had to take a moment to decide if this wasn't some trick. They were both vampire clones at different ages perhaps. "Come on. Let's stop loitering in the entryway. Do you need help with your bag?" She turned to the man on the couch. "Dale. Ashley is here."

"That's nice, dear. They're in overtime," the male voice called back. Schatzi scampered off to curl up on Mr. Schafer's lap.

"No. I mean where is Esther staying?" Ashley wrapped an arm around Esther's waist. Esther looked down at the floor, doing her best to will her cheeks from heating.

Suzie took Esther's suitcase and rolled it through the living room, past Mr. Schafer who grunted his disapproval, and down a hallway.

"She's staying in your room with you. I'm not *that* old-fashioned." She gave Esther another wink, and Esther smiled timidly back.

"What!" Ashley stopped halfway down the hall.

Her mother ignored her and continued to the room at the end and to the left.

"After all the lectures you gave me in high school about keeping my door open?" Ashley said. "Now, it's just anything goes?"

The disbelief and slight whine to Ashley's tone were not adult, and Esther had to pinch her lips between her teeth to keep from chuckling at their regressive banter.

"You're not in high school anymore," Suzie called over her shoulder. "You're an adult, and we trust you to be respectful."

They all piled into a pink and flowery room. Suzie rolled Esther's suitcase to the foot of the white metal-framed bed piled high with fluffy duvets and fuzzy throw pillows. Esther couldn't help noticing that she wore the only black in the entire room. The white wooden dresser and nightstands were draped in tissue-thin, pink cloth and covered in cutesy knickknacks from ceramic unicorns to a pink glitter lava lamp. On the walls were shelves of trophies and posters of late 90s' and early 2000s' pop artists.

"I'll leave you two to get settled." Suzie closed the door with a flourish to emphasize it was indeed closed all the way. On the back of the door was a small poster of Alanis Morissette, hair in her face and a microphone in hand. At least Esther wasn't the only one in black anymore.

"She's so frustrating already" Ashley flopped onto the bed, her body sinking into the many puffy layers.

Esther explored the top of a nearby dresser, ignoring the way Ashley's sweater tunic rode up, showing more of the thighs her black pleather leggings were doing nothing to hide. The room felt a little warmer.

Ashley slapped the covers on either side of her and sat up. "You know, she's only okay with this because you're not going to get her precious, little girl pregnant. This is still some patriarchal, heteronormative bullshit." Ashley cussing in this pink and white cacophony of millennial glory days broke away some of the nervous jitters building in Esther's gut.

"Did you just cuss?" Esther asked. "In your parents' home? What would Mister Unicorn think?" She lifted a ceramic unicorn from the dresser near her.

"You are quite mistaken. That happens to be Zenon, Unicorn of the 21st Century, and she has heard and seen much worse."

"Ah, to be a unicorn on this nightstand." Esther set Zenon back where she'd found her. "I can take the floor if you're uncomfortable sharing a bed."

"That's not the point." Ashley jumped up, using the fluffiness as a spring, and began unpacking. "And no, you're not sleeping on the floor. You're the guest here. I don't want to make you uncomfortable. That wasn't part of the deal when I proposed this plan."

"You know." Esther leaned against the dresser—watching for unicorns—and getting a good look at the bed-shaped cloud. "It's a pretty big bed."

Ashley met her gaze. Days ago, Ashley had pointed out she was mostly unkillable, and that reminder had Esther feeling a little braver. Like maybe she could suggest something reckless.

So Esther added matter-of-factly, "And I'm not uncomfortable."

Esther had messed up that night on the beach when she'd scared away Ashley's advances. She hadn't been dishonest. Esther had only dated men and, until that moment, hadn't seriously considered the idea of dating a woman. Because what was the point? She liked men. No sense in considering her sexuality any further. She didn't need to come out to her friends and family or enter the politics of another dating pool or take up space in a queer community. Uther would tell her there's no max capacity in the queer boat, but that didn't stop her from being unsure. She was still a cis woman who was attracted to men.

And Ashley.

But that night under the stars was an awakening. Like a curtain she never noticed pulled aside, and now that was all she saw.

Two quick raps on the door were followed by Suzie popping her head into the room. Esther and Ashley jumped apart. Great. Now Esther looked like she couldn't be left alone for two minutes with Suzie's daughter. What a terrible first impression. She hadn't even noticed how close they'd gotten in the last few seconds.

"Hot toddies are ready, ladies," Suzie said. "Did you two want some? There's also strudel."

"We're coming," Ashley said. "Geez."

"Well, don't take too long getting ready. Your father isn't much of a night person, and I bet he wants to see you."

She closed the door, and Ashley called after her, "And we will have a talk later about the proper way to knock!"

Esther covered her mouth to hide her giggling.

"Oh, this is funny, huh?" Ashley turned on her, lips tight and brow furrowed, but Esther saw how the corner wavered, edging toward a smile.

Esther schooled her face as well. "Of course not. All serious here."

They made it a whole three seconds before they both burst out laughing.

Esther padded down the hall, her fingertips loosely hooked to Ashley's as she led them to the kitchen. Mr. Schafer and Suzie were seated at the table, talking, mugs in hand. Susie jumped up as soon as they entered.

"I have your drinks ready." She ladled two steaming mugs from a pot on the stove and handed them to Ashley and Esther. Esther's mug had a cartoon cat saying, "To a PAWsome teacher."

"You two have perfect timing. I was just about to discuss Christmas plans with Dale." Suzie returned to her seat at the table. "The girls aren't going to make it to the big Christmas gathering, so we're planning something for tomorrow night—just the four of us."

"But don't worry." Ashley joined them at the table, taking the seat next to her dad. "We have the whole thing planned. It'll be so much fun."

"I'm sure it will be, kiddo." He wrapped an arm around her shoulders and kissed the top of her head. "It's nice to have you back."

Ashley smiled sweetly, and Esther wished she had a camera for this family moment. And then she remembered she was also in the room and standing awkwardly next to the table gawking at them. She grabbed the seat next to Ashley. Her chair scraped loudly against the linoleum floor, breaking the moment. Esther hunched her shoulders and tried to disappear, but Ashley took her hand. It was so sudden and natural Esther briefly forgot it was for show.

Ashley gave her a quick smile before turning back to her dad. "How'd the game go?"

He took a long drink from his mug. "I don't want to talk about it."

Suzie jumped up and rummaged through cupboards. She wasn't drunk, but Esther got the impression this wasn't her first glass.

"How about we bake cookies?" Suzie asked. "I have all the stuff for snickerdoodle. Or we could do chocolate chip."

"I think I'm going to hit the hay," said Mr. Schafer, rising from his chair.

"Mom, don't worry." Ashley took the jar of flour from her mother's hands. "Esther and I can make the cookies. You and Dad get some sleep. We'll see you tomorrow evening. You got my email about jet lag and time zones and everything, right?"

"She got it." Mr. Schafer wrapped a quick arm around Ashley's shoulders and kissed her forehead. "We know the plan. Night, you two. Come on, Suze."

Suzie wrapped Ashley in a tight hug. "Oh, I missed you, pumpkin." She kissed Ashley on the forehead as well. "It's good to have you home again. And you'll have to tell me what skincare routine you're using because it is working wonders on you."

"Thanks, Mom." Ashley let her go and gently pushed her toward the door where Mr. Schafer was leaving. "Night."

"Nice to meet you, Esther," Suzie called as she was hustled out of the room.

"You too, Mrs. Schafer—I mean, Suzie." Esther continued to cringe in general awkwardness until Ashley returned and confirmed her parents were in bed. It was just the two of them and a couple dozen cookies to bake.

Ashley pulled out ingredients, obviously familiar with the recipe.

Esther sat back and did what she did best—awkwardly supervised until someone gave her something specific to do. "Your parents seemed happy to see you. Were you staying here for the last five years? When you had to leave Plattsburgh."

Ashley dumped ingredients into a bowl faster than Esther could follow and plugged in the mixer. "No."

The whirring of the machine halted any further conversation.

"I snuck in once but couldn't stay. I didn't want to risk messing up again, but I needed to see them. Here." Ashley stuck a bowl of dry ingredients into Esther's hand. "Add this in slowly while I mix."

Esther let Ashley talk at her own pace. It wasn't Esther's place to push her. They worked together silently until the stuff in the bowl started looking like cookie dough.

"Okay, now we just need to—" Ashley looked at Esther and a smile broke across her face.

"What?" Esther touched her face. Her fingers came back chalky with flour. "Well, you're one to talk."

"What do you mean?" Ashley touched her clean cheeks. "I wasn't the one with my nose in the mixing bowl."

"Oh yeah? It looks like you have a spot right here." Esther smoothed a streak of white flour across Ashley's cheek.

"Hey! These cookies are for my parents. This is serious." Ashley couldn't finish the sentence without a smile breaking across her face.

They worked playfully, Ashley telling Esther what to do and the both of them working in tandem, and Esther couldn't help but think maybe this could work. No one was here to see them like this. Maybe, it wasn't just for show.

Esther scooped the last cookie onto the cooling rack. "Done."

"Success! Go, team!" Ashley raised invisible pom-poms over her head.

Esther smiled, but that faded when she realized morning was fast approaching. It was time for bed. One bed.

They took turns changing, and Ashley light-proofed the bedroom and bathroom.

Ashley hopped into bed first, nuzzling in deep so the only parts of her showing were tendrils of gold reaching across her pillow.

This wasn't going to be weird. Esther had been to sleepovers before. This wasn't the first time she'd shared a bed with another woman. True, it was the first time she shared one with a woman that made her stomach flex and her fingertips tingle when they held a gaze for too long, but Esther was a mature adult. And sometimes mature adults shared beds with people and didn't fantasize about making out with them.

She sighed and climbed into the squeaky, fluffy cloud

intending to stay on her side the whole night. She'd hug the edge if she needed to.

Esther sat on her side, sparing one second to see Ashley already snuggled up on her side of the bed. She turned off the bedside lamp and, with a deep assuring breath that all would be fine, laid down. Before she could get a grasp, the bed sank, and Esther tumbled to the middle. Free-falling until she rolled smack into Ashley's back. Ashley made one long luxurious stretch with a groan that sounded so good Esther nearly joined her. While bringing her arm back down to her side, Ashley's fingers tangled with Esther's, pulling her around to Ashley's chest.

"Night, Esther."

Esther's head filled static, unable to compute her present situation.

"Night." Esther suspected she would not be getting any sleep tonight.

20

―――――

Esther

Apparently, there was a pickle in the Christmas tree, and it was now Esther's goal to find it before anyone else.

Suzie had woken them promptly at five that evening, just after sunset, her voice a singsong as she proclaimed, "Christmas is ready." Esther had only the ghost of an impression that Ashley was a snuggler before Ashley leaped from the bed in shocked confusion, shaking the entire pile of fluff.

Ashley hip-checked Esther—bringing her back to the task at hand—as they both inspected a similar section of the tree. "You think you can beat me, love?" Ashley teased. "I've had years searching for this pickle. We have history."

She wore a white, cable-knit sweater she'd thrown over her sleep shorts and tank top before they joined her parents in the living room, the hem of the sweater hanging just lower than her shorts. Esther's eyes kept wandering from the tree to Ashley's long, toned thighs flexing as she squatted, the contours lit dramatically by the light of the tree.

"That pickle knows who bought it." Mr. Schafer, sporting some impressive bedhead to go with his red flannel Christmas robe, combed through the branches opposite Ashley. "Come to Daddy."

Ashley cringed. "Dad, you can't just say Daddy like that. I can't unhear it now."

"What?" His attention never strayed from the branches. "I *am* a daddy."

Suzie sat peacefully on the sectional, with a cup of hot cocoa in hand and nary a worry nor care on her face. As the designated hider, her part in the game was done, and now she reclined, listening to her family banter like this was her guided meditation soundtrack.

Esther wouldn't have thought something as out of place as a pickle would be so hard to find, but it turned out finding a small, green item in a large, green space covered in lights, ornaments, garland, and tinsel was quite challenging.

"Ah!" Ashley and Mr. Schafer both exclaimed, diving at a branch near Esther's elbow. The whole thing shook as they tussled. Esther backed away from possible tree-toppling range, and two ornaments plunked to the tree skirt below. Suzie sipped her cocoa, unfazed. A brief moment of slapping and name-calling concluded with Ashley raising a tin pickle ornament over her head.

"So there really was a pickle." Part of Esther thought it might have all been an elaborate prank.

"Mother," Ashley proclaimed in a grand voice. "I demand my prize."

"I let her have it." Mr. Schafer looked rather put out. Esther sensed the source of Ashley's competitive streak.

Ashley jumped up and down as Suzie pulled out a small,

wrapped gift from behind a throw pillow. She unwrapped it, revealing a small bag of chocolate truffles.

"This is about the time Oma would call us silly Americans for putting pickles in our trees," said Ashley, before cramming a truffle in her mouth. The three Schafers turned to a closed door off the living room with a small, cross-stitched verse hanging from it.

"When I was young," said Mr. Schafer in an exaggerated German accent, "you'd be lucky not to get a smack for being terrible that year." They all chuckled except Esther whose eyes widened in alarm at the casual child abuse joke.

"Gifts next." Ashley grabbed two packages from under the tree and shoved them into her parents' hands. "They're from both of us."

She plopped down on the couch next to Esther, crossing her legs so her bare knee rested on Esther's. A shiver went down Esther's spine as they touched. She wasn't sure what to do. How would a girlfriend act in this situation? She shifted her hands from folded in her lap to resting on her knee to stretching overhead so she could rest her arm over Ashley's shoulder. She made it to a fraction above their mark before chickening out and returning to her lap. She stared at her hands, wishing they were braver—that she were someone Ashley might actually want to date—when something soft dropped into her lap.

Esther blinked. "I get a stocking?"

"We weren't sure who to expect." Suzie tilted her head with a half smile.

"You're sharing my stocking." Ashley patted Esther's knee, and Esther's stomach clenched in response. The stocking was full of a stash of small gifts: nail polish, candy, a set of bookmarks Suzie's church friend had stamped, an

As Seen on TV device whose purpose Esther wasn't entirely sure of, and hand warmers.

"To keep you warm in Romania," Suzie added.

Once gifts were settled, everyone piled into the car and drove into town to look at Christmas lights. By the time they got back, Esther was on a first-name basis with Mr. Schafer—correction, Dale.

Suzie made everyone cocoa while Dale pulled out the peppermint schnapps and started a fire in the pit on the back porch. They gathered outside sometime around eleven, lounging on the deck furniture. Sparks from the fire leaped to meet the stars above. A cool winter wind blew at Esther's back, but the fire, the schnapps, and Ashley's arm draped around her shoulder on the two-seater couch kept the chill at bay. She couldn't think of any place she would rather be.

"Guess what I heard, Ashybear." Suzie continued without waiting for an answer. "The cheer coach at your high school says she's retiring after her daughter finishes college. They're going to be looking for someone new. That could be you."

"Mom, that doesn't have anything to do with micro science." Ashley shifted in her seat. Maybe it was the peppermint schnapps, but Esther couldn't remember Ashley's supposed doctoral program either.

"Yes, but you loved cheerleading." Suzie spoke with her hands, waving her free palm like she could summon Ashley's agreement. "You were always so good. We just assumed you'd make a career of it."

"That was a long time ago." Ashley's words were quieter now. Less certain than before. "I live in Romania now."

Esther considered Ashley's room lined with trophies and her old pom-poms. But she'd never said anything about cheering or wanting to coach before. Then again, she hadn't given Esther any indication she had any end goal, aside from joining that house of vampires.

And Ashley wasn't in Romania, not really. If cheering was her dream job, the only reason she couldn't go for it was because she was a vampire and couldn't go out in the daylight. Esther wasn't sure what to say, so she reached for Ashley's hand. Their fingers laced together. Ashley's hand was cold, but Esther pretended it was just the weather. She clasped it with her other hand to try to warm it and bring her back to life. Ashley smiled, and it was so bright Esther forgot what she'd been doing and where she was. She forgot the girl she was falling for was technically dead.

"What do you think, Esther, dear?" Suzie's question broke the spell and returned Esther to the moment. "You know our Ashy. Wouldn't she make a great cheer captain?"

"I, um. Well, the thing is... Haha." Esther reached for her earring, rubbing the cool metal and second-guessed everything. Sure, Ashley was outgoing and driven, but did her mom really know what Ashley wanted anymore? It'd been twelve years. Surely, cheerleading couldn't be Ashley's dream if she left it to be a vampire.

A montage of observations flashed behind Esther's eyes, the photos of Ashley at the beach with giant pink sunglasses and a blue bikini, raking leaves with friends in matching volunteer T-shirts, a framed acceptance letter from a university that wasn't PlattU with an education major. What if the only thing stopping Ashley was the sun?

Esther's mind clouded, losing the ability to form cohesive sentences. She had no right to interfere in Ashley's future. She couldn't possibly know the answer. Whatever answer Esther gave would be the wrong one, and Ashley would resent her forever. Esther's breathing increased, and she barely registered Ashley clenching her hand tighter.

"My career is my choice, Mom. Not Esther's."

"She can still have an opinion. She's clearly a special person in your life. Surely, she has a thought on how you spend your future."

Esther couldn't do this. It was all so clear now. Ashley was a vampire, and Esther was a ticking time bomb of bad luck. They were the worst possible ending for each other, even if it were possible for them to have a future. She would finish out this week, but no matter what, they were just friends at the end of this.

"Welp." Dale slapped both knees with his hands and stood. "I'm beat. Come on, Suze. Let's leave these two love-birds to their Romania time."

Suzie hesitated, clearly upset to leave the conversation but not enough to argue with her husband. "We'll see you two in the morning then for a quick dinner for breakfast. I'm making kielbasa sausage and scalloped potatoes."

21

————

Ashley

Ashley felt a familiar tightening in her skin as she watched her mom switch off the kitchen light for the small one over the stove and disappear down the hall to her parents' bedroom. Her mom's busybody tendencies, her dad's aloof dadness. Every memory was another final memory. But these memories deserved only happiness. So, she watched her mom until she turned out of sight and told herself she wasn't sad. Not yet. Because this was a good memory and she still had tomorrow to make another. She'd bottle up whatever sadness she might feel and save that for...well, for the end.

"I like your parents." Esther's comment interrupted Ashley's musing. "Your whole house, actually. How your room is still a shrine to you. There's a lot of love here."

"You like them, huh?" Ashley turned to the woman next to her, tucking her leg under her and dropping her arm from Esther's shoulder to the back of the patio couch.

The night sucked the color from them and dramatized

the contrasts. Esther's hair cascaded over her shoulders in a dark waterfall over pale cheeks, and Ashley's fingers itched to touch the silky ripples. The fire sparkled in Esther's eyes, drawing Ashley in like a beacon. But she held back. They were just friends, and making a move—again—when Esther was already doing her a massive favor, would be a dickish move on Ashley's part. The arm over Esther's shoulder had been pushing the generous boundaries Esther allowed. And there was no need to put on a show now that her parents were gone.

"What are your Christmases like?" Ashley asked. "Please tell me everyone's parents are in their kid's business like mine."

Esther huffed a quick laugh. "Hardly. I still tend to get a phone call on the big holidays. Christmas, Thanksgiving, and birthdays. Easter from Mom if she's at port."

"I just realized I don't know much about your parents."

"Well, Mom is a chef now for Mediterranean Cruise Line, and my dad raises Shetland ponies as well as a new baby with Marjorie in Nova Scotia."

"A new baby?" She looked Esther up and down. "Shouldn't your dad be getting kind of old by now?"

Esther shrugged. "He married younger, and I'm not sure the baby was planned." She shifted, looking uncomfortable. "Enough about me. What about you?"

"What about me?"

"Well, you're a vampire. Let's start there." There was a playful sparkle in Esther's eye that Ashley was loving.

"You're just cool with it? You know what comes with being a vampire, right?"

"I am familiar with the lore." Esther tucked her legs under her like a kid anxious for a story. "Would you tell me what comes with it?"

"I have a list!" A bubble of excitement filled Ashley at the realization. Esther was interested in her. Maybe not in the way she'd hoped, but she'd take the attention where it came. Plus, she never missed a chance to brag about her lists. She pulled her Lisa Frank notepad out of her coat pocket.

"What is that?" Esther flipped to the cover as Ashley tried to find the page. "Is this actual vintage Lisa Frank?"

Ashley pulled it back from her. "The nineties is hardly vintage." She continued to find her list, embarrassed she'd kept the notepad so long. *Oh god, it's older than Esther.*

"Wait." Esther stuck her finger in the way as Ashley flipped to the next page. "Was that my name?"

"No, definitely not." Ashley ripped the page from the notebook and stuffed it in her mouth.

Esther watched her chew with a look somewhere between disappointment and laughter. "Oh," she deadpanned as Ashley struggled to swallow. "I am definitely convinced now."

"Yes, yes, I'm a believable person. That's what vampires are known for. Their trustworthiness. Anyway, ooh look! A list of vampire things that Ashley wants to be able to do."

"Are we talking in third person now?"

"Sometimes we do that. Please, be distracted by this list of cool vampire things I can do."

Esther laughed and, thank everything holy, looked at the list. "You can change into a bat? That's a thing?"

"Okay, yes, it is a thing, but no, I haven't quite gotten that one yet. The closest I got was changing my arms."

Esther's eyes grew wide, and she sucked her lips into her mouth.

"Are you trying to not laugh at me?"

Esther's eyes watered.

"I am an intimidating vampire."

Esther held her arms to her sides, bending them so her hands were by her shoulders, and fluttered them. "With little bat wings?"

The question was barely out before she burst out laughing. And then they were both laughing, grabbing their sides and in danger of falling off the couch.

In a flash, Ashley grabbed Esther's chin and held her so they were inches away. "Okay. Enough of what I can't do. Time for the Twilight montage of cool and intimidating vampire stuff that I *can* do. You ready, spider monkey?"

"Yes, and please don't call me that."

"Okay, good." Ashley placed the notepad in Esther's lap, jumped to her feet, and rested her hands on her hips in a hero stance. "I'm ready. Call them out."

"Well, we can check off 'look hot,'" Esther mumbled.

"Oh my gosh, stop." Ashley pulled her scarf up to cover her cheeks and turned in an embarrassed half curtsy.

Esther blushed. "And super hearing?"

"Oh, that was nothing. Wait here." The next second Ashley was across the yard and pulling out her phone.

ASHLEY

whisper something and I'll answer.

"That white sweater you had on today was super sexy."

Holy fuck. Was Esther flirting with her? Did she just call her sexy? No. No, that was just the sweater. Esther had good taste. That was all. But she also called her super-hot just before that. That obviously meant something. Unless it was just a friend complimenting a friend? Female friends called each other sexy all the time. What was straight and what was gay anymore?

"I'm thinking of the number four," Esther added, a little

bit louder. She must have assumed her first comment was too quiet. How long had she been standing there struck senseless?

Ashley texted back the number with no other comment.

"I checked off running really fast, for obvious reasons." Esther spoke at a normal volume despite still being across the yard. "Next on the list is lifting heavy things and...ooh! Mesmerizing."

Ashley ran back to Esther's side instead of texting an answer. "There isn't anything impressive for me to lift around here." She scanned the grass and miles of empty cornfield, lit only by the moon. "I could bring the car over."

"Nah. Maybe tomorrow," Esther replied, as though someone carrying a car with their bare hands was a boring feat. "Let's try this mesmerizing thing." She scooted over and patted the seat next to her.

"We don't have anyone to mesmerize." Ashley ignored her signal to sit. She didn't like where this was headed.

"You can try it on me. Just don't make me do anything too embarrassing."

"You?" Ashley saw this coming, but the words still took her off guard. "I can't try it on you."

"Why not? I trust you."

Esther trusted her with her free will? Ashley didn't know what to say. After the incident on the plane, she wasn't sure if it was trust or Esther was just reckless. "Not to sound like a cliché hero, or basically any vampire romance, but you shouldn't. This is too much trust for one person to handle."

Esther took Ashley's hand, and Ashley let herself be pulled down into the seat next to Esther, as though this was something they did. Casually touching each other. "Really, Ashley. It's all right."

"I mean, I've never gotten this one to work before either. I've had better luck turning into a bat."

"Start small then." Hands on her knees, Esther faced Ashley. "Have me lift a hand or something."

Ashley took a deep breath. She could do this. Surely nothing bad would happen. This was Vampire 101. She just needed to clear her mind and force her consciousness into Esther. Oh god, it sounded violent already. She closed her eyes and tried to concentrate, but even with her eyes closed, all she saw was Esther's trusting eyes. This was too risky. Who knew what would happen?

"Hey." A hand fit into Ashley's, and she opened her eyes. "Let's take a minute. I don't want to force you to do anything you don't want to do."

Ashley gave a halfhearted laugh. "That's exactly what I'm struggling with."

"If you don't mind me asking, why did you become a vampire? Was it a choice?" Esther's hand was still in hers, rubbing her thumb along Ashley's knuckles, almost absent-mindedly. Did she know she was still holding Ashley's hand? Ashley wasn't about to point it out.

"It was my decision. I mean, how often do you get offered immortality?"

"Probably not often," said Esther. "I've never been asked."

Ashley tried to meet her eyes, but Esther was still looking down at their hands as she continued to draw circles. "What would you say? If you were offered."

Esther's nail drew a small circle around the freckle near Ashley's thumb. "It depends on who asked."

Ashley freed her hands and brought them to Esther's face. Resting her fingertips lightly along Esther's jaw, she used only enough touch to guide, not force her gaze up.

Esther's lashes lifted. She met Ashley's gaze like a magnet snapping into place. Concentrating, Ashley willed her mental bubble to expand and encase Esther. "Lift your left hand and touch your nose."

They waited, but Esther's hand remained on her knee.

Ashley tried again, concentrating harder. "Lift a finger."

Still nothing.

Her thumbs grazed along Esther's cheekbones. "Are you straight?"

They sat in silence. The last log on the fire crumbled into the embers, and a snowflake landed on Esther's cheek before melting into a drop of water.

Ashley wiped it away.

"I don't know."

22

─────

Esther

Four days sharing a bed with Ashley and it hadn't gotten any easier for Esther to keep her feelings in line. She had three more to go and was desperately eyeing her phone's calendar—avoiding the pair of long, smooth legs nudging her own on the couch as they considered what to do with their time in a small town where everything closed by nine.

Maybe it was the tilt of that traitorous bed, or maybe a subconscious part of Ashley sought out heat in the night. Either way, at some point in those dark, daylight hours, Ashley's chest ended up flush to Esther's back, her hand resting on Esther's hip. And one especially memorable morning, Esther woke to their legs tangled together, Ashley's cool thigh resting between Esther's.

And Esther knew she could say something. Conscious, Ashley was respectful of her space, but a part of Esther craved waking up like this. The weight of Ashley's arm draped over her side. The cool thrill down her spine whenever Ashley pulled her in closer, slotting Esther into the nook under Ashley's chin. There was the erotic rush of endorphins, like dark chocolate melting on her tongue, knowing the heat Ashley wore first thing in the morning was hers. But god, the dreams they inspired. Ashley using her cool thighs to part Esther's. Crawling down Esther's body and sinking her teeth into Esther's thigh. And the look in Ashley's eyes while she did it. The same look she gave Esther on the plane that had Esther's heart slamming into her chest. Like Esther had something that Ashley desperately wanted, needed, couldn't live without. And maybe that look wasn't just about blood.

Esther worried her showers were getting suspiciously longer, but no matter how hard she tried, she couldn't work that need out of her.

And now they sat on the couch together, the lights low and nary a conscious chaperone in sight, and Esther wondered—despite knowing she really shouldn't, that this was just how Ashley slept and not actual affection or even attraction—how would she make it through the rest of the night, let alone three more days, without throwing herself at Ashley and seeing where the chips landed.

"I have an idea." Ashley picked up her phone and dialed a number.

Praise Jesus, a distraction. "Who are you calling at two in the morning?"

"Don't worry." Ashley switched to speakerphone. "He said to call whenever."

Esther was skeptical but desperate enough for a distraction to allow it.

It rang a few times until, "Hello?" A groggy Uther answered the phone. "Ashley? I didn't think I had your number."

"Umm, that's because you don't." Ashley checked her screen looking puzzled. "Are you at August's place? At two in the morning?"

There was a pause. "It's three over here."

Ashley grabbed Esther's arm and they both screamed.

"What the hell is all that noise?" A distant, yet grouchy August mumbled in the background.

"In case you haven't figured it out by now." Uther spoke over Esther and Ashley's excited screaming. "We're kind of a thing. Also, why has Ashley called my boyfriend *twice* now while I have *yet* to receive a single call from my best friend?"

"Twice?" mouthed Esther.

Ashley shrugged and silently mouthed, *Bored.*

A muffled August in the background said something that sounded like "Boyfriend?" followed by a lot of shuffling and giggling.

"Witch," Ashley yelled into the phone, "if you have sex while on the phone with me, I will drown you for real."

"Listen." August was on the phone now. "I've got to let you go. Something just came up."

Another giggle in the background and more shuffling. Then Uther's voice. "Call again on New Year's. Toodles."

The phone went dead.

"Did he just say toodles?" asked Esther.

～ ～ ～

Ashley

"Is this too much for a karaoke bar?" Esther stood in the doorway in a little, black dress with long sleeves and diamond side cutouts, paired with black tights and gorgeous black pumps. Her lips were such a deep shade of purple they were nearly black.

"You're perfect," Ashley said. "It's perfect. Screw dress codes. Wear this always, please."

It was New Year's Eve, and Ashley's parents had ditched them for the Millers' annual euchre party. Which Ashley decided was fine, since she would much rather hang out with Esther in that dress at Peanut's Pub than enter the new year with her parents' friends and a stomach full of room temperature champagne and a dozen different kinds of pasta salad.

Esther pushed her hair behind her ear, providing a delicious view of the blush coloring her cheeks and—

"Where'd your cross earrings go?" Ashley asked.

"Oh." Esther flinched. "I umm... didn't think they were right for tonight."

"What's going to keep me from attacking you now?" Ashley joked.

"I-I guess that's just up to you now."

Sweet baby Jesus. Good thing Ashley was designated driver. She'd need all her senses tonight to remember to not take advantage of that opening.

By ten, they were in the car and on their way to the bar. Luckily, Ashley had a sequin mini dress from high school that still fit.

"So, what's the game plan here?" Ashley asked. She turned the radio down so they could hear each other.

"What do you mean?" Esther asked.

"Do you still want to be my girlfriend tonight? I never came out in high school, so we can totally pull off college friends, but you look super-hot, and I kind of want to show you off. But it's totally up to you. No extra hurdles either way."

"You're going to just come out tonight?" Esther sounded unsure.

Was she nervous about Ashley coming out, or did she not want to keep up the fake girlfriend charade when it wasn't strictly necessary? Ashley didn't want to push her. This night was supposed to be fun, and she didn't want Esther to be uncomfortable.

"Honestly, who cares? I never see these people, and I'll probably never see them again. I'm already hiding so much of myself as a vampire. I just thought it would be cool to throw this one piece of me out there, and what better way to do it than with a date looking sexy as hell. But this night is about having fun, so whatever you're comfortable with is what we'll do."

"Okay, let's do it."

"Yeah?" Ashley was caught off guard by how sure Esther sounded. She expected more uncertainty to wade through.

"Yeah. It's a lot of fun being your girlfriend. And you said tonight is about having fun."

"Hell yeah, it is." Ashley pumped up the music again. "Let's send this year out right."

They were easily overdressed for Peanuts. The noise rammed into Ashley like a semi the second she opened the door. Her heels crunched on the namesake's shells littering the floor. Straight ahead, the bar was crowded with people trying to get the bartender's attention. And to the right, the stage was currently occupied by Kyle, her one-time foray with the male species, singing that song about a heart in a blender. Everything was exactly how she left it.

"You still good?" Ashley yelled into Esther's ear.

Esther took her hand. "I'm good. Let's get a drink."

In a matter of minutes Ashley had procured two whiskey sours, claimed a table, and put in three song requests—all without vampire speed, thank you very much, and one of them a duet with an old cheer friend she ran into along the way.

"You sure you don't want to sing?" Ashley asked after returning from her second song of the evening.

"I'm not really the singing type." Esther sipped at the last of her whiskey sour. Ashley watched the motion, transfixed by the way her throat moved as she swallowed. Maybe she should be singing less and hanging out with Esther more. She was being a negligent fake girlfriend. "I don't know if I have any song that would be appropriate. And I'll need another drink first."

"I can get you that drink." Ashley jumped at the opportunity to do something for her. To make her happy in any way possible. "Name a song, and I'll put it in on my way back. You'll be finished with it before your name even comes up."

Esther took her time answering, running a finger around the rim of her glass and making Ashley sweat. What was in these drinks? Just being around Esther and her little movements made Ashley feel off-kilter.

Esther's fingertip paused, and it wasn't until Ashley looked up that she realized she'd been caught staring. "You get the drink." Esther's smile felt like a promise. "I'll put in my name. Just don't expect anything amazing."

Ashley swallowed before putting on a shaky grin. "I'm loving this surprise. Meet back here?"

"All right."

Casey behind the bar still remembered her and her drink, so Ashley ended up back at the table in record time. It was only a few minutes before she felt a familiar hand on her lower back. A hand much larger than the date she arrived with.

"Ashley? Jesus, you haven't aged a day." Kyle, on the other hand, looked ten years older, as was expected. He'd aged well. The skin at the corners of his eyes crinkled when he smiled like his face had recorded this regular habit, and she spotted a couple of gray hairs at his temples that sparkled when the party lights hit him just right.

"Not bad, yourself." She shifted so his hand fell from her back, but her smile remained genuine. As far as boyfriends went, he didn't suck. "What've you been up to?"

He planted an elbow on the table, making himself comfortable. "I teach math at the school now, if you can believe it."

"Seriously? You hated math."

"Nah, I was faking that. Thank god kids are allowed to be interested in things nowadays. But how have you been?" He tapped his beer to her glass before taking a sip. "Visiting family?"

"Yeah, I've been at my parents' since Christmas. We've—"

"Hey, I got the song... Oh." Esther noticed Kyle and startled, slipping on some shells and catching her balance on Ashley's arm. Ashley wrapped her arm around Esther's waist, steadying her. "Sorry, I didn't know someone was here."

"You have perfect timing." Her thumb landed on the open cutout of Esther's dress, and she took this happy chance to rub a slow circle on Esther's side. "I want you to meet my old fling, Kyle. Kyle, this is my girlfriend, Esther."

Kyle's gaze dipped briefly to Ashley's hand and back.

"*Girlfriend* girlfriend?" Even as adults, their vocabulary devolved into grade school vernacular.

Esther placed her hand on Ashley's chest, her thumb

brushing the underside of Ashley's boob, and Ashley thought she might short-circuit.

"Yeah, that kind," Ashley said.

He broke out the trademark smile that won him prom king. "Nice. I guess I wasn't the only one hiding something in high school."

"Next is Kyle with 'How You Remind Me,'" called the guy at the karaoke machine.

"I'm up." Kyle downed the last of his bottle. "Hey, Ash. It was good seeing you." He patted her arm before running to the stage and taking the mic.

The evening was a flurry of songs. Despite her newfound desire to stay quietly by Esther's side, Ashley kept getting called up for duets and group songs. Yasmine wanted to sing Dixie Chicks, and Stacy insisted she join her in "All the Things She Said" by t.A.T.u.

"All right." The DJ took the mic from Ashley and Stacy. "Last song before the countdown. I've got Esther with 'Head Over Feet.'"

Ashley's step faltered as she passed Esther. "Alanis?"

"I know you said 2000s, but I'm a sucker for *Jagged Little Pill*."

Esther took the stage, the music queued up, and everything else disappeared. What did it mean that Esther picked Ashley's celebrity crush for her song? She couldn't possibly have known that. It was clear Esther knew the song by heart. She even had Alanis's inflections. With Esther's hair in long, loose waves, Ashley could pretend she was at a concert. It was a little old and slow for their usual picks, but the crowd loved Esther's energy. Ashley waited anxiously for her at the bottom of the stage.

"I didn't know you could sing like that." She took

Esther's hand, needing to touch her and prove she wasn't dreaming.

"I don't usually. But you were having so much fun, I thought I should do one."

The screens previously displaying song lyrics switched to a countdown starting at thirty. Ashley pulled Esther closer as everyone crowded the stage.

"Ashley, there's something..." Esther's lips were moving, but the crowd was so loud she couldn't pick out Esther's voice through the noise overload.

"What?" she yelled directly in Esther's ear.

Esther put her warm hand on the back of Ashley's neck and guided her face to Esther's. Ashley wet her lips, but Esther moved past her mouth to Ashley's ear, her breath a warm puff to the shell of it. "I said..."

But the sound was drowned again as the crowd counted down from ten. She was being silly. This wasn't a real date. Esther didn't think of her like that.

Ashley pulled back to point at her ear and mouth. "I can't hear you."

"Three!"

Esther's hand was still at the back of Ashley's head, their faces inches apart.

"Two!"

She didn't try speaking again, but her gaze dipped to Ashley's mouth.

"One!"

Esther rose on her toes, the move so sudden Ashley almost shifted out of her way—her brain not registering why Esther's lips were at the corner of Ashley's mouth. Maybe she had moved a little.

It took the entirety of the room yelling, "Happy New Year!" for Ashley's body to fit the pieces together. Esther was sinking back down, eyes wide and cheeks blushing when Ashley swooped in, one hand on Esther's waist to pull her in closer and the other sinking into Esther's hair, tilting her so she could deepen the kiss.

If Esther was going to kiss her, Ashley would do it right.

The crowd cheered, confetti fell from the sky, and everyone mustered through the words to "Auld Lang Syne."

Ashley and Esther kissed, and it felt real.

23

Esther

Esther crashed, back first, against the front door of Ashley's parents' house—Ashley's chest pinning her to the cool wood, her blond waves blocking out the rest of the world. Distantly, Esther registered that they were still kissing, as Ashley scraped at the lock with her key.

Ashley was kissing her, and it was better than any other kiss.

Because this time, Esther knew she wasn't just being a good friend or admiring another girl's outfit or hair or body. Esther was kissing Ashley because she wanted to kiss Ashley. And as Ashley's hand found the side cutout in Esther's dress and worked her leg between Esther's thighs, a few other ideas popped into Esther's mind.

The door flew open, and they both fell into the house.

"Sorry, sorry." Ashley caught her balance on the catchall table by the door with one hand and Esther's waist with the other. "I always hated that lock. Tends to stick."

Now that they were separated and breathing again, Esther realized where the night was headed. They'd shared a bed all week, but until now, that was all.

Ashley must have seen her concern because she cupped Esther's cheek.

"Hey. What's going on?" Her eyes traced back and forth between Esther's, and her brows pinched together. "Listen, nothing has to happen tonight. I don't want to do anything you don't want to do. If you're not comfortable, we can just leave this where it is. I can even take the couch if...you know. If things are weird now."

Her phone buzzed, and she stepped back to glance at an incoming text.

It also gave Esther some space. A moment to take in what was happening and what she wanted to happen without the fuzzying effect of Ashley's nearness. Something had happened at that bar. Maybe it was singing on a stage in front of dozens of strangers. Maybe it was seeing Ashley come out in all her glowing bravery, but Esther wanted to be brave too.

And she wanted it all. No more hiding from herself, no more keeping her distance. Ashley was strong and indestructible, and she wanted Esther just as much as Esther wanted her.

"Okay. That was my parents wishing us a happy New Year. They decided to take up the Millers' offered guest room and go heavy on the champagne tonight, so it sounds like they won't be back until morning. Mom promises they'll be back in time to see us off."

Her voice was calm, but Esther knew Ashley had to realize what that meant. They had the house to themselves, and Esther had just kissed Ashley.

"Look." Ashley remained by the door, her hands grabbing the entry table behind her. "I understand that the power dynamics are off here. You're at my childhood home in a state you've never been to, and I happen to be a creature of the night. So, I'm going to be proactive and say I don't expect anything beyond our originally agreed upon terms of fake dating. I will default to sleeping in Oma's old room when the sun comes up like I should have been doing this whole week."

"Ashley." Esther took Ashley's hand, stopping her rambling before she ended up offering to chain herself in a closet or something. "I like you."

"You like me." Ashley said it like a statement, but her furrowed brows said she still wasn't sure what Esther meant.

She needed to be more explicit.

"I like you." Esther continued, stepping closer so she had to tilt her head up to look Ashley in the eye. "And not as a fake girlfriend or a classmate or even just as a friend."

She ran her thumb along Ashley's knuckles, trying to coax her into relaxing her other hand from the table, to let go.

"I like you because you're funny, and you're sweet, and you're sexy as hell. I like you because you notice things like a difference in power dynamics, but also that you come from a touchy family that enjoys hugs." Esther bit her lip. She was losing momentum and getting embarrassed by all of her declarations, but she needed to finish if she wanted this night to go as hoped. "I know at one point you seemed interested, and maybe now I'm coming off strong, but if you're still interested, I'd like to get rid of the fake part of our relationship."

"Yes, please." Ashley pulled their joined hands behind her back, pressing them snugly chest to chest, and tangled her other hand in Esther's hair. "Tell me what you want. Because I'll go as far as you'll let me."

A laugh escaped her at Ashley's eager answer.

"I haven't...umm been with a woman before," Esther said. "So, I was kind of hoping you could take the lead maybe."

"Damn it, Esther." Ashley looked up at the ceiling, and Esther worried she'd said something wrong. "You make the sweetest speech and dump all this trust on me. You're going to make me cry, and I really don't want to cry right now."

"Did you need me to sing some more of 'Auld Lang Syne'?" Esther joked. "Bring the mood back."

"Fuck that."

Before Esther fully processed the novelty of Ashley cussing, they were in her bedroom, standing at the foot of her bed, and Esther had an overwhelming sense of having moved without seeing it. Like being in a high-speed elevator. There was a click, and Ashley was near a Bluetooth speaker. A simple trilling piano filled the room, accompanied by a deep crackling baseline. The contradicting sounds were confusing but wildly sexy.

"Did you have this ready?" Esther asked.

Ashley walked to her. No, not walked. Sashayed? Maybe prowled. Yes, prowled was right. Her creature of the night comment was suddenly wildly appropriate. Ashley was beyond human. The glitter lava lamp on the nightstand cast pink undertones across Ashley's cheek and neck, her toned arms. And on the other side of her, the moonlight peeking through the open window played off the sequins of her dress, shimmering and highlighting her curves and the muscles of her thighs.

She was a sparkling, pink creature of the night.

Esther's knees threatened to fail her as this goddess drew near.

Ashley lifted a hand, brushing a lock of hair behind Esther's ear and running a nail along Esther's jawline until it tucked under her chin, lifting it to Ashley's face. "If you tell me 'stop,' I will stop. Immediately. Is that understood?"

Esther swallowed. "Y-yes."

The corner of Ashley's mouth curved wickedly. "I don't have any of my toys with me. Obviously, I don't keep those at my parents' house. But since this is your first time in a sense, we can keep things simple."

Toys? Esther was sweating. She was both frightened and horny.

And also thinking about what might happen when they got back to New York. What kind of toys? Maybe she should have done more research before initiating.

Ashley's fingers traced lightly down Esther's shoulders, the cool touch bringing Esther's racing mind back to the moment as they reached her waist. She couldn't help a gasp when Ashley's fingers touched skin.

"This dress." Ashley's words were a purr as she gripped Esther's hips and turned her to face the bed. "It's been driving me crazy all night. Long sleeves and a short skirt. You are full of contradictions, aren't you, sweetheart?"

Esther wasn't sure how to respond. She wasn't sure she *could* respond. Her heart beat a million miles a minute, and she forgot how to breathe as Ashley's icy fingers continued to wander across her stomach and hips. Craving Ashley's touch and scared that if she moved...if she moved, maybe she would wake up and this would all be a dream.

So, she held perfectly still and waited.

"Choices. Choices." Ashley was still inspecting Esther's curves with her hands, feeding Esther's growing desire for contact and fanning a flame for more. "I love these heels on you. Are you attached to these tights?"

The two thoughts didn't connect. Esther shook her head. She wasn't attached to anything except Ashley. Ashley and her hands that were all over.

She pushed Esther's hair to one side, wrapped it around her fist, and gently dragged Esther's head and then shoulders backward until Ashley's other arm around her waist was the only thing keeping Esther upright.

"I'm going to need verbal confirmation." The tone left no room for questions.

Oh, sweet Jesus. Ashley was bossy in bed. And they weren't even in bed yet. Esther's thighs heated. She was wet, and they were both still fully dressed. "N-no. I'm not attached."

"Is this all right so far? What I've been doing to you." For a moment, Ashley's eyes softened. "You remember what to say if it's too much?"

"Yes," Esther answered faster this time, glad she finally stopped her stuttering. "This is good—so good. And I remember."

Ashley smiled, baring her teeth, before kissing gently down Esther's exposed neck. She released Esther's hair and turned her to the bed again. "Good girl."

She put her hand on Esther's upper back and gently guided her forward until her middle rested over the cool metal bed frame and her hands, then her elbows, sank into the deep fluffiness of Ashley's bed. She felt the back of her dress rising to indecent levels—her heels doing no favors to hide anything. The idea alone of Ashley seeing her like this made her cheeks heat and her thighs clench.

"I think I'd like to eat you like this first," Ashley said.

"Wait, you'll what?" Esther squirmed, trying to look over her shoulder and fighting the bed for balance.

"Not literally." Ashley laughed.

"I mean...I wasn't complaining necessarily."

"I'm not doing that again." Ashley's voice was firm now. "I want you to trust me. And I still don't trust myself." Her cool hands trailed from Esther's waist down to her ankles, her sequined dress making a shushing sound as she moved, and Esther lost sight of her behind the bed. "I won't do anything to hurt you. Understood?"

"Understood." The word came out in a soft gasp as Ashley's hands continued their way up her thighs, lifting the hem of her dress over her ass.

Esther squirmed. Her tights were efficient, not sexy. She wouldn't have worn any, but it was so cold she couldn't go bare-legged. She was chilly and self-conscious and completely out of control as the downy nothing of the bed consumed her arms. She was forced to rely on the metal bar under her hips and Ashley's hands on her thighs for support, and the adrenaline of giving up so much control shot straight to her nethers.

Ashley slid Esther's tights down to below her ass. There was a sound, more like a pop than a ripping. Arms braced like Bambi on ice, Esther looked down her chest between her legs to where the middle of her tights was split in two, essentially making them tattered thigh-high stockings.

Ashley stared back at her, eyes wide and lashes batting. "Are you still all right?"

She had wrecked Esther's tights. The ugly tights that were blocking Ashley from getting in there and doing whatever she had planned.

"Very much so," Esther said.

Ashley smiled, and it was the bright and beautiful smile

she always had for Esther in class. The one that gave her warm, fuzzy feelings before she even knew what those feelings were and lit up the entire room. And then Ashley licked Esther's exposed thigh, long and slow, still matching Esther's gaze.

Esther would never see that smile the same way again. Ashley was the real contradiction. Her tongue went up, higher and higher until it reached Esther's panty line then stopped and moved to the other leg. There was a sound like a whimpering puppy, and Esther was shocked to realize the sound had come from her.

"How are you doing, sweetheart?" Ashley teased, fully aware of what she was doing. "Did you want to show me your pretty pussy?"

Esther nodded, mesmerized by what was happening between her legs. Ashley pulled down the silky, black fabric and let Esther step out of them. Then, in one quick movement, she grabbed Esther's ankles, pulling them wider than shoulder-width.

"God, your ass looks so good in this dress." Ashley gave said ass a smack.

Esther gasped and grabbed the sheets more from shock than the sting.

Ashley grabbed her cheeks, holding her firmly in place. She licked her from clit, through her folds, and all the way back to the pucker of her ass. Esther clung to the bed sheets for dear life.

"That's right, sweetheart." Her thumb slid through Esther's folds, picking up moisture before moving slow circles around her clit. "Let me take care of you."

Syrupy goodness coated Esther's inside, and she gave in, letting her body relax and allowing Ashley to take control. Ashley knew what she was doing. Her tongue set to work again, ministering long, luxurious glides across her seam, interspersed with feather-light flicks until Esther was writhing, grasping the blankets in her fists. She didn't recognize the sounds coming from her. Anytime she made an especially loud cry, Ashley went back and did it again, her cold fingers trailing fire and building a tightness in Esther's core that had her curling her toes until one heel and then the second lifted off the ground, her body begging for more. When she thought the pressure was too much, Ashley put her lips to Esther's clit and sucked.

Fireworks, crystal-sharp snowflakes, a scream as long as time.

Esther's body melted into a puddle, draped over the foot of the bed like a Salvador Dalí painting.

"That was beautiful." Ashley was up again, kissing Esther's neck, her back, her arms. "Do you have another in you? I got ahead of myself."

Esther mumbled into the covers, not sure what she was saying. Ashley had wrecked her, and she was still fully dressed.

"You want me to help you undress?" Ashley asked.

Was that what she'd said? Esther nodded, her face still half-buried in the comforter. It didn't matter what she'd said. She just wanted this dress off. She wanted to be free of clothes and melt like the proper puddle that she was.

Ashley's cool fingers grazed her neck, searching for her zipper. It made a soft purr as the clasp trailed down her spine, then Ashley was helping Esther to her feet. Standing upright, Esther regained some of her senses. She couldn't take this dress off yet. Ashley was still fully clothed.

"Wait, you first," Esther said.

Ashley did that thing that was half laugh, half smile, and Esther's heart did a little swoop.

"Same time?" Ashley was pulling up the hem of her dress to get to her pleather leggings.

Esther shrugged off her dress one shoulder at a time, trying to tease the moment, but her hands caught in the long sleeves. And of course, Ashley made removing leggings look like the easiest thing. Esther finally wriggled her hands free as Ashley pulled the sequin dress over her head, her gold hair cascading back in place around her shoulders.

"Jesus, are you kidding?" Esther said.

Ashley had the body of a Marvel superhero. The abs, the arms, wide hips leading to thick thighs, and a rack pointed straight at Esther. She knew Ashley had an impressive body, but she had no idea it was this impressive.

Ashley shrugged. "Did I mention I used to throw women around in my free time? The efforts start to show after a while."

"Wait." Esther shoved her own dress the rest of the way over her hips and down to the floor. "Do you still have moves? Could you throw me?"

She kicked her dress to the side and braced herself like she'd run and jump at Ashley. Funny that they were both naked together for the first time and Esther felt zero awkwardness. Ashley must have licked that out of her.

Ashley eyed her up and down. "Please. I could lift you before I even had vampire strength."

She motioned for Esther to run at her, and that was when Esther realized how ridiculous they were being. She'd never cheered a day in her life, and Ashley was standing there in all her naked glory, making it look like running and jumping was the simplest thing in the world.

But it was too late to turn back now. A reckless voice in Esther's head said she needed to see this through.

"Don't worry, sweetheart." Ashley smiled, arms raised and ready. "I've got you."

She ran. Ashley's hands met her hips, and Esther was weightless, and it was glorious. Not quite that orgasm from earlier, but she was still making comparisons. Just as she was savoring the novelty of seeing the world from a different angle and the feel of Ashley's firm grip on her waist, she was sailing backward through the air, free-falling onto the bed.

Esther lay, flung—no, splayed—across Ashley's bed in nothing but her ripped tights, which somehow made her feel more naked than if she simply had nothing on at all. There was this excited, bubbly feeling starting in her fingers and traveling up her arms. She could only describe it as restless peace. This was exactly where she wanted to be, here in this ridiculous bed with this silly, pink light and Ashley, so brave and strong and unapologetically herself—ready to fuck her to pieces again. She was so happy her body had growing pains making room for the influx of all this joy.

She looked up to find Ashley at the foot of the bed with a strange look in her eyes.

"Shit," Ashley whispered, running a hand through her hair.

Esther's heart raced at that word. Did Ashley regret this? Had Esther made a mistake? She stood on her knees and walk-crawled over to the end of the bed.

"Hey. Talk to me," Esther said. "What's going on?"

Water pooled at the corners of Ashley's eyes, and Esther thought she might break watching it happen. Her arms enveloped Ashley in a flash. Like maybe some of Ashley's speed had been transferred to her.

"It's just starting to really sink in," Ashley said.

Esther was never sure what to do in these situations. Not opening up meant she didn't have much practice handling other people's big feelings. But this was Ashley. She sank deeper into the embrace, wrapping her arms around Ashley's waist, keeping her in place. She would be an anchor if nothing else.

"Seeing you here on my bed where I couldn't have a girl before because then the whole school would hear about it and I'd lose everyone. All the fame and people I called friends. And then it's not just any girl here. It's you."

Okay, Esther needed to see her face for this. "Would you like to snuggle under the covers for a bit and tell me about it?"

Ashley sniffed and nodded. They both slipped under the covers and molded together, their week of sharing a bed providing them with the knowledge of each other's shape.

"I don't know why I'm such a mess," Ashley said, wiping the lingering tears from her eyes. "It's not like this is my first time. It was just seeing you here, on this bed, in this room. I guess I've always been hiding a part of me. First, being gay all through high school, and now, being a vampire from my parents, and...it means so much that I have one person right here that I can be myself with."

"Ashley," Esther whispered, softly kissing away the lingering tears on her cheek, "I'm so sorry you had to hide yourself for so long to feel safe."

"Well, I survived hiding through high school." Ashley laughed, waving away Esther's concern. "What's another eternity of hiding a part of me?"

Esther wasn't sure she liked this turn of the conversation. Ashley was a sun and shouldn't be hiding, but being a vampire wasn't Esther's secret to tell. Not for the first time, Esther wondered how much Ashley had thought through the decision to change and whether it was the right choice for her.

She opened her mouth to say something, though she wasn't sure what, when Ashley kissed her. Slow and sweetly nibbling at Esther's lip until she opened for her and all other thoughts abandoned her.

"You're so perfect, Esther." Ashley rolled their joined bodies so she was on top, trailing her lips down Esther's neck and shoulders. She gave a light nip on the top of Esther's breast, and Esther let out a little gasp, her back arching.

"You like that, sweetheart?" Ashley asked sweetly before licking Esther's nipple until it pebbled beneath her touch.

When her mouth continued to move down, Esther grabbed her wrist. "Wait."

Ashley froze, and Esther recalled Ashley's promise to stop whenever asked. She'd underestimated how serious Ashley's promise was. "It's my turn."

"Turns aren't a thing," Ashley countered, despite letting Esther roll her onto her back. "I like tasting you."

"Well, I'd like a try, if you don't mind."

"If you insist," said Ashley with a sniff, which turned into a gasp when Esther licked the underside of Ashley's breast.

"I insist." Esther kissed down Ashley's body, worshipping her with tongue and lips as she went. "Let me know if I'm doing it right."

"Just do what you...enjoy." Ashley's voice trailed off as Esther licked across her seam, opening her with her tongue. Esther knew what she tasted like, but Ashley was sweeter.

She explored, learning Ashley's body. First licking lightly near her entrance then gliding up to her clit listening when Ashley emitted a small gasp then going back to those spots for more until she felt Ashley growing tense, her thighs flexing under Esther's hands. Esther felt a rush of power—a drive to unravel her. Light flicks turned to building pressure until she was sure Ashley was near ready, and then she sucked on her clit until Ashley cried out and convulsed beneath her.

Esther sat up and wiped her mouth, hiding her smile. She was toppled onto her back, Ashley pinning Esther's arms over her head.

"You're amazing." Ashley's hand slid between them and down Esther's stomach, her other hand trailing behind Esther's head. A finger tapped twice playfully at Esther's clit, making her inhale sharply. "Tell me what you want, sweetheart."

Words? What were words? She still had the taste of Ashley on her lips, her body soft and snug against her. She wanted to be enveloped, devoured, which was a dangerous request to make to a vampire.

"Please," said Esther, pushing her hips up to Ashley's palm.

"You want me in you, love?" Esther's nod was interrupted by a gasp as Ashley slid one finger and then a second inside her, slowly easing in and out. "You want to let me watch you come again?"

Esther couldn't speak. The pressure built inside her as Ashley increased the speed, rubbing herself on Esther's leg as she curled her fingers, hitting that soft spot with each thrust.

"Ashley," she ground out as her body convulsed, flexing around Ashley's fingers.

Ashley's lips met hers, swallowing Esther's outcry. Devouring her like she wanted. She felt wholly herself and seen and no longer scared or embarrassed. She felt like a puzzle piece sliding into place.

Ashley collapsed on the bed beside her, smiling and

laughing again. Esther reached for her, not sure what she intended but needing to touch her. To feel Ashley and know that she was real. She brushed Ashley's hair from her face and ran her fingers along her cheek.

God, she loved this woman so much. If she were a cat, she'd be purring.

Wait. Love? It was much too fast for that. They'd only just decided they were dating for real. She couldn't possibly be in love.

But Ashley was stroking Esther's back, and the look in her eyes was earth-shattering.

Esther felt too good now to worry if her feelings were too big or too fast. A small part of her worried about loving a vampire, but with Ashley's arms wrapped tight around her, she felt so safe and comfortable just living in the present. They fell into sleep the way she knew they could.

Like two perfect halves.

24

―――――

Ashley

Moments after closing her eyes, Ashley woke to a buzzing on her nightstand. She hugged Esther closer to her chest, willing the buzzing to go away and leave her in this peaceful moment with Esther in her arms. Miracle of all miracles, it stopped. She gave a quick word of thanks before closing her eyes again.

The buzzing started back up, and Ashley's eyes shot open with a growl. Esther made a small sound in her sleep, so Ashley grabbed the phone before it woke her fully.

She hit answer without bothering checking the ID. "We're fine, Mom."

"So many questions," returned a male voice. "But first, I prefer Mommy."

"Who's calling you Mommy?" a gruffer voice asked in the background.

Ashley pulled the phone away from her face. Why was Uther calling her? Oh. Because this wasn't her phone.

"Let me talk to her. That's my girl, not yours," the second voice demanded.

There was some scuffling, then August was on the line. "Well, well, Ashley. Look who's on the wrong phone now."

"Shut up, witch." Ashley suppressed a laugh. Not even August's teasing could dull the high of waking up to Esther in her arms.

Esther stretched her legs, rolled over, and flopped an arm over Ashley's waist.

"Is that August and Uther?" Her voice was groggy with sleep. She cracked a single eye open. "And is that my phone?"

"Esther says hi," Ashley said into the phone.

"I didn't hear her." Uther's voice was small in the background.

Ashley rolled her eyes but switched the phone to speakerphone. "I thought you lot were Gen Z. What are you doing calling people on the phone anyway?"

"I can use a phone." Uther declared matter-of-factly. "I was trying to do video call with the camera off since no one can see my face this early in the day."

"Isn't August right there?" asked Esther.

"He's blindfolded," Uther answered.

"Don't tell them about our sex life, love," August teased. Or Ashley assumed it was teasing. "We promised we'd call in the new year. Remember?"

"I thought you would call closer to New Year's," said Ashley. "You know, when the sun is still down and vampires are still awake like a considerate friend?"

"I never claimed to be considerate," said August. "Plus, we were busy around midnight."

"Ashley," Esther whispered. "We were a little busy around midnight too."

"I heard that!" yelled Uther. "Omg, we're all going to double date. Tell me it's official, and I don't have to wait for the two of you to figure out why the other is making starry eyes."

Ashley turned to Esther, unsure how to answer. They never had a chance to discuss what happened let alone what that meant going forward.

Esther didn't look at her, directing her answer at the phone instead. "Calm down, Uther. We just woke up."

"Fine," he said, "but let me know the second you know what's happening, you crazy kids."

They chatted a little longer about their nights before hanging up. Ashley collapsed on the bed and threw her arm over her face. It was the middle of the day, but she was suddenly so keyed up—there was no way she could fall asleep now. She felt like a warm, shiny ball of fluff sitting here in her bed with the woman she was falling head over feet for, and now their two closest friends knew too.

It felt permanent. A good sign for the dawning year.

She took Esther's hand in her own, and Esther smiled in her sweet, closed-mouth way, with just the one side pulling up. Ashley wanted to kiss that secret smile and live in it forever. She wanted forever like this—her and Esther. The realization struck her, and she remembered the silver capsule Claribel had given her ages ago.

She thought about the last time she'd fallen for someone.

"Hey, what's the matter?" Esther asked. Of course, she'd noticed the change in Ashley's mood.

"It's nothing, just thinking about stuff."

"Any of it involve me?" Esther ran her hand up and down Ashley's thigh.

The heat of Esther's touch was intoxicating. "Yes. And also no."

Esther sat up, draped her legs across Ashley's lap, and wrapped Ashley's arms around her. "I'm here if you want to talk about it."

Ashley held her tight. They'd started something that couldn't be taken back or undone, but it could still be broken. Ashley would be gentle with it. "I make impulsive decisions."

A small chuckle escaped Esther at that comment. "You don't say."

"Hey now." She bit playfully at Esther's neck, enjoying Esther's squealed laughter. "I'm working on it." She took a moment to fit together what she wanted to say. "I've made mistakes in the past, and one of them really cost me. Well, probably more than one, but one of them cost me five years of my life, and I don't want to do that again."

"The last time you tried to join the vampires?" Esther lifted Ashley's hand, playing with her fingers before lacing her own in them.

"There was this girl. It's silly really. I was lonely after spending the last year banished from my first attempt."

"We'll put a pin in that story."

"And I just wanted to... Well, I barely made it to the second semester before I told her about me."

Ashley waited, but Esther stayed quiet. She assumed there would be comments at the end.

"Obviously, that was a mistake," Ashley continued. "She ended up telling a friend, who told another friend, and the next thing I knew, the supposed existence of vampires was the worst kept secret in Plattsburgh. I thought maybe if I controlled the spread until the end of the school year, I could still make it work. But one of the vampires caught word of it, and that's when I had to leave town while they did a city-wide sweep, cleaning people's memories of me."

Ashley shivered, thinking back on those early days when Hannah and John would interrogate people in the front sitting room, trying to follow the trail of the rumor and control the spread. Taking someone's memories—nonconsensual control over another person's body—never settled right with Ashley. There was a certain level of violence to the action, and that thought was probably what kept her from letting go and perform it herself.

"Geez, that sucks," Esther said.

"Yeah, it did. Anyway, this was all a long-winded way of saying, I trust you, and I'm all in. If that's something you're interested in."

Esther clenched Ashley's hand. "But? I feel like there's a but in there."

"But I want to take it slow. Or at least not my typical diving in blindly. You feel like something big, Esther, and I don't want to mess this up."

"That's fair and smart actually." She hugged Ashley's arms to her again. "I don't want to mess this up either. We have time. Let's just see where this goes, and if it doesn't work out, we'll cross that bridge then."

Ashley tucked a finger under Esther's chin and tilted her head up. "And if it does?"

Esther's eyes darkened. "Then we'll figure that out too."

Esther kissed her, turning to all fours and crawling over Ashley. Ashley grabbed the back of Esther's head and pulled her in closer, deeper, trailing a hand up and down the curve of Esther's back.

In the end, it was Ashley that had to break the kiss. "I would love to keep this going, but we should probably pack so we don't miss our flight."

Esther rolled off her and sighed. "If we must."

Ashley got up and tugged on a shirt and pants and wrapped a blanket over her entire body. As she headed to the door, she noticed the two crosses resting on Esther's nightstand.

"Your earrings are still off."

Esther stretched and scratched her head. "Well, I don't wear them to bed. That would be uncomfortable."

"Do you wear them most days?"

Esther's cheeks pinkened when she made eye contact. "I used to."

Three words. That was all it took to take Ashley's breath away. Esther said the earrings didn't fit her outfit last night, but it was clear now that it was for Ashley's benefit. And boy, had she benefited. Esther had literally made herself vulnerable, opened herself up to Ashley, and Ashley would not squander that level of trust.

"I...Esther." Ashley had to look away to control her tears.

She didn't know what to say, what to do with this. She was dangerous. Vampires were dangerous, and Esther trusted Ashley enough to leave herself bare.

Ashley walked back to the bed and took both of Esther's hands in her own, kissing her knuckles. "You are a treasure, Esther Green."

And the sweet smile that spread across Esther's face was worth every sunset.

"But..." Ashley pieced together what she wanted to say. Esther alone in a room with Hannah and how helpless Ashley had felt flitted through her memory. Esther may trust her, but there were still other dangers in the world. "I'd like it if you still wore them in Plattsburgh."

Esther studied her face but finally nodded, and a weight Ashley didn't know she was carrying lifted.

"Thank you, sweetheart." She kissed Esther's hand one more time before tucking the blanket tight around her and heading for the door.

"Where are you going?" Esther asked.

"To the garage before my parents get home. I stuck the last of my blood bags in the bottom drawer of the beer fridge for safekeeping. I'm about to go chug like five of them just in case. We're not having a repeat of our last flight."

"Good plan."

Ashley reached for the door again.

"Wait, one more thing."

"What's that?"

"What happened that first time you tried to join the vampire house?"

"Oh." Ashley laughed. "That was dumb. Someone caught me with a deer near the end of my second semester and ran off screaming. I told Claribel and Cynthia right away, and we managed to find the person before they told anyone else. But I still had to leave while the vampires did a sweep just in case. I didn't even need that deer. I just wanted to know if they tasted as bad as I remembered. So you know, they do."

Esther chuckled. "Well, go finish off the beer blood then." She flicked her hands at Ashley, waving her out of the room.

"I'm going, I'm going."

"Oh, and Ashley?"

"What?" Ashley groaned in mock frustration.

"We're real now, right?"

Ashley jumped and tackled Esther to the bed, giving her a quick and firm kiss. "We're very real, sweetheart."

25

———

Esther

Esther carved out a rhythm in the following weeks. Her time split evenly between coursework, her internship, and GA duties during the day and evenings spent wandering moonlit paths by a quiet lake, slipping between winter-cool fingers, and hushing each other's sighs and giggles in her attic.

The weekends were a constant tug between staying on top of the week's assignments and spending time with friends. Between catching up with Uther over brunch and laughing while Ashley and August fought over the popcorn bowl at movie night—despite August's protests that she wasn't eating it anyway—her work window shrank exponentially. She did very little sleeping and could see herself fraying at the edges. A snapping remark here, an ignored text there. More and more often, brunch was a chore rather than a way to decompress from the week.

And so, it was with a groan that she found her body curved over a desk and her cheek smooshed to a notebook on the night she'd put aside to catch up on schoolwork. A thin, college-lined page peeled away from her face as she sat up. She rubbed her cheek, hoping none of her notes transferred to her face. The only other student in this part of the library was two tables over and fully immersed in their project. An envious snake coiled in her gut, and a weight like the steepled space above her had solidified into a massive wood-paneled vulture to perch on her shoulders.

She wiggled the mouse, and the computer came to life. Her professor had assigned a project meant to help her better understand this program, but Esther didn't want to dig deeper into her student loans when the software was available for free on campus computers. So, she was at the school library trying to wrangle the massive workload her master's program had dumped on her before her last semester got out of hand.

A movement in her peripheral alerted Esther her late-night companion was calling it quits for the night. That was fine. She would channel the second wind her little nap should have given her and power through. She was on the cusp of a breakthrough. Just another hour tops and she could go home and get a couple hours of sleep before starting from scratch on another project due this week. If she didn't finish these two projects before Sunday, she'd have to miss movie night again, and Uther would disown her. She adjusted the number in her spreadsheet, and an error message flashed across the screen. The whole program froze.

"No, no, no." She clicked furiously, pushing every escape, backspace, undo-whatever-that-was button she could think of. Nothing changed.

Her phone buzzed.

ASHLEY

How's studying going?

ESTHER

Like crap. Might cry. Might just fail. TBD

She waited a few seconds without a reply before sliding her phone back into her pocket. If she turned the machine off and on again, she'd lose everything she'd worked on. Stupid, buggy, outdated program. Surely, someone had made something better that served the same purpose by now. As she was getting ready to throw the mouse across the table and screech at the computer screen, a light cough alerted her of another's presence. Her spine cracked as she twisted around to see who'd interrupted her melancholy.

"Hey, sweetheart." Ashley leaned against the bookshelf behind her as though she had only been in the other room the whole time.

Feelings blocked up Esther's throat, preventing her from replying. The legs of her chair skidded against the thin, faded rug as she leaped into Ashley's open arms, nuzzling in snug under her chin. Ashley's lips brush the top of her head, and Esther closed her eyes, letting herself breathe in Ashley's nearness and nothing else. Ashley was an anchor in the storm called grad school, a lifeline, a source of comfort, and a safe place to vent. People said grad school was a trial on a relationship, but those people weren't dating a vampire.

Ashley was everything but still hadn't asked Esther to change, to live forever with her. So, while all this support was comforting, a tight knot in the pit of her chest continued to warn her this was all temporary.

Although, if she was given the option, would she take it? As much as she skulked away from people, she wasn't a night person. But that was an easy adjustment. Her pale complexion had a rough relationship with the sun as it was. It was the potential to kill someone that held her back. Sunlight, she could take or leave, blood—she'd get over that—but after seeing the way Ashley was barely hanging on to her self-control on the plane, Esther wasn't sure she wanted the burden of keeping everyone safe from her tenuous hold on control. Or the repercussions and emotional toll of the outcome.

"Hey." Ashley touched Esther's chin, tilting it to meet her eyes. "Did you want to tell me what's going on?"

Esther turned to the end of the row where the librarian sat behind the help desk, clicking away at her computer. Ashley followed her gaze, understanding without Esther needing to utter a word that she was uncomfortable sharing vulnerable moments. She took Esther's hand and led her to a more secluded aisle.

"All right." Ashley leaned against the shelves across the aisle from Esther, the space small enough that Esther, leaning against her side of bookshelves, was still able to weave a foot between Ashley's, the contact keeping her grounded. "Are you ready to tell me what's upsetting you?"

What upset Esther was that Ashley was a fairytale. Here she was in her cute sweater ready to save the day, and there was this phantom ticking clock hovering over everything they did together. Esther couldn't focus properly on anything knowing that, as a human, this support, this encouragement, this friendship, this love would someday come to an end. And she had no clue when, but the not knowing only added to her stress levels. She couldn't implement some arbitrary rule to keep her safe here. All she could do was hang on for the ride and enjoy it while she could. And in the spirit of enjoying it while she could, she couldn't pressure Ashley into deciding on Esther's eternal state one way or the other because Esther still wasn't sure one way or the other.

So, she deflected to the next pressing item on the list.

"My program froze, and I'm about to lose everything I stayed up to work on." The words came out quiet, embarrassed by how frivolous it sounded in the shadow of eternity. Funny how one problem could be so massive until placed next to another.

"Ugh, that sucks." Ashley took her hand. "I'm not going to be much help in this situation. There's nothing you can do to at least save what you have?"

Esther shook her head. "At this point, the only thing left to do is turn it off and back on again. It took me forever to fiddle my way to this point in the project, and now I have to do it all over again, and I'll miss movie night again, and Uther will be pissed."

A tear escaped the corner of her eye before she even realized how worked up she was getting.

"Hey." Ashley stood, framing her feet around Esther's and cupping her cheek to wipe away a tear with her thumb. "You are brilliant. You did it once, and now you know you can do it again. This is just your sleepiness talking. Uther knows that grad school is not the same as undergrad and will understand. Just remember this won't be forever."

"It won't?" Frantic, Esther fisted the side of Ashley's sweater, pulling her closer. She felt like she was trying to grasp water, to stay in a moment that was steadily slipping away.

"Of course not." Ashley smiled, probably interpreting Esther's anxiety as a need for assurance and not that Ashley had just turned up the volume on their ticking clock. "In a few months, you'll graduate, and you'll have your life back. Or as back as working a full-time job to pay back the loan you took out in order to skip days of sleep getting a degree to get that full-time job to begin with."

Ashley chuckled, but when Esther couldn't find the will to join, her smile waned.

"Is there something else that's bothering—" Ashley started.

Esther kissed her, swallowing Ashley's concerns before they could be voiced. This was their moment. The clock could tick as loudly as it wanted, but it couldn't have this cluster of seconds forming minutes leading to an hour. This was theirs and Esther would take it. The kiss was too short, and when she opened her eyes, Ashley stood over her, their foreheads pressed together and breaths intermingling.

"Esther." The word was a single breath Esther consumed, and she tasted the truth in it.

Ashley heard the clock too.

26

─────

Ashley

Ashley stood in the doorway of the Platt House attic watching Esther snooze on her desk and wondering if she should just let her sleep.

She needed to make a decision soon though. She was quickly becoming a creepy vampire stereotype, watching her unsuspecting lover while she slept. Maybe she'd give her a few more minutes. She backed out of the room when a loud crash from downstairs broke Esther from her sleep.

What were Uther and August up to down there?

Well, since Esther was up. Ashley rapped at the doorframe to get Esther's attention. "Hey, sweetheart, do you have a minute?"

Esther ducked her head to wipe her mouth on her sleeve before turning around.

"Ashley." Esther's gaze slid across Ashley's body, and she couldn't help subtly flexing and hamming up the moment. "I have all the minutes for you, babe."

"How's your project going?" Ashley scanned the desk.

Esther had nearly buried her laptop in a mountain of paper, and Ashley would bet money whatever was in that mug had gone cold a while ago.

Esther sighed, tapping at her computer. "Slowly."

"Do you need the night? I know we had plans, but if you need to work..." She had big plans for tonight, but if Esther wasn't in the right mindset, it wasn't worth pushing the moment. She could wait.

Esther's eyes widened, and her brows shot up to her hairline. "No. Oh my god, I almost...No. This can wait."

She shuffled piles around, taking a distracted sip from her mug and cringing. Definitely cold.

"Hey." Ashley walked to the desk and crouched into Esther's line of sight. "Are you sure? This is just a day on the calendar. I won't be offended. You've been working so hard on this project, and you're almost there."

"No, I'm fine." Esther drained the last of her mug and slammed it down like a shot. "This can wait."

Ashley wasn't sure she believed her. Esther was making that smile that was supposed to be comforting but was too teethy for an Esther smile. She was going to argue further when Esther took her hand.

"I know you've been working on some Valentine's Day surprise," Esther said. "Show me."

That familiar intoxication whenever she was around Esther took over. They'd been together for real now for over a month. Surely this sparkly, hard-to-think feeling would dull and she could function like a normal human—or vampire—around her. In the meantime, Ashley bid rational thought adieu and led Esther to a smaller set of stairs at the back of the attic. Ashley had requested romance, and Esther had requested a quiet night in relative privacy. Since neither of them had exceptionally private housing, Ashley had enlisted the help of August, who'd lent them the upper floors for the night.

At the top of the stairs, Ashley pushed open a trapdoor, letting in a wave of cold air and exposing a box of starry sky. She helped Esther through the door and closed it behind them. She stayed silent, letting Esther take in her work. Twinkle lights were strung around the railing of the widow's walk, and a corner was piled with soft blankets and the plushest pillows Ashley could find while scavenging through August's surplus of guest rooms. Ashley had even tucked the heated blanket from her room into the pile.

"You made this for me?" Esther asked.

"Do you like it?"

"Oh, Ashley." Esther tucked her head under Ashley's chin, hiding her face. "It's beautiful."

Ashley wrapped her arms around Esther and kissed the top of her head. She led Esther to the blankets and pulled her down beside her. "I wanted to give you that quiet time you were hoping for, and I thought you might like this. It's a little cold, but the stars were so bright tonight."

"It's perfect. Thank you so much."

"Oh! I nearly forgot." She reached into the pillow pile and pulled out a thermos and two mugs. "Cocoa?"

Esther laughed. "Yes, please."

She poured the mugs, and they sipped in comfortable silence. "So, I didn't mean to wake you up earlier."

Esther snort-laughed into her cup of cocoa. "I didn't mean to be asleep earlier."

"Could this have something to do with our string of late nights?"

"Surely not," said Esther, taking a sip.

"Esther, talk to me." Ashley hadn't meant to say it so sharply. Sometimes, it was hard to get Esther to share her feelings instead of keeping them all bottled inside. It must be exhausting. "I know you don't like to demand or even speak up for yourself, but I care about you. I don't want to dance around landmines, trying to avoid unknowingly stressing you. You're not going to hurt my feelings."

Esther lowered her mug. "It might be too many late nights."

She mumbled so quietly it was only with Ashley's enhanced hearing that she caught what Esther said. Ashley kept forgetting how much work Esther had to do. Ashley's weekly workload could all be finished in a couple of hours on the weekend, and they were really just for show. Passing her classes wasn't a requirement for getting into the Family. But Hannah and Claribel had hinted it would piss John off if they could brag about her grades, so she should at least try.

"That's no problem," Ashley said. "We can cut back to once a week. We could actually sleep at night." They didn't have anthropology anymore, which only made Ashley more desperate to see Esther during the week. She needed her Esther fix. But she wouldn't keep Esther back from her dreams either, and graduating—and graduating well—was important to Esther, so it was important to Ashley too.

"I highly doubt that will happen." Esther chuckled, all too aware of how difficult it was to keep their hands off each other. "It's not just the sleep though. We don't have any privacy. I have my uncle and Jason, and you have all the vampires. The only place we can find some privacy is here at August's place, and this isn't even that private."

"What are you talking about?" Ashley gestured around them at the empty darkness. "We have plenty of privacy."

The door to the roof smacked open, and August poked his head up. "Hey, Ash. Have you seen Uther's bag? He said you might have moved it."

"Do you know how to knock?" Ashley demanded. "I could have been topless up here?"

"A nice set of tits never scared me off." August winked.

Ashley threw a pillow at his stupid face. "Get out of here before I drown you."

"Hey, August. I found it." Uther popped up through the hole beside August. "Oh wow. It's so cute. Why haven't you shown me up here before?"

"Because it's literally freezing outside," August said, "and only a cold-blooded narcissist would make their date freeze to death for the sake of some stars."

Ashley stuck out her tongue, and he returned the gesture.

"I'd sure like to go somewhere warm." Uther ignored their antics. "We should go somewhere for spring break. All of us. We could split the cost."

"That would be perfect, actually," Esther said. Ashley hadn't expected this level of enthusiasm from Esther. Not when her schoolwork was building up. "It gives me something to work toward while buckling down on my final project. Something to look forward to besides graduation."

"Graduation high five." Uther and Esther air-fived across the roof.

"And it would be an escape from schoolwork and your uncle," added Ashley. "Did you have any place in mind?"

"It's a little last minute to be reserving stuff." Uther already had his phone out and was scrolling. "People reserve beach houses months, sometimes a year in advance. And we only have a month now."

"Actually," said Esther, "I have an aunt with a beach house in South Carolina. I bet she would let us borrow it for the week. She's almost never there anymore."

"That would save on our budget too." Uther was

vibrating with excitement. "Now, how are we getting there? Were you thinking plane, or should we rent a car? If we rent a car, we'll have it for the rest of the trip, which could be good for going out and getting groceries, but flying will leave us more time at the actual destination. We could rent a car once we get there. Now, what were you thinking for meal plans? Should we plan a menu to eat at home, or were you picturing eating out? What is your imagined budget?"

He made to climb the rest of the way up the ladder when August grabbed his arm.

"Or we can discuss this later," August said, "and you and I can go downstairs and...work on that project we were talking about earlier." He lifted a brow.

Uther scrambled back down the ladder. "Right, the project. Talk soon, ladies. Happy Valentine's Day."

August slammed the door behind them.

"Now, where were we?" Ashley cupped the back of Esther's head, drawing her closer.

Esther brushed her lips against Ashley's. "I think we were watching the stars."

They sank into the blankets. Ashley toyed nervously with the item in her pocket. She'd waited weeks for this day, but now she worried Esther would think it was too soon.

"Esther?"

"Hmm?" Esther with stars in her eyes was heartbreaking.

"This is real, right? Us, I mean?"

"I sure hope so."

Right. This felt right. "I got you something."

Esther sat up. "What is it?"

Ashley paused, not knowing how to describe it. "It's really weird now that I think about it."

A curl worked its way free of Esther's messy bun as she

turned her full attention on Ashley. "Well, you have to tell me now. I like weird."

"Yeah, but this is creepy weird." In all the weeks she'd pictured giving Esther this gift, she hadn't considered the optics. "There has to be a much cuter way to go about this."

"Ashley." Esther took Ashley's free hand in her own. "I'm dating a vampire. In case you didn't know this already, I like creepy."

"And you're okay with that? You know what I am and what that means. What a future with me would be like. Even a temporary one."

"Ashley, you're once in a lifetime. I'm not letting you go while I have the chance." Esther kissed her, firm and deliberate—their lips speaking a silent promise as they moved together.

Bolstered by her words, Ashley broke the kiss and held up a silver necklace.

Esther took it and raised an eyebrow. "This is it? I thought you had a dead rat for me, based on the way you were acting. Jewelry is a pretty standard gift."

Ashley scrunched her eyes shut so she didn't have to see Esther's reaction. "So, it's kind of a vial—of my blood."

Silence followed while Ashley waited for Esther's reaction. Maybe she would scream or throw the necklace off the roof.

"Okay," said Esther.

Ashley cracked open an eye to see Esther still sitting there, not panicking or running away screaming.

Esther nodded encouragingly. "I like where this is headed, but I'm going to need some more backstory."

Ashley opened her second eye. Esther hadn't left, and she didn't look like she was tensing to run. Maybe this was okay? She breathed in through her nose and out slowly through her mouth, rotating her shoulders to loosen up again. She needed to get this story right. "So, I kind of got the idea from Claribel."

"And Claribel is...an ex?"

"No!" exclaimed Ashley. "No, of course not. That'd be an inappropriate way to start this story where I'm trying and failing to be romantic."

"Okay." Esther waved her on. "Get to the romantic part then."

"I'm working on it." So bossy. "Anyway, she's a vampire, and she had this guy she liked a couple hundred years ago —a human. And she knew he would die, so being the true goth girl she was, she collected some of his blood and keeps it in a vial around her neck."

"So, you mean to woo me with your vampire blood?" Esther turned her head and touched a fist to her chin in a thinking pose. "Yes, I think I'm wooed. Good work. A quality Valentine's gift." She unlatched the necklace to put it on.

But Ashley grabbed her wrist and stopped her. "There's still a bit more to this story."

"Continue," said Esther, setting the necklace back in her lap.

Ashley opened her mouth to continue then registered what Esther had said. "Wait? That's it? Someone gives you a vial of their blood, and you are wooed?"

"Yeah," said Esther—rather firmly, in fact. "It's kind of hot."

"You're kind of a creep. Did you know that?" She nudged Esther's shoulder.

"Takes one to know one." They both laughed.

"I'm falling for you, Esther. Like, hard, and it scares me, but not as much as the idea of losing you." She swallowed. *Here goes nothing.* "Part of becoming a vampire is to drink a vampire's blood, so that's what this is—a vial of my blood. And I don't expect any final decisions now. I don't want that. This is a symbol of how serious I am. I just hoped you'd consider it. Because I want to spend forever with you."

"Ashley." Water pooled at the corner of Esther's eyes.

Ashley was dying. Not literally, obviously. But emotionally, Ashley was falling apart waiting on some clear answer from Esther.

Finally, Esther handed the necklace back to her. "Will you help me put it on?"

27

Ashley

"It's cozy." Ashley rested a pensive fist under her chin.

"And conveniently close to groceries." August joined with additional praise. Ashley gave him a look of thanks.

"Are we seriously staying here for a week?" Uther received an elbow in the side from August and a glare from Ashley. "What? Esther, I love you, but this place is a dump."

Uther wasn't wrong, but Ashley was so proud of Esther for speaking up and suggesting a place for their spring break trip. She didn't want to ruin it by pointing out that to get to the beach they had to cross two highways, a mall, and a parking lot that was strictly mall parking only. Not to mention that the proximity of said highway meant that they had the unique challenge of yelling to be heard over semi-engines and the wailing of horns while pretending they weren't yelling. Maybe it was just the evening rush hour, at eight pm in a beach town.

The house itself was on a sandy, grass-speckled lot—the

entire yard flooded by the white LED light of a neighboring streetlight—with a chipped, cement path leading to a gray-paneled box of a structure that looked as though a swift breeze would end it.

"We haven't even seen inside yet," said Ashley in a voice she hoped was both audible and passed as a casual register. "I'm sure it's nice inside."

"Did you say there are lice inside?" yelled Uther.

"Nice," repeated Ashley.

"Rice?"

August pushed past both of them and walked up the path to the door. He jiggled the knob, and the door opened.

"Was it not locked?" asked Esther. "I have the key here."

"I guess not—" August froze in the doorway, and Ashley put herself between the door and Esther.

"Wait there," August yelled back at them. "Let me get a light first."

He disappeared through the doorway, and Ashley waited, acting as a human—vampire—barrier between Esther and the door. A yellow light streaked through the yard from the open doorway, then several loud thuds interspersed with a string of curses.

Uther pulled out his phone. "There has to be a hotel open in the area."

A few minutes later, August appeared in the doorway, a metal dustpan dangling from his hand. "All right, I think I got them all."

Uther scrolled more furiously. "Shit. Does anyone have a charger I can borrow?"

"We're here for a week," said Esther. "You didn't pack one?"

"Mine broke like a week ago."

"How is your phone not dead?"

He held up his phone. "It *is* dead."

"And how have you not bought a new charger in a week?"

Ashley walked past their bickering to the doorway. August had left the door open and she peered cautiously through. She wasn't as squeamish as Uther, but—

"Ouch!" Her head bumped something in the doorway.

But there wasn't anything there. She held her hand up. An all-too-familiar wall blocked her entrance. Esther and Uther were back at the car digging through Esther's bag.

"Damn it," Ashley said. "Hey, witch! Let me in."

August strolled down the hallway with a smirk as he leaned just inside the doorjamb and out of her reach. "Well, well, well. What have we here?"

"Don't be an ass. I'm getting in there one way or another, and the longer it takes, the more you're going to regret sleeping in the same house as me."

He pressed a hand to his chest. "I would never." He kicked the door open the rest of the way. "Come on in."

"Thank yo—" Her face slammed into a still present invisible wall.

August bent over cackling.

"Damn it, witch!" She slammed her fist against the empty doorway, which made no sound and only made her look like an angry mime. "What did you do?"

Between gasps, he answered her. "You have to get Esther. She's responsible for the house."

"Freaking hell, August." She kicked the doorway. "You knew that this whole damn time."

"What's going on?" Esther called from the car as she pulled an endless string of charging cords from her bag.

"I'm going to beat up Uther's boyfriend," Ashley said. "That's what's up."

"Have I graduated from drowning?" August had finally recovered himself.

"The night is young."

Ashley helped with the bags, and this time, Esther's permission did the trick. They all piled into the living room.

It could have used a thorough dusting and run-through with a vacuum, but the space didn't seem so bad. Or perhaps her bar had lowered so far that, as long as it wasn't a literal pit or home to a hungry tiger, it was exceeding expectations. To the left was a simple open kitchen including a yellowing fridge, a worrisome-looking gas stove, and overhead cabinets with most of their doors intact. To the right was a sitting area, complete with a lumpy and mildly stained futon and a TV stand with no TV. Straight on from the front door was a hallway that she assumed led to the two promised bedrooms and shared bathroom.

"This isn't so bad." Ashley was feeling better and better about their situation. "Give me a night with some cleaning supplies, and I can shine this place up to homey levels."

"What do you mean by homie?" asked Uther.

"You know, comfy, hygge."

"Are you speaking Dutch?"

"I think it's Danish." August took Uther's bag for him. "Come on, Uther. I've called dibs on our room. Just think of it as our own personal hobbit hole."

"Hobbit holes are known for their *cleanliness*, August." He reluctantly followed him down the hallway.

Ashley took Esther's hand and led her to the other unoccupied room. Praise Jesus, she'd thought to pack a sleeping bag because they were not sleeping on those sheets. She was making a mental list of supplies for Esther to get from the mall during daylight hours.

"Ashley, I'm so sorry." Esther plopped onto the bed then winced, rubbing the spot where she landed. That wasn't a good sign. A silver chain escaped her top with the motion, catching in the overhead light. "I've never actually been here before, but the way my aunt talked about this place, it sounded amazing. I just wanted us to have a relaxing week away."

"And we will, sweetheart. Don't you worry. I'll have this place fixed up in no time." She was excited about the challenge, but her attention had snagged on the vial around Esther's neck. "But in the meantime, let's go check out the beach."

"Did you want to unpack first? Maybe give the guys some time to unpack as well."

"I thought we could go, just the two of us."

Esther squinted at her as though assessing Ashley's true motive but agreed, and they headed out. Esther locked the door behind them when they heard a thunk. They opened the door to find the inner handle rolling across the short beige carpet.

"I'll fix that too." Ashley fit her hand into Esther's. "Don't worry."

Getting to the beach was as much of a headache as Ashley had suspected. The highway between the mall and the beach had a pedestrian overpass, but the first highway between their house and the mall required walking three blocks out of the way to a convoluted five-way intersection. Despite being less than half a mile from the beach, the walk took them a half-hour. The moon was full and bright by the time they were taking off their shoes and sinking into the sand, but the beach was blessedly empty.

Ashley led them down to the water until it licked at their toes. Her fingers laced with Esther's. The water lapping at the sand provided the soundtrack to their night as they walked along the shore.

The wind whipped across the waters, and Esther's hand trembled slightly. It wasn't near as cold as New York, but it was still chilly. Ashley hardly noticed the cold anymore. When she first changed, the feeling of constantly being cold frightened her. She remembered living in Konstantine's heated blanket that first week, shivering under a UV-free mood light.

"So." Ashley wasn't sure how to start this conversation. She decided to go with her usual technique of diving right in. "Are you still considering my offer?"

Esther didn't respond but touched the vial hanging around her neck. They hadn't spoken of her becoming a vampire since Valentine's Day. The only indication that Esther was still considering Ashley's offer was that Esther continued to wear the necklace.

"I am," Esther said after a moment.

The words drifted out with the tide, a hopeful message in a bottle. At least it sounded hopeful.

"In that case, you should keep regular human hours this week," Ashley said.

"Wait, what?" Esther's hand clamped tighter around Ashley's. "I thought we were spending time together this week. This was supposed to be a relaxing getaway together."

"I know, but if you're seriously considering changing, I want you to know what you're giving up. I want you to be human while you still can. Don't just jump into it like I did."

"Ashley." Esther moved in front of her, blocking the path. "What are you going to do all week? I don't want to be out having fun while you're at home by yourself."

"I'll be fine." She took Esther's hands and raised each to

her lips, kissing her knuckles. "I'll have plenty to do in the house. It's a blessing it's such a mess. I've started a list of things to do, starting with our room."

The corner of Esther's mouth wavered.

Ashley had hoped to coax a smile out of her with the list comment. On to her next plan to lighten the mood. "Plus, we'll still see each other in the mornings and evenings. I might have brought some toys for us to try out."

"The boys are in the house!" Esther scanned the empty beach, confirming they were still alone. But the blush on her cheeks told Ashley she wasn't immune to the suggestion.

Ashley wanted Esther to take this week seriously. To really consider her decision. Because if she was serious about being a vampire, she was serious about Ashley. The two went hand in hand.

"I guess we'll have to be quiet, won't we," Ashley said.

"You're terrible." Esther wrapped her arms around Ashley's neck, standing on tiptoe to reach her.

Ashley bent, catching Esther's lips with her own. "You like it when I'm terrible."

～ ～ ～

Ashley

The next day, Ashley was awakened to the pleasant caress of warm hands pressing circles into her back. "Mmm, that feels so good. Please, tell me this is Esther. Actually, it's too good. I don't even care who this is. Just don't stop."

"Hey!" Esther laughed. The mattress sank as she

mounted Ashley's back, her thighs warm against Ashley's sides.

Now Ashley was feeling more than just relaxed. "What time is it?"

"Okay, so it's noon. But I cleaned our sheets this morning, and the boys decided to eat out for lunch." She nipped Ashley's ear.

With that, Ashley was wide awake as all the information sank in. She leaped from the bed, racing for her bag.

"Oof."

Ashley glanced over her shoulder to see Esther tumbled on the floor. "Crap, are you all right, sweetheart?"

Esther rubbed her shoulder, which had taken the brunt of the impact. "I wasn't expecting your reaction to be to toss me from the bed."

Ashley held up the pink vibrator she'd retrieved from her bag. "I was actually planning on making you come until you begged me to stop." She turned on the vibrator for dramatic effect and watched Esther's eyes go wide. "Get back up there and lay down for me."

Esther scrambled to comply, and the power rush of that kind of obedience was Ashley's own kind of foreplay.

"You like doing what you're told?" Ashley asked.

Esther sat at the head of the bed, one knee up and her gaze flitting between Ashley and the thing in Ashley's hand. She blushed but nodded like a bobblehead.

Perfect. "Then undress for me." An idea was forming, but she needed Esther fully on board. "How would you feel about some light bondage?"

Esther paused with her underwear halfway down her knees. A pink blush worked its way from her chest up to her cheeks. "Fuck."

"We don't have to." Ashley hastened to amend. She didn't want to overstep. But a part of her craved to know how far Esther would let her go. "It was just an idea. No worries."

"That is—" Esther pinched her eyes shut. "Ashley, you're too sexy. I would love that, but I should warn you, I might finish fast."

"Are you sure? That is definitely not a problem." Ashley rushed to her bag, digging for her satin sashes. "I was planning on getting you off more than once anyway. I would love the confidence boost of a fast one." She pulled the sashes out and ran back to the bed. "Not that you need to hurry."

"Now what do I do?"

Esther sat against the headboard, fully naked. Her lanky limbs curled around her, and her dark hair fell loose over her shoulders. A shudder trickled down Ashley's spine.

Ashley took a moment to savor this image. She pushed Esther's hair to the side, running her lips down Esther's pale neck. Esther's breaths grew shallow. She tilted her chin as Ashley licked and sucked down her throat. She smelled so good. Ashley wanted all of her, just as she was, for as long as she had her.

"Lay down for me and grab the headboard. Yeah, just like that. Good girl." She fastened Esther's wrists to the wooden rails, checking to be sure they were tight enough to hold her without being uncomfortable. "Now, you're in charge of this, but don't worry. I'll tell you when to start." She pushed the remote into Esther's hand, resting her thumb against the control panel. "Up and down control speed. Left and right will switch up the pattern. Got it?"

Esther nodded again.

"Good. Did you want to give yourself a little speed?" She placed the vibrator on Esther's sternum, waiting until it started before working it over to circle one nipple and then the other. Esther took a stuttering gasp and her chest rose from the bed. Ashley worked the wand lower, circling Esther's navel then her inner thighs.

When Esther pulled at her binds, Ashley put a hand on her chest, gently pressing Esther to the bed.

"Shh, just relax." Ashley repositioned herself lower on the bed so her arm with the vibrator rested across Esther's stomach, restricting Esther's movement and giving Ashley a prime view of what she was working with. Her free hand snaked under Esther's thigh and up to slide through her luxurious wetness. Esther was squirming and pinching her mouth shut, holding back the full sound that Ashley was determined to draw from her. When Ashley's fingers were good and wet, she trailed one down the valley of Esther's ass, circling in time with the vibrator around her clit.

"Ashley, I-I'm so close."

"That's right, sweetheart. Let go." She kissed the dip at Esther's hip as Esther's moaning grew and her hips bucked and Ashley continued circling, drawing out Esther's climax.

"Ashley." Esther's voice was so soft and sweet, Ashley's heart melted just hearing her name.

"I'm right here, sweetheart." She shifted up the bed alongside Esther, her hand caressing Esther's cheek and petting down her side. Ashley was still in her pajamas, making Esther's nakedness an extra treat. "That was beautiful."

But Esther continued to fidget in the binds. Her eyes trailed down Ashley's body. "I want to taste you."

"Is that right?" She stood from the bed and pulled down her pajama shorts and underwear in one tug. Her long T-shirt fell to the top of her thighs. She crawled onto the bed and threw a leg over Esther's waist, making small circles with her hip and enjoying the heat of Esther's body against her most sensitive skin. God, she missed this warmth. "You're going to have to ask nicely to get this pussy."

"Please." Esther's words came out in a desperate whisper. "I want to taste you. I want you to come on my face."

Ashley didn't need any more persuading. She crawled up Esther's body until her knees were notched under Esther's arms. Before Ashley sat up into place, Esther opened her mouth, her tongue resting eagerly on her lower lip.

"Jesus, Esther." Ashley pulled off her T-shirt, flinging it across the room, and lowered her hips.

Esther lapped energetically at Ashley, who tilted her hips to give Esther just the right angle. Esther was licking and whimpering, and Ashley rode her face, and even though Esther was the one tied up, Ashley was the one losing control.

Ashley braced a hand against the wall as she pinched a nipple with her other, pulling and teasing herself. And the whole time, words spewed from her. "Yes, right there. You like how that tastes? Look at you begging me to ride my cunt on your face."

She rode her hips back and forth until her toes were curling. There was nothing in the world more important than Esther's warm tongue against her. Esther caught Ashley's clit between her lips and sucked, and that was it.

Ashley cried out as she came, her forehead pressed to the wall to hold herself up as she chanted "Don't stop, don't stop, don't stop." She collapsed at Esther's side, panting as she regained herself. "That was amazing."

Ashley found Esther's lips, kissing and demanding.

To kiss her deeply and taste herself on Esther's lips, on

her tongue, and know that she was there. That she had marked Esther in this intimate way.

"Ashley, I—" She paused and blinked as though confused by what she was about to say. "Could you untie me? My arms are starting to tingle."

"Sure, of course." Ashley hurried to loosen her bindings and turned Esther on her side, lining herself up against Esther's back and slotting one arm under Esther's neck and the other over Esther's waist so they lay skin to skin. "This was the perfect wake-up call, sweetheart. Thank you."

"'S no problem." Esther yawned and hugged Ashley's arm closer, but her breathing was deep and slow.

Esther's skin was so smooth and warm. Ashley couldn't get enough of the contact. One hand cupped Esther's breast while her other trailed down Esther's stomach. It felt so good to be warm again. To savor in Esther's body. Ashley wasn't quite done. Her middle finger slipped between Esther's thighs, moving easily through the slickness. Esther gave a small sigh and turned, leg opening for Ashley's hand. Ashley gave Esther's nipple an appreciative pinch, and Esther groaned, her eyes still closed as she neared sleep.

"That's right," whispered Ashley. Her finger dipped between Esther's folds, spreading her and moving around the wetness. "Relax. Let me take care of you."

With one hand, she pinched and circled Esther's nipple, holding her firmly to Ashley's chest. With the other, she sank one and then two fingers deep inside her, slowly pumping in and out, matching Esther's rhythm as she ground her ass into Ashley's crotch. Ashley waited, keeping up her small slow movements until Esther's mouth parted and her breath hitched. Ashley captured her whimpers with a kiss and pressed down with her thumb against Esther's clit, riding her through another orgasm, until her body finally relaxed boneless into the bed.

"Ashley, I..."

Ashley waited for Esther to finish. But her breath had slowed again, and nothing more came. She pulled the blankets over them and held Esther close, feeling alive for the first time in forever.

28

───────

Esther

A loud thud smacked Esther out of her sleep.

"What, huh?" She shifted, and a wet spot smeared under her cheek. Oh god, she was drooling.

"We're going out." August stood in front of them, tapping a flyer in the middle of the table and blocking the movie she was watching with Ashley.

Crap, she was using Ashley's thigh as a pillow. What were the chances Ashley hadn't noticed this wet spot?

"What's all this noise about?" Uther shuffled down the hall in his fluffy purple robe, rubbing at his eyes, his blond hair sleep-mussed.

"This is about you two." August sent accusatory fingers at both her and Uther.

"Me?" Uther squeaked. "I just got here."

Esther pushed into a seated position, stretching a kink out of her shoulder. "I think I missed something."

Ashley still hadn't said anything but reached past Esther for the flyer lying on the table.

"It's ten pm on a Thursday night, and you both are asleep." August's scolding was just warming up. It was too late in the day for this kind of energy. Although, she did feel bad about sleeping through the movie again.

Uther pulled his robe up tight, muffling his words. "You know the sun makes me sleepy."

Esther nodded along. It was an energy drain.

"We are still in our twenties." August wasn't having any of Uther's valid points. Now he had hand gestures to go with his rallying cry. "Our week of fun and forgetfulness is almost up, and what have we done? Gone to bed early so we can be up at a reasonable hour? Sleeping by the beach?"

"Well, this *is* a vacation..." Uther mumbled.

Esther nodded again, pointing at Uther to show her support.

"Love." August bundled up Uther in his arms, kissing him gently on the forehead. "You are so smart and so cute, but that's not the answer I'm looking for. Ashley?" He pointed to the couch, and Ashley looked around, as though unsure she was the Ashley he was talking to. "What is this?"

She looked down at the paper in her hand, and Esther watched in real-time as a spark lit and caught flame in her eyes. "This is spring break."

Oh no. What was on that piece of paper?

Ashley hopped up from the couch, full of energy. "We're on spring break!"

She tossed the paper in the air, letting it flutter back to the couch. Esther snatched it before it landed, reading quickly.

Carnival in the Moonlight, one night only, beachside.

"Help me rally the troops?" August was alight with

excitement, and for a moment, Esther thought the two of them might hug.

"We should do shots," Ashley cheered.

Esther rose and shuffled toward Uther while Ashley and August strode to the kitchen discussing rum shots.

"It only took a few months and locking them in a shack together," Esther said, "but I think they're finally getting along."

"Don't let them fool you," Uther whispered. "They text each other constantly. They're both just too stubborn to admit they've been friends for ages now."

"Esther," Ashley said. Esther turned to see Ashley with a shot in each hand. "Prepare yourself, sweetheart. We're going out."

Esther sighed and accepted the small cup Ashley handed her. For her and only her, she would take off her comfy pajamas and don her outdoor clothes again. "All right."

She clinked Ashley's glass and took the shot.

⌄　⌄　⌄

Esther

Pop, pop, pop. "Die, ducks!"

"Esther, I don't think I've ever seen you this bloodthirsty. It's a bit of a turn-on." Ashley's cool hand rested lightly on her lower back, but Esther's attention was on the row of carnival ducks merrily quacking across the stand in front of her. To her right, Uther lined up his shot.

"We've got a close race here, folks." The carnival worker

was eating up the attention they attracted. "One more round to find our winner."

"You've got this, sweetheart." Ashley kissed her cheek as the guy behind the booth stood to the side and counted down. "And I hear you mumbling over there, August! No cheating."

August pressed a hand to his chest. "I would never."

But Esther was no longer paying attention. The obnoxious carnival music, *the tick-tick-swish* of nearby roller coasters accompanied by a chorus of screams, and the salty sea breeze mixed with stale popcorn all faded as she lifted the small, plastic rifle to her shoulder and ground the ball of her foot into the hard-packed sand. A horn sounded, and the back of the stand clanked into motion as three rows of two-dimensional, wooden ducks crisscrossed in and out of view.

Pop! The first duck she lined up disappeared in a spatter of pink powder before she pulled her trigger.

"Keep up, Esther." Uther lined up another duck and fired.

The game only lasted a minute. *Pop, pop, pop!* Three ducks disappeared in a cloud of green. Esther had never held a gun in her life, and she wasn't even sure this counted. But the adrenaline coursing through her said not to stop shooting.

Another blast from the horn and the ducks stopped their journey.

"A close game folks, but we have a new record tonight. Congratulations to Player Pink!"

"Yes!" Uther jumped into August's arms.

"Damn it!" Esther threw her gun onto the counter. The clang of plastic hitting wood startled her out of her red haze of frustration. "Oh my god." She turned to Ashley, a terrible realization coming to her. "I'm a terrible sport."

"You're a bad loser." Ashley wrapped her arms around Esther's waist, a smile spreading across her face and warming the night. "I did not see this coming, but I love this about you."

Esther pressed her face into Ashley's shoulder, hiding her smile and the way her cheeks warmed when Ashley looked at her like that.

Tonight was what this week was supposed to be when Esther pictured a week away. The two of them out of the house, having fun. It was Ashley's limitless energy that had first drawn Esther, and tonight under the flashing lights and sounds of the carnival, Ashley was alive and glowing.

"All right, lucky winner." The booth keeper gestured to the wall of hanging stuffed animals. "What will it be?"

"The goat." Uther pointed to a floppy goat hanging from the ceiling, a flower fastened to its collar. The man pulled it down for him, and Uther hugged it close. "All right, what next?"

"I vote Gravitron." Ashley pointed to the nearby spinning-and-flashing spaceship. Screams filled the night from the hidden interior.

"Sure." Esther shrugged. "I haven't been on one in forever." She took Ashley's hand and started to the metal corral to join the line for the next group.

"Actually." August's voice stopped her, heels shifting in the sand as she turned back. "Uther was saying he wanted a churro." August's eyes flicked between the flashing ride and Esther, his throat working. "So, we'll...umm, we'll just meet you two afterward."

Uther tilted his head and squinted before August

elbowed him. "Oh! Yeah, I definitely need a churro. Right now."

He nodded firmly, threading his fingers through August's.

Esther recognized the way Uther's lips pinched at the corners to hide a smile. She shrugged. "More time with Ashley."

She grabbed Ashley's hand and dragged her to the corral, anxious to not miss the next ride.

"Did that feel fishy to you?" Ashley looked back to where August and Uther disappeared into the crowd. Yellow and red streaks flashed through Ashley's hair as the ride slowed, and Esther realized she couldn't care less if August was scared of roller coasters.

"Hey." She took Ashley's hand and wrapped it behind her, pulling Ashley close. "I don't think I've seen you in a crowd before. I'm kind of enjoying the novelty."

"Is that so?" Ashley's free hand slid behind Esther's neck, her thumb tracing Esther's jawline. "Are you a fan of PDA, Esther Green?"

Esther bit her lip. She couldn't recall being into public kissing, but at this moment, she wouldn't say no to whatever put that spark in Ashley's eye.

"All aboard! Step right up folks, tickets here. Come defy gravity in our Gravitron."

Esther fumbled in her pockets for her stash of tickets. Why did her shorts have to be so tight? Her fingers touched crumpled paper as Ashley stepped up to the doorway. Esther passed the ticket taker two wilty tickets and slipped inside after her.

Ashley had laid claim to two adjacent panels on the far side and was flagging her over.

"Ready?" Ashley took her hand.

Before she responded, techno music blasted from the speakers, and the ticket taker hopped into the center console, instructing them to take their positions because they were blasting off. Esther leaned against the hard pleather, meeting Ashley's eyes as the room started spinning. This evening, with the lights and the crowds and this ridiculous music, with the sticky sweet carnival smells and just being young with her friends, and now here in this tiny moment with Ashley. It all felt so horribly, beautifully normal in every way Esther could have possibly hoped for.

Esther gripped Ashley's hand as they picked up speed. Gravity pressed her body against the hard plastic cushion until her panel flew up to the ceiling, shaking loose a startled scream.

29

———

Ashley

Ashley's panel shot up a second after Esther's.

With Esther's freckles darkened by the sun, the lights from the ride shining in her eyes, and her teeth flashing in full-bodied laughter, Esther was a galaxy, and Ashley couldn't take her eyes off her. Fighting gravity, she slid her arm against the wall until their pinkies touched. Esther snatched her hand.

The force of emotion that one small action elicited was like a punch to the chest. This was what Ashley wanted, Esther's warm hand tight in hers, always. Her imagination wandered to them walking along the lakeshore, to museum trips and restaurants, and laughing as Esther tried to convince her she only needed one carry-on as they packed for far-off places, to finishing school and sharing a home, a life she was proud of, together. Ashley would give anything —her life again if she had it—for that dream. But it was just a dream. She would take whatever she was offered and make the most of what she had.

The ride slowed, and Ashley landed on shaky feet.

"Come with me." Esther took her hand and dragged Ashley off. Something about the possessive way Esther held on to her knocked butterflies loose in Ashley's gut. Like Esther was fully aware that Ashley's hand and the rest of her were all Esther's.

They left the fairground and tripped through the loose sand, her sandals sinking deeper as they moved farther inland to a nearby cropping of trees. Finally, in the shadows of the foliage, Esther pulled Ashley by the hips so she was flush against her. She looked up at Ashley through her lashes, her eyes dark and her gaze scouring Ashley's face working its way down her neck and chest.

"Was there something you wanted, sweetheart?" Ashley pushed a lock of hair behind Esther's earring-free ear, resting a hand against Esther's throat before tilting her head back and exposing her beautiful neck.

Esther swallowed, the movement mesmerizing beneath Ashley's fingertips.

"Yes." Her answer was a whisper in the ocean breeze.

That was all the direction Ashley needed. She never was one for teasing. In the next second, Ashley had Esther's thighs wrapped around her hips and her body pinned to the nearest tree as her hands explored Esther's waist, her ass, the annoying way that Esther tucked that thin white tank top into her shorts. She needed more skin to touch. She slotted her fingers along Esther's ribs and coasted upward. Exploring, she caressed the shape of Esther's breasts before pinching her nipple through her shirt, eliciting a gasp followed by a groan that made Ashley nearly lose her footing. Esther, for her part, seemed just as intent to do damage as she latched on to Ashley's neck, biting and licking like it was her personal mission to find out if vampires could get hickeys. Like this moment was sand in an hour glass and they would squeeze every last second out of it.

"You're so fucking hot, sweetheart." Ashley ground her hips into Esther's, eliciting a gasp before she clawed down Ashley's back. She loved when Esther went feral.

"I want you, Ashley."

Esther's lips took Ashley's before she could answer, leaving Ashley's mind spinning with lists and plans. What she would do to Esther, how much they could get away with before they required the privacy of the house, how long it would take for her to run them both back. She could be throwing Esther on their bed in seconds. Right, first she'd—

White-hot fire lanced through Ashley's calf, and she dropped to the ground, Esther falling on top of her. Her dark curls curtained their surroundings, and for a moment, all that existed was the confused look in Esther's eyes.

"Ashley, what—" Esther's startled scream ripped through the night as she was tugged from Ashley's body into the shadows.

"Esther!" Ashley screamed and tried to stand, but the pain in her calf brought her straight to the ground, her nails digging into the sand as she fought the pain.

Impaling her calf was a wooden bolt. This wasn't an accident.

Breathing deeply, she wrenched it free, the wood coming out dry. Finally, a convenient vampire trick. At least she didn't have to worry about bleeding out. But the dart had torn muscle, and there wasn't time to wait for it to heal. That could take all night, and she couldn't hear Esther anymore. Bracing herself against the tree, she used her arms and one good leg to hoist herself up.

"Esther!" Her cry sank into the hungry forest, trapping any hint of an echo or reply. "Est..."

Shifting in the foliage knocked loose a sob in her chest. Whatever had grabbed Esther had let her free. She wiped at the tear tracks on her cheeks.

One shadowed figure emerged from the shrubs followed by another.

Neither were Esther.

Two crossbows loaded and pointed directly at Ashley. "That's enough out of you, bloodsucker."

Magic oozed from them, clawing its way down Ashley's throat and making her gag.

Witches.

"This the stray you were talking about?" The first witch, a Latina woman who came to Ashley's chest, squared her crossbow to Ashley's heart.

Her companion, a gangly copper-haired woman with freckles so thick she looked tan, stepped into the moonlight and nodded. "That's the one. I can feel her new blood a mile away."

"Where's Esther?" Ashley needed to know Esther was safe. She took a step toward them, and her leg gave out beneath her. She fell to the sand, the pain making her fangs come out.

"You're not getting your food back, bloodsucker."

"Don't talk to her," the shorter woman scolded. "Let's just finish this up quick and get out of here. I wanted to actually enjoy the carnival."

"Fine." The redhead lifted her crossbow to Ashley's heart and shot without a moment's hesitation.

Despite her speed, her aching leg left her weighted to the spot. She could do nothing but watch as it shot straight for her heart.

The bolt ricocheted off nothing inches from her chest, sinking harmlessly into a nearby tree. The three of them stared in confusion. Was this some new vampire power she hadn't heard of before?

"Stop!" August came tripping up the sand from the direction of the carnival, the lights casting strange shadows across the dunes.

Ashley never thought she would be happy to see a witch in her life.

"Stop," he said again. "She has a Family."

Ashley stilled, his words not fitting together quite right. She had a family? A family was there for you when you were scared and alone, when you needed someone to talk to or laugh with. A family was people you counted on and trusted. Sure, she had her parents, but who was here to protect her now?

August climbed his way through the shrubs and stood between her and the witches, his hands raised like a human shield.

"She has a Family," he repeated, gasping for breath after his uncoordinated trek through the loose sand.

Shuffling came from the woods along with an "Ow!" and "Is that a knife?" from a voice Ashley didn't recognize. Then Esther tumbled out, her hair in knots and her switchblade out and ready. She was back and she was safe. Or as safe as they could be while confronting armed witches. Esther joined August in the human blockade.

One of the witches stepped forward, the one who'd shot the second dart which Ashley only now realized August had blocked. "We monitor vampire Families in this area, and no one recognizes her. Not to mention she's dangerously young. You can feel that, can't you?"

From this angle, Ashley could only see the back of August's head as he nodded, his words still coming out between gasps.

"We're traveling," he said. "Just here for the week."

"We?" The redhead looked from August to Esther, and finally Ashley as though trying to solve long division.

"Psst." Uther appeared nearby, tucking his prize goat into his back pocket. "Do you need help?"

He offered a hand to Ashley, and she took it, grinding her molars when she put weight on her bad leg. Between Uther and the tree, she was able to regain a standing position. He tucked himself under her arm, which was only mildly awkward as they were about the same height but did make standing much easier.

"I figured we should just start moving while they deal with this." He nodded back to August and Esther, who were still talking to the witches, their bodies a wall between them and Ashley. "We were just coming to find you. Good thing you and August have that magical sense-each-other-anywhere thing or we'd never have found you back here."

"Will they be all right?" She glanced back over her shoulder, searching the dark for Esther. The crossbows were out of sight, and no one was following them. All good signs.

"Are you kidding me? *They'll* be fine." The sand slowed their pace as they worked to keep from falling over each other. "Of course, neither of them were shot with a crossbow, so I'm not as concerned at the moment."

"Thanks, Uther. For coming and finding me and... Well, for everything." The pain in her leg was dulling to a light throb. She could probably let Uther go. She only pulled his bony shoulders closer, his body serving as an anchor as some unnamed wave thrashed against her shields.

"Sure, of course," he said. They reached the hard-packed sand of the fairground and stopped a moment to rest and wait on the other two. "What are friends for?"

30

Esther

The sun sparkled off the ocean, and Esther thought of how radiant Ashley was at the carnival last night.

What followed was a burglary.

A precious moment forever tainted by violence and fear.

She'd tried to get Ashley to talk about it that morning. Just a check-in to make sure she was okay. But how could she possibly be okay after something like that?

"It's just something that happens." Ashley had shrugged. Shrugged. Like a crossbow through her leg was the least of her worries. "It's not like I can do anything about it. This is my life. Even if I wanted to, I can't take it back."

If Esther was honest, a thought had rooted in her mind for months, slowly digging deeper. The way Ashley's energy doubled when she was in a crowd, her college acceptance letter and room of trophies, the way Ashley kept failing to join the Family because she couldn't help being human, the mix of terror and frustration on her face when the witches appeared, ready to hunt her like an animal.

Ashley regretted becoming a vampire.

The thought continued to pop up at the smallest provocation. Uther would tell a joke or she'd happen upon a pearlescent shell and she'd turn to Ashley, hungry for her reaction, her thoughts, only to remember Ashley wasn't there. Or when they were back at the beach house in the evening, winding down while watching a movie, and next thing she knew Ashley was helping her back to bed while the credits rolled and she couldn't recall what they'd been watching. It snuck in like a whisper, and what followed was a growing itch of a thought.

Ashley regrets becoming a vampire.

It remained a floating thought. A brief cloud drifting across the blue skies of her week, and when it passed, Esther nearly forgot the thought had happened until it popped up again.

"Did you hear another Plattsburgh tourist went missing?" Uther lay on a towel next to her, the two of them sharing the beach umbrella. While neither was a vampire, they were still too pale to handle direct sunlight.

She rotated her head to see his face. "I didn't. What do you mean *another*?"

He turned his head to her as well, his cheek resting on the sea foam-and-clam-spotted beach towel they'd found in the house because he forgot to pack one. "Just people reported missing. The only connection they've found is they were all last seen at the Plattsburgh City Beach."

"But it's March. What are people doing at the beach in March?"

"There was a recent and supposedly very credible Champ sighting, so all the cryptid hunters are coming out hoping to spot him." Uther adjusted his sunglasses, turning to face the underside of the umbrella.

Esther had only recently learned about the mythical sea creature, Champy, that lived in Lake Champlain from Uther—Plattsburgh's own Nessie. But if vampires were real, who was to say a freshwater dinosaur wasn't swimming around upstate New York?

"The rumor I've heard, so far, is that a couple poor swimmers underestimated the icy waters," Uther said. "I was planning on going to the beach when we get back and taking some photos for my photojournalism class. Maybe talk to some people. If there really are any people on the beach in March."

"Hey, Uther, Esther. Get in here," August called from the water.

Simultaneously, Esther and Uther sat up and lifted their shades as August rose from the ocean, water catching the light as it dripped from his sun-bronzed body. With both hands, he brushed his shoulder-length hair back from his face, his biceps flexing from the movement and the ocean sparkling around him.

"Holy Mary," whispered Esther. "This never gets old."

"This man is going to wreck me." Uther fanned himself with his hand.

August jogged up the beach to them, water glistening off his body. By the time he made it to their umbrella, both Esther and Uther were perspiring.

"Hey, love." He dropped onto Uther's towel, taking his chin and giving him a quick kiss.

In their two seconds of contact, Esther's mind raced to Ashley, wishing she was there on the beach with her.

Ashley regrets becoming a vampire.

Uther and August parted, and Esther shook her head, clearing the wayward thought.

"So, how's your lady love, Esther?" August's eyes creased at the corners, fighting off the sun. "Is she doing all right after..."

"She didn't say much this morning." Other than requesting Esther stop fussing over her and go to the beach. "Her leg looked better."

He grunted like he knew there was more to it. "Maybe I'll check in on her tonight and bother her while she packs. Lord knows I owe her a headache."

"Hey, what about me?" Uther pouted.

"I have other evening plans for you." August pressed his forehead to Uther's.

They stayed that way for several seconds, and Esther looked back at the ocean, uncomfortable in their private moment. Being the surprise third wheel on a romantic getaway was not always fun. The moment dragged until she decided she wouldn't be missed and got up and walked to the ocean.

It was still in the lower seventies. Too cold to be in the ocean. She didn't know how August could stand it. But Esther waded in to her knees, not willing to miss a chance to be in the water. The waves tugged her in farther, but she held her ground, letting the receding water erode the sand around her feet, sucking them into the ocean floor.

"I was hoping I'd get a chance to talk to you." August was back in the water.

She hadn't heard him over the crashing waves. She looked back at the shore to see Uther lounging, a book in hand and his hair slightly more ruffled than before. She looked back to the blue horizon. There was something entrancing about the ocean. The rhythmic give and take of the swells, the silent spark of the sun dancing on its surface. The way the breeze gently pulled at her hair, pushing the heat of the sun from her shoulders.

"I know she's asked you." August didn't have to elaborate. There was only one she and only one question. "And I know it's not my business..." He trailed off, as though expecting her to stop him.

The corner of Esther's mouth lifted at that. He was used to talking to Ashley. *Ashley regrets becoming a vampire.*

August continued. "Don't. Don't do it."

"What a shocking opinion coming from a witch."

"It's coming from a friend." August rested a hand on her shoulder, and she turned to look at him. Even his concerned face reminded her of Ashley. The way they both knit their brows and looked down at you in the sternest of ways. It was almost parental. A sure kind of concern. "If I had been there when she was asked, I would have said the same thing."

Ashley regrets becoming a vampire.

"But you weren't." Esther turned to face him fully, and his hand slid from her shoulder. "You weren't there, and I wasn't there. And now..."

Looking at him was a mistake. He was too focused when he was like this. Like this was the only conversation that mattered. She looked back to the horizon, doing her best to ignore the feel of his stare, and reached for her earlobe to caress a cross that wasn't there.

"I love her. And we both know what that means. Either I join her or it's over." Except that Ashley regretted becoming a vampire. Would she grow to regret Esther changing as well?

"What if there's another way?"

"I can't even begin to wade through the social stigma of what our relationship would look like if I continue to age and she doesn't, how that would leach into our daily lives. It'd erode our trust. Me, worried I'm not what she asked for, getting tired, and losing mobility. And her young as always and getting bored with the choice she made but feeling obligated to stay. If she didn't change her mind on her own, I'd end up pushing her away."

"And you think an eternity together is a better solution? Humans are lucky to manage a lifetime of love together. What are you going to do if fifty, a hundred, two hundred years down the line, one or both of you decide to call it quits? What then? You'll still be a vampire."

"It would be worth it." Esther scooped water into her hand, watching it spill through her fingers before she balled it into a fist. "She would be worth it."

"Esther."

"Look, I don't have an eternity of life goals. The plan was just to lie low and carry on, and then Ashley..." Esther trailed off, the words, her feelings, impossible to pin down.

"And then Ashley," August said with a huffed laugh. "I love her too, Esther."

Esther reached under the waves and took his hand. She knew he did, and Ashley in her way loved him too. It wasn't a romantic love, like the way Esther felt for her, but they had built a sort of family, the four of them, and it struck Esther how painful it would be to lose August and Uther.

The horizon wavered as her eyes watered. "I don't want to lose you. Either of you. Any of you. I just... I don't know what else to do."

"There's another option." He was animated now. Not in movement necessarily—he stayed in the same spot, and his hand still held hers—but there was an energy about him like every atom in his body was vibrating with the need to express this thought. "We could cure her."

"What?" Esther took her hand back and stepped away. She'd never seen a fire like this in August's eyes, and something about it scared her.

He continued, using his hands to shape his words and freeing small drops of water back to the ocean. "There's a cure. We could turn her human again."

"What are you talking about? What cure?" She was getting all of her vampire knowledge from pop culture, but there was one common denominator: Vampirism was permanent. Her body chose fear over hope—the safer of the two options.

"That page we got from the vampires," His words came in quick bursts, like a horse pulling at its tethers. "Do you remember? The missing page from the grimoire. It describes a potion that can reverse the effects of the vampire curse. It can return her to before. We just need one more ingredient."

"We? You mean the witches." Esther was backing away, but August continued to follow. He probably didn't even notice they were moving, he was so engrossed in the topic. "The witches that hate vampires. The witches that were looking for this book before you even knew Ashley."

But August wasn't listening to her.

"And you happen to have that final ingredient." His gaze dipped to the chain around her neck, and a hungry look she didn't recognize crossed his face.

Without thinking, she grabbed the charm, blocking it from his view. "It's a weapon, August. You have to see that. Those witches don't care about curing Ashley. They just want to be rid of vampires."

"And a cure would do that."

"No."

"Esther," he said. They were barely in the water, enough

to cover their feet. "Just think about it. Think about Ashley as a human, here on the beach with us." He opened his arms wide, taking in the sun and waves. "Think about growing old together. Never having to drink blood or lie about your age."

No. There had to be a catch to this. The offer sounded too good.

She couldn't trust those witches. But now that the words were out, she couldn't block the picture of Ashley splashing in the waves, her hair whipping in the wind, and her smile lighting up Esther's heart. She could be free.

"All we need is that vial of blood," he said, "and you two can live happily ever after."

"No." Esther shook her head and stepped fully out of the water.

August didn't follow her, but his shoulders slumped.

"I can't betray her like that. This vial is a symbol, and you want me to give it to people who actively hate her. I would never hurt her like that, and I can't believe you would ask me to."

"The choice is yours, Esther. But I think you've known for a while now that Ashley shouldn't be a vampire."

"Is that how you rationalize your friendship?" She stomped back into the water. "You can't like vampires; therefore, Ashley shouldn't be a vampire. Is that how this works? You love her *despite* what she is?"

"That's not what I mean."

They were both yelling, and an external part of Esther acknowledged that it was ridiculous to be in a shouting match with her friend over who loved Ashley the "right" way.

"Are you two all right?" Uther walked over with a look of concern.

They were loud enough to reach him up the beach. Or he had seen them fighting. Either way, Esther didn't want to make a scene.

"We're fine, Uther. Just a disagreement. I'm going to go back and check on Ashley. I'll see you two for dinner." She padded off to grab her towel and head back to the house.

"Esther," August called. "Just think about it."

She continued walking. Not responding or even giving him a parting glance, but the vision of Ashley laughing under a sunny sky was forever burned into her mind.

31

Esther

Esther refused to think about it.

Finals were a month away, then weeks, then days. She doubled down on her studies, spending every daylight hour, and most of the night, finishing her final report. She hated avoiding Ashley, but Ashley had her own finals to look to. If there was ever a time to buckle down and stay busy, it was now.

But she still couldn't escape the dreams. She stood in the shallows, but instead of August with her, it was Ashley laughing and splashing in the waves. As Esther drew near, the sun brightened, a burning blaze lapping at their skin, until they were both set aflame.

She woke up screaming and sweating.

Esther avoided sleeping over, not wanting to worry Ashley with her nightmares.

The day wasn't any better. Anytime she leaned over her desk for another paper, the vial beat at her chest like a drum, reminding her of the choice she was given. She started keeping it in her pocket, only taking it out when Ashley was around.

She didn't tell Ashley what August had said about the cure. She didn't need to. She knew what Ashley's answer would be—a firm and resounding no. There was no way Ashley trusted witches with a cure. Which was exactly the answer Esther was sticking to. But a part of her worried about keeping a secret from Ashley. That she would want to know, even if the knowledge of Esther considering the option might hurt her.

Needless to say, when Esther stepped out into the rain that afternoon, she was actively not thinking about that day at the beach.

She'd forgone an umbrella, opting instead for her black hooded raincoat. She was in the mood to feel the rain pounding against her hood. Water filled the gutters, streaming down the sides of the roads so she had to leap to cross the street, and still, her boots splashed on the landing. Her black jeans were soaked through by the time she made it to campus, and she was sure the lecture hall's air-conditioning would freeze her, but maybe the sensation would keep her mind from wandering.

She gave up navigating around puddles and was clomping through an especially irksome moat when she found a flowering purple crocus sprouting through the cracks on the brick path. Esther first considered how strange it was to see a crocus in May before considering that crocus were not weeds and someone had to purposefully plant it under the sidewalk for this flower to sprout here.

"Esther. How lovely to see you." The woman in front of her wore a bright yellow raincoat and white rain boots spattered with flowers. She smiled at Esther, as though they knew each other.

There was something familiar about her, but for the life of her, Esther couldn't place her.

It wasn't until the woman behind her joined in, that Esther recognized them as a set. The witches from the island on the lake.

"We're here for the necklace, Esther." Meg had on her usual Carhartt with the hood pulled up and a scowl across her face. As though Esther, through some unknown negligence, had inconvenienced Meg's day, and now she was in the middle of setting it right again as quickly as possible. "You've made your point. Now hand it over."

"Made my point?" The request was so out of nowhere, Esther could only parrot a response. They shouldn't even know about her necklace and what was inside.

"You have no people skills," sighed Gwen. "You're supposed to build up to the request."

"It's not a request," Meg said. "We've waited long enough. She may know that August is a pushover, but I'm not as patient."

The pounding rain on Esther's hood made it hard to make out what they were saying, but she was certain she'd heard August's name. Her eyes widened in understanding followed by a tightening in her chest as she pieced the information together. August had told them about Ashley's blood.

"I need to get to class." She changed course to walk around them, but Meg shifted to block her path. So much for the easy route. "I already told August you can't have it."

"I know," replied Meg. "And I'm not August. We need that blood before the situation gets worse."

"Get your own blood." Esther shoved past Meg, and this time, Meg let her pass.

"Esther." Gwen jogged to keep up. Esther tugged her

hood tighter over her head. She reached her building and pulled the door open. "The vampires are taking people."

Esther froze in the doorway. The eaves blocked the rain from them, but there was still the enveloping sound of rain. Esther wished it would wash Gwen's words away. The disappearing people. Uther had noticed months ago, but that didn't mean it had to do with the vampires.

"You're just speculating," Esther said.

"They've been doing it for years," said Gwen. "It used to be just one missing person a year, but the numbers are growing. They've gotten greedy. That's why we were trying to find the spell. We knew the Platt grimoire had to have an answer, and it did. It doesn't even kill them. It just reverses the effects of the vampire curse. We've collected everything to make it except the vampire blood, which you have on you right now."

"Why can't you get your own blood?"

"We've tried. It's rather difficult." Gwen kicked her rain boot at the sidewalk. "They don't bleed. Not unless they're bitten by a vampire. Something to do with their venom. So, you can only get it from a cooperative donor, and vampires don't usually cooperate with witches."

Esther touched the swell in her pocket where the charm rested, seeking comfort in the knowledge that it was still safe. "I can't give it to you."

"More people will be taken, Esther. You could save so many with one simple act." A trail of water slipped down Gwen's cheek, and Esther couldn't tell if it was rain.

There was no proof. That this spell would work, that Ashley and the other vampires would be safe, that the vampires were even involved in the missing people. And even if the vampires were responsible, she didn't want to be involved in their deaths. She had a choice before her with no clear correct answer.

"I have to get to class." Esther closed the door on the witch's face, but not before her words slipped through the crack.

"Make the right choice, Esther."

But what was the right choice? Not even the freezing blast from the air-conditioning on her wet clothes could distract her from this new fuel. She could talk to Uther, see if he knew anything more about the missing people. He'd followed leads for weeks. Surely, if there was a connection he would have a lead by now. She'd call him after class.

She took notes robotically, but it was a review class, and reviewing best practices on ingesting data and the pros and cons of different digital storage options was not keeping her gaze from flicking to the clock every couple of minutes. She started packing her bag five minutes before the bell.

"Esther." A voice hissed in her ear.

Esther barely had time to grab her bag before August was dragging her out of the room.

"August, what's going on?" She couldn't see his face while he navigated them back into the rain and under a window eave, but she felt the panic in his motions. What had happened in the time she was in class? "Is it Ashley? Is she okay?"

Esther regretted not calling Ashley that morning. She used to be so diligent, calling Ashley each night before she went to sleep, but with Esther's fear of sounding suspicious, she'd fallen out of the habit. If something happened to Ashley, Esther would never forgive herself. Or August, for that matter, for involving the witches to begin with.

August finally turned to her but didn't meet her eye as he raked his hands through his hair. "Uther's missing."

"What do you mean?" A million questions raced through Esther's mind, each less helpful than the one before it. "Did you try calling him?"

"Of course I called him. I've been calling him for hours, and he hasn't picked up."

"He probably let his phone die again."

It wouldn't be the first time, but the way August was pacing made her think there was more to the story.

"He went to the damn beach again. I told him it was getting risky, his questions were drawing attention, but he wouldn't listen to me. He was supposed to be back hours ago."

"Hey, listen. We'll go to the beach. We'll retrace his steps." She tried to speak calmly, but August's pacing was getting to her. "He's fine. We'll find him, okay?"

"Okay. Okay, okay." He was nodding, taking in what she'd said. He still wasn't himself, but he didn't seem as hopeless.

"I'll get us a car." She pulled out her phone to order a rideshare and sent an update to Ashley. The clouds were thick, but the sun was still up there somewhere, so she doubted Ashley could help for another hour or more.

Still, this conversation only made Esther realize how much she missed her. She'd see Ashley tonight and explain everything. The witches, the cure, everything. Keeping the secret was keeping them apart, as much as she tried to compartmentalize. She wasn't going to lose Ashley because she couldn't communicate properly.

August's anxious demeanor had turned darker, but he was determined to continue with the search. "If they touch him, I'll kill them. I'll kill every last vampire."

32

Ashley

A ping woke Ashley from her sleep. It was a text from Esther, and she couldn't help the excited smile when she read the name.

They hadn't spoken that day, and Ashley missed her. In fact, since their beach trip, she'd seen less and less of Esther. It was probably the approaching finals. Graduate students had quite a workload. She recalled Esther's call for help in the library at the start of the semester. But there was a part of Ashley that worried there might be more keeping Esther away. Maybe the vial was too big a gesture too soon. What if Esther had made her decision and was avoiding telling her? Ashley was wary when she opened the text.

> **ESTHER**
>
> Uther is missing. I'm going with August to the city beach to look for him. Meet us if you can?

That question mark nearly killed her. Of course she'd

meet them. She checked the clock. Sunset was still an hour away, but it was cloudy and she could layer up. She'd make it work.

"Hey, Cynthia?" Ashley called down the hall. "Have you seen my trench coat?"

No answer. She might still be sleeping, but Ashley guessed she more likely had her music on too loud. Sure enough, as she trotted down the hall, the drums and dirty guitar of Joan Jett blasted from behind Cynthia's door.

"Cynthia." Ashley knocked harder.

The door flew open. "What's up?"

"Have you seen my trench coat?"

"Sure thing. Just give me a second." Cynthia disappeared into her room, leaving the door open for Ashley to linger in. It was annoying that Cynthia borrowed her stuff without asking, but she was so close to getting into the Family. She could have a talk with her in a week when the school year was over and she was officially a member.

A light flashed on Cynthia's nightstand, drawing Ashley's attention. It was a text message, and obviously, Ashley wouldn't have read it—except the name of the person texting popped up on the screen, and Ashley did a double-take.

"Hey, Cynthia. You've got a text." She swallowed. "Who's Konstantine?"

Cynthia continued to dig through her closet. "Oh, that's some chick that was here a couple of years back. She was in and out for a while and finally decided to try nomad life. Maybe the year before you came back, actually."

"Do you have a picture?" It couldn't be her. But a vampire with the name Konstantine. And spelled like that. No, it was impossible. Konstantine was dead. "I think I might know her."

"Got it!" Cynthia pulled out a long, tan trench coat that Ashley had forgotten was her purpose for being there. "Here you go. And one more second." She threw Ashley the coat and swiped through her phone. "Here."

She passed Ashley the phone, not sure what she wanted to see. But there on the screen, in some bar with their arms wrapped around each other's shoulders, were Cynthia and Konstantine. From her long, black curls and signature smokey eye to the black vintage Pink Floyd T-shirt Ashley had helped her style years ago, there was no mistaking her. Ashley felt an extra sting when she noted Cynthia was wearing her Farrah Fawcett costume from Halloween in the picture.

"H-how?" Ashley coughed, clearing her throat. "How did she end up here?"

Cynthia chuckled, taking her phone back and thankfully not noticing Ashley's distressed state. "She had some crazy story about ditching this clingy ex. She supposedly paid off a witch. Could you imagine? How crappy was that ex? But it worked out because we only had room for one more person at the time, what with Gus not taking up much space anymore."

Pieces fit together lightning fast. The overwhelming residue of magic at their apartment with no sign of a struggle or body, the business card in Konstantine's stuff that led her to this house. It was all just a ruse to leave her. And a sloppy one at that.

But it had worked.

For twelve years, Ashley had fallen for it. She'd given up her life, and Konstantine couldn't even tell her to her face that she was done.

"So, do you know her?" Cynthia's question drew Ashley's attention back.

"No." She put the coat on and backed out of the door. "No, I don't know her."

She raced down the stairs, needing to get away from the knowledge that someone she cared about had left her. Konstantine. They were supposed to be in love forever. That was the entire point of changing, and Ashley's death and rebirth had meant nothing to her.

"It's still too bright to go out." John sat in the front sitting room with a book in his lap.

Ashley didn't have time for this. She was spiraling and needed to compartmentalize. Her friends needed her. Her friends that loved her. "I've got layers, and the sun's nearly down. I'll be fine."

"There's no reason to be rushing out at this hour. You may sit and wait." He gestured at an open chair, but Ashley couldn't wait.

"One of my friends is missing." She cinched her coat, checking for openings. "I'm going to go help look for him."

"Friends? Not another human." The way he drew out the U in human had her cringing. "Or is it that witch you've been seen with?"

Instinctively, Ashley wanted to defend her friends. To speak of their quality, but she knew, despite his puritan upbringing, moral appeals wouldn't reach John.

"They're good people. In fact, Esther is talking about becoming a vampire as well." She blushed, knowing how intimate transforming a human was and the significance of the gesture.

John scoffed. "Pray tell. How does she expect to accomplish this?"

Ashley took a deep breath. She'd meant to wait until Hannah was there to have this discussion, but Esther was a sure thing. "I offered to change her." Her cheeks heated, excitement coursing through her veins, as she finally said the words aloud. "I plan on being with her forever."

John stood, setting his book down on the seat he vacated and drifting toward her. "You told a human about us and offered to make her a vampire? Without consulting us first, the Family you hope to be a part of?"

"Well, I figured it wasn't really your business," said Ashley. "It's something personal, and we don't really have that share-personal-things kind of relationship."

John closed his eyes and sighed the sigh of fathomless weariness. "An initiate creating another vampire in the town where we strive to keep our presence relatively unnoticed is most certainly *my business,* as you say."

"Oh." Ashley wasn't sure what else to say. She hadn't considered the issue from this angle.

"And so, to clarify any misgivings, you will not be transforming your human companion. No matter how *familiar* the two of you have become. Furthermore, you should be made aware that your acquaintance with such unsavory characters has been noticed and is not seen in a favorable light. You would do well to remember your precarious state in this household and the image you are meant to portray if you hope to become a member."

"Do you have a problem with my friends?"

"You are meant to be *breaking* your human ties, not creating new ones."

"Why did you send me to school if I'm not supposed to talk to anyone?"

"That was precisely the point. The objective of this exercise was to demonstrate your ability to engage with humans without drawing attention. To live amongst while maintaining your life apart."

She didn't have time for this. While they discussed her

failures as a vampire, her friends were waiting for her. Esther's question mark of doubt continued to haunt her. "I need to go. I can talk later when I get back."

"Leave now, and there will be no need for you to return."

"Is that a threat? You're kicking me out?"

"That's up to you. But know that if you leave now, there will be repercussions, should you return." His hand curled like claws around the banister.

Ashley paused with her hand on the doorknob, reeling at another person so casually throwing her away.

And now she had to choose.

Everything she'd worked toward for years—everything she was so close to having—or the people who had grown closest to her. The people who had stood up for her and shown they cared.

"Fine." She opened the door and left.

Ashley was still a hopeless romantic after all.

33

Esther

Esther stepped from the rideshare directly into a puddle and scanned the beach parking lot. A soft mist shaped the gentle waves of her hair into serpentine ringlets, but at least she didn't need her hood anymore. Only one eyesore, Uther's electric-blue Nissan LEAF, occupied the lot, but Uther himself was nowhere to be seen.

"Maybe his battery died," Esther suggested as August waved the driver off. "Or he ran out of gas and called a ride home."

"How could he call a ride if his phone's dead?" His soaked hair was starting to dry, curling the small hairs by his ears. He shook his head disapprovingly at the lone car. "There're too many coincidences for my liking."

"Well, what do you want to do?"

The plan was to ask people at the beach if they'd seen anyone matching Uther's description, but with no one to ask, that plan flew out the window. The rain had done its job of clearing out any beachgoers.

"Let's split up and search the beach." August shoved past her before she anticipated his move. "You take the right. I'll go left. Meet back in the middle in ten minutes or if you find something."

Esther jogged to catch up. "It sounds a little Scooby and the gang, but I guess that'll work."

They reached the sand, and despite the chill, the clouds, and the foreboding tone a missing friend made of the evening, Esther couldn't help recalling the last time she was on a sunny beach with August, given an impossible choice that still haunted her. She cared about August, but some tension in her shoulders loosened when they parted ways.

She wasn't sure what she was looking for. Tracks? Dropped clues? Neither of them were trackers. She hadn't even been a Girl Scout. And was she supposed to turn around in ten minutes or be back at the middle in ten minutes? She couldn't recall. It would take more than ten minutes to search all of the beach.

Continuing south, woods blocked her view of the parking lot. With the lake on one side and trees on the other, she imagined she was the only one for miles. Despite the clouds and a crisp breeze, Esther was lulled into a calm tranquility by the chittering of birds and crickets and the shushing waves across the shore. Her boots sank in the sand, making her calves burn by the time she came to a path of creeping vines. They crawled a path from the tree line into the lake.

As she approached, tiny white buds bloomed, unfurling in a wave that drew her eye to the forest. She may not be a tracker, but she got the message. Following the green trail, she let it lead her to the woods as Meg and Gwen emerged from the shadows.

"Were the theatrics necessary?" Stress sapped her energy. She crossed her arms, gazing up the small sandbank to the tree line. "You could have just come out and spoken to us."

"We can help you get your friend back." At least Meg remained blunt. "But first, give us the vial."

Something wasn't right, but Esther was having a hard time piecing it together. Did they know where Uther was? Was he actually in danger? Taken? Hurt? Who had him? Everything was processing slowly, her mind shutting down under pressure. She wished Ashley was here. Her calming presence and steadfast confidence were exactly what Esther needed.

The soft grind of steps in sand alerted her someone had found them.

"What's going on?" August asked.

It wasn't Uther or Ashley, but Esther still took comfort in having someone she trusted there at her side. Even if that someone was an emotionally compromised August.

"They know where Uther is." Her hand sought his, but he didn't notice, stepping past and engaging in a silent war of wills with Meg. Esther crossed her arms, shielding herself from another brisk breeze that rattled the leaves overhead.

"She wants the vial," he said. His gaze remained on Meg, which meant he didn't notice when Esther rolled her eyes.

"I know what she wants," Esther snapped. August was officially useless. "And I want Uther back."

He turned back to her, and that fire she first noticed the last time they were on a beach was back. "Well, it looks like that's only happening if you give her the vial."

"So, this is a ransom."

"No, it's the key to a problem." He took her hand. "Why are you fighting this? You know Ashley would be better as a human."

Esther pulled her hand back. "Ashley is fine as she is."

"Come on, Esther. She's a walking parasite. You want to be like that?" He pointed to the sun, finally released from the day's cloud cover and painting the sky streaks of red as it burned its way into the lake. "She can't even be here to help you find your best friend. My boyfriend." His voice broke at the last syllable, his eyes tearing up, but he kept going. "Why? Because she can't be in the sun without bursting into flames."

He was hurt and scared. Esther knew this, but she was scared too. And there was nothing to guarantee this spell worked.

"She's not getting older," he continued. "You'll never grow old together. She can't offer you a life, only an eternity to eventually get it wrong."

"What makes you think we would get it wrong?" She meant the words to come out stronger than they did.

"Look at you." And he did, his gaze almost cruel. "You're offered one choice, and you clam up in your little shell and hide from the world. Did you even tell her about the cure?"

Water dripped on her cheek, and to her utter horror, Esther remembered it wasn't raining anymore. "I didn't... She wouldn't—"

Words were failing her. Or maybe the words were fine, and it was Esther that was failing. August was right. One small pressure and she'd crumbled beneath it, and now she was taking Ashley, Uther, and who knew how many more innocent people down with her.

In a softer voice, he spoke so just Esther heard. "If you won't do it for the two of you, do it for Ashley. You heard about her first two tries to join the vampires. They're not going to let her in. And she's not going to last long on her own. Remember the night carnival? That will be her every day. Give them the vial, Esther, and she'll never have to go through that again." August's shoulders dropped, and the hard edges of his words softened. "We won't force the cure on her. I promise. If you still want to be a vampire with Ashley, she can get you more blood. But this is the only way to beat that house of vampires and get Uther back."

"Just"—she shoved him back a step. He was too close—"be quiet for a minute. I need to think."

Esther pulled the vial from her pocket and held it in her fist. The metal casing was warm from being so close to her all day. She took a couple of deep breaths and closed her eyes, clearing her mind of August and Uther and the witches and any ticking clocks to look at this problem properly.

She had a choice to make. The way she saw it, she could hand over the vial or empty it into the sand right now so they'd never have it.

Ashley regretted becoming a vampire, and Esther had a growing fear she'd regret Esther changing as well. This was a chance, no matter how small and messy and dangerous. It was one small chance at a happily ever after they both could live with. But it meant making a choice, and historically her choices never turned out the way she'd hoped. She clenched the necklace in her hand, a piece of Ashley, and thought of the night Ashley had told her to be brave and make suggestions—that Ashley was indestructible and not afraid. She saw a vision of Ashley standing in the waves, smiling eyes closed as she faced the sun and thought of how good it would be to stand in the surf, holding her hand.

And she had her answer.

Opening her eyes, she dropped the necklace into August's offered hand. In one swift motion, August tossed the necklace to Meg. Then Meg was gone, vanished into thin air.

34

———

Ashley

Konstantine was alive. And Ashley was banished from the vampire family forever. She was lucky she'd gotten out of there alive. She'd put these feelings in boxes, but now that she was out and moving, they pushed at their walls fighting to break free. So, Ashley let them out, just a little. Enough to channel her anger into more speed.

So, Konstantine had faked her death instead of talking to her.

So, John wanted to kick her out of the Family.

Fine. She didn't need them. She'd found her own family. Maybe they didn't have the access to blood banks and forged government documents that the vampires had, but she could figure that out. They would figure it out together. Because no matter what, her friends would stick up for her. Esther, August, Uther. They were a unit, and together they were untouchable.

Ashley ran, sticking to the shade of buildings and

wooded areas whenever possible. Her layers were working, but her face still felt overheated. She slowed when she heard voices in the woods near the beach. Better to be spotted as a lost hiker than someone running at super-human speeds. She recognized the voices as she grew nearer and corrected toward the sound. The tingling in her throat whenever magic was nearby was stronger than usual.

Something had August heated to be this loud. Uther was still missing. He was bound to be tightly strung. Ashley would be. She could almost see them through the trees now. But with the sun breaking from its cloud cover, she couldn't risk the last few steps.

"Come on, Esther," August was saying. "She's a walking parasite. You want to be like that?"

Ashley froze. Her mind was static as August viciously listed every fault Ashley had, and Esther said nothing to contradict him. Because there was no contradicting him. She couldn't go out in the daylight. The sunset on the other side of these trees was keeping her from joining them. She had to drink blood to survive. She could never offer Esther a life together because technically she was not alive. She'd given that away to someone who couldn't care less about the gesture. She'd been reckless with her future, and now she had nothing to offer.

"Did you even tell her about the cure?"

The cure to what? Was Esther keeping something from her? Ashley was back in motion, moving for the tree line and the sound of voices, heedless of the setting sun. She broke through the foliage in time to see a glint of silver flying from August and Esther—a burning glint of sunlight catching it as it sailed—and land in the hands of a woman in a beige Carhartt jacket. The woman turned to Ashley before flashing out of sight.

A witch.

A witch had her blood, and there was no way Ashley could get it back or know what she would do with it.

Another piece of her that she'd entrusted to someone she loved—tossed away like it was nothing. Pure rage coursed through her body as the heat of the sun disappeared beyond the horizon, her welting skin cooling with the darkening sky. There was only one witch left on the beach, and he happened to be the one who'd thrown the necklace.

In the next second, Ashley had her hand around August's throat as she pushed his head under the water. He didn't even deserve deep water to drown in. Let him die in the shallows.

She'd trusted him. She'd loved him like family. She'd given up everything, and now her blood was in the hands of witches. She pushed harder until bubbles came up from the water. Fleetingly, she noticed someone pulling at her arm.

"Ashley, you'll drown him!"

That was exactly the idea. Why didn't he break one of her limbs like before? She heard his heart still beating, but he continued to not fight back. Why wouldn't he fight her?

"Ashley, stop!" Esther called. "Stop, it's my fault. I gave them the charm. Let him go."

But she couldn't fight Esther. And that was the whole point, wasn't it? The water blurred out of focus as Ashley's eyes watered, and her grip loosened. August shot up, turned on all fours, and began puking up water. He wasn't fighting back because he knew she needed a fight and he was the only one that could take it. Esther went to check on August, and that was the last Ashley saw before she laid back under the water, letting the waves block out the sounds of encroaching twilight and the sight of the two people closest to her who had just crushed her dead heart.

She had no one now. No vampire Family, no friends, no love. She was alone. Again. Abandoned by the people closest to her and doomed to walk the world alone for all eternity. How melodramatic. She considered staying here, letting the lack of oxygen put her in a form of hibernation. But they would drag her out eventually and hurt her all over again.

Or worse. They would leave her alone.

That left her with one option. She needed to sever all ties.

She rose from the water. Esther and August had made it to shore, Esther rubbing August's back as he continued to rasp in air. They both looked up as she approached.

"In case it wasn't clear," she said, directing the words to Esther. She wasn't sure if it was lake water or tears streaming down her face, but it didn't matter. She had to get this out. "We're through. I knew I couldn't trust a witch." She directed this at August. "But I guess I can't trust humans either. Thank you for reminding me why I'm better off alone."

With the last of her dignity, she walked past them and into the woods. She didn't think they could hurt her more than they already had, but the silence as she walked away sliced her in two.

Ashley

Ashley was in the woods now. Literally.

She'd stormed off, before remembering she had nowhere to go. Her tie to the vampires was burned to the ground. The love of her life and her closest friend had betrayed her and ridiculed her in the most personal way. She was exactly where she was all those years ago when she decided to follow that business card to the Family in Plattsburgh. Because her girlfriend at the time had thought staging her death was an appropriate way to break off a relationship.

So why did this time hurt so much more? She really wasn't cut out for being a vampire. Not for the first time, Ashley cursed herself for making that decision so long ago. She was such an idiot. She'd tried so hard to measure up to expectations that never fit and continuously stumbled to maintain the bare minimum of a grasp on her life. She was sick and tired of striving for benchmarks that didn't fit her.

Ashley walked deeper into the woods until there were only trees and underbrush before dropping to the ground and laying in the dirt. Overhead, specks of stars glinted between the branches, no longer dimmed by the town's light. An owl hooted somewhere farther in the trees, and a single bat fluttered haphazardly through the open branches.

What was she going to do now?

As if to answer her query, a high-pitched hamster cut through the quiet night with his nonsensical singing.

A laugh bubbled up inside her. This was quite possibly the worst song for this moment. Ashley remembered listening to it with her mom when it first came out so many years ago and the two of them laughing and dancing to the silly tune. Her mom had promised it was impossible to be sad while listening to it. So maybe it was the perfect song for this moment. Ashley may be alone, but there was still one person in the world that wanted to talk to her.

"Mom?" Ashley held the phone to her ear, trying to keep her voice from wavering.

"Hey, honey, what's wrong?"

Of course, her mom saw right through her. "I think I messed up."

A clink came through, probably her mom setting down her coffee mug. "Tell me everything and start from the beginning."

So, she did. Well, not everything. But she told her the important stuff. About how her mom's disregarding comments about Ashley's sexuality made her feel invalidated and forgotten, about convincing Esther to come home with her and pretending to be her girlfriend, and about falling for Esther for real in the end. She talked about August and how annoying and fiercely loyal he was, about Uther and his endless compassion and humor, about her roommates—roommates, not vampires, because her mom didn't need to know that detail—and how she never quite fit in with their long-established group.

Ashley told her mom about the breakup, about hearing her friends saying the worst things about her before giving up a token that was supposed to mean their future together.

"And now I'm alone." Ashley wiped a sleeve across her face because, if she couldn't cry on the phone with her mom, who could she cry on the phone with? "And I don't know where to go or how to move forward from this."

"Ashley, honey." Her mom took a minute before answering. "I want to apologize for my part in that. I was just joking, but I see now that my jokes were more harmful than funny. I didn't mean to hurt your feelings or make you feel forgotten. I couldn't forget you, sweetie. I love every last bit of you. You don't need to prove anything. Tell you what, what if we both met up in Europe somewhere and had a girls' weekend. My treat."

Right. Ashley still hadn't mentioned the not-actually-in-Romania thing. But that seemed less pressing when the sun would come up in only a handful of hours and she still wasn't any closer to a plan.

"That sounds like fun," Ashley said. "But I'm trying to figure out what to do next first. I've burned all my bridges, so to speak."

"Oh, honey. This is what you thrive under."

"I don't think I've ever been in this situation before, Mom. So, I'm not sure what you're talking about."

"Ashybear. You're the most organized and focused person I know. I have no idea where you got it either. Lord knows your father is a scatterbrain, and I'm always trying to juggle a million things at once. Just get that notebook of yours and make a plan."

A list. Of course, a list was the answer. A plan would guide her back on course.

She just needed a place where she could safely start it. "But where will I go? My roommates kicked me out."

"It sounded to me like just the one did. What if you talked to one of your other roommates? Even if it's only temporary, I don't doubt you'll get back on your feet in no time. There's no way I would have been okay with you halfway around the world if I didn't trust your survival skills, honey. You'll make it through this."

She'd make it through this. "All right, I'll come up with a plan. Thanks, Mom."

"No problem. Call me when you're all settled again, and we'll discuss a girls' weekend."

"Sure thing, Mom. Oh! What were you calling about before I took over the conversation?"

"Just calling to catch up. It's good to hear from you, dear."

They exchanged a few more platitudes because she couldn't just hang up on her mom, then Ashley started walking. She had a quarter battery on her phone, the clothes on her back, her favorite notepad, and most importantly, a heading.

She pulled out her phone and scrolled to one of the few numbers in her contacts.

ASHLEY

Hey. I need your help

35

———————

Esther

Esther was stunned silent by how quickly and drastically her decision had turned for the worst.

Thank you for reminding me why I'm better off alone.

Esther had done that.

She could say she was confused and pressured, but at the end of the day, she'd been sure this was the right choice. That giving the witches the necklace solved all of her problems and Ashley's as well.

And now she had nothing to show for it.

"Let's go." August had caught his breath and was pulling himself from the water. "We can catch up to Meg and Gwen at their place and start work on the potion. It should only be a couple of days to finish, but more hands will make it go faster."

Esther felt a burning sensation in her stomach that she was unused to.

Rage.

She wished she had Ashley's strength and speed or August's magic. She wanted to destroy something. To mark the occasion in an irreversible way. She let out a scream that started at her toes and threw it out across the water reaching as far as her human strength let her.

When she was finally out of breath, she sank into the water, the weight of her wet clothes and full boots anchoring her to the ground. The small waves from the lake lapped at her fingers, her arms, but she wasn't moving from this spot.

"I'm not going to help you," she said.

"They still have Uther. If we don't finish this potion, all of that was for nothing."

Esther bit the words out between her teeth. "I'm not going."

"Esther." Whatever his comment was going to be, it was interrupted by a ringing in his pocket. He pulled out his phone, shook off what water he could, and answered it. "What?"

His entire body shifted when whoever was on the other end spoke. He turned from her to face the trees. Esther only heard one side of the conversation, but it was clear who was on the other side.

"You're all right? Jesus, love. I've been worried sick over you. Well, yeah, we just found your car abandoned here. What was I supposed to think? You *walked*? That's... How many miles is that? Where was your phone? All right, stay there. I'll be over soon."

"How's Uther?" asked Esther.

Because of course, after all of this, Uther was fine.

She gazed out at the lake. The sun had set, and the moon cast a streak of glittering white across the black water. "Are the vampires treating him well?"

"So," August said, "I might have overreacted."

It wasn't an apology. She didn't know how they'd fix this, but she knew she needed to be alone.

"Just go," she said.

The sound of insects threatened to drown out her words, but she was confident August understood her. There was splashing, then she was being lifted, warm hands under her legs and back and her head cradled against a strong shoulder.

She punched said shoulder but was too tired to put up a good fight. "I'm not going to the witches."

"I know," he said. "But I'm not leaving you out here to catch a cold. Uther's back at my place. You can dry off and take one of the guest rooms."

He carried her to the parking lot before setting her down to call a car. They were waiting in silence when August walked over to Uther's car and pulled something dangling from the front hood. A dead vine.

"Damn it, Gwen." He crushed it in his fist and growled before stomping back. "Esther, I–" His fist with the vine shook, but she wasn't going to comfort him. "For what it's worth, I'm sorry I involved them without your notice. I was just..."

Esther shook her head. "I'm not ready for this conversation."

"Right." He met her gaze a second longer before turning back to the car.

They returned to August's place, and she went through the motions of showering, borrowing a large shirt to sleep in, and crawling into bed. A few minutes later, the door creaked open, and someone crawled in with her.

"Hey there, friend," whispered Uther. "I heard you came to my rescue."

Despite all her anger from earlier, it all washed away hearing her friend's voice. She wrapped her arms around him, letting him be her little spoon. "I love you, Uther."

"I know."

She held him tighter, trying to hold in the tears. "That tough guy Star Wars nonsense will not be accepted here."

"I know," he repeated then chuckled. He took her hand in his and kissed a knuckle. "I love you too, Esther. I'm sorry you're hurting."

She snuggled into his neck, and they lay in silence for a while.

"I shouldn't have given up the necklace," she said. "This is all my fault."

"It didn't help that my car and phone both died at the same time. I swear I charged it. It just died out of nowhere. August says it wasn't my fault, so I'm going to have to get that in writing when he's not as huffy. The whole thing really did a number on him."

"Yeah, I saw that."

"I think he has a crush on me."

"Oh, you think?"

They both laughed, but there wasn't any real heart to it.

"If it counts for anything," Uther said, "I think you made the best choice with the information you had."

Esther didn't believe that for one minute, but it was nice to know at least one person wasn't disappointed in her. "Where's your boyfriend now anyway?"

Uther shifted and pulled the blanket over his mouth before answering. His words were mumbled but clear enough to understand. "On his way to the island."

"He's still going through with it." It wasn't a question.

"After what you two gave up? Yeah, he's going to see this through."

"They told us the vampires had you. They took advantage of that missing person situation you were looking into to scare us into acting. What makes him think they wouldn't trick him again?"

"Because it'd all be for nothing if we didn't try. And if he's there, he'll make sure they do it right. That it's safe. He wouldn't do anything to hurt Ashley."

"We already did." Esther swallowed back a sob as she recalled Ashley's closed-off expression, standing over her in the water. "I'm not letting my choices hurt anyone again. I'll buckle down and mind my own business like I should have from the start."

"Doing nothing is still a choice."

36

Esther

Esther hit send, her computer made a swishing sound, and that was that. Her final project was turned in. Provided everything was there and looked good, she would receive her Master's in Library and Information Science come graduation.

Sitting back in that creaky chair, she let the moment sink in. Physically, she was relieved. If she could melt into a puddle, that was exactly what she'd do.

Through the window, the sky lit blood-red as the sun sank below the horizon. She relaxed her shoulders, tensed from days of tunnel-visioning through the rest of the Platt collection. She was mid-stretch, her guard completely down when everything from the past week swept back in.

The witches, the potion, Ashley.

She hadn't seen or heard from her in a week.

At first, she just sat there, letting the emotions wash over her, building one on top of the other. With a few clicks of her laptop, she switched her music from lo-fi to the other song in her history. It only took a few bars of the banjo before feet pounded on the stairs.

Uther burst through the attic door. "We're back to the Taylor phase? Honey, this is the same as the original version."

"But it's not." The screen blurred, but she held her tears from tipping over. "She's older now, and I'm older, and we've been through so much, but the feelings are still there."

"I thought you didn't like country."

"She's pop now. See? We've both changed so much. Taylor is just out there making music and reclaiming her songs."

"Esther, you're being unnecessarily philosophical again." He closed the door and took her hand. "Do we need to go make cookies?"

Her lower lip wobbled as she sang along to the part about crying on a staircase, begging her love to please not go.

"Oh my god. Are you changing the pronouns to fit you personally? We need something faster than cookies. This is an ice cream and wine kind of situation."

The door slammed into the wall, making both Esther and Uther jump.

"It's done!" August stood before them, a dramatic fist raised above his head.

"August, this isn't the best time." Uther gestured at Esther with his head as though she was blind and wouldn't notice.

"Are we back to Taylor again?" He crinkled his nose at the screen. "I'm going to be honest. I didn't really see you as a Taylor fan."

"Where do you think I got the name for this chair?"

Esther angrily gestured at the arm of Trouble, who squeaked with the movement.

"Never mind. It's ready." He lifted his hand, letting a chain dangle from his fist with a familiar silver bulb hanging at the end. "I put a dose in here for you. Figured two birds, one stone."

He dropped the necklace into Esther's hand and stood back with his hands on his hips and an expectant look on his face.

Esther waited for further explanation. "What is this?"

"The cure, obviously," mumbled Uther.

"An excuse to go get your girl back," said August.

Esther threw the necklace on the desk like it had burned her. She didn't want anything to do with that day. Digging through her bag, she pulled out her earbuds and phone to queue up more Taylor. Without her classwork to carry her mind away, she was exposed, drowning in the floodgates of feelings. She hated feelings.

August looked between Esther and the necklace on the desk. "What are you scared of, Esther?"

She glared at him. They really hadn't figured it out. "I give terrible advice and ruin lives with my bad decisions."

Both boys looked skeptical.

"When have you ever given bad advice?" August's question was more challenge than anything else, but Esther was ready.

"Aside from the obvious and most pressing one?" She gestured at the silver necklace.

"Sure, we'll round back to that." August leaned against a bookshelf, crossing his arms in front of him.

"Well, you both remember the beach house, right?" she asked.

August nodded. "I remember having a lot of fun with my friends for a week and saving money on housing to do it."

"Uther?" Esther snapped her attention to her best friend.

He returned her look with a sad smile. "Yeah, I hated it at first, but I ended up having a lot of fun that week. Ashley did a lot to fix up the place."

"Okay, well." Esther racked her brain. "What about my idea to throw a Friendsgiving and you and Ashley decided to start a food fight and nearly tore each other's heads off?"

August avoided eye contact until Uther elbowed him in the ribs. "Ow! Fine. I might have given Ashley my number that night. It was sort of the start of us actually trying to get along and might not have happened if you hadn't given us one more push. Now, how about some good decisions you've made."

"Ooh!" Uther hopped onto the desk and swung his legs back and forth. "What about that day you decided to go to a board game café to make friends? Anything good come out of putting yourself out there that day?" He poked her shoulder, and she swatted his hand away with a smile.

"Okay, yes." She nudged Uther's knee with her shoulder. "But you were also kidnapped because you're friends with me."

"Okay, one, I wasn't. How many times do I need to remind you? You just thought I was. And two"—he spread his arms wide—"I'm fine. I'd even go so far as to say your presence in my life has made it better."

"See?" said August. "It just needed time to resolve itself. Now, what about that time you agreed to go home with Ashley over Christmas and the two of you finally stopped awkwardly flirting and just made out already? That was good, right?"

At first, Esther's mind blessed her with a vision of Ashley in her white cable-knit sweater and long, toned legs smiling at Esther, her blue eyes sparkling in the Christmas lights.

This vision shifted, dragging Esther back to the unforgettable look of betrayal on Ashley's face when she found Esther and August with the witches—and the way that look morphed into the purest of anger. Ashley had trusted her with a literal piece of her, and she'd given it away right in front of her to the people Ashley hated the most.

"She hates me," Esther said.

"Maybe." August's voice was quiet. "You're not alone there. But I don't think we're done yet." Grabbing the new stool he'd bought, he took a seat closer to the desk. "There's something that all these situations have in common. They all get dark before working out for the best in the end. I think we just need to see this through."

Esther placed a hand on his knee. "Not everything works out in the end."

"Not for everyone," August said. "But it does for you."

"August, that's—"

"Esther." Uther took both her hands. "You still have time to fix this. When you look back at this day, are you going to be satisfied? You have a whole lot to gain and not much to lose."

August picked up the necklace, and Uther let go of her so August could place it in her hand.

"Remember what you were saying about Taylor?" Uther continued. "You're both different now. You don't need to hide anymore. Sometimes, you have to do something scary to make a very mildly different song. I think I lost the metaphor at the end there. But you get what I'm saying."

Esther nodded. "But what would I say?" The words

congested in her mind, tangling until it was impossible to find a start.

"What would Ashley do?" Uther turned to August.

August passed Esther a pen. "Write it down. When you've worked it out, go over there."

"We'll give you some space." Uther took August's hand, leading him out of the room.

Esther set the silver necklace on the desk. Fear knocked at her heart. This letter was an apology. She should have told Ashley the truth about the cure from the start. Now Esther had broken Ashley's trust. There was no getting around it, and Esther would do whatever it took and wait however long Ashley needed to earn that back.

Ashley had given Esther a piece of herself when she had already given away too much. This was Esther's chance to give her something back. To give her a second chance at life.

It was scary writing the words, but for the first time in a long time, she was excited to give someone a choice. To not fade into the background and let everything they'd built crumble into nothing.

Esther tore the page out before her nerves bogged her down, grabbed the necklace, and hurried from the room.

"I'm off. Wish me luck," she shouted to Uther and August as she ran out the door.

"Have fun storming the castle," shouted Uther from the porch as she jogged down the sidewalk and around the corner.

The streetlights flickered on one by one.

Esther wasn't sure why she was running except that the moment seemed to require it. She was going to tell Ashley she was so sorry for breaking her trust, and Esther always wanted the best for her, whether that included Esther in her life or not. She was still practicing her lines as she climbed the steps to the vampire house. She'd start with a classic like, "Hi, Ashley," then wing her way through her highlighted points from there. She knocked on the door and waited.

Hi, Ashley. Hi, Ashley. Hi, Ashley.

Someone that wasn't Ashley answered the door in distressed denim shorts and a knit crop top.

"Hi, is Ashley in?" Of course she was in. Where else would she be? The sun had just set.

"Have I seen you before?"

Esther was pretty sure she'd never seen this woman. "I was hoping to speak with her."

"You're Esther, aren't you?" The woman leaned against the doorway, getting annoyingly comfortable in this unhelpful limbo they were in.

"Yes?" It wasn't meant to be a question. Esther was caught off guard by the vampire knowing her name.

"Awesome." She offered her hand. "I'm Cynthia."

Esther shook Cynthia's hand. "It's nice to meet you. Do you know if Ashley is in?"

"Why would I know where Ashley is?" Cynthia spoke loud and dramatically, her gaze darting behind her into the house. "She's probably out."

This wasn't the outcome Esther had hoped for. While her note was solid, she'd still hoped to speak to Ashley in person.

"One second." Esther pulled the letter out of her pocket, folded it into an envelope, and slipped the necklace inside. "Here." She handed the package to Cynthia. "Could you see that she gets this?"

"Sure thing, dude." With a brief finger gun, Cynthia sank back into the house and closed the door.

And that was that. Esther walked back to August's house

with a feeling of incompleteness. So, she hadn't gotten to say her speech. Ashley would still get the note. She couldn't bring herself to text Ashley. Not after her awkward exchange at the door. Maybe she'd text Ashley tomorrow. Just to make sure Cynthia had a chance to get the letter to Ashley. There wasn't any reason to rush.

37

Ashley

"There." Ashley stuck the last notecard to the wall with washi tape and wiped her hands together. The color-coordinated cards and cheerfully contrasting tape really brightened up the room. As long as she only looked at this one wall. Not even her extensive collection of office supplies could fix all the chipped plaster and dusty cobwebs.

The door to the basement opened. Before the creak of the top step, Ashley had pulled shut the curtain she'd rigged across her card wall and taken to her designated hiding box.

"It's just me," called Cynthia.

Ashley sighed. This whole setup was very demoralizing. When she'd texted Cynthia for help, Ashley hadn't considered that she'd be spending her days in the basement, a few feet below everyone she was hiding from. She wasn't sure how much longer she could stand it down here. But that was what her card wall was for.

"I have something for you." Cynthia held up a small piece of folded paper.

Ashley eyed it suspiciously. She was always waiting for the other shoe to fall with Cynthia. When Ashley's mom had suggested calling another vampire, her first thought was Claribel. While her stories may be all over the place and her mind two hundred years in the past, Claribel was at least reliable. Cynthia, on the other hand, could ditch Ashley at any moment with the smallest excuse. But Claribel was closer to Hannah, and it was Hannah—and John—that Ashley was hiding from.

"Your girlfriend was here," Cynthia said.

Electricity zinged down Ashley's spine at the mention of Esther, despite everything that had happened a week ago.

"She left you something."

"What?" Ashley was out of the box and in front of Cynthia. "I'll take that, thank you."

Cynthia laughed as she passed the note. "Way to play it cool, chickee."

Ashley sat on her hiding box and picked at the folded corners of the note while Cynthia pulled back the curtain to Ashley's card wall.

"Careful with that," Ashley called. "I ran out of tape, so some of the cards aren't as secure as I'd like them to be."

"What is this anyway?" Cynthia poked at a card. Ashley joined her at the wall, too nervous to leave Cynthia with it unsupervised. "A flow chart?"

"This"—Ashley gestured grandly—"is my life plan."

Cynthia nodded, eyeing the cards appreciatively. "What do the colors indicate?"

"Those are different life courses, so I can visually follow each flow."

"Sure, sure. I can see the accessibility benefit from it."

Cynthia was studying the wall like this was an art exhibit. "Does it come with a color key?"

"Of course it comes with a color key." Ashley hadn't expected an appreciative audience. Maybe she could have been bonding with Cynthia over charts and lists this whole time instead of just using her as a party buddy.

"But I'm going to..." Ashley lifted the half-opened note again.

"Right. Go on ahead." Cynthia brushed her off. "I'm going to look at this a little longer."

Ashley sat back on her hiding box—an embarrassing designation but apt—and opened the folded envelope. She was pleased to see the art of folded notes hadn't dissolved with the rise of cell phones and texting.

A flash of silver fell out.

Ashley caught it before it hit the floor. It was her necklace from Claribel. Ashley covered her mouth, holding in a sob. The exchanging of things meant they were really over. But would Esther really have bothered going back to the witches just to get Ashley her necklace back?

She scanned the letter. It was an apology.

"Anything good?" Cynthia sat down on the box next to her.

Ashley didn't answer. She read in silence then read the whole thing again before looking at the necklace in her shaking hand. "This is the yellow cards?"

"Yellowcard? Like the band?"

"Not the band." Ashley paused. "Wait. How have you heard of Yellowcard?"

Cynthia rolled her eyes. "I'm not dead. Well, no, technically I am. But I still listen to music. Just because I died in the seventies doesn't mean that's the only music I'm allowed to listen to forever."

That was another fascinating subject Ashley didn't have time to dig deeper into right now. "Whatever, I'm not talking about the band." She pointed to the colorful wall. "The cards. Yellow is the life plan I'd take if I were human. Yellow for sunshine. I don't even need my color key for that one."

"Why would you even make that plan?"

She shrugged. "I had a lot of free time this week."

Really, she couldn't get the comment August made that day on the beach about a cure out of her head. She thought she'd misheard him. But it looked like it really was what she'd thought. That was why she'd made the yellow cards. Once she'd started on the plan, she couldn't stop. It was the easiest of the card choices. She walked over to the board and followed the yellow blocks.

She'd get a teaching degree—her hands trembling at the thought of creating lesson plans, of buying school supplies —and maybe get a position coaching cheer at the local high school while she was at it. The idea of organizing while being part of a team, a community, where she didn't have to prove herself by hiding who she was, was everything and more than she hoped for. This was the ultimate life plan. Everything else was a patchwork of making do with what she had. She held the necklace in her hand, the key to her happily ever after. She could take it right now and get everything.

"So that necklace will make you not a vampire? How do you know it'll work?" Cynthia's words pulled Ashley back to the present.

This potion was the work of witches. Witches, who were out to end vampires. Despite knowing that witchcraft didn't kill Konstantine, Ashley didn't trust them. A decade in the vampire world had given her a lifetime of distrust. And how could she take a potion made by people she couldn't trust?

But this was coming from Esther. And despite everything that had happened, she still trusted her and valued Esther's opinion.

"I don't." Ashley considered the wall. "I'll have to make another list."

Cynthia nodded in agreement, and Ashley returned her attention to the wall. Maybe if she made a points system to rank the pros and cons of each choice, she'd have tangible evidence if the rewards outweigh the risks.

"I'd love to see what you come up with." Cynthia headed for the stairs. "But I have a phone call I need to make. Text me when you're done."

This shouldn't take too long. Ashley pulled out her colored pens.

Only an hour later, Ashley had the numbers tallied and beautifully organized in her notebook. She pulled out her phone and texted Cynthia.

ASHLEY

It's ready!!!

CYNTHIA

just finished my call. omw

Ashley reread the figures while she waited, but the numbers didn't lie. The rewards of possibly becoming human again far outweighed the risk of potential death, which she had designated as the worst possible outcome of taking the potion.

The door to the basement creaked open, and Ashley tensed to hide. She needed to get out of this basement.

Cynthia closed the door behind her. "What did you decide?"

"I'm taking the potion. I'm going to be human. Or maybe

dead. It's not clear. But I did the math, and the numbers don't lie."

Cynthia gazed thoughtfully and nodded along with Ashley's words. "Right on."

Ashley lifted the vial to her lips.

"Wait." Cynthia held out a hand, stopping her. "Should we do a toast or something? This feels big."

"Sure." Ashley paused to think. "I'm not sure what to say. Cheers?"

Cynthia pulled a flask out of her back pocket. "May this moment bring you a new awakening. With the morning comes your new life."

Ashley smiled. "Thanks, Cynthia. That was beautiful."

They clinked glasses or did their best. Ashley's tiny vial was rather difficult to handle.

"Cheers then." Ashley shot it all in one go.

They waited.

"Any idea how long it takes?"

Ashley shrugged and shook her head.

They waited a little longer.

"I don't feel any different. Do I look different?" Ashley looked at her hands, flipping them back and forth, but everything looked the same. She consulted her risk-and-reward notebook. She hadn't considered an option for the potion to do nothing.

"Well, I guess I can tell you my news." Cynthia lifted her flask. "I'm leaving the Family." She took another swig.

"What?" Ashley dropped her notebook. "What do you mean you're leaving? Why? Where will you go?"

"That was the phone call I just left for. Remember that person I was texting earlier? That chick that used to live here."

Ashley's skin tingled. "Konstantine?"

"Yeah, that's her." Cynthia screwed her flask shut and stuck it back in her pocket. "We've been talking lately. She's on the ground floor of this tech startup in Seattle and wants me to join her team. I'm flying out tonight. Just finished confirming the details."

"I-I don't know if that's such a great idea. What will you even do?"

Cynthia tilted her head. "I've been studying UX design since the dawn of home computers. She wants me on her design team."

"Oh." There went that excuse to keep her from leaving. Why did Cynthia have to become so interesting the second she decided to leave? "But are you sure? It's dangerous out there. And you'll have to start in a new Family."

Cynthia placed a hand on her shoulder. "Let me tell you a secret. Some vampires get stuck in their ways, and that's fine. We should all do what brings us joy. Hannah still lives in the town she grew up in, Claribel hasn't changed her fashion sense in centuries, and you're still listening to music from 2001 and wearing skinny jeans, even though I hear they're on the outs."

"Skinny jeans are not out! Kids these days just don't know what they're—" *Gasp.* Ashley wasn't ready to pick any further at that revelation.

"But that's not me. I have enough experience to know what I'm doing. It's time to spread my wings and move on to the next adventure. If you want to tag along while you're figuring stuff out, you're welcome to."

"But you're leaving tonight? I need to recalibrate my numbers and find the next option in my queue." Ashley grabbed her notebook, comparing the color key to the cards on the wall.

"I'm heading out now actually." Cynthia threw a thumb

over her shoulder toward the window. "I have a long way to go and don't want to waste night hours. Text me if you want to catch up." She opened the window, and before Ashley could reply, Cynthia poofed into a bat and fluttered out into the night.

Ashley sat back on her box. There it was. Just when she thought maybe she could build a stronger relationship with Cynthia, she was gone. Ashley was on her own.

And that was when she puked blood all over her card wall.

38

Esther

The streetlights were on by the time Esther made it back to August's house. Uther waited for her on the porch. She hadn't even finished climbing the steps before he bombarded her with questions.

"Did you talk to her? What did she say? Is she taking the potion? Are you back together again? Are you going to be a vampire?"

"Okay, hold on." Esther walked past him to the door. "Let's go inside, and I can catch you up."

"Oh." He took a step, blocking her path. "Um, what if we just sat out here for a bit and caught up?"

"Is something wrong?"

"No, it's just..." He glanced at the front door. "Okay, so August has someone over."

"What do you mean, August has someone over?" She walked around Uther and peered through the window, cupping her hands to block the glare.

Uther grabbed her arm and pulled her from the glass. "Can you be less subtle?"

"Probably." An idea that sounded a lot like Ashley popped into her head, and she grabbed the doorknob and yanked it open. "Hey, August." She spoke so her voice traveled through the house. "What are you up to?"

August appeared in the kitchen doorway, followed by a much smaller woman in a severe bun. "Esther, you're back." His voice was annoyed and grumbly. "You remember my Aunt Hannah."

"Ms. Comstock." *Crap.* "Yes, we spoke once before, about the journal from the collection. Thank you again for the interview. It was instrumental in clarifying discrepancies in my final report."

"Indeed." Hannah sniffed dismissively and walked back into the kitchen.

August and Uther shared an obvious and wordless conversation. From what Esther deduced from their body language and facial expressions, Uther had been tasked with providing August with privacy while entertaining his aunt and could he please try harder next time, and Uther made gestures toward Esther that seemed rather rude in her opinion.

"Your friends may join us," Hannah called from the kitchen.

Esther pushed past August before he could interject and joined his aunt at the table. A few moments passed before August and Uther joined them. They were probably silently arguing again.

"Are you sure you want them here for this?" August remained by the doorway, shifting his weight back and forth, as though he'd run right out the door again if it were socially permissible.

Hannah met him with a stern look, and he took his seat next to her.

"You say it's in the tea." Hannah nodded to the cup in front of her.

Esther hadn't noticed until then that tea had been served.

August glanced at Esther before answering. "I'm not sure we should be talking—"

"I know they are familiar with vampires." Hannah folded her hands gently on the table in front of her. "You are all terrible at keeping secrets. But it is not an issue at present, so please, continue."

"I, umm…" August blinked repeatedly, before regaining his momentum. "Yes. You drink the tea, and it will reverse the vampire curse."

"I see." She turned the glass ninety degrees, as though inspecting every angle for abnormalities.

It was only then Esther pieced together the very private moment she'd barged into. Her attempt at making a bold choice had led to an awkward intrusion into a personal moment. *Classic Esther.*

Esther stood again, her chair scraping against the kitchen linoleum. "I can give you some privacy."

"Don't you want to know what happens?" The way the woman said it was a challenge.

Esther looked to Uther, but he was mirroring her expression. It was her choice. She sat back down.

August gestured to the innocent-looking cup. "You've lived hundreds of years this way. Maybe there's no reason to take the cure. But I had one made with you in mind because…"

He paused and looked around the room.

Whether the look he gave Esther was embarrassment to

have an audience or seeking comfort, Esther wasn't sure, but she nodded encouragingly all the same.

"I hoped we could be aunt and nephew in the typical sense of the word. I'd stop by for tea and cookies, and we'd catch up on each other's lives on a regular basis. I'd shovel your sidewalk in the winter so you don't slip on your way to the car. We'd buy each other Christmas gifts, and I'd introduce you to my boyfriend. It's all selfish stuff, but you're the only family I have in town, and I can't stop by except at night, and then it's all this drama with you being a vampire and I'm a witch and what a mess my parents made of things." He stopped to take a breath because his words were picking up and his shoulders were hunching like a shield. "And I can't help but hope a part of you wants a normal relationship as well."

Hannah kept her gaze firmly on August. They were both the same set of hazel, and for some reason, this observation was what finally connected them for Esther. Hannah was tiny and blond to August's broad shoulders and dark hair. But over a few hundred years of adding and subtracting family genes, this one marker still connected them.

Hannah picked up the tea in both hands and held it close. There was a domestic innocence to the move. Just an older woman having tea with her nephew and wanting to warm her hands.

"I saw the page," she said. "From the grimoire. I've had it for decades. But you must have realized this, or you wouldn't have taken it."

"I'm sorry, I just—"

Hannah lifted a hand, cutting him off.

"I am old." She chuckled at her tea. "At first, the days fly by so quickly. Then the years, then decades. I understand you think it's the witches and vampires that keep us apart, but I have been separate from our family for much longer than your parents' generation." She took a sip from her tea before continuing. "You are correct in your assumption. I do miss having a family."

August smiled and his eyes were watering, but he kept silent, waiting for her to continue.

"But I should tell you, this won't work."

The smile dropped from August's face. "What do you mean it won't work? Why are you drinking it if you know it won't?"

Hannah took another sip. "I would like to have tea with my nephew, while he introduces me to his friends. Is this that boyfriend you mentioned?"

"Hi." Uther gave an awkward wave that turned into hand wringing, and Esther smiled.

"Yes." August's features reanimated. "Aunt Hannah, this is Uther."

"Uther," she replied and reached out to shake his hand. "How Arthurian."

He shot up from this seat to take her hand. "I didn't pick it."

"No, I doubt you did. But it suits, I think. Are you good to my nephew? You treat him well, like a prince should?"

"Oh my god, Aunt Hannah." August covered his mouth, red splotches covering his cheeks.

Esther didn't think she'd seen August embarrassed before.

"Of course," Uther replied, all serious.

"See that you do." She turned to Esther, and Esther sat up straighter. "And I've already met you. Do you keep his confidence as well?"

"I like to think so."

She nodded and placed a hand on Esther's arm.

Esther understood the tea then. Whether the potion worked or not, her hands were warm now. They could pretend this was a human moment, being properly introduced to August's aunt for the first time.

"See that you do." She turned back to August. "And that chatty vampire, Ashley. Is she good to you as well?"

"Ashley?" Esther studied August, looking for a reason for Hannah to be asking about her.

His brows furrowed and he shook his head. "What do you mean?"

Hannah took another sip of tea. "That girl could befriend a teaspoon. If anyone could break you out of this reclusive hovel you buried yourself in, it was her."

Uther snickered behind his hand. "That sounds about right."

She finished her tea. "I like this aunt business. I think I might have been rather good at it, given the chance."

"You're a natural," said August. He was back to smiling. "Did you want some more tea?"

Hannah smiled, and wrinkles framed her eyes that Esther hadn't noticed before. "No, thank you, dear. Actually, it's a warm night, and if memory serves, you have a lovely garden out back. Would it be terribly rude if I asked you to take a stroll with me?"

"No, of course not."

The three of them—Esther, Uther, and August—leaped from their chairs, the room filled with the sound of wood scraping as they stood like this was a Jane Austen novel. Hannah took August's arm, and the two of them went out back. Esther and Uther remained behind in the kitchen, wanting to give them a private moment together.

"How long do you think they'll be? Should we make some tea? Start a movie?" Uther asked.

"Let's put on some tea and give them a few minutes." Esther glanced out the window.

It was dark, aside from a decorative streetlight over the bench in the backyard. August and Hannah sat side by side, their backs to the window.

Tea was made, and Uther and Esther entertained themselves, sharing videos on their phones.

"No, wait!" The call came from outside, but they both recognized the panic in August's voice.

Esther and Uther sprinted out the back door. August was alone on the bench, his fingers raking through his hair and his shoulders heaving.

Uther got to him first. "August, are you all right?"

"Don't sit there!" August shot up and grabbed Uther, pulling him from the bench.

"What happened?" There was no sign of Hannah anywhere.

August was bent over sobbing into Uther's shoulder. "She's...she's gone."

"Where did she go?" Esther tried rubbing August's back, but she wasn't sure that was any help.

He pulled back from Uther's shoulder, tears streaming down his face. "I didn't want this. I would have tried harder if I'd known. I just wanted to fix her. To fix us."

"August." Esther put her hands on his shoulders, trying to anchor him. "Just point where she went. We'll find her."

He hiccuped and pointed at the bench. Brow furrowed, Esther released August and approached the bench. They hadn't noticed before with August in tears, but there was a pile of gray soot on the side of the bench where Hannah had been sitting.

Esther gasped when she recognized what it was. "What happened, August?"

His breathing was slowly coming back under control. Uther had taken over rubbing his back and helping him stand upright.

"I didn't notice at first. The shadows were blocking her face. She started to slow, so we sat down. It all seemed normal. But then her voice changed, and that's when I noticed." He sniffed, and a tear tracked down his cheek. "She was aging, right there in front of me. Then she just dissolved into dust."

"Jesus," whispered Uther.

Esther covered her mouth.

Hannah was right. The potion didn't work.

"Ashley."

Esther ran like her life depended on it.

39

———

Ashley

This was fine. She was fine.

Ashley wiped blood off the blue card, which—according to her color key and risk/reward system—was the start of her next best course of action now that yellow was out. She'd planned on taking a picture of the wall so she could carry it with her when she left and zoom in on the cards when she needed to reference them, but now blood covered half the words. She tried to gently wipe another card with her shaky fingers, and her perfect calligraphy smudged. Or maybe that was just her eyesight going a little fuzzy. She dropped onto her box, both exhausted and frustrated. Why bother salvaging her plan if she was dying anyway?

The puking had stopped, but she was shaking, and her vision was blurring. Still, it might just be a bad reaction. Maybe she wasn't dying. In which case, she needed her cards and color key. Maybe she could number the cards and use a clip to keep them with the key. It wouldn't be as convenient as seeing them all in order, but she could recreate her wall when she reached her next location. Wherever that was...

Yes, numbering the cards was the best solution. This solved all her problems. She pulled out a silver gel pen—the obvious choice for blue—and started numbering.

There was a banging at the front door. Ashley obviously couldn't answer it. She was in hiding. It was rather insistent though. Didn't matter, she continued numbering.

"Ashley!" That was Esther's voice.

It was more muffled than she was used to, but she'd recognize that voice anywhere. One person had left the house while she was talking to Cynthia—she wasn't sure who—which left a fifty-fifty chance that either Hannah or John answered the door.

Please, go away, wished Ashley.

The upper stairs creaked.

Tell her to go away.

The front door opened, but Ashley's ears stuffed up like she'd left a concert after camping out in front of the speakers.

But she recognized that deep voice—John.

She crept closer to the stairs, hoping to get a better sense of what they were saying over the sound of footsteps. Had Esther come inside? There was shuffling, a loud crash, then Esther screamed.

Ashley's limbs felt like they were moving through water, but she ran up the stairs and burst into the living room.

John had his arms locked across Esther's chest as she tried vainly to block her neck.

"Ashley." John's voice was its usual slow and proud cadence. "I had a feeling that was you stowed away. You think I couldn't hear you scuttling around down there like a rat?"

"Leave her alone, John. She isn't part of this."

Esther continued to fidget in his arms. Ashley wished she'd stop drawing attention to herself.

"I told you there would be consequences." He leaned, his fangs inches from Esther's neck.

Ashley clenched her fists, but there wasn't anything she could do. John was hundreds of years older than her, and with time came speed and strength. He could snap Esther's neck before Ashley took a single step. A wave of dizzying nausea passed over her—as though she needed another reminder of her disadvantage. It took all her concentration to keep from swaying on her feet.

"Take me instead." Ashley clenched her fists. "You want someone to take your anger out on. Why not go to the source?"

"Your blood is not as sweet," he replied.

He grazed a fang along Esther's neck, leaving a small, red trail behind. A single drop of blood leaked from the opening. Ashley concentrated on controlling her breathing, holding back the urge to fling him from Esther, to curl her body around Esther's and never let anything harm her ever again.

With dramatic slowness, John dragged his tongue along Esther's neck, cleaning away the drop of blood.

"Stop it!" Ashley screamed, dropping her fangs.

Her cheeks felt wet. She hated to think she was crying, showing weakness in front of John, but that was what she was—weak.

Esther turned her nose inches from his, her face blank. Had John mesmerized her as well? Were there no boundaries he wouldn't cross? Esther's hand lifted, reaching for his cheek.

John said nothing, looking only at Esther, his lip curling in an amused smile.

Her hand continued past his cheek until she smacked it against his forehead and held it firm. John's eyes went wide. An inhuman roar bellowed from his chest. He released Esther, backing away and scratching with both hands at his face as steam rose from where her palm had been. Through his fingers, Ashley barely made out the black outline of a cross.

Esther's earring.

Ashley's laugh came out as a sob when she recognized the shape. No wonder Esther was fidgeting with her ear while John held her. She had a weapon the whole time.

Esther reached Ashley while she was still distracted by John's face. "Ashley." She was panting. "Are you all right? I came to tell you not to…"

Her words trailed off as her eyes wandered down Ashley's front.

Right, she was still covered in blood from her earlier puking stunt.

"It's fine," Ashley said. "I'm fine."

"Ashley." She touched Ashley's cheek, and the care in Esther's eyes was worth everything.

Ashley had missed her so much.

"You haven't taken the potion yet, have you?" Esther asked.

She couldn't stand it anymore. Ashley ran her hand along Esther's arms, her cheeks. This day felt like a dream, and she had to know it was real. That Esther was really here in front of her.

"Ashley." Esther took both of Ashley's wandering hands

in her own, focusing her back on the question. "Did you take the potion in the necklace?"

"Don't worry, sweetheart." Ashley pulled a hand free, still not satisfied, and brushed Esther's hair back behind her now empty ear. "I gave it a lot of thought first, and the numbers don't lie. It was worth it. Just to have a chance with you."

"No." Esther was crying, too. "No, I'm too late? Ashley, I'm so sorry. I didn't mean for this to happen. I didn't know it wouldn't work. I came as soon as I found out."

"Shh, it's all right, sweetheart." She continued to brush back Esther's hair trying to soothe her. "You were all of my yellow cards."

Esther shook her head, her brows pinching in confusion. "I don't know what you're talking about. The band?"

"Not the band." Geez, maybe picking yellow was a confusing choice after all. "I made a color key. I can show it to—"

Ashley was pulled by the roots of her hair, her scalp on fire, and flung through the air, crashing into a column in the foyer. There was a booming crack that knocked the air from her lungs before she tumbled, her head smacking the floor as she landed. She gasped, trying to suck in air. From her fallen place, her cheek pressed to the cool wood, she saw two boots step toward her. One swung back before burying in her gut. There was a pop in her chest that she guessed was a rib, though this had never happened before so she couldn't be sure. That was what it would have been in the movies.

Esther was screaming, and Ashley needed to get up and tell Esther to run. But the boot swung again, and this time it caught her in the chin. Stars blocked out her vision.

She pinched her eyes shut, trying to make them work.

When she opened them, Ashley had to blink repeatedly before they focused on the scene before her. Esther swung from John's back, her arms locked around his throat as he spun, trying to fling her from him.

Ashley needed to get up. She needed to help. Esther wouldn't survive being flung against a wall like Ashley. She was human.

Her side burned, but she forced herself to move through the pain. Bracing a hand against the column, she stood. The old oak sported a deep crack where she'd hit it, like the jagged lines of a map. On the ceiling, holes marred the star-speckled plaster and littered the floor around her.

An idea slowly formed. Ashley pushed at the column below the crack. The wood groaned but wouldn't budge. This should have been easy, even without the ready crack, but her body was so tired she wasn't sure how she would do it. A movement in her peripheral drew her attention back to the fighting as Esther was flung across the room and hit the wall by the door.

Esther fell limp to the ground, a small gash leaking a crimson tear down her cheek.

Ashley ran and leaped at John, her arms locking around his neck and her teeth clamping onto his throat. She'd tear out his jugular and leave him gasping until she found something that worked as a stake.

But something was wrong.

Her fangs wouldn't descend, which meant her teeth wouldn't sink in.

John laughed and flung her from him. She hit the column again with as much force as before, and this time it was enough. The column cracked, and the small tendons holding it together snapped one by one as the pressure from the ceiling pushed the column into its final bow.

John's chin tipped to the ceiling as the column groaned, but he was too late. Ashley shot out and grabbed him around the ankle. He fell to the ground. They grappled, both clawing and elbowing, one to get free and the other to hold in place.

"Ashley." The sound was barely more than a whisper.

Ashley looked up to see Esther, propped on an elbow, her dark hair sticking to the blood on her cheek. She tossed a small, silver object through the air. It slid across the floor and landed a foot from her—Esther's second earring.

Keeping a fistful of John's button-down in one hand, she dove and grabbed it, ignoring the pain that burned through her side at the movement. Half the ceiling's plaster crashed where the earring had been moments before, leaving a cloud of dust and blocking her view of Esther.

John ripped himself free, leaving behind scraps of his shirt in Ashley's fist. It was just the two of them now as more plaster fell and a second column cracked and bent under the weight of the crumbling house.

Ashley stood, the cool metal grasped firmly in her palm as she circled the last of the open space, John mirroring her on the other side.

"I always knew you were a terrible vampire," he said, narrowly dodging a piece of falling plaster. His shirt hung in tatters around his lean frame, and his thin, brown hair was covered in so much plaster it looked white. It was the most disheveled she'd ever seen him. "I only regret how much I underestimated that first assessment."

"I really am a terrible vampire." She ducked and somersaulted away, narrowly missing a support beam as it crashed between them. "Good thing I was always a decent cheerleader."

She vaulted over the beam and landed knees first on

John's chest. Before he could move or say anything else, she pressed the second cross to his exposed chest, right where his heart would be, and didn't let go until it sank beneath his skin.

The second floor gave way around them, drowning out his scream.

40

Esther

Someone knocked on the front door.

Muffled words carried through from the other side. "Are you kidding me, Uther? Look at the house."

August and Uther had found them.

Esther tried to get up, but something pinned her in place. She called out, her voice a dry rasping sound that broke into a cough.

The door creaked open, and more dust and plaster fell around her.

"Esther." The cloud settled, and there was Uther crouching over her, his face more serious than she ever recalled. His warm hands traced her cheeks. She hissed when his thumb brushed a cut. "You're going to be all right, okay? I've got you. Everything is fine."

For some reason, the shaky way he said "everything is fine" while scanning her body and avoiding eye contact made her think that everything was not, in fact, fine.

The last few moments ran through her head. Ashley covered in blood and being flung across the room by that reaper of a vampire. The sound of her body hitting the column not once but twice. That last image of Ashley grasping, nails raking the floor for the earring Esther had tossed before it all went dark.

"Ashley," Esther said.

"Is she here? Do you know what happened?" Over Uther's shoulder, August climbed through the rubble.

The ceiling was gone, leaving a giant chasm in the middle of the house. A rug hung precariously from one side, and on the other, water spurted from somewhere unseen and trailed in a waterfall to the floor below before disappearing in the litter of timber, plaster, and splintered furniture piled in a heap.

"Ashley!" August screamed her name and flung chair legs, then a whole bed frame, from the pile.

Esther focused on his movement. If she just concentrated on his actions, she could ignore the sinking feeling in her heart the longer they went without a reply.

Maybe Ashley had made it out. Or she got to the basement before the collapse. Maybe she finally turned into a bat and flew out a window.

"I'm going to move this off you." Uther was talking to her.

She pried her attention from August flinging chunks of plaster to see what Uther was fussing over. A wooden beam pinned Esther's thighs to the floor.

"When I lift it, can you slide out of there? Hey!" He called to someone outside the front door. "Come help me already."

The pressure on Esther's legs eased, and Uther pulled her out before it crashed back to the ground. Confused,

Esther looked up at the newcomer in the doorway. Meg shoved her hands in her coat pockets, and behind her, Gwen fidgeted with the skirt of her dress as her gaze darted between August flinging furniture and the open space above them.

Esther wasn't sure what to say, torn between, "Thanks," "How dare you show your faces," and "Go, help him!"

Meg nodded, as though she read all three options in Esther's face, and walked to August, putting her hand on his arm so he'd pause. They exchanged a silent conversation that Esther couldn't follow before August backed up and let her take over.

Esther had always been impressed by August's little flashes of magic. The way he casually wove it into his every day. His magic was small: flicking the lights on or off, locking the door when they nearly forgot, opening a window when it got warm. Little things that required a bit of pressure, but the way he used them was natural and domestic. She'd sensed Meg and Gwen were stronger when she'd first met them—their magic originating in their bones and leaking from them like it was too big to keep in without constant vigilance—but nothing they'd done so far prepared her for when Meg bowed her head and held out her open palms.

The entire room of debris trembled. It was the same kind of magic August used, the manipulation of pressure, but instead of flicking on a light switch, her fingers contracted into claws and sweat formed on her forehead as she pulled everything—the plaster, the pillars, a tub, and several more chairs—up from the floor until the only thing left below, like a puppet with its strings snipped, lay Ashley.

Her body was coated in blood and plaster, and her gold hair was matted and covering her face, but it was her.

August stepped like he'd run to her, but Gwen grabbed his arm and pulled him away.

Meg dropped the still floating rubbish into the space he'd recently occupied. The floor vibrated beneath Esther's fingers as it settled in its new place.

Esther needed to get up. She needed to see Ashley, to know if she was breathing. The pure volume of stuff Meg had pulled off her, not to mention the work August had done by hand, was beyond what any human could handle.

But Ashley was a vampire. Sure, she was dying from some faulty witches' brew, but vampires couldn't be crushed to death. Could they?

Esther went to stand, but her leg firmly refused to hold her weight. Her arms were intact, so she army-crawled her way across the floor, paying no mind to Uther, who fussed over her the entire way.

August was there by the time Esther made it and had brushed Ashley's hair from her face, his hands now coated in blood and his wrist pressed to her lips. "Ashley, I'm so sorry. I was wrong and you were right, okay?" His shoulders shook and tears dripped down his face. "I overstepped, but you can't...you can't leave. Who's going to threaten to drown me every time I'm a crappy friend?" He shoved his wrist at her face. "Drink, already."

Uther dropped to the floor and wrapped his arms around August, gently pulling him back into his lap and cradling August's head to Uther's shoulder.

"Ashley." Esther tucked two fingers under Ashley's chin and checked for a pulse. She sighed with relief when she found one. "She's not dead."

August's head shot up. "What do you mean she's not dead?"

Her eyes watered with relief, clearing tracks down her chalky cheeks. "She still has a pulse."

"A pulse?" His hand shot to Ashley's neck, tracing around Esther's fingers until he found the spot where a gentle but steady beat ticked under Ashley's chin. "It worked?"

"What do you mean..." Realization dawned on her.

Ashley shouldn't have a pulse. She was a vampire. Or she had been?

Esther took in the rest of Ashley's body. Nothing seemed out of place, but a large shard of wood pierced the side of Ashley's abdomen. Blood coursed from the wound and pooled around her middle.

Ashley was alive and bleeding out in front of them.

"Gwen!" called August. "Gwen, get over here."

The witch pranced over, her green skirts flaring prettily as she dropped to the floor beside them.

"Help her," August said.

Gwen shook her head, but her face showed remorse. "I don't work with humans."

"Your power is life. Just stop the bleeding. That's all we need. Turn her into freaking Poison Ivy, and we'll drop her off in the city to haunt Batman. I don't even care. I just can't let her die."

41

Ashley

The first thing Ashley noticed was a gentle burning in her side. The sensation morphed into a slicing pain as something was tugged from her. She hissed instinctively, but her fangs still wouldn't descend.

"Ashley?"

Gentle fingers touched her cheek, and she turned her face, urging the cool touch to soothe the throbbing building in her skull. It felt like a house had fallen on her.

"I think she's waking up."

"Esther?" Ashley croaked. She hardly recognized her own voice, her throat was so dry and scratchy. She coughed and tried to pry open her eyes, but they were just as dry.

"I'm here, Ashley." Cool fingers encased her hand. "We're all here. You're going to be okay. Are you almost done?" The last comment sounded like it was to someone else.

Who was here? Ashley was having a hard time remembering.

"Just about." Ashley didn't recognize the second female's voice.

She tried opening her eyes again, but they remained cemented shut. Rubbing at them left her free hand coming away sticky.

"Uther," said Esther's voice. "Can you get a wet cloth for her face? Hang on, babe."

Moments passed while she tried not to think about how she physically could not open her eyes. She startled when a damp cloth, soft like a T-shirt, touched a corner of her eye.

"Sorry, sorry." Esther's quiet coos were as soothing as the fabric cleaning her. A few swipes and some heavy blinking and she could see again.

"Esther," Ashley sighed.

It was dark, the shadows deeper than they should have been. She just made out Esther's face, the cut on Esther's cheek. A movement behind Esther drew her eye to water running from the ceiling then the piles of debris littering the floor.

Everything came back in a rush.

"Esther, are you all right?" Ashley tried to sit up, but her side burned, and a hand on her shoulder pressed her back down.

"I'm just about done here." The voice was gentle but firm.

Ashley followed the hand to the source. The woman was familiar, but in this setting, she couldn't quite place her. Her dark curls were braided back into a low halo, her button nose focused down on her work. The hand that wasn't on Ashley's shoulder hovered over a torn slit in Ashley's blouse where a bouquet of tiny white flowers sprouted from Ashley's torso.

"What the hell are you doing to me?"

"August..." the woman said, not looking up from her flowers.

August jumped to action, bracing his hands on Ashley's shoulders and gently but firmly holding her in place. "Give her another minute, Ashley. We don't need you opening it back up again."

"What are you doing here, witch?" she snapped. She tried shaking him off, but another wave of nausea had her seeing spots. "Did you bring your witchy friends to finish me off this time?"

"There," the woman proclaimed, wiping her hands together and inspecting her work. "That should hold for now. Try not to move too much, and it should fall off naturally in about a week. You'll probably have a decent scar from this though."

"Would everyone stop touching me," Ashley said, "and just tell me what is going on?"

"Ashley." Esther reached for her hand and paused, presumably because of Ashley's demand for people to stop touching her, but that was hardly the case for Esther.

Ashley took Esther's hand and waited for her to continue.

"I don't know how to explain this." She was smiling, and tears carved tracks through the dust on her face. She placed Ashley's hand on her chest. "Just feel this."

This was a weird time to share a new kink. She lifted a brow to Esther.

"Not that," she laughed. "Do you feel anything different?"

Her chest was warmer than she was used to without Esther to warm her. She waited a few seconds then felt a small, rhythmic tapping. Was that the flower growing out of her stomach? What was inside her?

"Ashley," Esther said, "you're alive."

"Alive?" She looked between the familiar faces, Esther to August to Uther, trying to find someone to deny what Esther had said. "Are you saying the potion worked?"

"Of course the potion worked." Another figure walked forward.

This one, she recognized as the witch that had caught Esther's vial. Ashley hissed, but again her fangs didn't come.

"Not *of course*." August left Ashley's side and went toe to toe with the witch in the Carhartt. "The first batch...that one didn't work."

"Yeah, it did."

"Meg." The witch with the flowers scrunched her eyes and pinched the bridge of her nose like she had a headache coming. "Stop being curt and just explain it to them."

"The potion reverses the effects of the vampire disease." She looked incredulously at them like this explained everything and they were all being obtuse.

The flower witch planted her face in her hand and sighed. "What Meg is poorly explaining is that, once the virus is removed, the effects it had on the body are removed. Advanced hearing, eyesight, speed. All gone. As well as freezing your age. So, if you've been a vampire for two hundred years, once the potion takes effect, you'll age two hundred years."

"So, if I've been a vampire for twelve years." Ashley sat up, and this time, no one stopped her. "Are you saying I'm in my thirties now?"

The witch placed her hand sympathetically on Ashley's knee. "I'm afraid so. You'll want to watch your alcohol and get a good eye cream."

"Esther," Ashley called, even though Esther was sitting right next to her. "Guess who's the older one in the relationship now." She shoved a thumb at her chest. "This guy."

Esther broke out in laughter, and it was music to Ashley's ears.

Holy shit, she was human.

"Christ almighty, what in the ever-living fuck happened to my house?" another voice said.

Everyone turned to the front door, which was still open. Framed by the twilight was Claribel.

"Well," said the flower witch, clapping her hands together. "It's been lovely, but I think that's our cue to leave. Don't forget to take it easy for a couple of days—two weeks to be safe. No heavy lifting. Meg?"

She held out her hand to the grumpy witch, who helped her up, before the two of them sidestepped around Claribel and out the door.

Claribel stepped inside and slammed the door behind her. A small chunk of plaster fell loose and plopped to the floor next to her. "Who is responsible for this?"

"Okay," said August, standing and pulling Uther with him. "That's a long story, and a lot of people, so I think we'll leave you to that, Ash." He had the audacity to shoot her finger guns and wink as he hurried past.

"Et tu, August?" Ashley yelled as they scampered out the door.

Claribel's steps echoed as she approached, her eyes scanning the debris and the chasm where their home used to be. By the time she reached Ashley, her shoulders had slumped, and her face had fallen. "What happened to you, Ash?"

"Esther, can you tell August to bring his car back while I catch Claribel up?" Ashley said. "We're staying at his place today. All of us. That witch owes me big time."

Esther nodded and started texting.

Right, thought Ashley, looking at Esther's legs. Neither of them would be very mobile for a while.

"Is that the necklace I gave you?" Claribel touched the silver charm around Ashley's neck. In all the confusion of the evening, she'd forgotten that she'd put it back on. "Did you get her to fill it for you?"

Ashley laughed until her side hurt and she worried she'd split it back open again. And even then, she held it in agony while trying to hold back her giggles.

"Oh boy, did she ever," Ashley said, wiping her eyes. "Listen, Claribel. There's something you should know."

By the time she'd finished explaining the cure, Cynthia leaving, the fight, the deaths—with Esther filling them in on Hannah—the boys had returned with the car. August carried Esther, while Uther acted as a crutch for Ashley, and they all limped their way to the car. Claribel grabbed an umbrella from the surprisingly still intact front closet and claimed the middle seat, ordering August to step on it before she burned to a crisp and set them all on fire in the process.

Back at the house, Ashley set August and Uther to work light-proofing a guest room for Claribel.

"It's been a long night," Claribel said, turning down Ashley's offer to keep her company and help her settle in. "We can talk in the evening. For now, I want to forget everything and just sleep."

Ashley was exhausted as well and left the boys downstairs to their brunch and snuggle or whatever they got up to on a day without schoolwork. She continued past Claribel's room and across the hall before knocking and peeking inside.

Esther was propped up on the bed, her legs properly

bandaged and tucked under the sheets. "Do you get your knocking etiquette from your mom?"

Ashley smiled and leaned against the doorway, grimacing slightly when she bumped her flowers. "I can go back and try again."

"Get in here. I want to be with you for this."

"For what?" Ashley walked inside and carefully crawled onto the bed next to Esther, cautious not to jostle her legs.

Esther turned back to the window facing the bed. "For you to see the sunrise."

Ashley gasped as the sun slowly rose over the house across the street. Muscle memory told her to run for cover. She had to fight the instinct and stay in place. Cautiously, Ashley reached out to the sunbeam that tracked its way onto their bed. Her fingers dipped into the light, casting shadows, and her hand warmed with a gently soothing touch she'd nearly forgotten.

"It's beautiful." She turned back to Esther to see tears in her eyes.

"Ashley, I'm so sorry. You gave me your heart, and I...and I betrayed you in the worst way possible. You're this sunbeam that deserves everything good in this world, and I don't know how, but if there's anything I can do to earn back your trust, I'll do it."

"Shh." She ran her thumb along Esther's cheek, wiping away the tears. "Sweetheart, that's not how this works."

She pressed her forehead to Esther's, and a tear trace down her own cheek.

"I love you, Esther. If someone was going to be my downfall, it had to be you. It's all right. We'll figure this out. Together."

"All right." Esther nodded, and they kissed as the morning light filled the room.

EPILOGUE

Ashley

shley pushed away her syrup-soaked plate, resting a hand on her stomach. "I'm stuffed. Stop giving me food. I couldn't possibly fit anything else."

Esther chuckled from the wobbly stool next to her, the sound so soft Ashley hardly heard it over the din of chatter and scraping cutlery from fellow brunch-goers.

"Was it worth it?" Esther asked.

"God, yes." Ashley had missed food so much.

A cloud shifted across the sky, releasing a stream of sunshine through the street-side window and spilling onto her empty plate. Her hand twitched back to the shadows under the table. No, this was all right. She didn't have to be afraid anymore. Being human took some getting used to. A warm hand on her thigh told her Esther had noticed.

Ashley captured Esther's hand in her own, lifting it to her lips and placing a small kiss on her knuckles. "It was all worth it."

"Get a room." August barely looked up from his plate, a smirk on his lips as he shoved another forkful of breakfast into his annoying face.

"Watch it, witch." She pointed through the sunbeam at him, showing both who was boss. "I can still take you."

His reply came through a mouthful of food. "I'd like to see you try."

"Ashley." Esther's voice was soft, but the warning carried.

Right. They were here to celebrate.

She released Esther's hand and sat up straight to clink a fork to her glass, careful not to spill what was left of her mimosa. "A toast!"

Uther was quick to raise his glass, elbowing August to follow suit.

"To Esther and Uther on somehow making it through this year with the grades to graduate."

"Hear! Hear!" Uther chimed as they clinked glasses, weaving and reaching to make sure each drink touched. Ashley hadn't finished her sip before Uther continued. "On to the next order of business. Esther." He pointed his glass across the table at her. "How did your interview go?"

Ashley held her drink tight. Esther's interview with the historical society had finished that morning, making her a couple of minutes late for brunch. Typical Esther, she'd said nothing on the subject, happy to let Ashley rattle on with her regular nonsense. Her reluctance to offer any details was nerve-racking, but Esther was a shoe-in. She had her degree, and she'd worked with the very collection they would be hiring her to continue.

"The interview?" Esther fidgeted with her fork, stabbing at a piece of arugula that refused to be pierced.

"Esther Green, do not play coy with me." Uther had

abandoned his seat to lean farther over the table. "You've let us stress all of brunch, and I will have no more of it." He slapped the table, the force barely enough to rattle a fork, but enough to draw Esther's attention.

"It was fine." Esther took a sip from her mimosa while they all waited.

"Fine?" Shocking Ashley, August was first to break the silence. "What does 'fine' mean?"

The corner of Esther's mouth twitched. "I got it."

"You got it?"

They screamed in tandem while a rosy blush worked its way up Esther's neck.

Esther's shoulders hunched as she stared fixedly at the plate in front of her. "The interview was a formality, I guess. They interviewed a couple of other people, but knowing the collection was what won them over."

"Sweetheart, I'm so proud of you." Ashley looped an arm around Esther, her heart melting as Esther leaned into her touch.

"So, when do you start?" August asked.

"That's still...umm, soon." Esther's shoulders stiffened under Ashley's embrace, and she shifted back to her seat. "I have a couple of things to work out first. What about you? Are you and Ashley taking summer classes together?"

"Hell, no." They both said in tandem.

Ashley tried to glare at the witch, but the corner of her mouth twitched into a smile. "I'm waiting until the fall semester to start classes."

"And I wouldn't be caught dead in the teaching program." August waved his fork in Ashley's direction, in case anyone there wasn't sure who had chosen to pursue a teaching degree.

"As opposed to the millions of other programs you've burned through," Ashley said. "What are you majoring in now?"

"Hey now." Uther placed a hand on August's thigh, shielding him from Ashley's truthful comments. "This brunch is about celebrating accomplishments, not criticizing future paths."

"I could use a walk." Esther abruptly stood from the table. "Ashley, would you like to walk with me? Digest all this food we just finished?"

Alarm bells sounded in Ashley's mind, but she nodded. "Of course." She wrestled out of her chair and grabbed her purse. "August, I'll Venmo you for the food."

He gave her a two-fingered salute as she led Esther out of the restaurant, her hand at the small of Esther's back while Esther waved goodbye to their two best friends.

Esther didn't say anything as they made their way to the lakeside path. Spring was in full bloom, and a pocket of tulips waved at them as they crossed the last intersection. The lake had a wet, humid smell from the heat of the day, and another couple walked hand in hand in the opposite direction as they started down the path. Patches of green light poked through the leaves overhead, birds chittered, and every daytime detail filled Ashley's heart to bursting. She was alive and she had Esther, and life was good.

Esther led them to a familiar log by a pebble beach, the waves making soft splashes against the rocks as the occasional boat sped by. "So, I'm just going to say it."

Ashley brought her attention back into focus, taking her seat by Esther.

Esther took a deep breath and scrunched her beautiful face into the most ridiculous expression. "Would you be interested in taking a month or two this summer to travel with me?"

"Oh my god, yes!" Ashley braced herself. Was she for real? "Where, when, how? Also, did I mention, yes?"

Esther worked her bottom lip between her teeth, fighting a smile. "So, my mom's been saying she can get me a room on one of her cruises. I was thinking since you haven't been able to travel internationally this past decade, maybe we could catch this transatlantic one that's leaving in a couple weeks and backpack Europe before your classes in the fall. I had some ideas for places, and you'll have to pack much lighter than you did for our beach trip. But what do you think?"

"Esther." No longer able to keep her hands to herself, Ashley cradled Esther's cheeks in her palms. "Did you just plan a multi-week, multi-location vacation for the two of us that involves meeting your mom?"

Esther pulled her lips in between her teeth and nodded between Ashley's cupped hands.

"Have I told you lately how I'm ridiculously in love with you?" Ashley asked.

That earned her a laugh, teeth and all. "You're not scared for your life?"

Ashley's hands drifted down Esther's neck, her thumbs playing along her delicate collarbone. "Esther, you gave me my life back. I'd brave the world if it meant doing it with you."

She pushed a lock of hair back from Esther's face, tucking it behind her ear and jostling the new hoop earrings she'd gifted Esther as a graduation present. Esther smiled and ducked her head, nuzzling under Ashley's chin as Ashley wrapped an arm around her.

"It still feels like a fairytale." Esther's words were quiet over the lapping water. Ashley couldn't see her face from this angle. "I keep thinking I'll wake up and none of this will have happened."

She tilted Esther's chin up so she could see her face. "This is real, sweetheart. It'll just take some getting used to."

Ashley brushed her lips against Esther's to the tune of a world awake and future plans on the horizon.

ACKNOWLEDGMENTS

I first started drafting this book in the summer of 2019, if that gives you an idea of how old this story is. Although, if you were doing the math, the book does take place during the 2020-2021 school year in a timeline in which there's no global pandemic but there are vampires and witches hidden among us.

This book would be nothing without all the amazing help I received over the years. I want to thank Jeni Chapelle for being the first person I met in the writerly spheres of social media back when I had nothing but a NA/YA(?) fantasy romance with five POVs and the dream of some day being published. If there's anything wrong with the editing, I probably ignored her sage advice.

Michelle Rascon! Thank you thank you for being the first person to pick up my book and say this is actually good (other than my husband who is biased on the matter). Sunsets would not be the same without you.

To Jessica Lewis, who dropped into my DMs after a pitch event and offered amazing advice. I can't thank you enough. I wish all the orange cats find your stoop. Or whatever a reasonable number is. And to my amazing alpha reader Katie Erin of Erin Rose, who read this book back when it was so baby and said "what if they did something over spring break like go to a carnival or something?" Brilliant. Game changer. A hero.

To my many beta readers and critiquers and "can

someone look over this just one more time?" readers over the years that got me to a point where I wasn't cringing at the idea of letting someone read this book: Mae Bennett, Debbie Exton, Rachel Berros, Fulton Wald, Stephanie Adamakos, Maria Millage, Maggie North, Amanda (A.B.) Wilson, Mallory Marlowe, Dallas Stotland, Sarah T. Dubb, Jamie Z, Victoria Levine, Ana Mae Wright, and Amber Roberts, a million thank yous to each of you.

And I can't forget Luly (@lulybot on IG) for making such amazing character art and being a dream to work with and Kels and Ada at Archetype for marketing and branding. Honestly, I really rode on all your hard work. Thank you for making me look a little put together.

And one last big thank you to my live-in husband, Mr. Dani, aka Patrick who might not be as plugged in with the romance community but certainly knows more about grammar than I do. You've been an amazing cheerleader, dear. I'll keep you.

And to you, dear reader, for getting this far. This book would just be my own personal fever dream without you.

ABOUT THE AUTHOR

Dani Frank is doing her best. Her writing tends toward the humorous side of millennial angst, be it paranormal vampires or small-town contemporary romance. She is the "small-town girl moves to big city" trope where she lives with her husband and fluffy cat. She is still trying to visit every museum in the area and has visited four sites where Edgar Allan Poe lived. She is still salty to have not been voted the friend "most likely to have touched a human bone."

If you, enjoyed what you read, or even if you didn't but still want to support an indie author, leaving a review makes a world of a difference.

For more updates, visit my website
www.Dani-Frank.com

And if you would like to be the first to know about upcoming books in this series, or potential ARCs, my newsletter is a good source for that.
https://danifrank.substack.com/